MAJOR MARKETING CAMPAIGN

75,000-COPY ANNOUNCED MARKET DISTRIBUTION

Author Appearances · National Print Publ

Launch Advertising · Trade A

Pre-Order Campaign with Incentive

Early Reader Review Campaign

Bookseller Mailing · IndieBound Campaign

NetGalley Promotion · Goodreads Giveaways

Influencer Outreach · Wednesday Books Promotion

Social Media Promotion · Email Marketing

YA Festivals & Conferences · Discussion Guide Posted Online

Author Website: LaurenBlackwood.com

𝕏 @LJ_Blackwood   @LaurenBlackwoodWrites

LAUREN BLACKWOOD

is a Jamaican American living in Virginia who writes romance-heavy fantasy for most ages. When not writing, she's a musician and a tiramisu connoisseur. She's the *New York Times* bestselling author of *Within These Wicked Walls* and *Wildblood*.

On Sale 5/14/24 · Young Adult Fiction
Hardback: 978-1-250-89107-5 · 368 pages
6 ¹⁄₈" × 9 ¹⁄₄" · $20.00/$27.00 Can.
eBook: 978-1-250-89108-2 · $11.99/$12.99 Can.
Digital Audio: 978-1-250-35049-7 · $26.99/$35.99 Can

Also by
Lauren Blackwood

Wildblood
Within These Wicked Walls

THE
DANGEROUS
ONES

Lauren Blackwood

WEDNESDAY BOOKS
NEW YORK

First published in the United States by Wednesday Books, an imprint of St. Martin's Publishing Group

THE DANGEROUS ONES. Copyright © 2024 by Lauren Blackwood. All rights reserved. Printed in the United States of America. For information, address St. Martin's Publishing Group, 120 Broadway, New York, NY 10271.

www.wednesdaybooks.com

Designed by Devan Norman
Petal art © Shutterstock.com / ChoChe

The Library of Congress has cataloged the hardcover edition as follows:

ISBN 978-1-250-89107-5 (hardcover)
ISBN 978-1-250-89108-2 (ebook)

Our books may be purchased in bulk for promotional, educational, or business use. Please contact your local bookseller or the Macmillan Corporate and Premium Sales Department at 1-800-221-7945, extension 5442, or by email at MacmillanSpecialMarkets@macmillan.com.

First Edition: 2024

10 9 8 7 6 5 4 3 2 1

Dedication TK

Some of the thematic material in *The Dangerous Ones* contains depictions war and slavery, blood and gore, murder, death, physical abuse, hate crimes, racial discrimination, gun violence, and references to sexual abuse. For more information, please visit the author's website.

THE
DANGEROUS
ONES

1

JERUSALEM

Virginia
June 29, 1862

he sky was pitch, and my tears blinding, so out-running them hounds was tricky. Three times faster than the men, but just as hateful, trained from pups to big old beasts to despise dark skin as much as the rest of them. But it wasn't so much the dogs I was worried about. It was getting through these daggone woods in the dead of night. I'd been born with better night vision than anyone, but the brush was harsh, and the trees grew close, making it hard to keep a pace. My stupid full skirt kept catching on branches. Thank the Lord the thunder and wind that had been threatening for hours hadn't yet turned to rain. And that I was still faster than anyone on any day.

My bare feet hurt, was probably bleeding, but I couldn't

stop. Not unless I wanted to be torn to shreds like they'd just done to my brother—

I swiped at my tears and ran on. There wasn't nothing back there for me but death. Maybe if I'd kept my head down like Pa had always said, they would still be alive. If I'd just held back and not indulged in using my abilities, the mistress wouldn't have punished them. Lila, Matthew, Mama, Pa. They'd still be alive.

Alive and enslaved. But alive and with me, at least. Alive.

I couldn't hear the howls no more, so I slowed. My lungs burned; my tears ran hot.

My family. Dead. 'Cause I dared to defend them.

Now you know good and well it's 'cause you killed the master.

I laughed at the thought, muffling it with my hand when the trees echoed back.

Why you laughing, dumbass?

I let out a breath and swiped at my eyes again. At least that demon of a man was dead. His wife was worse, but I wasn't going to see her evil ass again. Besides, my family was with God now. Safe. Free. Better off.

I was the only one still in hell.

"What you going to do now, Jerusalem?" I murmured. Them hounds would catch me up soon, just sitting here. I needed a plan. I thought hard, trying to remember the things I'd heard whispered about at night when there wasn't no risk of prying ears. That the closest free state wasn't too far—Pennsylvania, I think they called it. If I kept heading north, I'd hit it eventually. Black people could make a living up there. Wasn't no whips or overseers. Maybe people like me, with inhuman strength and speed, didn't have to hide what we could do.

Hold your horses. You ain't even out the master's woods yet.

Naw. I had to stop calling that man master. I was free of him. No more chains. It wasn't his woods no more if he was dead, anyways; it was the mistress's.

You want to be free, Jerusalem? Then talk like it.

Adelaide. Not mistress. Adelaide.

I pressed my collar into my eyes to soak up tears that wouldn't stop. Adelaide Troy. She deserved a death worse than anything, except I couldn't have killed her if I tried. Her husband had been a human, flesh and beating heart. But she was a literal bloodsucking monster. Soulless, wicked as the day was long. Who'd hanged Mama and Pa, let them hounds have Matthew—

A howl sounded not too far off. *Speak of the devil.* I straightened and lifted my chin. I outran them once; I could do it again. And this time, I wouldn't stop.

But resting had dropped my pulse, eased the tight feeling in my body that told me to run.

Instead, I turned around and rushed toward the barking.

I didn't know what I was doing, what I was *going* to do. All I could think of was my big brother. Of Matthew.

"*Show them how fast* you *can run,*" he'd whispered in my hair as I'd held on tight around his waist. It was the last thing he said before they dragged him away from me . . . and when I couldn't save him, I did exactly that.

More tears gathered, and I tripped over some branches, falling hard onto my hands and knees, panting, the howls dangerously close. I felt for the branch—it was heavy, trailing off like massive antlers—and snapped off usable pieces.

They had seen my speed. Now they would witness my strength.

I'd seen them hounds plenty of times before, but up close,

even in the dark, I couldn't rightly call them animals. It wasn't even that they was huge—a horse was bigger without being terrifying. I'd seen wolves before, too, and as wild animals, they wasn't as ferocious. I'd even seen these very hounds as pups but was convinced that somewhere in the middle of maturation, they'd been swapped out for monsters fit to match the ones who owned them. No question, they was hell's creatures—spawned from a fiery pit.

The shadow of a beast ran toward me, and I held the antlered end of that branch and ran right back, a crack of thunder blocking out my yell. It didn't even have a chance to scream as I nailed it right in the mouth, running it through with a wet noise.

One down.

The second hound was farther away, but I threw a small log at it, missing. I threw another and clipped its leg, enough to make it trip to a stop with a whimper. I wasn't no good at throwing, looked like, so I switched to a club-size branch. These beasts wanted to make it up close and personal, and I'd give them that last request.

I rushed up to the one I'd nicked and crushed its lungs in before sinking my fingers in its fur and lifting it in time to use as a shield for the next. When that one's teeth was good and sunk in flesh and fur, I cracked it over the head, snapping my club, a chunk splintering off and flying past my face.

Three hounds dead. There was one more, but I was down all my weapons. The last hound wasn't running—it must've known something was off 'cause it kept pausing and sniffing, its ears going up and down. I used a loud crash of thunder as cover to sneak over to my first kill and broke off a piece of the branch still shoved right through it. But the cover didn't last, and the last hound jerked up at the *snap*, charging at me. I quickly put the stick in my apron pocket and ran back to the hound I'd hit with the club. If something worked once, I could do it again. Use this one as a shield while stabbing the last hound in the back of the neck. Or wherever I could aim. Anything to stop it enough to land a killing blow—

The last hound didn't move as well in the dark as I did 'cause it slammed into a tree snout-first, howling as it fell. I raised my brows—wasn't hounds supposed to be good hunters? There was a bit of squirming, the brush beneath it disturbed, and then it was still.

I didn't see nothing else move. I paused to listen, my swallow the loudest thing in my ears aside from my pulse. But I didn't hear nothing else, neither.

I released a heavy breath.

Four. There was only the four. And now they was dead.

Except, Lord, there wasn't only four. I saw another run toward me, but this one wasn't big and bulky. It was quick as a shadow, with an artful run that dodged around trees instead of a charge like a dumb, bloodthirsty beast. I swear it was only a second that I looked down to find a weapon, but when I looked back up to where the hound had been, it was gone.

Light met the edge of my eye, and I spun quickly, but a cold hand clamped around my wrist before I could back away.

When I seen the man's face, my body went stiff as a scared possum. My blood felt like sludge, and yet my heart raced hot. I recognized him as the overseer—well, one of them. The head of them. The *worst* of them. He held an oil lantern and had a big old knife strapped at his hip. He *snuck up on me*, even with that lantern, and now I knew why a man stood before me and the hound had disappeared. I knew why I was so scared to move it hurt, why my breath came out in terrified gasps. 'Cause this monster wasn't no man.

He was a vampire.

Red hair like his pa, flaming in the lantern light like a demon's, and green eyes that looked more animal than human. He was one of them New Bloods, vampires that was turned in the past fifty years or so, instead of one of them Ancients from Europe. One year ago on his twenty-first birthday, he'd asked his bloodsucking step-mama Adelaide if he could be turned 'cause he wanted to be able to beat us all better. And, Lord, could he—his pa had to make him ease up 'cause he kept killing us, and they didn't have no money to keep throwing around buying more people to torture.

He'd been that monstrous before he'd been turned, to be honest. But now he was strong as an ox, too.

"You killed all four hounds?" he asked, and his voice was violent already without him doing nothing, like them nasty beasts meant something to him.

"One to go," I said, tipping my chin at him.

What in the hell, Jerusalem! my body screamed inside. My muscles tightened, forget how brave I sounded. *How you expect to kill a vamp?*

"Never could control that sass of yours." The edges of his mouth was raw and scabbed, and when he smiled at me with them fanged canines they threatened to tear open. "And to think, I had planned on bringing you home alive."

He set the lantern on the ground, sending stark shadows to haunt the woods around us. I tried to jerk away while he was off balance, but he was too fast, too strong. I hit the ground, so sudden that I didn't feel no pain till he had me by the hair, half dragging me to my feet. And next thing I seen was nothing but darkness with a flash of blurred light . . . then stinging, throbbing pain hit like a brick, and I realized he done slammed the side of my head into a tree. My face was wet with something thicker than tears, warmer than rain.

Killing his human father and them hounds made me forget this man—this monster—was beyond my physical match.

He dragged me to him, and for a second, I felt dizzy from the movement. My back was at his stomach, my hands locked in his crushing grip, as he forced me down with him to kneel on the ground.

"I'm going to enjoy ripping the life out your little body. But first . . ." His bony fingers dug into my hair to the root, pulling my head back and sideways, stretching my neck painfully. He inhaled deeply. "You sure do smell a whole lot better than you look . . ."

"No, no, no . . ." I whimpered, kicking and fighting and crying—we was back to crying, but everything within me was revolting, my disgust of what was about to happen too much to stomach. I couldn't die, not like *this*. Not eaten alive by this monster.

I shouldn't have turned back. I should have listened to my big brother and kept running. My quiet, brave brother . . .

My sweet, logical Mama.

Pa, my anchor, my strength.

And pretty Lila, with so much hope.

I was about to see them again, wasn't I? I was going to die slow, in agony, sucked dry. Forgotten. Dead and gone to the world, and no one would care. But I'd be with my family after . . . and maybe that'd be better.

But then . . . who would make Adelaide Troy pay?

I was stronger and faster than most men. I could make her

regret the day she took my family, along with any other vamp who got in my way.

And dying was no way to do it.

I felt the tingle of his nasty cold lips at my skin, and I jerked my elbow back. Must've hit somewhere good, too, 'cause he cussed and let up his grip a little—enough for me to tear my hand from his and pull the jagged stick from my apron pocket. It was in his neck before I even knew what I was doing. The sound from him was vile, but I didn't think to stop. I snatched the big knife from his belt and plunged it into his chest, the force shoving him to his back.

My head throbbed, and my hands shook. The vamp cussed as he tried to remove the knife, but he stayed on his back, like he was pinned there.

I didn't know if it was my blood or his, but I wiped my hands on the monster's shirt.

"You disgusting rat," he gurgled, twitching, the shadow of his hand reaching for me in the lantern glow. "You don't know the lashing you're about to get!"

I moved out of his reach and stood. I done missed his heart, I think, 'cause he wasn't dying. Not fast enough. Never killed no vamp before; maybe they could get up again. Maybe he'd recover.

I opened the lantern door but wasn't about to burn myself trying to get at the oil. Instead, I looked around for a stick and lit the end of it.

"What do you think you're doing, girl?"

I threw the lantern on the ground hard so it busted, oil running out from the bottom. The flame, oddly, stayed put.

"I said, what you think you doing?" his voice rose shrill, shifting to a scream as I set the lantern on his stomach, the hot oil and lard burning through his shirt.

Finally, he got the message. His eyes went wide as saucers as I picked up the flaming stick.

I smiled down at him. "Enjoy hell."

I dropped the stick on his oiled belly, and an inferno leapt to life, fueled by the monster's body and the burning wick in the lantern.

After that, I hightailed it out of there, no looking back, till the edge of the flame's light faded to pitch night, till the screams no longer carried. All I heard was my breath, my steps, and night noises.

Mama once told me, "Jerusalem, you can't sew like Lila, can't cook like me, and you got a smart mouth to boot. Find you something useful you love to do and perfect it."

Reckon she didn't think it'd be killing.

2

ALEXEI

Pennsylvania
June 29, 1863
One year later

American prey was less exciting than the prey back home.

But then, vampires were still considered Creatures of the Night over in Russia. Superstitions, myths, terrifying stories parents used to get their children home by sundown. There, hunting took planning. Skill. Here, we were a common part of life. Owning plantations, wandering where we pleased, *when* we pleased. Still at the top of the food chain, but with far less need to stalk our prey.

So when I caught the eye of the woman picking berries behind her house, and she immediately succumbed to my hypnosis, I nearly changed my mind. No chase, no excitement. Just me, looking very much human despite my incredible beauty, enthralling a woman with only a look.

To be honest, I was bored.

But I needed to drink *something*. Odessa had been gone on a stealth mission this entire week, and as a result, I'd been tasked with keeping Jerusalem under control. As if anyone could control Jerusalem—she'd sooner break your arm than listen to anyone but Odessa. So I just made sure she slept enough and stopped her from brawling with every soldier who looked at her wrong. It left little time to feed. And seeing as I was only in this country to assist the Union army in the War Between the States, I couldn't very well feed on a random soldier. I had to venture away from camp, but only when Jerusalem was sleeping, which left me less than a four-hour window to scour the area. Not to mention animal blood was disgusting. All that to say, I hadn't had a proper meal in a while.

It wouldn't have even mattered if Jerusalem wasn't . . . well, Jerusalem. If her blood wasn't the sweetest thing I'd ever smelled in my life. I was an Ancient, not some stupid New Blood who couldn't control his thirst. But her scent drove me mad in a way I could hardly process.

It was better to be safe than devastated.

And since Odessa and Gael had arrived from their mission this morning, I felt safe leaving to catch up on my hunting.

I held out my hand, refocusing on the woman, and she took it without question, as if in greeting. I sighed—this really was too easy—and leaned down, raising it to my lips.

Inches away, I turned her wrist slowly. She watched as if I were about to perform magic, and she didn't want to miss the trick. It *was* a trick, I supposed, hypnosis.

I sunk my fangs into her wrist, where I knew the blood

would flow freely, and drank. And she let me. As long as I kept her looking at me, she would let me suck her dry if I wanted to, without even processing what was happening. My kind preferred their blood from the throat, but breaking the connection resulted in frantic prey who would struggle and ultimately need to be killed. I hated wasting prey—and her blood tasted good, as far as American blood was concerned—she would make more blood for me later if I chose to find her again. So I stopped before the point of her eyes fluttering, her vision going black. She looked a bit trembly, but nothing a glass of water wouldn't fix.

I licked her blood from my lips. She hadn't been able to give enough before becoming light-headed. I'd have to find dessert elsewhere.

"I'll give this back to you," I said, pressing her apron to her wrist and resting it against her stomach.

"Thank you, sir," she replied, dazed.

I smirked. I didn't think I'd ever get used to how some of them did that. Despite the revolution, the politeness of their former Mother England remained, and it was odd to say the least.

"You're on your way home," I said, her hypnotized mind clinging to my every word, "and have not encountered anyone on your way."

And then I shifted into one of my other preferred forms—a black crow—and took off, snatching the basket of berries from her other hand as I rushed upward.

Flapping my wings was a nice relief from the heat. Not that I could feel hot or cold in that way—they didn't affect me negatively, at least. But this was the northern territory of *North America*, and for some reason I'd always thought it would feel . . .

I don't know, a little milder. Their Julys were hot enough that the odor of sweat filled the air just as thick as the smoke that veiled the sun. At least flying kept the stench away.

Even after two years out here, I still hadn't found much to appreciate as far as views were concerned. Perhaps it was beautiful elsewhere, but there were only so many woods and farmlands I could look at before it became monotonous. I'd heard so many good things about America, but if wartime couldn't make this country more interesting, then I couldn't recommend it.

Go easy on it, Alexei. After all, the things I might have found beautiful as a human tended to become old news after three hundred years.

I shifted to my human form as I reached camp, carrying the berries with me. My arrival must have been awaited because a young soldier rushed up to me.

"Welcome back, sir," he said.

John? No, Nathan. Something like that? There were a lot of those running around. I held the basket of berries out to him, hung on one finger. "Put this in my tent."

"Of course, sir." He cradled the basket like it was a baby and rushed off.

I scoffed and headed toward the war tent; I could smell Odessa, Gael, and Mills waiting for me. On the outskirts of camp, Jerusalem stood on a small boulder, doing her daily training exercises with her spear.

"That brat is training without me," I muttered, grinning despite her betrayal.

I immediately changed targets and headed toward her, staying out of her eyeline. As a vampire, I had a way of being light on my feet when I wanted to be, no matter how heavy my boots, so I simply walked up behind her. The boulder made her a few feet taller than me, and her waist was in perfect grabbing range . . . My fingers ached to touch her, but she would kill me for startling her while she was training, so I kept my hands in my pockets. As long as she didn't turn around, she would never even notice I was there.

But where was the fun in that?

"You're finally a normal height, I see," I teased, but I'd barely finished my sentence before she turned and quickly launched her spear at me.

If my heart could pound, it would've as I lunged sideways, barely in time to avoid the weapon, watching it slam into the boulder behind me, shattering to pieces.

Not your brightest idea, Alexei.

If that had hit me, it would have cut me in half just from sheer force. A human her size, throwing a weapon far larger than herself, with that much speed and power . . . it was inconceivable. I'd never had a Saint come so close to killing me, and it was both unsettling and admirable.

"Alexei, what in the hell?" Jerusalem lifted her leather beaked plague mask to scowl at me, planting a hand on her hip, thumb forward. "You raring to get killed or what?"

I tried not to grin too broadly, but her Southern accent was music to my ears. "Good morning to you, too, Saint Jerusalem."

She gave me a grimace of a smile. "Wouldn't mind killing you, come to think of it," she muttered as she leapt down from the boulder to retrieve her spear. I didn't need to breathe to live, but I held my breath anyway as she passed so the scent of her blood wouldn't drive me absolutely feral. Sweet, a little spiced. I swallowed quickly to keep myself from drooling. I don't remember much about being human, but surely I had more self-control than this when it came to food.

I would need to finish my breakfast to ease the edge.

When she was safely beyond me, I turned to her. "Why are you training without me?

She yanked her spear out of the hard ground without any trouble despite it being wedged in by at least a foot. "You was gone when I got up."

"You woke up too early. Perhaps you should start sleeping the proper length a human should."

"How do you know how long humans got to sleep? You ain't been human since Jesus resurrected."

"I'm not *that* ancient."

"No, you right," she said, a playfulness in her eyes if not her expression. "If you was older, maybe you wouldn't be such a dumbass."

I grinned. "I love when you provoke me."

"Oh no," she said, deadpan. "The White Wolf fittin' to risk mussing up his hair—run for cover!"

I snatched her up and threw her legs over my shoulder, my arm around her waist. A laugh burst out of her as the back of her head hit my stomach, and I reveled in her joy.

She sat up using only her abdomen muscles, scowling at me as if she hadn't just been smiling. "Put me down; you interrupting my training."

"I'll interrupt all I like. Next time, wait for me."

"Next time I'll stab you, how about that?"

I released her waist, allowing her to land on her feet. "You still don't look before you throw."

"Oh, I saw you," she said, and flicked her finger up and down at me. "Giant-ass tree. Who could miss you?"

I gestured to the shattered stone behind me. "And yet?"

She raised a brow. "And yet." With that, she climbed back

up on her boulder and returned to spinning her spear, as if she hadn't just awakened something inside me ready to worship her.

I grinned, backing away so I could watch her work before suddenly remembering I was expected elsewhere. What a distraction this girl was . . . "Vengeance will be had, Tiny Saint."

"Just try it, Silver Fox," she called after me, as I hurried on to the war tent.

She always did like to bid me goodbye with her most cutting insult.

After she found out the papers had taken to calling me the White Wolf, Jerusalem had seen fit to downgrade me whenever she wanted.

"You ain't *all that*," she'd said with a disdainful purse of her lips. "More of a whiny fox than anything."

When I pushed aside the tent's flapped opening, Odessa and Mills were sitting at the war council table and Gael was standing with his wide-brimmed hat held politely against his stomach. Odessa shook her head at me, so I knew I'd done something wrong. I gave her a winning smile and she smirked. Whatever it was, she'd forgive me.

"How was it?" I greeted Gael in Spanish (you couldn't help but pick up a few languages when you'd been around as long as I had). He spoke English, too, but the first time I'd ever spoken Spanish with him was the first time I'd seen him smile while talking to me, so I'd kept it up. And in return, he didn't avoid me like the other Saints did, which seemed to be the greatest show of friendship he would ever afford me. It was enough, considering the Northern sentiment on vampires.

He nodded in greeting, his dark eyes twinkling. "You'll see."

Vague, but promising. Clearly good news.

Odessa and Mills stood to join us—the colonel couldn't have

been more than twenty years older than her, but he pushed himself up from the chair much slower and with a small grunt. Human knees decomposed quickly.

Odessa pulled me in for a hug. She wasn't one to go up on her toes, even if I was six-foot-five and had to lean over quite a bit to get to her. When we were first on hugging terms, I'd tried to pick her up, and she'd yelled at me. It was the first time someone had ordered me around in three hundred years, and it had been confusing to say the least.

"I'm a grown woman," she'd said when I'd asked why. "Not a toddler. Not a puppy. Not an object. You don't just pick me up."

"Plenty of grown women have practically begged me to pick them up, Dess," I'd said.

"You see the difference?" she'd asked, giving me a disapproving look.

I think . . . no, it was. That was the first time I'd been told *no* in that way by a human since I'd been human myself—of course, every human I'd encountered since had either been terrified, seduced, or hypnotized, so there really was no room for rejection. To be frank, my entire friendship with Dess was the first time I'd viewed a human as more than just a business partner or a food source.

If a Black woman could make me change my ways hundreds of years in the making in a matter of seconds, it was no wonder the white men here wanted to keep an entire race of people in check.

"You're ten minutes late," she chided, for my ears only. "You do love to embarrass me."

Late?

"The meeting begins when I arrive, my friend," I said, squeezing her. "How was your trip?"

We disengaged, and she tugged down her blue jacket to smooth it. "Fruitful."

There was a finality to the way she said it that excited me. If I gathered nothing else, it was that we were in for quite a battle.

"A handful of Southern soldiers have taken up a stronghold in Gettysburg, a few days' journey from here," Odessa said, unfolding a worn, yellowed paper and handing it to Mills. "General Lee plans to march his troops there and gain ground in the North. What Saint Gael and I propose is sending a small group—"

A small group? Why was I in this meeting? This didn't concern me whatsoever.

But what I *did* think about—*still* thought about—was that tiny traitor training *without me*. When did she start doing that?

Mills handed me the report, and I pretended to scan through it. English was a foul language that I hadn't bothered to master in written form, and so I could only pick out a few words and phrases. I assumed it was everything Odessa had just told us, which didn't pertain to me, anyway. Why would I ever want to go on a mission that would lead me *away* from the army, running ahead of them only to kill those few soldiers manning the stronghold? Naturally, I'd be staying behind to meet the army head-on. My blade was thirstier than I was at this point.

Humans weren't much sport, but at least there would be—

I stared at the four names of the vampires listed. No, not at all four, one in particular . . . the only one I could make out because his name consisted of just five letters, and one of the English words I could recognize with certainty was *the*.

"Zamir the Mangler?" I muttered aloud, shock coating my voice. And yet, just saying his name, I felt a soft fondness return, of memories long forgotten.

Zamir . . . I hadn't heard his name in a long time, let alone seen him. He'd be a thousand years old by now, a true Ancient who had never left Eastern Europe his entire life. And now he was *here* in America. At precisely the same time I was. It couldn't have been a coincidence.

And if he was here, that meant—

A sharp sound slipped out of me. I quickly cleared my throat to cover it, but that didn't stop my hand from pressing into the side of my stomach where pale scars burned with as much stabbing pain as the day they'd been inflicted.

Don't let them see, Alexei.

I put the paper down on the large table full of maps and diagrams, then folded my arms across my chest so there'd be no evidence my hands were shaking. I'd moved quickly enough, I think, because with half my ears, I heard Mills continuing to blab on as if nothing had happened.

But I couldn't move on. I had thought that part of my life was well behind me, but if Zamir was here, that meant so was *she*, and I never thought I'd have to worry about seeing the one who'd turned me ever again. The one who'd kept me captive for months.

Pain bloomed all over me, and even though I knew it was imagined, my mind wouldn't let go of it. Of the metal shackles digging into my wrists, tearing my skin raw. Of the sharp shards of bone stabbing through my skin as she broke my limbs, allowing them to heal just so she could do it again. Of the starvation draining my body within an inch of insanity—

"What about Zamir?" Odessa asked—*again*, it seemed, since I hadn't heard the first time in my panic. She was giving me a narrow-eyed look, like she was realizing something about him was significant. Gael looked at me, too, but only because

Odessa did, and it was less accusatory and more confused. Mills didn't look suspicious whatsoever, so all I had to do was redirect the two Saints, and quickly . . . if it wasn't already too late for that.

"He's not the battle type, that's all," I said dismissively. "Last I saw him, he was back in Russia making art out of human bodies." That was a lie—the last time I saw him, I was . . . it didn't matter. Not to Dess or Gael. Not to the colonel. I should have lied even more, in fact. They didn't need to know everything I knew about Zamir. He wasn't even the problem. "Just surprised he made the journey."

That seemed to satisfy them. Either way, I didn't hear anything that was said next. There was no way Zamir had come here alone. He only spoke Polish, Tuvan, and passable Russian. His understanding of English barely existed. His favorite hobby was heavily reliant on the fact vampires weren't part of human society over there. And America was far too loud for him.

I suppose one could change in three hundred years, but when I'd met him, he was already seven hundred years. He wasn't the type to break from his routine. No . . . there was no way he'd come to this country alone. As much as I wished I was mistaken, I knew Zamir too well.

He wouldn't leave Red Mask. He was here because she was.

I felt a hand on my elbow and looked down to find Odessa taking my arm.

"Time to gather the Saints," she said.

The meeting was adjourned, then. I'd missed everything. Hopefully nothing pertinent.

"Oh. Yes." I flashed a grin. I would rather die than show how I was screaming inside. "I'll catch up."

Gael held the flap open for her, then exited behind, and as

soon as the flap shut behind them, I leaned over the colonel. I sensed his pulse pick up, and it reminded me I was still a little thirsty. *Not for drinking, Alexei.* I didn't derive pleasure from making humans nervous, but it certainly never hurt negotiations.

"I will lead the mission," I said, smirking inwardly at his shocked expression since men never took smiles seriously in situations like these. "And I'll pick my own team."

"What?" Mills paused, looking a bit pale in the face. "Your talents are wasted on a covert mission such as this. Wouldn't you prefer fighting?"

"Which part of what I just said confused you?"

His jaws snapped shut.

"This is our priority, colonel," I said. "Without that stronghold back in our possession, your army doesn't stand a chance."

Sometimes the nonsense that flowed from my mouth to manipulate humans scared even me. This was, in fact, the most trivial mission I could ever think of participating in. If we headed off the army before they got close to the stronghold and ran them back south—or better yet, killed them all—they'd never get to use it as an advantage. It would be easy enough to steal back later. But truth be told, this silly mission was all that was standing between me and having to face my former captor.

It was better than the risk of her catching me and taking me back. She had been . . . *unfathomably* strong when she'd turned me, and a vampire's strength only increased the longer they inhabited the earth. It would take a miracle to defeat her, even with an entire battalion. Except she didn't care about the battalion.

She was here for me.

So if I had to make it sound important enough for me to waste my time on, that was what I would do.

My nonsense must have convinced Mills without my having to hypnotize him because he nodded. "Yes. Of course, Alexei. Whatever you think is best."

I left the tent before he could question me again.

It was fine. Everything would be fine. In an hour or two, I'd be heading far from the Southern army.

Which left me open to worry about something more immediate.

Vengeance.

I looked out at camp, my eyes on Jerusalem, training again, and made sure her back was still turned before rushing over to her tent. I kicked off my muddy boots and left them blocking the opening before continuing to my own.

3

JERUSALEM

*T*he Saints laughed at me the day I picked a spear as my weapon. Harder to aim for the heart, they said, and even I knew my aim was bad. Tall as a person, so how was my short ass going to spin it? Could never move as fast as a sword in up-close combat. Hell, maybe that was why I *did* choose it—to prove to myself I could do it.

Anyway, men didn't need much reason to tease me. I was a five-foot Black girl born into slavery—everything they'd been raised to underestimate. So each morning and evening, I took my spear just outside of camp and did fifty spin variations, fifty thrusts, fifty slashes, fifty throws. A few months into training, they stopped laughing.

Threats ain't so funny.

Lucky for them, I had bigger fish to fry.

This morning wasn't no different. I spun my spear, the head flashing like a wild, silver spark. I'd done most of my spin variations and throws already when something caught my nose.

I breathed in, picking up an awful stench. I could smell

it through the burning thickness of soot and sulfur in the air, through the herbs and medicines and such in my beaked leather plague mask meant to filter out the smoke. I raised my mask to rest on my head, my lips settling into a satisfied grin. I recognized that smell, and without my mask, I recognized the source, too.

A plume of smoke was working its way heavenward. Only leetles and bry did that—a root and a stone that, when combined, burned pitch and thick without fading away for weeks. There was plenty of plumes down South—vamps had taken to making the bonfires to veil the sunlight so they could be up during the day to do business with humans without getting hives.

So they wouldn't miss out on torturing their slaves, more like.

The Northern states seemed only minorly affected by it— the smoke drifting up from the South, making everything up here a little cloudy, a little hazy, but not real dark and stormy like the skies in Virginia. But this was the first time I'd ever seen an actual plume in a Union state.

Now it was looking like the Southern army was bringing the war to us and had some vamps with them. But this was Pennsylvania. Them graybacks was fools to think they could hold a Northern territory for long, not if me, Lex, and Dess had anything to say about it.

"Jerusalem!"

I pulled my attention from the plume and turned on the worn-down heel of my leather boot to look over at camp, at the woman waving at me. Odessa. Relief settled on me, warm and cozy. *Finally.* If I had my way, that would be the last mission she ever did without me.

"You never stop training, do you?" Odessa asked when I

reached her, shaking her head with that pretty, fond grin. She had her heavy bow slung across her shoulders, a leather quiver at her hip full of arrows. Saints toted their weapons everywhere to be recognized from regular soldiers. Wasn't why I kept *mine* handy, but to each their own.

"Got to be ready, Dess," I said with a shrug. "But how was your spying? Man, I wish I could've gone with you."

"Next time, I promise," she said, giving me a squeeze around the shoulders. "In the meantime, the colonel is calling a meeting of all the Saints."

"Them graybacks is building a new bonfire," I said, pointing over my shoulder with my thumb, "so I'm sure it got to do with vamps."

"They're getting bolder of late." Dess pulled me in close with the arm still around my shoulders before adding, "I have a present for you."

"What is it?" I asked, barely able to hold in my excitement.

She hugged me even closer. "Everything I tell you must stay between us," she whispered. "You can't tell a soul, nor can you talk about it where anyone could be listening. Not even to me or Alexei."

"Yes'm," I said without question.

I knew good and well how to keep a secret—living under masters my whole life, most all my secrets were life and death, ones to keep my family safe. So none of what she'd said gave me pause or made me nervous. It was that she'd said it was a present that truly got me, and my body vibrated with excited nerves. When Dess gave presents, they was always memorable—cake, the boots I was wearing. Hell, even my spear was a gift.

And something told me this would be the best one of all.

"When the colonel explains the mission," she said, "he'll say a small group must overtake an enemy stronghold. That's the plan we want everyone to believe. Instead, we are going straight for the army to launch a sneak attack against the vamps when they least expect it."

My vibrating risked turning into hopping, and I forced my feet still. But even so, I frowned. Part of it didn't make no sense to me. "Why a small group?"

"You don't want another Saint to steal your kill, do you?"

"My kill?" My body lit up, all that vibrating bursting my insides into glorious, enrapturing flame. But there was rage right along with it . . . rage I'd had to keep to myself for so long, too long, finally breaking free. "Naw, Dess, it ain't never Ade—" Dess shushed me, and I dropped down to a whisper that felt like a growl leaving me. "Adelaide finally joined the army?"

Finally.

Every night for the past year, I done prayed to God to punish my enemy the way that monster had punished my family—in a slow, brutal death. It was what she deserved. And I wasn't ignorant enough to believe I could kill her after a few months' experience. I was strong, fast, and capable, but I knew I'd need at least a year to develop the skill to kill her in the way I wanted. And I'd prayed to God to not let me see that murderous monster till the day I was ready.

And now, a year later, here was my enemy, delivered right on a silver platter.

Wasn't sure whether to thank God or Dess, but in this state, I'd thank the next bird that flew by. "Thank you, God!" I wrapped Dess in my arms, squeezing her tight as she chuckled. "Thank you, Dess!"

"I knew you'd be pleased."

"Can I lead the mission? I know more about that vamp than anyone, I reckon."

"You'll have to ask the colonel." She held me at arm's length like a proud mama. "Now, remember what I said. This is between me, you, Alexei, and Gael."

I groaned. "Gael got to come, too?"

"He's the sweetest man in the world; what could you possibly have against him?" asked Dess with a sweet smile to match her words. A little too sweet for a married woman to be talking about some man that wasn't her husband. He was a nice guy, but not all *that*.

"He ain't been in the army but three months, and already you trust him more than me."

"He's a seasoned soldier, shares the same goals as me, and is even-tempered. What's there not to trust?"

Fine. That *was* true.

Still, I scrunched up my nose. "Well, he don't barely talk. It's weird."

Gael was the only brown-skinned Saint other than me and Dess, and he didn't so much hang out with us as show up whenever Dess was in need of service—like Dess was the vamp recruiting familiars instead of Alexei. He was handsome but in a fatherly sort of way, with silky black hair and a dark beard that hid how young or old he could be. He wore a cross but smoked like a sinner. And the only time I ever heard his voice above a murmur was when he sang, pretty as a songbird. I could like him, really, if the quiet didn't freak me out . . . and if I didn't get the feeling he was fittin' to steal Dess's heart right from under her husband's nose.

It always be the quiet ones you had to look out for. Not to

mention the ones in hats, and Gael's was well and big enough for some good secrets.

"He doesn't feel the need to speak unnecessarily." Dess raised a playful brow. "I wish that mindset would rub off on you, to be honest."

"What you trying to say, Dess?"

"That you need to learn to control that mouth of yours before it gets you into trouble."

Boy, did I know that to be true. My mouth had gotten me into more than just trouble. Still, we was living in a world white folks had created . . . and if white folks was going to try to silence me, well then I would be fittin' to holler even louder. But they already hated us, so why not make them miserable along the way?

But I said, "Fine," for Dess's sake, and played like I was locking my lips up and threw the invisible key over my shoulder.

She smirked. "Let's go gather the Saints."

My smile might've been a bit too big as I walked with my captain back to camp.

Even smirking at me like an amused mama would at a toddler, a look I'd kill any other Saint for trying, I still couldn't help but think she was the prettiest woman I'd ever seen. The kind of pretty that came from being born free. Free and noble and just, like how an archangel might look. Strong limbs with good fat cushioning muscle, that could switch from handling a bow so heavy an arrow shot from it could tear off heads, to a motherly touch that could put a baby to sleep—could and did, since she had five children back home. And she had an angel's attitude and grace and devotion. She was pure power and glorious purpose. Only thing the woman was missing was wings.

But even if she didn't look like she broke bread with the

angel Michael, I had this belief—and ain't nobody could tell me nothing to change my mind—that you could tell the most about someone just by looking at their hair. From status to who they sided with, it was different from person to person in texture, condition, style. Moods affected it. Nutrition, even more.

And Odessa's coily hair was immaculate. Healthy and moisturized and pinned into a neat bun at the back of her head. She kept trophies from each vamp she slayed—their fangs, long like wolves' teeth—attached to the pins she used to keep her bun tight. Having begun her collection at the start of the war, two years later, her bun was circled twice over, like a vicious, razor crown.

All the Saints kept trophies, and Dess had the most. But I couldn't stomach the thought. Not 'cause of the killing—Lord knew I liked the killing, maybe a little too much. Just the *keeping*. I didn't want no part of them bloodsucking monsters. Why should any memory of them be kept for future generations? Let them be forgotten, I say.

It was the least they deserved.

The rest of the camp was up now and getting ready for the day. What used to be working farmland now housed hundreds of tents, soldiers with blue coats, artillery, and fussy horses. I'd been with the Union army a full year, but I still wasn't sure I'd ever get used to it. Hanging around so many white people, I mean. Me and Odessa was the only Black women in the battalion, but Odessa was captain of an all-Black company made up of about eighty soldiers. They didn't sleep side-by-side with the white soldiers, and I'd've joined them if I didn't want to be closer to the action—with no rank or position, I had to tag along with Odessa into the Saint meetings, and those were very white affairs—other than Gael, but he was so quiet, it'd be easy to forget he was even there if he didn't manage to loom still in all that silence. All that to say, up North, whites didn't believe in human slaves, but that didn't mean they considered Black people equals.

Still, that they was fighting for the freedom of Black people at all was good enough for now. One problem at a time.

I looked down and grunted. The colonel was going to give me a problem if I showed up to the meeting looking a mess without my blue Union coat. It annoyed him enough that I was in the meetings in the first place—I was a Saint 'cause of naturally enhanced skills, but not a soldier and definitely not one of his captains like Odessa. Mills could die mad for all I cared, but I respected Odessa too much to embarrass her. And besides, I needed the conditions to be just right before demanding I lead the mission.

"Have you seen the latest?" Will rushed over to us, waving a newspaper. Looking like a walking piece of chalk. "I have a code name."

"Congratulations," said Odessa, her tone diplomatic.

"Just two years into the war, huh?" I said, meeting his butt-hurt scowl with a sort of non-smile.

"Just because you were given one six months into your career," he said, "doesn't make you a better Saint than me."

"It do, though."

"What do they call you?" Odessa interrupted, subtly squeezing my hand to hush me.

I rolled my eyes. It did, though. Every Saint out there on the front lines, doing their part, had a code name given by the papers. Usually had something to do with their Saint weapon or how they chose to kill vamps. To them, I was the Demon Saint 'cause, as the papers first put it almost six months ago, I was "like some unstoppable menace spawned from the depths of hell." At first, I'd hated it—I'd been called demon spawn before, and not in a good way—but then I realized I always wore my mask during battles and nobody could even tell I was Black. Even Odessa, who mainly stood back and killed her targets from a distance without having to join the fray, was known as the Specter on account her arrows just came out of nowhere like they was shot by a ghost.

Anyway, even if code names didn't mean nothing, trophies sure as hell did, and Chalk Boy didn't have but ten sets of fangs sewn to his belt in two years. Gael already had that many circling the band of his wide-brimmed hat, and he'd only been here three months. Just sad, really.

"Wait until you hear it." He cleared his throat and read, "'The White Wolf led our boys into . . .'" Blah, blah, blah. "'The Southern army was forced to retreat, thanks to the quick actions of the White Wolf and his Saints: the Demon Saint, the Specter, and the Butcher. Torch was also seen there.'" He beamed, pointing to some words. "Look at this. 'Torch was also seen there.' They call me Torch."

"That's nice," Odessa said.

Torch. I mean, he used a fiery club for a Saint weapon, so it made sense. Still, if I was him I'd be embarrassed to show my face on the battlefield.

"Sure they ain't just missing an *A*?" I said, trying to hold back a laugh. "''A torch was seen there'? You know, 'cause it was dark out.'"

Will dropped his arms, the paper slapping his leg with a small crinkly crunch. "You know, people might actually like you if you made yourself agreeable."

Made myself agreeable. As if I had any interest in changing myself to make this chalky child happy.

My days of burying my spirit to stay in the good graces of white folks were over.

"Don't you got an alley to light, Torch?" I asked, walking away before he could say something else ridiculous, and yelling over my shoulder, "Imma get my blue coat, Dess."

But I tripped to a stop at my tent's entrance, staring at a pair of boots there. Big, muddy boots, too big and muddy to be mine.

I knew them big old boots anywhere.

I growled and snatched them up.

"Here we go . . ." muttered Odessa, but I didn't stick around long enough to be teased. Instead, I stormed right over to Alexei's tent.

Two young volunteer soldiers lingered around it—one looked as red faced as a farmer, the other looked like he'd never worked a day in his life. They was probably older than me but looked green and bushy-tailed and stupid. I rolled my eyes and shoved passed them, slapping the tent's flap aside and storming in, barely looking at the dumbass sitting inside as I threw the boots at his head.

He knocked the boots away without any effort, his reflexes lightning fast like mine—clearly he'd smelled me approach and expected as much. His blue eyes were bright, welcoming . . . mischievous.

Annoying.

"Good morning, again, Saint Jerusalem." He smiled, his voice velvet with the tinge of an accent that wasn't quite American. "Don't you look like a vengeful angel of death."

I shifted my hand on my spear, my senses spiked. Alexei might've been able to effortlessly scare every person we crossed paths with, but I wasn't one of them. And it wasn't just 'cause I knew he wouldn't try to hurt me. It was 'cause monsters became significantly less intimidating after you've heard them complain about bedsheet thread counts.

Still. That didn't make him any less a vampire.

He stood, the movement fluid and quick like his sword in battle. Pale as seashells, white-blond hair that fell well past broad shoulders and glinted like a freshly cleaned blade, muscles sculpted as if he actually put effort into them. He was the type of pretty all those great painters of old had tried their best to capture but never could.

But he was also the type of annoying where his looks was never going to get in the way of me wanting to kick his ass.

"We was getting along like normal people this week," I said. "But now Dess ain't been back from her mission but one hour and you already back to leaving your stank-ass boots outside my tent?"

"I think you mean, 'Good morning, Alexei, thank you for calling me beautiful and powerful, even though I am also very bitter for my age.'"

"Clean your own, like the rest of us," I said impatiently. "Or get one of your many eager familiars to do it."

"You know I don't keep slaves."

That he said with no hint of teasing. His anger at my accusation—like owning people was the worst thing he could think of, 'cause it was—was about the most decent thing I'd ever heard out of a white boy.

But then, vampires were experts at fooling human prey.

Besides, he didn't get no blue ribbons for basic human decency.

I shrugged. "So you going to tell your little admirers out there to get lost, then? 'Cause we both know you ain't never turning them boys into vamps, so why not put them out of misery so they can stop following you around camp like hounds waiting for scraps. It's embarrassing."

Alexei smirked. "Don't tell me you're jealous."

"Ew."

"Listen, Tiny Saint. Listen." Alexei shook his head, approaching me casually, like he had the right. "I know I'm the first friend you've ever had—"

"Touch me, and you die," I growled, my killing instinct rising within me as his hand reached toward my chin.

"So let me educate you on the topic. When people care about each other, they do each other favors."

He didn't take my warning seriously, and I shifted my spear down to slice his arm with the razor head. My Saint reflexes were fast as if the world was slow—but Alexei was faster, drawing his knife and blocking the attack before I could so much as nick him.

"What makes you think we friends, Silver Fox?" I snapped, as we held each other there, weapon to weapon.

"Your scent," he said, with a slow smile, "lingering on every piece of fabric in this tent."

It didn't matter that I was a liar—I did consider him my friend, as unbelievable as it sounded to befriend a vamp, and a white one at that. And, true, I *had* shared his tent all week, so I didn't doubt he smelled me on everything. But that didn't mean nothing special; I just didn't like sleeping around all them men while Odessa wasn't here. And 'cause she trusted him, I did, too. So yeah, we was friends. But he made me mad as a dog when he wanted to, and I couldn't let that lie.

"Well, I don't do no free labor for no white man these days. So quit leaving your boots like you expect I'll clean them. This has got to be the third time this month."

"And it's the third time you've thrown them in my face." He rested his hand against the shaft of my spear, taking its weight before lowering his knife. "I like this consistency between us. Don't you?"

I didn't go no farther with my weapon, didn't even try. 'Cause I could see what he'd done—he'd made himself vulnerable. My spear could've easily been dampened in holy water—which was really nothing from the Almighty, just water infused with silver dust—and burned his ungloved fingers off. It usually was, before a battle. I could've killed him, and he knew it.

But Alexei had taught me to use my spear, to fight, when I'd showed up here a year ago with nothing but my brute strength and anger. He'd taught me the best ways to kill his kind—to kill *him* if I wanted He was still the better fighter, but I knew his secret weaknesses now, whereas he ain't know none of mine. He was in more danger than I was. Still, I wasn't about to betray his trust that way. It was the one olive branch I'd ever afford him. He had taught me to kill my one true enemy, and in exchange, I'd never thought to hurt him with cruel tricks. I was loyal to my allies, even if he was a bloodsucking pain in my ass.

I backed out of his presence with a scowl. Lord, I should've lowered my plague mask before I came in here so I wouldn't have to smell him. He smelled like blood and sweat and adrenaline. Like battle. But also a hint of shortbread? All the things I loved rolled into this cocksure monster, and I hated it.

"I catch any of your things by my tent again," I said, "you better trust and believe Imma burn them."

He smiled, his pointed canines gleaming. "We both know you won't."

That. *That.* If I didn't have somewhere to be *Lord*, I'd hit that boy in his pretty face so hard. "Quit messing around. Colonel

Mills want to see us," I snapped, storming out of the tent before he could say another word. I was so annoyed I almost smacked right into Odessa.

She was grinning.

"How'd it go?" She'd clearly listened in and knew exactly how it went, only she found it more amusing than I did.

I rolled my eyes. "Stupid, prideful donkey. As usual."

She handed me my blue coat. "He knows how to get what he wants."

"Which is?"

"More time with you."

I adjusted the collar of my worn coat with a scoff. "You talking crazy, Dess."

"I have eyes. He's smitten with you."

"And hundreds of years old," I argued. Not that it mattered so much with vamps. *Everything* seemed to stop aging the moment they turned, organs and hormones included, if they even used those things anymore. So I knew Alexei had to've been at least young enough that his brain hadn't finished maturing, the dumbass. Still, I rubbed at a sudden itch on my cheek that wasn't there. If I didn't hide any sign of embarrassment with my hand until I could get rid of it, she'd never let me live it down. "Besides, the boy'd be smitten with a daisy if it grew where he could see it."

Odessa barked out a hearty laugh, hugging me around the shoulders as we made our way to the colonel's tent.

A hundred years ago, smoke didn't shroud the sky. I'd seen paintings in the big house that proved there was a different kind of life before this hellscape. Paintings of graceful, kind-faced white folks with their little lap dogs, sitting in green grass with a blue sky and the sun crowning them in light.

Or maybe them paintings was just fantasy. Until I came to the North, I ain't seen more than two white people in my life with any hint of kindness or a dog that wasn't trained to hunt dark skin, I could tell you that. And you couldn't convince me the sky was ever blue. Sorry, that just didn't make no sense.

And there was no vamps walking among us, either—or if they was here, they kept to the shadows like the monsters they are. It was only after the vamps decided to live like humans—and realized they could keep slaves openly without having to hypnotize or seduce anyone—that they invented them God-awful plumes.

They nearly took over, then, these monsters roaming around like they was people. They used to be human, and so look it enough from over yonder. The devil making poor copies of life, playing like he was God.

But up rose the Saints, with the first ever being the legendary Van Helsing. Just as fast and strong as the monsters. Not immortal, but then, you couldn't go to Heaven without a soul to save. God's own creations to match the devil's.

Sometimes I think about that . . . how out of anyone God could've picked, I was chosen. He couldn't grab no nurse or preacher? No, he picked the scrawny girl in chains who daydreamed about killing the people who put them on her.

But maybe that was why He *did* pick me.

'Cause I knew I was different from the time I could walk. Faster. Stronger. Could work them fields longer with less fatigue. *A miracle*, Pa called me.

Mama wasn't so impressed.

"Now you know your pa and I can't get you no house position, on account of your mouth, so you better not be acting a fool in those fields," she'd said. "Everybody got to keep pace with the fastest. Don't you run around dooming your people by picking so fast no one else can keep up."

And Mama's word was law, so that was it. I stopped picking quick, stopped running places, pushed down the urge inside to do all my body was capable of. Anything I could to keep from standing out. At least until that last week . . .

I didn't know then that I was a Saint, but I knew I was *something*. Something stronger than the overseers. Someone who could save my family, maybe even every enslaved person on that plantation.

Lord Jesus, don't let it be too late for me to be that Someone.

'Cause now I had nothing. No family, no home, no knowing what Imma do after the war. Only my name, my spear, and my hair were truly mine.

My hair, with lots of braids that reached the base of my shoulder blades, except my cornrows wasn't in no straight lines along my scalp but swirling and circling like a kraken set loose. A chimera, more like—big old creatures with the parts of different animals, like God couldn't decide on what He was making. Or maybe He knew *exactly* what He'd made 'cause chimeras was the only creatures vamps was afraid of. Which was why I'd felt mimicking one in my hair was fitting.

'Cause a chimera was a vamp's natural-born enemy.

And, after what them monsters had done to my family, so was I.

The war tent was bigger than the others, but it still only just fit the colonel and his eight captains, plus me, what with the table full of maps and figurines and such. Not that being squished in made any difference. We'd all seen the plume, so we had an idea of what was coming.

Well, *they* had an idea. I already knew and was forcing myself not to fly to heaven in excitement.

"We all know what's coming," said Colonel Mills. His big, old mustache covered his mouth, but I could see his brows drawn down clear enough. "The Confederates have taken up a stronghold near Gettysburg, set up in preparation for the rest of the army. They plan to keep headquarters there to extend their reach and occupy the North. We can't let that happen."

And there was the lie. I kept my mouth shut but looked over at Gael standing at the back cool as a cucumber as he casually rolled a cigarette. Not that I expected *him* to spill the beans.

"As we speak," Colonel Mills went on, "General Lee is on his way with his army, plus multiple vamps. Thanks to Saints Odessa and Gael's thorough intel, I have the names of the vamps in question." He waved the paper. "And what little we know about their stronghold."

The colonel handed Saint Thomas the list to pass around the room. I bounced a bit on my toes, waiting for this pointless meeting to be over while he went on about how Alexei would lead a covert group of Saints to go in first and overtake the stronghold. Then the battalion would follow behind to face the army. Everything was shaping up just as it should; now if only he would stop blathering so we could go.

The tent's flap slapped open noisily, pulling a few of the Saints' attention, and before I could turn, I smelled shortbread and felt slight pressure wrap around my upper arms. Even through my coat I knew the hands daring to touch me didn't have no body heat.

"You love to block my entryways, Pocket Saint," Alexei

whispered, shifting me back toward him to make space in front of me. And then, quick and slick, he crouched in front of me and tied the lace of my ankle-high boot.

"Boy, if you don't get off me, your face about to get real friendly with my knee," I muttered to the top of his head. "And you late. *Again*."

He stood up and smirked. "Nothing important is ever said without my presence."

Alexei made his way over to stand near the colonel while I fought the urge to grab the shaft of my spear and prod him in the back of his smug head.

Finally, the paper came 'round to Odessa. I peeked at the scribbles on it, even though I couldn't really read none, even though it didn't matter.

"Just curious," I whispered. "Who's on that list?"

"You know, I wrote it and don't even remember." She gave me a small smile as she ran her finger along the paper to find the names. "'Silas Barton,'" she read quietly.

They let that lazy-ass bard be a soldier? He didn't own no slaves, but Adelaide enjoyed his music, so he had visited the big house often. As threatening as a June bug, but maybe he'd learnt a thing or two since I last seen him. From what I remember, he'd be an easy kill.

"'John Carter.'"

He was a true Virginian and had visited Adelaide once or twice. Even so, I didn't know much about him except he talked a lot about planets for some reason? Guess I'd have to wait and see, but the name alone sounded pretty flimsy to me.

"'Zamir the Mangler.'"

Ah, that's more like it. He was one of them *old*-old Ancients, like very old world. They was more my speed, strong and smart fighters like Alexei, except the Mangler wasn't so vain and petty from what I'd heard. He'd be a fun challenge, all right. Plus, he was a literal serial killer, coming out of hiding every fifty years or so to give law enforcement a run for their money, so God knew he deserved to die already.

"Jasper Whitlock."

Jasper *Who-the-Hell?* If I ain't heard of him, he couldn't be no threat.

Dess passed the paper on.

I raised my brows. "You didn't include Adelaide?"

"I swapped out one of the names," she whispered back. "You've talked enough about having it out for her; I just wanted to avoid any suspicion of what we're truly after."

I nodded and kept my mouth shut. Every time Dess opened hers, she impressed me. A daggone genius.

At the front of the crowd, Colonel Mills cleared his throat. "Alexei will select two or three Saints to join him. Secrecy is of the utmost importance. If the Confederate army catches wind of our plan, they may change tactics . . ."

Alexei ran his hand through his long hair, looking like he was actually listening. 'Course he was listening; the colonel was talking about *him*. Selfish, prideful . . . *pretty* monster. Just looking at him riled me up. Maybe 'cause I was used to his kind being the enemy, and it was still hard to wrap my head around any of them wanting good for people who looked like me, even after knowing him for a year.

Or maybe 'cause he was an arrogant donkey.

Look at him. He thinks he's God's gift.

Alexei's gaze wandered across the circle and found mine. He winked, so I showed him my middle finger, at which he bit back a laugh.

Next thing I knew, everyone was leaving. I waited until the tent emptied out, and it was just me, Dess, Alexei, Gael, and the colonel. Dess said something to Gael in Spanish, and he nodded, putting on his hat, and stepped out to smoke. But his shadow on the tarp said he didn't go far.

"Begging your pardon, Colonel," I said, walking around the table toward him. The old man sighed impatiently, but that wasn't going to stop me from going on. "I know you already said Alexei would be picking people, but I've come to put myself up as leader of the mission. "I—" Dess's words flashed through my head—I couldn't reveal the real mission, not even in the colonel's tent. Anybody and their uncle could be listening. "I escaped from the South with not so much as a rat catching me. If anyone should be leading a stealth mission, it should be me."

I didn't mention I'd spent most of my running time in the swamp and with the Underground Railroad, so there was no way someone was going to see or catch me no how. That wasn't white folks' business to know.

Instead of answering, the colonel looked at Odessa. "Saint Odessa, please control your charge."

But Odessa crossed her arms, nailing him with a look. "She makes a good point, Colonel. You should consider what she has to say."

He tightened his already thin lips, exhaling heavy through his nose. "Alexei has hundreds of years of experience. This isn't even a discussion."

"With respect, Colonel," I said, fighting to keep my tone as respectful as I claimed to be, "Alexei ain't been in this country much longer than I been free. What he know about navigating hereabouts any more than I do?"

"Alexei is a vampire," said the colonel, scoffing. "And you—a girl we picked up a year ago, *trained* by him, with no rank—presume to be the better choice?"

This man done ignored everything I just said.

I bit my tongue against giving him a lashing with it. Wasn't like being disrespected was new for me. If only I could tell him my real qualifications. That I *knew* these vamps, not as a species but as individuals. What made them tick; what choices they might make. Not to mention, I *was* much better than Alexei at stealth situations, so my plan of attack was bound to be better, too. And even if all that wasn't true, hell if I cared. I wanted it more than him.

I *needed* it.

So all I said was, "In this case? Yes, sir."

That response probably wasn't much better than telling him off.

Colonel Mills was seething like a baked snake. "Let's get one thing straight, girl. If you had a decade of training under your belt, you would still never stack up to Alexei's capabilities."

That hurt. And admitting it hurt, even just to myself, made it hurt even worse. As if everything I done went through, all that training and practice, didn't mean nothing. I swallowed, gave myself a second to turn that hurt into anger. I wasn't going to let no white man I could easily kill tell me I wasn't good enough.

"You're not giving Jerusalem enough credit," Odessa cut in, her hand planted on my shoulder like she thought I might spring on him. "To be as skilled as she is after only a year of training? And someone who can escape slavery and attempts on her life, to travel that far to freedom without getting caught, understands subtlety and stealth better than any of us could."

"I know you're soft on her," the colonel said, sighing like a tired cow. "And she may be a fearless fighter, but she's also a child—"

"She's standing right here," I said, forcing my tone not to get me into more trouble. "And eighteen ain't no *child*."

"This doesn't have to be an argument," Alexei said, his voice only bordering on patient. "I would bring you anyway, Jerusalem."

"Then you won't care if I take the lead," I said, and Alexei's glare was bloodthirsty enough to turn the bravest man to stone.

But a glare wasn't nothing to me after a life of enslavement.

"Regardless of who leads," said the colonel, "it doesn't change the fact that if you can't keep this covert and deal with it quickly, the battalion will have more than a little trouble on our hands. One slip up, and the mission is compromised."

"'*Regardless of who leads?*'" Alexei repeated in disbelief.

"Have I ever steered you wrong, Colonel?" Odessa said.

He rubbed his mustache with a heavy sigh. "I trust you with my life."

"Then hand command of the mission to me."

"You just returned from a mission, Odessa."

"I'm not tired, sir. I'm used to doing important tasks on little rest."

No one in the tent said a word, but only 'cause Odessa gripped my wrist when I opened my mouth to start. That sure as hell was right—she'd reared five babies, something this old man would never understand. Dess knew what it was to be tired.

"Fine," the colonel said finally with yet another deep sigh, and my heart leapt

Alexei's jaw dropped. "'*Fine?*'"

"*Fine.* That's a compromise I can live with."

"Thank you, Colonel," Odessa said.

"Keep the girl out of trouble."

"This is absolutely insulting," Alexei growled—why the hell was he overreacting like that? "I did not come all the way across the world to be sidelined."

The colonel cleared his throat. "We value your assistance, Alexei. The North owes you a debt, and we won't forget that. But Saint Odessa has led many missions—many of which you've been part of—so I see no offense in her leading. You two work wonderfully together, and I have no doubt this time will be more of the same."

I scoffed. Leader of a whole-ass battalion, and this vain monster made him nervous? Mills was practically falling all over himself to compliment him. You'd never catch me doing that.

"And I'm sure," the colonel added, pushing aside the tent flap, "you'd enjoy a break from babysitting the little one."

After that, he left in a hurry.

"'The little one' fittin' to carve a new face on the back of your bald head," I mumbled after him, grinding my fingers into my spear shaft. Odessa squeezed my other hand to keep me still.

"Why did you do that, Jerusalem?" Alexei asked, his voice sharp, sounding somewhere between annoyed and disappointed. "I taught you to use your weapon when none of the Saints took you seriously. I've never asked for anything in return."

It was his disappointment that really got to me. More human than all his arrogance. More personal because I knew his weaknesses, and he trusted me anyway, as much as he could. It was hard even looking at him with that tone, so I pushed my annoyance through even more, not letting the thought that I cared what a vampire thought of me settle in. "And what, I ain't never said thank you? You know I'm grateful."

"Then how could you betray me like that, when you know I would've brought you with me, anyway?"

"You need to calm down," I said, rolling my eyes. "Odessa is the best Saint in this battalion. She's killed more vamps in two years than anyone. Ain't no shame in being led by her."

"That's not the point," he snapped. "He gave away my mission. I am not some lowly foot soldier. Your army is lucky I'm here to help at all."

"So don't come," I snapped back, squaring up to him—I didn't care how much taller he was. "What the hell is wrong with you? Why you acting up over this?"

His eyes were so fiery he could've cooked an egg by staring at it, but I'd seen hell on earth before. Ain't no way this boy could scare me. "We both know that with Odessa leading, it'll be the same as you taking command." He literally growled. "She listens to everything you say."

"Get some smart ideas, and maybe she'll listen to you."

"You are *not* a ranking officer."

"You ain't, neither, bloodsucker—"

"You had no right—!"

"Alexei, stop!" Odessa warned, snatching up an arrow as her voice climbed beyond firm, and the head of my spear flashed as I shifted it to rest beneath his jaw.

'Cause he really did look like one of them just then. A monster. His eyes tinged with animal rage, like I wasn't nothing to him but something to be butchered. I felt my hands shaking something awful. I'd seen that look so many times, but it made me feel different coming from him. It . . . I didn't know. I didn't know what I felt. Not fear of him or nerves from a fight.

I just . . . after all we been through, I hated he could ever look at me like that.

But he must've knew what he'd done 'cause he backed away from me like I was hot coals. I saw the moment his eyes softened, but mine never did. I hated him. I hated that he could make me feel so helpless.

It wasn't a feeling I wanted to have ever again.

Gael must've heard it all from outside 'cause he grabbed Alexei's shoulder and dragged him farther away from me, then stepped in front.

"Everything fine here, Alexei?" he asked, and I would've been more shocked to hear his deep speaking voice at all if his tone didn't sound like he knew good and well everything wasn't fine. He gripped his Saint weapon, a big old machete, ready to make a move if needed. There was a reason the papers called him the Butcher—he preferred his enemies in pieces. He and his weapon made a deadly combination, and that he'd threaten Alexei with this fate wasn't lost on me, or on Alexei, who put himself a safe distance from it.

"Fine," Alexei replied, his voice tight.

From the corner of my eye, I saw Odessa lower her bow and arrow.

Wasn't no vamp in this world who wasn't a potential enemy, and we all knew it well.

"This mission is time sensitive," Odessa said, "so we *will* have to leave in the next hour."

Alexei didn't fight the command. My muscles stiffened in discomfort as he transformed into a dark wolf and bolted from the tent—he *would* choose the form I was least comfortable with, just to get under my skin for going after what he happened to want.

Let him throw his hissy fit. It wouldn't change that I was going on this mission. That I would finally get the chance to confront Adelaide. Tear the immortal breath from that wicked monster's body. Watch her expression of horror and disbelief and—God willing—*fear* as the undead life left her eyes.

And now that God had given me the go-ahead, that was exactly what I intended to do.

4

ALEXEI

My muscles twitched as I paced the walls of my tent. Why was I so agitated? I was still going on the mission. I was still headed away from the army, exactly as planned. Admittedly, it even made sense that I wasn't leading—I didn't know where Gettysburg was. And I'd be with Jerusalem, besides.

But, historically, taking orders from someone had never ended favorably for me.

I didn't like it. I didn't like handing over control. Moreover, I didn't want to.

And, as I'd learned long ago, that was reason enough.

I had to crush this anxiety before I saw the girls, especially Jerusalem. I'd never shown nerves in front of her before, and I planned on keeping it that way. I laced my fingers behind my head and sighed up at the tent's fabric ceiling. *Think of sweeter things, Alexei.*

Like Jerusalem.

How I'd fallen for her was beyond comprehension. She

hated my kind, for one, and even if we were friends, tenuous ones at that, it should've been plenty of reason to move on. She also smelled incredibly delicious, which should have created at least some sort of divide, making me see her as food instead of an individual person. But I couldn't make myself stay away.

She was beautiful, downright adorable at times, and that she never let me say it without wanting to kill me just increased the attraction for me. She was strong for a Saint, both because she was diligent in training—which was admirable enough alone—and because she disregarded danger as if it didn't exist. I'd never met a human who lacked fear to the point where I thought maybe she believed she was as immortal as I was.

Normally, too much of a height difference would be an issue for me, but she was perfect. The world could not have handled a taller version of this tiny angel of death. Imagine if she could reach things without jumping or assistance? I'd be of no use to her at all.

And I would die for that smile. Others already had died for it—she smiled the most when she was driving her spear through an enemy during battle. And I would willingly let her stab me just to hear her war cry.

I rubbed my hands down my face, laughing.

Should I have been disturbed that such things could make me horny for a girl who told me she hated my kind daily? I supposed being self-aware enough not to voice it or do anything about it was more important. Jerusalem's trust in me had been slow going in the beginning, and I had enough of it now that I would rather choke than betray it.

But . . . if I loved her in my own mind, unrequited, who had to know?

"Daydreaming?"

My jaw tightened. I hadn't even noticed Dess's approach; I'd been so wrapped up in my thoughts. "I'll be ready when it's time to leave, if that's what you're worried about."

"Really?" she replied with a scrutinizing raise of her brow. "Because you're late for everything."

"Time passes differently for vampires."

I didn't know if that was true. I was going to live forever . . . maybe I just didn't care. I snatched up my pack, sitting cross-legged on the floor. I didn't need to sleep or eat the way humans did; a change of clothing was a waste of space—my weapon would be on my hip anyway. I had learned long ago not to treasure possessions, so I proceeded to fill the pack with food for the girls. Mostly for Tiny, as she ate like a full-grown horse, and who knew what sort of hunting there was to be had between here and the stronghold.

All the while, neither I nor Odessa spoke. I loved her dearly, but that didn't mean I was going to make an apology any easier for her after she stabbed me in the back.

Not that she ever apologized. Even if the way she worded her reply made you feel better, she never actually said the words unless it could be proven by facts and evidence that she was wrong.

Finally, she said, "Did you skip breakfast, Alexei?"

I raised my brows at her. "Don't you have something to say other than mothering me?"

"I'll mother all I want; you nearly bit Jerusalem."

"I didn't *nearly bite her*. My thirst flared, that's all, and I'm well in control of it. I would never bite her."

"You're the one who told me her smell was irresistible. That I should check you if I saw something was off, that you're not to be around her if you haven't eaten your fill beforehand. So don't make me ask you again—"

"I had breakfast," I snapped. She didn't look convinced, so I added, "Fine, I'm still a little thirsty. That doesn't mean I would hurt her."

"This didn't happen while I was gone, did it?"

"It's never happened before, and you know that. This was a one-time mistake. I was . . . I was mad is all."

She sighed. "There are better ways to use your anger, Lex. Now, make sure you finish eating before we leave."

I looked down at my pack, feeling nothing but shame. Shame that I worked quickly to extinguish. To slip up so badly, nearly lose control . . . Jerusalem was fast and strong, but I edged her out. And when thirsty . . . ? As much as I pretended to disagree with Odessa, we both knew she was right. If I hadn't caught myself in time, Jerusalem's blood would be on my tongue.

A shiver went down my spine at the thought, but it wasn't completely from disgust.

Treat her blood as sacred. Off limits. Not for drinking.

"So are you going to apologize or not?" I asked, a salty edge to my voice that wasn't all meant for her.

"The colonel trusts me blindly. I did what I thought would settle things. If anyone else was assigned this mission instead, we wouldn't be able to support Jerusalem in her goal."

"She'll have better luck encountering her enemy if she stays with the battalion."

"Then you would stay, too. You know you would. And we wouldn't be having this discussion."

But I wouldn't stay. Normally yes, but now . . . ? There was no sense in telling her the truth, though, not when I already had what I wanted.

Odessa ran her hand along the curve of the small, round, wooden table in the corner. "Fine craftsmanship."

"Some of these boys seem to have a lot of their parents' money to throw around." Most of the clutter in my tent was gifts from familiar-hopefuls. In fact, so was this very tent—most Union tents weren't tall enough for someone of average height, let alone me, and it was a relief not to have to lean over all the time. It didn't matter how often I said the idea of keeping a familiar disgusted me; they kept fawning, so I just kept accepting. Because why not? No sense in letting their parents' money go to waste.

"You really should stop leading them on," said Odessa. "You have no intention of turning them."

She'd clearly been talking to Jerusalem.

"You get bored after three hundred years. And it's not as if I'm hurting them." I stuffed the last of the jerky into my bag and buckled it. "Besides, you don't find it funny? We're literally fighting to abolish slavery, and they're pining to be my slave."

Odessa gave me a disbelieving look, as if I should know better. "At this point, it doesn't matter whether we're able to abolish it. You know as well as I do the vampires overrunning the South don't care about laws. They'll enslave the entire country if given the chance, no matter what President Lincoln has to say."

I scoffed. "Yes, America's colonizing ways has clearly rubbed off."

"I seem to recall that particular ideology being inherited from *your* side of the Atlantic."

"Touché." I smirked. "But believe it or not, most vampires don't want to conquer the world. They just want to be left alone to live their lives."

"At the expense of the rest of us."

"It's no different than animals and habitats being destroyed by humans."

She raised her brows at me. "*Humans* are not the same as animals."

"All I'm saying is you eat animals just as we feed on humans. And, in fairness, most of you are vile gremlins." I gave her a teasing grin, but she wasn't having it. "Not a world's worth, Odessa. They're taking advantage of legal slavery because they have humans to run it, but once it's abolished, they won't continue that lifestyle. I promise you."

"I pray that's true, Alexei. For all our sakes." Odessa put her weight on the table, arms folded across her chest. "So. You asked to lead that mission after I left the tent this morning."

"I didn't *ask*. Though I suppose I should have given you the option first, seeing as you went through the trouble of gathering the intel."

"I don't mind. But you usually never miss a battle. What made you decide to take a mission headed in the opposite direction?"

"This seemed more important."

She raised her brows. "Does it have anything to do with the Mangler? You seemed a bit thrown off, seeing his name on the list."

I attempted a casual shrug, but my shoulders felt stiff. "Just shocked he'd travel all this way, that's all."

She gave me a disbelieving look. "Alexei. It's me. You can tell the truth."

But I couldn't. Because *Zamir isn't the problem* and *I'm terrified to face the captor I thought I'd left behind in Russia* wasn't something I could ever admit aloud, not even to Dess. "You like to meddle too much. Every time I tell you a secret, Jerusalem hears about it."

"Only when it concerns you both," she said, grinning. "How was she while I was gone, by the way?"

I sighed, then shrugged. "The usual. Irritable. Distant from the men."

Sad. Angry . . . Beautiful.

"Did she sleep enough?"

"You know she didn't. But she slept in my tent, so I could at least keep track of her."

Odessa gave me a sly grin. "How was that for you?"

"Ha!" I slouched, staring at my pack. "Every time she's near, I'm never sure if I want to kiss or consume her." Hearing Dess laugh, I glared. "I am in love with a girl who smells to me the way you obsess over steak and pecan pie. That's not funny."

"You're right; it's very tragic."

"Stop *laughing*, Odessa."

"Do you think maybe she smells better than anyone else to you because you love her so much?"

"Listen to what you just said. Do I want to taste her so badly because I love her?" I smirked at my own innuendo while Odessa looked on unamused, just shaking her head. "Maybe, yes."

"Why don't you get it all out in the open already and tell her how you feel?"

"I'm beginning to wish I never told *you*." I tugged on my hair a little at the root to comfort myself. "She trusts me . . . somewhat. Enough to feel safe in my tent. And you want me to tell her that not only am I in love with her, but she smells so delicious I wish I could literally drink her blood?"

"Ease in the latter part, of course. You know how headstrong Jerusalem is; a confession of love from a being she's determined to hate will be hard enough for her to swallow."

I cringed. "You're right. I think I'd prefer to continue loving her in secret."

"You have to tell her before the end of our journey. It'll only be the four of us out there, and I will gladly make an excuse to go off somewhere with Gael when you give the signal. Just do yourself a favor and get it over with."

"I don't want to lose her completely, Dess. She hates vampires. She'd stake me in the heart if she knew."

"It's clear she already has . . . metaphorically."

I shot my so-called friend an unamused look. "Please show yourself out."

"She does like you, you know. More than that, she needs you. More than she'll ever admit." She took a step out of my tent and paused. "I love you, Alexei, and I might have been laughing earlier, but you will make an enemy out of me if you bite that girl. So go eat something. We're leaving in thirty minutes."

I sighed and stared at the place Odessa had vacated. She was right. I had pulled myself back this time, but it was foolish to think I was immune to my own thirst, especially when it came to a scent as intoxicating as Jerusalem's. If I had to drink animals, I would, as much as the thought made me want to gag. Because if anything ever happened to Jerusalem . . . and it was my fault? I couldn't live with that. I wouldn't want to.

I got up and stormed over to the tent's flap, shoving it open. The two boys jerked their heads in my direction. Had they nothing better to do than stand outside my tent? Was that really what familiars did all day? It would have annoyed me more, except I actually needed them at the moment.

"One of you," I ordered. "Here. Now."

They practically shoved each other out of the way to get to me, but I simply grabbed the closest one by the wrist and dragged him halfway into my tent. I locked him with my gaze, barely waiting to make sure he was under before I sunk my teeth into his wrist.

Too hard. He was going to bruise terribly; I was lucky the pressure of my bite hadn't broken his wrist.

I'd sworn to the colonel when I joined the army that I wouldn't drink any of his troops. But no one mattered except Jerusalem. And the last thing I wanted to be the next time we saw each other was a threat.

My prey could give more than the woman from earlier, so I took it. Less of a dessert and more of a second meal, but I'd rather be over full than not have enough. Besides, he ended up tasting a little better than he smelled.

I finished and covered his wrist with his uniform, pressing his hand to the wound to stop it up. I didn't feel like touching him to make him look away, so I snapped my fingers at him impatiently, startling him out of hypnosis.

"Go," I said, waving him from my tent.

"Thank you, sir," he murmured, disoriented and baffled, and left.

And, I don't know why, but this time hearing the strange thankful response made me laugh.

New Jersey
Two years earlier

The colonel's fear was palpable in the small, enclosed carriage as we made our way to the battalion I'd call home for the foreseeable future, the musty scent of his sweat thickening the already pungent air, the tremble of his hands creating vibrations. To be fair, I wouldn't have enjoyed being contained with me, either.

Mostly because I hated being contained.

"Do you have any questions so far?" asked Mills.

It was a miracle I'd fully understood any of what he'd said. I spoke English, but not often, and certainly not in the last twenty-five years. Also, I'd learned English in Scotland, and, unless I happened upon Scottish immigrants, most Americans had strange accents, comparatively.

"Is there more I should know?" I asked.

He looked nervous, as if my question had been a test, and there should be more. But then, I'd been told I looked intimidating, even when I was smiling—worse when I was smiling, some said, as my fangs made humans uneasy.

"No . . ." He cleared his throat, and said with more certainty, "No, that's about all for now."

"Very good." I caught him in hypnosis, then. It wasn't something I felt good about doing to my allies, morally or ethically, and I saved it for only the direst of situations. But I'd just gotten off a warship, having traveled weeks on the open ocean, and had already ridden an hour in this carriage. It felt dire enough. "Don't speak to me unless it's important. Remember that when we reach camp."

It was a petty command, but I'd much prefer silence than tedious small talk with a stranger. Besides, if he was this afraid of me now, knowing that I was fighting on his side, I highly doubted our interactions would be much more tolerable in the future.

I didn't know how I'd caught wind of the Russian navy heading west to the Americas to aid in a civil war, but they were fighting to abolish slavery from what I'd heard—and it was all I'd needed to hear. The next day I found myself stowing away on a warship to head west.

Reaching the shores of New York had brought a new kind of freedom into my life—the sky in America was constantly gray up North, full of smoke and ash the farther south you traveled. I no longer needed to only hunt at night or cover myself from the sun. But with that truth came another—everyone was afraid of me, whether I had any intention of hunting them or not.

This was partly distressing, as it would be difficult to make allies in the very army I came to assist. But, at the same time, people tended to do whatever I wanted without much protest. That, I could use.

The carriage halted, and I exited without waiting for him.

The battalion was settled at the base of a hill, which seemed a poor choice, strategically. Then again, we were nowhere near a battlefield, and most of these soldiers had had probably never seen war in their young lives. I had a feeling I'd have to be the one to inform them of the dangers of selecting the low ground later.

A boy holding the reins of two horses cowered between the animals' necks, as if blocking his face made him invisible.

I scoffed. "Tell the colonel to meet me at camp."

I shifted into a crow and took off. It would be useful to explore the camp myself, no guide to spout their own biases.

But as soon as I landed within the camp, I wanted to immediately turn around and go back to Siberia. I loved the thrill of a good fight, and abolishing slavery was important to me . . . but I had assumed on the Northern side of this civil war, where there was no enslavement, things would be, well, a bit more diverse. To be fair, the only thing I'd seen of America was New York and New Jersey—neither of which looked like York or Jersey—but this was a country composed of immigrants from all over and yet from what I could see from here their army was decidedly monochromatic. If I was honest, it made me uncomfortable.

Don't be ridiculous, Alexei. They all look like you.

And that was the problem.

Physically, I was the epitome of white. My skin was fair, unchanging with moods or the sun, though I liked to imagine that when I'd been human, it at least had had a healthy, pinkish hue. My hair was nearly silver from birth, my eyes as sapphire as the clear, deep sea.

But for years, I'd wanted to be as far away as possible from Russia, any country bordering it, and frankly any other place in the vicinity of Eastern Europe, to avoid . . . her. So I spent most of the first two hundred years of my life more or less circling Russia. East Asia to South, through all of Africa, up along the coasts of Western Europe. And though I did finally end up in Scotland, I'd only stayed long enough to learn English before deciding I hated the weather and endless grass.

So, suffice to say, I had always been the whitest person in the room, whether with my Tuvan coven in Siberia or the vampire friends I'd made during my travels.

Now, even in the army, I was keen to gravitate to what was familiar. And I saw it in the form of a lovely dark-skinned woman tending to a mule's ankle. This was my chance.

"May I be of assistance to you, Saint?"

By then, the woman had lifted the mule across her shoulders—clearly something the creature was used to because it looked incredibly content.

"Does it look like I need your help?" she asked.

It was a question only a petty, pathetic person would answer *yes* to. Still, her tone made me glance at the arrows at her hip.

"Not even remotely," I said. "But as a gentleman, I cannot allow a lady to lift a finger unnecessarily."

"As a lady who is devoted to her family, I must decline." She, with the authority of a captain commanding a crew, added, "Now don't get under my feet while I'm working."

I grinned and leaned on the end of the wagon to give her space, watching as she placed her injured mule down beside the rest of her supplies on the wagon. Only when she was finished did she finally look at me. Recognition flashed in her eyes before her gaze shifted slightly, not quite looking me in the eye. "They sent word a vampire would be joining our ranks."

This wasn't her first time dealing with vampires, clearly. I noticed how casually she suddenly had need of her knife—it was small, but I could feel the subtle warmth of the silver blade from here—as she went about trimming excess rope from her supplies. And avoiding eye contact was generally the best way to avoid hypnosis. But I wasn't looking for someone to attack or control.

That was the last thing I ever wanted from a relationship.

"News travels fast," I said, although you really only needed to be faster than the colonel's extremely slow carriage.

"I'm sure you'll want to see the colonel," she said, and gestured off in the opposite direction from where she seemed to be headed. "The war tent is that way."

"Perhaps I could see where the Saints stay, instead."

"I've lost count of how many harassers I've had to run off since touching foot in this camp," she said firmly. "Do me the favor of not being the next."

"Harassers?" I asked, and she seemed confused by my genuine confusion. "You're a Saint."

She shrugged. "I'm a Black woman."

"Then allow me the pleasure of running them off for you."

She looked thoroughly unimpressed as she rounded the wagon to take hold of the front. "I'm a poor choice for a familiar. I don't take orders."

"Neither do I," I said with a grin. "And I'm not looking for a familiar."

"What are you looking for, then?"

"'Friends,' I think is the English word."

That at least elicited a smirk. "You're serious."

"No, I'm Alexei." I held out my hand while she sighed and shook her head at me. "And you are?"

"Odessa." She didn't shake my hand, but I suppose that was a lot to expect from a human on day one.

"Hey! Girl!" I looked up to see a man thundering toward us. "You can't be here, little miss. We're in the middle of a war." When he came close enough to identify us, I saw his face blanch, and he immediately turned another way as if he hadn't just been speaking to her.

Whether he saw her Saint weapon on her hip or recognized me as a vampire, I didn't care.

"Where do you think you're going?" I asked him, and my voice held enough of a warning that the man tripped to a stop despite passing me. I could smell the sweat at his hairline, hear his heart pounding blood close to the surface as he hesitated. He turned to look at me. Odessa looked at me, too, a bit of curiosity veiled by a stern reserve. They were waiting for what I'd say next . . . but I wasn't sure myself. "Do you know who she is?"

The man hesitated. "Um—"

"'Um' is not an answer. No, shut up," I added as the man opened his mouth. He snapped his jaw shut just as quickly. "You saw her Saint weapon, so why is it you have not yet kissed the very ground she treads?"

I had agreed not to harm any of the Union soldiers, but perhaps he didn't know that. I was used to using humans' fear against them, as much as that made me a hypocrite—I certainly didn't like it done to me. But I hated bigots even more.

And this one was looking increasingly flustered. Good.

"Get on your knees," I said, "kiss the ground at Saint Odessa's feet, and apologize."

The man didn't even hesitate, falling to the earth so immediately, that I barely held in a laugh, taking the moment he spent muttering on the ground to shake the amusement from my face.

When he finally stood, I took him by the collar, and his face ducked behind the neck hole a bit like a scared turtle. "This is your only warning. You will show respect to Saint Odessa, or I will make you do more than grovel in the dirt." I shoved him away from me, his racing heart palpable even from a distance. "And pass the word around, will you? I would hate to have to repeat myself."

"Yes sir," the soldier murmured, then ran off.

I grinned at Odessa, but she didn't look amused. "I don't need anyone to fight my battles."

"You certainly don't," I agreed. "But isn't it nice to have?"

She raised a brow. "Yes, well, there was a less humiliating way to deal with that."

I shrugged. "He humiliated you first."

She appraised me for a moment, and then she shifted to one side of the wagon. I grinned and held the other side level as she lifted and rested her side on her shoulder.

"The Saint tents are this way," she said, and we carried her wagon through the crowded field.

5

JERUSALEM

The four of us headed out on horseback. Since it was a stealth mission, we left our blue coats behind. Me and Dess wore split skirts—they looked real enough, but without all them crinolines and petticoats underneath and room to wear my leather pants—with hidden slits that could open if we needed to move or got caught on something and had to leave it completely. And I wore my lightweight cowl that kept half my torso and arms good and covered, so nobody would notice I only had on a white undershirt—well, mostly so *Alexei* wouldn't notice, seeing as it was his. His vain ass had cut the sleeves off to expose his strong shoulders, granting the perfect amount of circulation and freedom that I just couldn't pass up.

Alexei had on a Henley like a working man, probably 'cause he knew it made his arms and chest look good. Gael looked the least obvious, with a worn shirt and his hat blocking his eyes. 'Course, people would probably still stare or stop us, seeing as two Black women and a Mexican man riding around with a white man was a strange enough sight, not to mention we all had our slaying weapons on us.

But for the first few hours, we didn't run into nobody. Just vast fields of crops and such, too early on to be picked. And between all that land was woods. Dense and wild, no real paths and not easy to ride through. It was a bit like Virginia in looks, I guess— not that I'd seen much of the state, except when I was running from it. Like Virginia, but without the humidity and annoying gulls.

And without the slaves.

There was *white* people out there, working hard in the heat, sweating, in anticipation of money instead of a whupping. White people, doing they own work, minding they own business. Imagine that.

"Can't *wait* to kill me some vamps," I said, fighting the urge to dance on top of my horse.

I also might've said it too loud on purpose 'cause I wanted Dess and Gael to stop *whispering* like that. It'd been nonstop since we set out, and it rubbed me the wrong way, to be honest. He'd only been here three months; there wasn't no way them two could be *that* close.

"You know, we won't even run into the Southern army," said Alexei, annoyed like the spoiled brat he was. "We're supposed to travel ahead of them, remember?"

I bit the inside of my cheek. Dess had told me not to say nothing, and here I was screaming to the mountain tops that we was heading toward the vamps instead of away, to anyone who might hear out in the open.

Thank the Lord for Alexei. Still, there wasn't no need for the tone.

"Why you so salty?" I asked. "You still mad about the meeting?"

"It was wrong of you, Jerusalem, and you know it."

"Aw, go on, you big baby. Neither of us is leading, so what's the big deal?"

"The principle," he said.

"Just 'cause it inconveniences you don't make it wrong."

"Why not?"

A vein ticked in my temple as I glared at him. "Acting like God's gift to this war."

"I *am* God's gift; thank you for noticing."

"God ain't got nothing to do with you," I snapped, and he was lucky I was on a horse, or he'd of gotten smacked. "You a soulless monster. And a coward, at that, so no spine, neither."

"Are you acting out because you skipped breakfast again or because you don't want to admit you *like* me?"

"You wish that was the reason, you pompous ass."

"Enough, you two," said Odessa, like a tired mama—not that she didn't always sound like a tired mama. She should've known better, to be honest. Not sure why she expected more from us.

Quick as anything, Alexei grabbed my horse's reins and pulled my mount toward his so they was side by side. It took everything in me to not kick him—but it wasn't the horse's fault his rider was an ass. "Then why are you blushing, Jerusalem?"

"That's what warm-blooded humans do when they're angry," I snapped. An overreaction, but yelling was all my body could think to do, 'cause . . . what the hell? I *was* blushing, and even if it didn't show, I knew he could sense my pulse rise. But I didn't even know *why* I was, and I sure as hell wasn't about to fess up to no soft feelings for a *vampire* of all things, let alone this arrogant jerk. Just the thought of it sent my heart thundering.

"Now let go of my reins, or Imma put this spear right through your pretty face."

He smiled the slightest bit. "You think I'm pretty?"

"I said *enough*." Odessa's voice boomed just as I was about to lift my spear, but I knew better than to disobey a fed-up mama. She halted her horse in front of mine. "I'm not going to travel for days with you two behaving like toddlers. Alexei, ride ahead."

Alexei winked, but urged his horse forward before I could kick him off it.

"Gael," Dess said, "will you keep him occupied, please?"

Gael let out a patient breath. "Por ti, querida." And he rode ahead to join Alexei.

"*What'd* he call you?" I asked, more than a little annoyed.

"It's just a nickname," said Dess.

"You ain't smiling like it's just a nickname," I accused, the urge to throw a rock at the back of that man's head growing by the second.

Odessa sighed, and she sure wasn't smiling no more. "Can we focus on the real problem children of the group?"

"Alexei started it," I grumbled.

"I don't know why he insists on annoying you instead of being straightforward," Odessa said, shrugging. "Been around hundreds of years, yet he's still an eighteen-year-old boy."

"Eighteen?"

"That's how old he was when he was turned." She said it like it was normal, like it wasn't one of the worst things I could imagine.

Just thinking about Alexei—or anyone for that matter— being turned so young put a foul taste in my mouth. And since

I was real determined to hate him at the moment, I shoved it from my mind.

"Hormones, or whatever, ain't no excuse," I mumbled.

"To be fair, he did try being nice to you for a while. You didn't like that, either."

"I didn't like his white, bloodsucking ass."

"When you first arrived, that was more than understandable. But it's been a year, sweetie."

"And I *still* don't like his lily-white, bloodsucking ass."

Dess sighed. "You're not innocent in this, you know. He knows exactly which buttons to push to rile you up, but you let him. If you hate it so much, stop giving him what he wants." She gave a small smile, then shrugged again. "Or fess up already and accept that you enjoy your little spats."

"Like hell I do."

"Could've fooled me."

"I don't love him or nothing, Dess," I snapped. And then I scowled 'cause *Lord*, where did the word *love* even come from? "I *don't*."

"I'm a firm believer in saying things out loud," she said. "The things you want, but also the things you're feeling. 'Cause then they're out in the open, and you can focus on achieving them rather than continuing to doubt them."

"What you trying to say?"

"You know what I'm saying. You have feelings for Alexei other than annoyance. And the sooner you fess up to them, the less anxious you'll be."

I swiped sweat from my neck and wiped it on the big, stupid skirt. "Of course I do, Dess—he's my friend. And it ain't like he's annoying *all* the time. But there's no changing the fact he's a vampire."

"And?"

"*And?*" I lifted my mask so I could give her a look like she should've known—'cause she should've. "Immortal monsters? Who enslave people that look like us? And eat humans?"

"You shouldn't judge people by what they are, Jerusalem," Odessa said, shooting me the look my mama used to all the time, the *I know you're not rolling your eyes at me* look. "I'm serious. Being angry at the world is too exhausting not to pick your battles. I should know."

"With respect, Dess, you know good and well you ain't never met no good vamp before."

"Not before Alexei," she said with a bit of a shrug.

"Then how do you know he really is good?"

"Because I've been friends with him for two years. Because he's never given me a reason to think otherwise." She shook her head at my scowl. "I judge him by who he is, not what."

"He's an arrogant ass, is who he is."

"Who treats Black people like equals. Who cares about our cause. Who has lived a full life and has interesting stories to tell if you can get him to, and is really sweet and generous when you get to know him. Besides, if he's arrogant, so are you. It's something I happen to love about you both— matching confidence."

I sighed. "I don't get why we're even talking about this."

"Because you are going to need each other to complete this mission." She raised her brows at me when I gagged. "You make a great team."

"Well, the second part is true. But every step forward he takes by being sweet, he takes five back by driving me up the wall. Matching confidence my ass, I can't stand him."

The boys had halted their horses, waiting for us to catch up, and I felt a sudden prick of guilt that Alexei might've heard the last thing I said.

We was still friends, even if I hated his kind.

But he didn't say nothing about it. Instead, he said, "There are two riders headed toward us from the south. One is human, the other a vampire."

I looked off beside me and squinted. Sure enough, two riders were headed in our direction. I couldn't tell vampire from human at this distance, but I trusted Alexei's nose.

One of the few things I did fully trust about him.

"You might get that fight you wanted after all, Tiny," he said.

"Only two against our four," Gael mumbled through another fresh cigarette in his lips, casually striking a match to light it. "That's no fight."

Odessa shook her head. "No one is fighting. We'll wait in the trees for them. I'm sure they have valuable information."

Alexei sighed, shoving silver hair away from his face. "If I can smell them, they can smell us."

Odessa took her bow off from across her shoulders. "They won't get close enough to hurt us."

"Why can't we just meet them halfway?" I asked, impatiently. "It would be quicker."

"I'm with Jerusalem," Alexei said with a small laugh. "I'm getting a little thirsty, anyway."

My muscles stiffened at his words. Once, almost a year ago, Alexei had said he was going to feed, and when I said I hated that kind of stuff, he said he'd wait till I was sleeping. After that, he never really talked about feeding—to the point I wondered sometimes if he did it at all anymore. But today he'd said it to get on my nerves; I was sure of it. Wasn't nothing funny about a person getting the blood sucked from them by a monster.

"I'd prefer we not fight out in the open and give ourselves away," said Odessa with a sigh. "Patience, children."

"Yes'm," I grumbled.

Gael leaned over and whispered something to Dess, who nodded. "That's probably a good idea," she whispered back, grinning.

"*What's* a good idea?" I asked with more of a biting tone than was needed, but hell, I needed them to stop *whispering* like that. Like they had intimate secrets or something 'cause they didn't.

Dess raised a brow at me, but that was all. One thing I knew for sure about her, there wasn't no way of getting her business out of her if she didn't feel like telling it.

"You," Alexei answered for her. "Minding your business."

The tension in me broke as I busted out laughing, leaning on my horse to catch my breath. "Your white ass with that Black answer."

"Is that a Black answer?"

"It's what I would say."

"Yes, well," he said, grinning as he flicked his long hair behind his shoulder, "I aspire to be just like you when I grow up."

"Dumbass."

He pursed his lips. "Or I guess I should say when *you* grow up. As in a few more inches."

"Lex, I swear to God," I said, lifting my spear.

Despite my threat, Alexei laughed before leaping gracefully from his horse and strolling toward me.

"Don't start nothing," I warned him.

"Too late, Tiny," he said, still grinning. "We're already in the thick of it."

"One day you going to walk too close to me at the wrong time."

"There's no wrong time with you. Every moment is a potential land mine."

I raised a brow at him. "And yet?"

"And yet." He adjusted my loose shoelace before tying it as I sat on my horse. "Why do you wear brogans? Just wear riding boots and you won't have to worry about laces."

"Long boots make my legs sweat. And I *don't* worry about laces."

"Right, because I do."

"Who asked you to?"

You did, Jerusalem. Why else would you always leave them when they come untied?

Why do it myself when I can get a white boy to do it for me? Reparations.

"Look at that," Alexei said. He crouched in the brush, holding his finger out to a small plant. "This one's about as small as you."

"A snail?" I asked, sounding childish. I bit back my excitement, so it wouldn't show on my face, but leapt off my horse too fast to fool anyone. "Let me see."

I jogged over to where he crouched and leaned my hands on my knees to look. It was a snail all right, smaller than I ever seen. The shell was no bigger than a pebble with a clean spiral.

A high-pitched sound came out of me, and Alexei laughed a little, but I didn't care none. "Gimme," I said and touched my finger to his cold one so the tiny cutie could climb on. "You always spot the best snails."

He grinned at me. "Happy to offer my services."

"Bless you, Lex." The little eye stalks moved, and I felt my heart grow three sizes. "Gah! So cute!"

"Get ready, you two," said Odessa, though she hadn't even lifted her bow yet.

"Look at the baby," I cooed, showing my companions.

Odessa sighed and shook her head, turning back to her prey.

"She's cute, mija," Gael said gently, and I didn't want to think about how much his encouraging grin reminded me of how Pa used to look at me 'cause it made the back of my eyes burn with tears.

But it made me mad, too, 'cause Gael wasn't Pa.

I looked down at my snail for a second and heard a small slap, only to look up and see that Odessa had already let an arrow fly. Fast as anything, Alexei transformed into his wolf form and dashed off, followed quickly by Odessa on horseback.

That boy distracted me with a cute-ass snail so he could get to the enemy first. Son of a dick.

"Hey!" I glared up at Gael, who shrugged like he didn't seem in no rush to join in the action. I put the snail back on her leaf and leapt up onto my horse, kicking it forward. "You best save me some action, cheater!"

ALEXEI

I hadn't meant to use The Littlest Saint's love of snails against her. Well . . . I had, but only because of how quickly she tended to become bloodthirsty around vampires, and who knew if we would get what we needed out of this one if she had it her way. I admired her vigor, but if the Southern army was planning something, we needed to know about it. Especially if that information would keep me away from their ranks.

The force of Dess's arrow had thrown the vampire from his horse, and he huddled on the ground, hand gripping his heart. I glanced at his comrade cowering a small distance away, horse dead beside him—the thick arrow had gone cleanly through the vampire's heart and pierced the horse's neck. I shoved the cowering man to the back of my mind—he hadn't reached for his musket or tried to escape yet, so he was not a threat.

Instead, I ran over to stand on top of the vampire before shifting to my human form, pinning him there—the arrow's silver tip had cauterized the bleeding, but I wouldn't wish a never-healing wound on anyone, especially not this boy . . . the terror in his eyes was not what I'd been expecting.

It was the kind of fear I'd only ever seen from a New Blood.

"Where were you headed?" I asked, shoving my hair over one shoulder so it wasn't in the boy's face—I needed to see him, otherwise I would've left him to experience my hair in all its glory.

"The stronghold," he gasped. He could barely catch his breath to get a word out, but who could blame him with that sort of pain. "In Gettysburg. There's a letter for them in my front coat pocket. But that's all I know," he added, frantic, as I searched his pockets. "They didn't tell me anything else, sir, honest to God," he said. For a moment, I thought he might vomit from the pain of his wound, from the effort it took to speak. "I don't fight on the front lines; I repair roads and bridges."

Whether or not I believed him was irrelevant. I retrieved a sealed envelope. It was weighty—definitely more than just a letter inside.

I looked up as Odessa dismounted and stood by the human, not bothering to keep her weapon at the ready—the man was in a sad state. Pathetic.

But then, most soldiers recruited during dire times were rarely built for war.

"Dess," I heard Jerusalem say, and I cursed myself that she'd caught up so quickly—I knew better than to doubt her. "This vamp ain't on the list."

I paused and glanced at Odessa. She always had a stellar poker face in front of the enemy, and I couldn't tell if the sweat I smelled from her was newly filled with adrenaline from withholding information or from the general excitement of the situation. Gael was off in the distance acting as lookout, so I couldn't question him about it. All I knew was that Odessa had never brought back false information from a spy mission. Ever.

So where had this New Blood come from? How could they have overlooked something so significant?

Either she had lied to my face when we'd met with the colonel, which was unlikely after two years of friendship, or . . . or her intel had been wrong.

"When were you turned?" I asked.

"A few weeks ago."

My gut twisted, and for a moment, I couldn't breathe. "And they sent you out here?"

"They thought I'd be safe as a vampire." He had started crying. "But I don't feel safe at all."

I swallowed. "You're safe from me."

He nodded, more tears gushing from his eyes. He didn't deserve this. Any of it. A familiar pain and anger grew in my gut. And disgust.

"Please don't let your Saints kill me, sir," he said, as Jerusalem walked over to us. "I just want to go home."

"I can't promise we'll send you home," I said.

"Like hell," Jerusalem muttered.

"Don't move until we finish questioning your comrade." I held out the sealed note to try and occupy my violent girl's hands for a moment. She was agitated, ready for action. To be fair, I'd *promised* her action, and I hated to disappoint. But this was different.

This felt too personal.

My distraction didn't work for long, because she tossed the letter to Odessa and asked, "What's this vamp got to say?"

"The letter is communication from the army to the stronghold," I said. "Beyond that, he has nothing we need."

And that much was true. Still, I didn't move away from our captive. The last thing I wanted was to give Jerusalem an opening.

"How many vamps you got in that army of yours?" Jerusalem demanded. "'Cause you wasn't on our list."

"Of course he wasn't," I said, and she ground her jaw at me. "He's a New Blood."

"So what the hell they doing over there, biting people to make a vamp army?"

"Let's ask *him*," I snapped, gesturing to the cowering man in the distance.

I waited until Jerusalem was storming in that direction to stand.

"Hey, you," she called, but the way she paused when he looked up at her as she got closer raised my hackles. The New Blood would be fine if he did as he was told and stayed put. Now my mind was full of nothing but Jerusalem. I looked at the two of them, resting my hand on the hilt of my shashka. Not that I needed it to tear him to pieces.

Had he been one of the men to raise a whip to her? And how often?

Hang the questioning.

I wanted him dead.

JERUSALEM

I knew this man. Garfield, Adelaide's stepson, the oldest one who was still human—and Lord, if that redheaded gene wasn't strong in that family. His hair was less neat than I remembered, growing out a little long with the beginnings of a rusty beard on his cheeks. But beyond that, all I could think of was my Lila. My baby sister. Fourteen, and full of life and hope.

It was the only reason I remembered his name. 'Cause he and his wife had taken my sister in, sheltered her as a house slave in their little cabin away from the big house where the evil lived.

At least . . . sheltered her until there was no one left to shelter.

And that was the only reason I didn't introduce my spearhead to his face right away.

Garfield looked shocked to see me, but a little relieved, as if I'd let him live any more than my companions. "Dido?"

"I don't go by that slave name," I said coldly. He deserved it, fighting in the Southern army, even if he had been good to my sister for the most part. And for that same bitterness, I didn't offer him my true name. "Never pegged you for the fighting type."

"Didn't have much choice, what with the draft and all."

Liar. The war'd already been going before I escaped, and he was living at home, not even thinking about it. I'd've bet anything it was Adelaide that forced him to join up when she did. So maybe, in that way, he didn't have no choice—nobody said *no* to Adelaide and walked away unscathed.

He seemed uncomfortable, not attempting to stand, as if any movement might set me off. Always was the smart one of the family. "Glad to see you made it North. Toby said you would."

"His name was Matthew," I growled, pointing my spear at his throat so quickly he looked stunned, like his soul done left his body. "And don't you talk about my brother like you didn't stand there and let your Pa's hounds tear him to pieces."

"I-I didn't!" He fell back, cowering behind his arm, as I moved my spear closer. "Wait, wait, wait! He's alive!"

"We're wasting time," said Alexei, scowling at me as I stopped him with my arm before he could do something to Garfield he'd never dream of doing to that vamp.

"You lying," I said to Garfield, trying to shove away my hope. *My brother . . . alive?*

No. He couldn't be. I saw them hounds lunge at him. I heard him cry out in pain. Garfield was bluffing, saying whatever would keep him topside longer.

There was a small *smack* like something slapping the air, and when I turned, a bat was fighting to fly but was clearly too injured to get far.

"Foolish boy," Alexei hissed, but I got to the vamp first, smacking him out of the air with the shaft of my spear like swatting a fly. He skidded, little squeaks changing to weeping as he shifted to his human form.

The vamp looked at me, wide-eyed. He hadn't done that to Alexei. 'Cause he was a pretty silver-haired white boy talking low and gentle, one of his kind, and I was . . . a Black girl. That was enough for some to look at me off, like I didn't belong where I was. But give a Black girl a spear and enhanced strength, and that look turned to fear real quick.

Just how I liked it.

So I didn't care what Alexei had promised him, didn't wait for nothing. "Jerusalem, no!" I heard Alexei yell, right as I stabbed my spear into the monster's neck and tore it aside, disconnecting the head from the body.

Alexei's voice cracked, but I didn't linger over it. I stormed back over to Garfield and grabbed him by the shirt, my agitation higher than before, my spear hungry for more blood. "What you mean he's alive?"

Garfield eyed my bloody spearhead, like he didn't know the fist gripping his shirt was the more immediate threat. "When Adelaide saw—I mean, we *all* saw it—how fast you done ran out of there—"

"Talk faster."

"She called the hounds off him to send them after you," he went on, almost in a panic this time. "And then you killed our hounds and Walter, and I-I think she realized what you were— *are*. A Saint. She reckoned you'd be back for your brother."

I was stuck between staying put and throwing that man as far away from me as I could. My fist at his shirt was shaking, and for a second I didn't think I breathed none 'cause the next second, I was breathing in heavy.

"You seen him with your own eyes?"

He nodded. "I was home a few weeks ago. I seen him, all right, swear to God."

Tears burned at the backs of my eyeballs. My brother. My Matthew. Alive?

"Jerusalem," Odessa reminded me sternly.

My heart pounded loud through me, but I got up, dragging Garfield up with me. I shoved him away, and he stumbled back on his feet. "'Cause you was good to my sister—and *only* 'cause you was good to my sister—Imma let you go."

"*What?*" Alexei growled.

"But if I catch you on the battlefield, best believe you a dead man."

Garfield nodded over and over, like his head was about to come off. "Oh my God, thank you, Saint." He bowed to us, like we was royalty or something as he backed away. "Thank y'all—"

Odessa grabbed him by the collar before he could hightail it, and he yelped and cowered in her grip. "He'll warn the Confederate army. We can't let him live."

"I know him," I said. "He won't say nothing."

Alexei shook his head, his glare deadly. "That poor New Blood had to die, and *this* cretin gets to live? You can't be serious."

"I am serious," I said, squaring up to him. "And if you don't get the difference, maybe you fighting on the wrong side."

"He was a victim."

"You should know better than to let a young face and a couple tears fool you. And he couldn't even follow simple directions." I shifted a glare to Garfield that made him twitch. "Whereas this man knows Imma do to him what I did to his brother if he breathes a word."

"I'll go straight home," Garfield offered in a panic. "I swear."

Odessa frowned. "And be labeled a coward for deserting?"

Alexei scoffed. "Well earned."

Odessa gave him a look I'd seen plenty of times from my own mama, and if he'd've remembered ever having a mama, he'd of shut up right then. "And if the vamps catch him first?"

"Look at him, Dess. The mere *threat* of torture would make him squeal."

"You really trust him to keep his word, Jerusalem?" Odessa asked.

You couldn't trust nobody in this world, but Garfield was a simple man, no tricks up his sleeve. Work, results. Actions, consequences. And I sure bet he'd seen the aftermath of what I'd done to his wicked brother.

"He talks," I said, "I burn his ass alive."

Garfield's eyes were wide, as if I'd do it right then and there.

Odessa released his collar, and he stumbled, shifting terrified glances at the three of us.

"You best get going," I said. "'Cause you got to take the long way around the army."

"Thank you," he murmured.

"Get!"

"We're not actually letting him go?" asked Alexei in murderous disbelief as we watched him run.

"This is a mistake," Odessa murmured, playing with an arrow at her hip. She was thinking about killing him anyway, despite my promise.

To be honest, so was I.

I watched him run, feeling madder and madder with each second, each step. 'Cause with each one, I thought of my sister.

Lila was taller and prettier than me, and much more skilled at household things, and so at only twelve years old, Garfield's wife, Millie, took her in to be her lady's maid. Matthew was already Garfield's personal valet, so they trusted my family to know what they was doing. It was the best thing for her, to be honest—she wasn't fit for no field work, the dainty thing. It was hard work in the house but not the same kind of brutal, and at least it was all in her wheelhouse of talents. And Millie was nice compared to the rest of them, so I felt safe leaving my baby sister with her.

But I should've known better . . . ain't no safety for us nowhere.

'Cause she was only fourteen when we found out she was pregnant by the master. Lord, I was steaming to kill the man right then and there, but my baby sister stayed trying to see the good, even while crying.

"Remember how Miss Millie can't have no children?" she asked, squeezing my hands tight. "She and Mr. Garfield going to take the baby for their own if it ain't too dark."

"*Look* at you, Lila," I said, smirking a little, just enough that I wouldn't scare her with the rage burning my insides raw. "That baby fittin' to be dark."

"But you and Mama ain't as dark—there's something in us that might give this baby a fighting chance. And just think, Jer! My baby won't be no slave, and I'll get to nurse and care for it and everything. Someone in our family finally going to own something instead of being owned. And then maybe, when the baby's grown, it can help make things easier for us."

My sweet, hopeful Lila.

Never did find out what the baby looked like, if it was a boy or girl or healthy or even alive. 'Cause by the time Matthew came and told me she was in labor it was too late.

We was too late.

Lila lay on a wooden table, dressed in a bloodstained burlap gown, her skin and hair still sweaty . . . her face still marked by the struggle and agony, not of childbirth, but far worse.

Matthew ran to the table, held her face, cried over her. I should've done that, too. Instead, I stood a bit apart, fists gripped, vibrating with hate and anger as I watched the blood drip from the table to the floor.

My baby sister. My Lila. Something had gone wrong with the regular labor of pushing, maybe the baby had been facing the wrong way or something. But they hadn't bothered to fix it . . . instead, they'd cut my sister's belly right open to remove the baby by hand. And I know good and well they didn't use no numbing drugs, didn't care if they punctured organs, didn't care that she felt every second of being carved into. They'd slaughtered my baby sister like she didn't mean nothing.

"We got to sneak her out," Matthew said, already positioning her body to pick her up, swiping his eyes with his sleeves so he could see what he was doing.

"Who you think held the knife?" I asked. "You think it was the master?"

My brother paused to look at me. He wasn't confused, only horrified. He knew me better than to ask what I meant.

He rushed to me, taking my face firmly, leaning over so we was eye to eye. "You ain't taking on no white man, you hear me? I lost one sister. I ain't losing the other."

"He got to pay for what he done."

"You strong, Jer, but going up against the master's a death sentence, plain and simple." He glanced around quickly, then went to Lila to lift her from the table. "God Almighty going to make him pay, someday. Till then, we got to hold on."

He rushed out the front door. I followed, nearly knocking into him, he stopped so suddenly.

Garfield stood there, a small parcel in hand. He looked horrified, like he might vomit up all his insides. As he should. His family and their doctor was the ones that did it, and he probably knew it, too.

But the first words from his mouth was, "How's the baby?"

How's the baby?

While my brother stood right in front of him holding our sister's ripped, breathless body? How's the *baby?* Dead, I hoped. He didn't deserve my sister's child—that was brutally forced on her, anyway, that was heartlessly torn out of her when they was done using her as nothing but a casing. He didn't deserve nothing more from my Lila. Least of all a poor baby who was probably much too dark for them to bother keeping alive.

Them people tolerated and used my sister till they didn't have to no more, Garfield and Millie included.

Monsters.

Even human as they was, they was monsters, too. Complicit, selfish monsters. 'Cause what was the difference between the ones who killed the innocent and the ones who simply stood by and let them die?

Only took a couple seconds for me to come to my senses. Odessa was about to string her bow, but I beat her to it. Barely paused to measure or aim, just threw my spear. My target was a good few hundred feet away, but went down quick and hard, with barely a sound.

From the corner of my eye, I saw Odessa look over my head at Alexei, and I was sure he was looking at her, too, but didn't stay to find out if they thought I was crazy. Instead, I leapt onto my horse and rode over to retrieve my spear.

I looked down at my work as I reached it. My spear had gone clean through his upper back, out his lower chest, and— 'cause I'd arced it—pinned him to the ground. Or it would've, if the force of impact hadn't cut him nearly in half, spreading mushy red all over. I slipped down from my horse and gripped my spear. It was wedged into the ground pretty good.

"I thought you wanted to spare him." Alexei's voice came from above as I finally yanked it out—I'd've stabbed him for being so stealthy if my spearhead was facing the right way.

"Said I'd let him go." I knelt and cleaned my spear on what was left dry of Garfield's coat. "Never said I'd let him live."

"Jerusalem." From the corner of my eye, I saw Alexei crouch down on the other side of the body, and I willfully didn't look his way. "Are you all right?"

"Why you asking?"

"You threw your spear pretty hard. It doesn't take that much force to kill a human."

"What's your point?" I snapped, standing to glare down at him.

He stood slowly, my glare trained on him all the way, till I was looking up at him, a tower as tall as the sky.

"You're not all right," he said, which made me want to stab him even harder. Who cares that it was obvious from looking at me, that he sounded like it bothered him. He didn't get to tell me how I felt.

Tears burned the backs of my eyes, wavering my glare. I wanted a hug real bad . . . a childish urge I couldn't afford. I wasn't about to cry, not even—*especially* not—in front of this great warrior. I wasn't about to show my weakness. "So I changed my mind about killing him. A girl can't change her mind if she wants?"

"Seeing him again must have been difficult—"

"Don't act like you know something about what I been through, Alexei," I said, stepping away as he stepped closer. "'Cause I can tell you right now, you don't."

He held his own hands back, then put them behind his neck,

like they had a mind of their own and would touch me without him even knowing. "I understand more than you know."

"No, you don't!" I shoved him, and that was me checking myself and not killing the boy 'cause I was mad enough to do it. "No, you don't, white boy. Look at you, all blond and blue eyed. You don't know what it's like to be called subhuman. To be enslaved 'cause a whole race of people think the color of your skin and the size of your nose and what your hair looks like make you lesser. Or 'cause a whole race of people think horses and dogs are worth more than your life. You don't know nothing."

"Fine. That's fair. Maybe I don't. But that doesn't change the fact that I care about you, Jerusalem. That I care how it affects you."

I'd turned back to my horse before he finished—anything to not look at him—but the last of his words stopped me from mounting. I wanted his words to be true more than anything. Beautiful, powerful Alexei who could do anything, *kill* anyone. I wanted him to truly care, as needy as that sounded.

"We're a team, Jerusalem, and yet you still speak as if you don't trust me. I'm on your side."

I spun to face him, all the soft feelings I'd had for him a second ago disappearing on the wind. "Like hell. If you was on my side you'd've killed that vamp as soon as you got the info we needed. Not make no deal with him and let him live."

Alexei shook his head. "He was a New Blood, turned in the past few weeks. It was clear he didn't want any part of this."

"He was delivering a secret message for the Southern army; can't get no closer to 'part of this' than that."

"He was terrified—"

"Good! He should be. They should all be quaking in their boots, pissing their pants, at the thought of us. Besides, my first kill was a New Blood, and there wasn't nothing innocent about him." I swallowed, pain in my heart just thinking about that night, and turned back to my horse quickly to mount. "Ain't no mercy in war, Alexei. Can't be. Else what becomes of the innocents caught in between?"

And I rode off to get away from him and my thoughts.

ALEXEI

Russia
Late 1500s

The innocents caught in between.

I awoke naked and shivering to my core. There was only darkness, a thick cloth giving me a headache from how tightly it was knotted, blocking out all light, if there was any. And silence, except for a whispered conversation somewhere in the hidden corners of the room. My hands were bound behind my back with a crude rope, my bare legs kneeling on something hard and cold, grained like wood.

I forced down a spark of panic. I was eighteen, had a new wife and a good, steady job. That made me a man, and men didn't panic.

Besides, there was a rational explanation. It was obvious my father-in-law's debts had finally caught up to him. No one would've ever dared mess with me otherwise.

Heavy footsteps approached, and the floor creaked as an unseen person crouched in front of me. "Drink," he said, his voice quiet and heavy. I spoke enough Polish to make out the word. That old man's debts were worse than I thought if someone from a completely different country was here looking for him.

"What is it?" I demanded, feeling the rim of the glass against my bottom lip.

"Only wine, boy."

I accepted the wine, like an idiot, then promptly squeezed my lips tight not to allow anymore in. Tinny and bitter, thicker than any wine I'd ever tasted.

The man suddenly squeezed my nose shut, forcing the liquid in my mouth as I opened it to gasp for air. He dragged my head back by the hair. I spit the liquid out as best I could, but he poured more in after it, and I cringed as my body was forced to swallow a little before I spit the rest out to run down my chin.

What the hell . . . no, it can't be . . .

But I had gotten into enough fights in my youth to now recognize the taste of blood.

He released my hair, and I heard the pound of his boots as he left me alone.

Or maybe not, because my head tipped as the blindfold was snatched from my eyes. There was a little candlelight. As sparse as it was, it still felt glaring, but I didn't need to see clearly to gather the remainder of bitter liquid in my mouth and spit it at my captor. There was just enough light to make out a figure cloaked in furs crouching before me, a blood-red mask reflecting glossy in the firelight with nothing but dark slits for eyes, nostrils, and mouth. It was made all the worse by the liquid I'd spat running down the smooth surface . . . liquid I was now certain was blood, making the mask look more like a flayed face.

The figure didn't move to wipe away the blood. "That was rude, Alexei."

Finally, some Russian. Her voice was unsettlingly calm, undoubtedly due to overconfidence. The mask had been a clever move, but I could figure out her identity soon enough simply by watching her body language. I lived in a small village, and that she knew my name had more than given her away.

"How much does my father-in-law owe you?" I asked, my confidence rekindled now that I knew I was dealing with common thugs. "I can get it for you, but this little intimidation game you're playing isn't the way."

The figure paused, as if regarding me. "I am not interested in money."

"Well, then, I don't know what to tell you. You have the wrong man."

"Oh, I don't think so. I think you are exactly what I'm looking for."

Looking for . . . for what? Panic threatened to rise again, but I had been conditioned since adolescence to suppress such weakness in my expression. "The fact that you think you can threaten me is ill-conceived."

"Ill-conceived?"

"You know my name—you must know my reputation. So what you're looking for is trouble if you don't give me back my possessions and let me be on my way."

She turned her head and said, "He's perfect," to the shadows. Someone within them moved—and it must have been the first man. But all I saw was the back of a large black fur cloak as he opened the door and exited into the dark hall.

"Do you cry, Alexei?" the masked figure asked, turning back to me. "On command, I mean?"

It was becoming increasingly clear that I didn't know anyone who spoke this way. Still, any liar could play superior from behind a mask. "I will happily make *you* cry if you don't release me."

She chuckled. "I do enjoy your threats."

"You won't when I do more than threaten."

"I must disagree with you." The figure leaned a bit closer. "I will ask nicely again. Cry for me, Alexei."

It wasn't asking, nicely or otherwise, and it was such an unsettling request I felt dread at even acknowledging it. I looked away with a scoff, secretly searching for a way out, but it was a windowless room, and the only door was the one the man now blocked . . . this time holding the shoulders of a young woman with wide, familiar eyes and as pale as a sheet against his dark cloak.

And suddenly, my heart pounded in my throat, threatening to suffocate me.

"Leave my wife out of this," I said, but a sharp pain cut off my words, and I cried out as four blades cold as icicles went into the side of my stomach, freezing me to my core. They shifted a bit, as if alive, then left me as quickly as they'd entered.

The figure lifted the red mask, just enough to expose a pale chin and red lips, and I watched her—as if in a fever dream—lick my blood from her fingers. And then that hand touched my throat, and a shudder went through me. The flesh was cold, not from lack of gloves against the snowy climate, but cold as stone . . . as if there was no life beneath the skin.

The figure crowded me, and then there was more pain but worse, far worse. My scream was stifled, sharp and painful pressure on my throat, as fanged teeth sunk into my neck. The wound burned, as if poison was creeping through my body, replacing my blood. It went on and on until I was weeping in a panic, my body begging for it to stop.

Finally the pressure let up on my neck. Through the haze of my own searing pain, my panting breaths and throbbing throat, I heard, "Next time I tell you to do something, you do it. Is that understood?"

I couldn't answer, couldn't have stopped the tears if I wanted to, my fear as immediate as my pain. Next time. So there would be more of this. *More of what, Alexei? . . .* If someone had asked me to describe what had just happened, I'd have no idea what to tell them.

"I'll return with some proper clothing for you after you've eaten and regained your composure." The figure stood, but I was in no position to look up with how I was bound, and I didn't want to. I didn't ever want to look at that monster again . . . "My dear Alexei. I am going to thoroughly enjoy breaking you in."

The woman left the room, and the man blew out the few candles that were lit, throwing the room into darkness as he shut the door behind them.

"Alexei." My wife gasped in the pitch blackness, nothing but a small amount of moonlight underneath the door revealing her silhouette. She felt her way over to me, and I groaned in pain as she put her arms around my bloodied frame. She was shivering in her simple dress. She needed warmth, and soon. "That woman . . . she . . . she *bit you.*"

I couldn't respond with words, my throat so raw even the slightest sound sent tearing pain through it. I tried to nod through my trembling, but there was no way she would see it in this darkness.

"We must get away from this awful place." I winced at the volume of her voice, so close to me, but barely noticed through my panic as she stood and looked around. "There was a window just in the hall. The snow outside is deep enough to break our fall, I'm sure . . ."

"There's something wrong with me," I tried to reply, my voice coming out as a pained gasp—the pressure of the monster's bite must have done damage beyond bruising. But I could speak, which meant I was in better shape than I had been in a moment ago.

She didn't listen—or perhaps didn't hear—as she tried to tear at the ropes around my wrists. My pulse felt sluggish despite my panic. I watched my wife as she worked, her brow creased in determination. I saw her clearly now in the dark of the room . . . and the unlit fireplace, the walls, the chair against the wall. I saw everything now, as if we weren't covered in darkness.

The rope dropped away from my wrists. "Something is *wrong* with me," I said again. My body didn't feel like mine—quick, painless, and, despite my nakedness, not at all cold. I could hear the snow swirling outside, smell the remnants of the candles across the room, see everything crystal clear despite the room being bathed in night.

I'm dreaming. Or drugged.

Either way, we had to get out of that house. Immediately.

"Have your eyes adjusted?" I asked quickly.

"A little," she said. "Not well."

Meanwhile, I could see her worried expression perfectly, and *that* worried *me*. "Stay close to me."

She cried out as I took her hand, and I dropped it quickly, covering my ears with my hands at her volume.

"You were crushing me," she protested.

"I was not."

I tried to take her hand again and she began crying. "Alexei, stop!"

"Stop yelling, my God!" I covered my ears again, my mind in a panic, my senses overwhelmed. "I barely touched you."

"You were *hurting* me."

"Hurting you . . . ?" I looked at my hands. They didn't look any different. Perhaps fear of the situation had made me grip too tightly, and I hadn't even been aware of it.

Except everything smelled too strongly. Everything sounded like horns blasting in my ears. All the pain I'd felt from being stabbed, being bitten, was completely gone, and that wasn't . . . that wasn't normal. None of this was normal. I fought against the tears forming at the backs of my eyes. "We have to get away from here."

This time, I let her take my wrist and led her toward the door, the entire time thinking she . . . didn't smell right. Normally, she smelled of our vegetable garden, like the rye we used to make our vodka. But now a bitter, unappetizing aroma enveloped my nose. *Unappetizing? What a strange word to use in reference to your wife—*

But by the time I reached the door, all I could think was that I was thirsty, so thirsty, too thirsty, and there was something *alive* in this room, beside me, heart beating hot . . . And I *needed* it.

"Alexei, what is that?" I barely heard over my growling. "It sounds as if they have turned a wolf loose in the—"

And I sunk my teeth into my prey's hot, pulsing throat.

6

JERUSALEM

I've decided you're ready," Odessa said on my third day in the Union camp. By then, I'd been more than sick of the inside of a tent, of following Dess around while white men stared at me like I wasn't a Saint who belonged there just as much as they did.

But then, she'd handed me a big, old history tome full of drawings of weapons, and I knew my revenge plot was finally in motion.

"How come y'all don't use silver bullets and be done with it?" I asked, opening the book.

"It's nearly impossible to construct a functional silver bullet—they're more of a myth than anything. Besides, a Saint's weapon should be seen. It's your calling card," she said, and gave me a knowing grin. "Choose wisely."

I flipped through the book, knowing what I was looking for without really knowing at all. All I had was my encounter with the monster I'd killed to know what I wanted in a weapon and what I didn't. Sharp, for starters. Silver. But any of these weapons could be those.

Lots of knives and swords on the pages, but . . . I shivered, remembering the feeling of the pointed stick going into that vamp's neck. You had to be close to stab the enemy, and I didn't ever want to be touched by one of them monsters again. Dess's bow and arrows was good for distance, but there was something about it that felt impersonal. And there was nothing impersonal about what I wanted to do. Anyhow, I knew my aim wasn't good enough for that.

"Ain't there any longer weapons than this?" I asked, looking up as Dess stepped away from her weapons and over to me. "Something where I don't got to get too close to the vamps to use it."

"What about a spear?" suggested Dess, but I must've looked at her sideways 'cause she chuckled as she flipped a few dozen pages over and pointed at a gloriously long staff with a pointed metal end.

"That's the one," I said. I didn't need to consider any others. It was the most beautiful thing I ever did see.

'Cause it was one step closer to avenging my family.

"I've never used one," she said, which made me instantly deflate. "So we'll have to ask one of the other Saints if they can teach you."

I didn't mean to let it out where she could hear, but I groaned. "You mean I got to spend a bunch of time with a *white man?*"

"They're not the same as down South, I promise you."

"You been saying that since I got here, but they still all look at me cockeyed when I walk by."

"To be fair, I think that has a lot to do with your height.

They think you're younger than you are and are probably wondering why you're here."

"I'll give them something to wonder about," I muttered.

Odessa made a small sound of chastisement. She took my chin in her hand, and I almost missed what she said next, the fight not to cry blocking everything out. Mama held my face like that when she was trying to tell me something important—she did that a lot, and I was suddenly sorry I gave her a hard time about too many things. I just wanted to apologize face-to-face, to be wrapped in her arms and forgiven. For what, who knew. I ain't done nothing. I just wanted my Mama's arms.

"Do you understand?" Dess asked.

I shook off the memories, the childish desires. I hadn't heard a daggone thing Dess said but nodded anyway. "Yeah."

"Repeat back what I just said."

Yep. She sure as hell was a mama of five babies. "Behave?" I mumbled.

"Close enough." She gave me a reassuring grin. "Let's be off, then."

I followed her out of the tent.

All the Saint tents sat in one section, but the camp was huge, and the Saints really could've been anywhere. The only thing that helped was they hung around in little groups, so look for one, and you got three or four for your trouble. We came across a group of three standing in a little triangle talking about their dogs. What was with white people loving dogs?

The group greeted Dess enthusiastically, even before we'd finished approaching. I ain't never seen a white man greet someone who looked like me like *that*, let alone three of them. That a Black woman could be so beloved here was almost enough to make me believe what she'd said, encouraging in the most unreal way.

"Have any of you used a spear before?" Dess asked them.

"A spear?" said one of them in distaste. "How very barbaric."

"Ain't that a spear?" I asked, tipping my chin at his weapon, and he gave me a look that made me feel downright murderous—like I was stupid. Like I didn't belong.

"It's a *lance*," he said. "That's why the papers call me Lancelot."

He said it like I knew what the hell he was talking about.

"You never just lance *a bit*?" I asked, and everyone laughed except Fancypants, who looked real annoyed.

Well. *He* wasn't going to teach me nothing.

"Is this your daughter, Odessa?" asked one of the Saints, looking chalky as hell—Will was his name, I found out later.

"She looks feral," said Fancypants, looking me up and down. I was starting to think he should be my first practice target.

"Well, you look like you start crying after a single beer," I retorted, looking *him* up and down.

Odessa grabbed my hand, and I froze. Suddenly, I couldn't hear nothing else again. 'Cause her hand was firm and gentle at once, strong and calming. Like Mama's.

I had to stop comparing this woman to my Mama . . . but it was something familiar in this strange land. And I needed something familiar.

A ruckus broke through my thought then, and I winced at the three Saints in front of us, practically crying from laughter.

"Is *that* why you asked about spears?" said the first Saint.

"This *little girl*," said Lance-a-dick, "can't wield a spear."

"I want to see it, at least for a little bit," said Chalk Boy. "Think of how cute it'll be to see her holding a weapon taller than her."

I didn't know why Dess had said these people was any better than the ones I had left. They didn't enslave people up North 'cause the law said they couldn't . . . but that didn't mean they thought of me any better. All the dirty looks, and now they was laughing at me, even though I should've been their equal—I was a Saint, too, wasn't I? And why was a spear something to sneer at when a lance was the same thing?

Fancypants was bigger than me, probably more experienced at fighting than me, and was holding a big-ass blade against his shoulder, but it didn't stop me none from storming up to him and punching him upward right in the jaw.

He stumbled back a step, caught off guard—he'd been in the middle of laughing at me, so served him right. Everyone got quiet then, even the regular soldiers around us, waiting for what I'd do next. Fancypants looked hellbent on killing me. I'd seen that look too many times before, and used to be I'd have to appease it just to survive.

But I was free now.

I didn't immediately go after him again. I had better things to do, like finding someone to train me. But I stared him down all the same.

Dess stepped in front of me, blocking him from approaching. "Stand down, Colin. She's not a trained fighter."

"Let her learn, then, Odessa," he said.

And that did it. My fighting instinct leapt up above any other rational thought as I shoved past Dess and stormed up to the man who looked like he had no intention of standing down.

There was a dark rush of movement in the air, and I stumbled to the ground as I watched a black bird shift form into a man. Light as anything, he dropped down between us, facing my enemy. It was the vamp I'd met my first day here—I only knew 'cause of that long silver hair and the curved sword at his hip. But Lord, I ain't remember him being so *big*. Fancypants backed away fast, like the vamp standing there was enough of a deterrent.

Wasn't Saints designed to kill vamps? Size shouldn't've mattered to him at all.

Using the distraction to get to my feet, I looked the vamp up and down. I could see why someone might be afraid. He was tall as an elm—I had to back away to even see the whole of him. A giant. And he didn't slouch like taller people tended to do to get closer to the average people. I knew he could tear off a person's head with his bare hands 'cause vamps could do stuff like that, but he *looked* like he could tear off heads, his hands big and strong.

"I wasn't going to hurt her," said Fancypants, like anyone'd asked. Lying through his teeth, the coward.

"Just like I'm not going to hurt you," said Alexei, a terrible calmness to his voice that I recognized immediately.

I seen that sort of power before—it wasn't hypnosis, only a look. A threat. Any human confident enough could pull it off, too, but coming from a vamp, it went from a threat someone might challenge to a scary-as-hell encounter you wanted to get away from as soon as you could. I had to admit, it was satisfying seeing the wariness in Fancypants's eyes, the uncertainty. It thrilled me beyond reason to see white folks squirm.

"We're all allies here, Alexei," said Odessa, firmly but carefully. "Let's not do anything we'll regret."

"Of course, Odessa," said Alexei, though he didn't move to stand down. "After all, I did promise the colonel I wouldn't eat anyone."

I swallowed back my disgust and fear at his words—easier

here than with the vamp I'd killed a week ago only 'cause they weren't directed at me. I couldn't afford that kind of fear, not when I'd be living with the enemy.

He turned to me, that quick, animalistic movement I was used to in vamps, and two thoughts went through my head at the same time—one that told me to behave despite my body wanting to run. *Hold still. Keep your mouth shut. Obey.* Lord bless 'em, Mama and Pa been trying to cultivate that part of me all seventeen years of my life. But that thought left as quick as it came.

The one that lingered, though, that one was me. The one who had talked back to Donald, had killed the master, had burned his vamp son to death. The one who had waited seventeen years to be set free.

Well, hell. I could take this pretty boy.

As if hearing my thought, Alexei smiled. Seeing his fangs made my skin crawl. "I hear you've selected a spear as your Saint weapon. Excellent choice."

"I take it you ain't got none of them laying around?" I said, my voice stone cold.

"No, but I can make you one to practice with for now."

Naw. I wasn't trying to be indebted to no vamp. *Like hell.* But I didn't have no options. I had to think of the end goal—I had me a vamp to kill. And who could teach me to kill my enemy better than one of her own kind?

So I took a deep breath and swallowed any protests I had waiting on my tongue. 'Cause a week ago I'd been enslaved, lost my family, was nearly killed. Learning what I needed to know from a cursed vamp was a thousand times better than anything I'd just left behind.

"Whatever you got," I said, and he nodded.

"I need a broom," he told the air without ceremony, never taking his eyes off me, and a young soldier scampered off to do his bidding.

Disgust budded in my stomach. "You can't keep familiars up North, I thought."

"I've never had a familiar in my life."

"Then what the hell was that?"

"I can't help that people are friendly." He shrugged, and I hated him for it. White folks was always so unbothered while dishing out commands, vamps especially. And his command was the type that wasn't one at all. Just a spoken desire, as if he knew people would go running to please him. 'Cause people *would* go running to please him. He kept familiars, right enough, whether or not he wanted to call it by name. 'Cause that boy sure as hell brought him the broom.

Alexei took it without ceremony and popped the bristle end off quick and easy, leaving a long staff. And I didn't know if he was testing the weight or showing off—after I got to know him, I would swear it was the latter—but he spun the thing, and my breath caught in the most glorious way. Time seemed to slow as I watched his hands control the stick, it spinning quick as lightning in response. It wasn't hypnosis, at least not the vampiric kind. It was just . . . beautiful. Fluid in a way I couldn't describe. And all I could think when he finished was, *I want to do that.*

He stopped abruptly and murmured, "Good enough," then held out the stick. He at least had the decency not to step any closer, to hold it at length from the end. I took it from him quickly, gripping it close to my body with both hands.

But maybe I'd shown too much awe on my face 'cause he grinned at me in a way that was half genuine kindness, half teasing, a grin I might have loved if I loved him, but at the time didn't do nothing but leave me more determined than ever to prove everyone wrong. "Well, then, Jerusalem, what do you say we find somewhere with a little more space?"

A few months later, I'd been training with Alexei almost every day—*almost*, 'cause he forced me to have rest days. I would've trained every day if my body could keep up. That was how much I wanted this.

Still didn't trust his ass too much, though. Vamps didn't like wasting their time, and so his devotion to training me told me he didn't have no intention of killing me. *That* I trusted, at least. Still, I never trained with him without Dess present.

I didn't trust him *that* much.

And he was vain as a flower in bloom—beautiful and knew it, the showoff. And his *audacity*. As I warmed up, so did he, no longer the polite boy who remained considerate despite my vocal protests.

Now he was just plain annoying.

"Do you need me to take that from you yet?" he called casually from the creek bank.

I didn't know what had possessed me to let this white boy put a giant bolder on my shoulders while I stood on some slippery rocks in the middle of a rushing creek, but after ten whole minutes of holding the thing I was good and well over it. "I *need* you to shut up before I throw this boulder on your head."

"What's that?" he yelled, exaggerated, hand to his ear, like his bloodsucking ass didn't have advanced senses.

"Alexei," Dess said with a heavy sigh. She sat on a blanket

weaving flowers into a crown. "Her legs are shaking. Get closer to her, at least."

"Stay over there," I snapped, adjusting my grip on the boulder. "I don't need your help."

"Don't be stubborn, Jerusalem," Dess said firmly. "Part of being in a battalion is relying on each other when you need it."

"It's okay, Odessa," said Alexei, sounding genuinely encouraging until he added, "Technically, she's not a soldier, so the army won't be liable if she's crushed by a rock."

I growled and threw the boulder at him—I'd had it with him and his irritating comments. He looked completely befuddled, gaping, but managed to catch the boulder before putting it down. A shame, really. Immediately, I felt lightheaded and could barely control my fall as I went forward onto my hands and knees.

"Easy . . ." said Alexei, suddenly far too close. "Your body needs to recover from all that weight."

"I'm fine," I snapped. But when I tried to shove his hand off me, my vision went black, and next thing I knew, something hard was resting on my shoulder and across my chest to my hip, holding me.

I blinked my vision clear, looking up to see that Alexei sat in the water as far away as he could while holding the end of my makeshift spear—the only thing keeping my face from plunging into the water. My arms and legs for sure couldn't hold me, shaking like they was. So I let them rest in the cold water, giving my spear the weight.

"I'm not coming any closer," Alexei assured me gently. "I'm not going to touch you. I'm just going to sit here until you can lift your body safely and reach the bank. Okay?"

"Okay . . ." I murmured. And then I closed my eyes to get rid of the dizziness. 'Cause the wild part was . . . I believed him. I wasn't worried about him breaking his word, and that left me time to get my sorry self together. The boulder couldn't have been *that* heavy.

But through my pounding heart and light head, I vaguely heard Odessa telling Alexei off for making me lift too heavy, for overdoing it. I would have laughed if I didn't think I'd throw up instead.

I watched as a Black soldier ran up to Dess and whispered something to her. She smiled and nodded. The soldier glanced our way nervously—probably at Alexei—and ran off.

Finally, I placed my own weight on the creek floor, and Alexei let up a little on his assistance. I took hold of my fake spear and stood it upright, using it to help me stand. Alexei stood along with me, although he didn't step any closer. My legs felt a little shaky still, but I was able to make it to shore without embarrassing myself, even if I did have to waddle a little.

"No more for today," Odessa said, like an order. She'd started cleaning up her flowers.

"What's next?" I asked.

"Something a little more fun."

Alexei's eyes lit up. "It's here?"

Odessa grinned and led the way back to camp.

My legs was so sore, my knees didn't bend without wanting to collapse on me, but I managed to follow Odessa out of the trees and over to her tent. And as soon as she opened the flap, I screamed in giddy glee. 'Cause resting across the bed mat was a brand-new shiny spear.

I wanted to run to it; instead, I turned to Dess quickly to double check. "Is that for me?"

It was a silly question—of *course* it was for me—but I had to know 'cause . . . hell. Nobody other than my family had ever given me nothing. And certainly nothing like *this*.

I started tearing up before Dess even answered and wrapped my arms around her neck. "Oh, thank you, thank you, thank you!"

Odessa chuckled. "You're very welcome, sweetie."

Now I gave myself permission to run to it. I snatched it off the bed mat, but as soon as I got it in my hands, I slowed. It felt too special, too sacred. There was intricate etching on the silver head, its angles smoothed, giving it a narrow teardrop shape. Blue jewels sparkled just below where the blade began. It was elegant, but not too showy. Perfectly sized and weighted for me.

I tested a thrust, but Odessa brought the blade safely upright again. "Let's keep that kind of activity outside of the tent," she said.

"This is way too generous, Dess, really," I said, hugging it to myself. "I mean, look at them jewels! Must've cost a fortune. I hope you charged the army for it and didn't spend none of your money."

"Don't worry about that. Alexei called in a favor to a friend. All we paid for was postage to send him your specifications."

I felt myself stiffen at her words. "A favor?"

Alexei smirked. "You tend to collect a lot of those after three hundred years."

I hesitated, staring longingly at the beautiful weapon. I fell for this spear at first sight . . . but hell if I was going to be indebted to a vamp. "I can't take this."

"Of course you can," said Alexei right as Odessa said, "It's yours, sweetie."

I looked at Alexei coldly. "What do I owe you? Say it now so I can decide whether it's worth it."

Alexei's brows lowered slightly, as if he was confused. "It's a gift, Jerusalem."

"I promise you," Odessa added, taking my shoulders gently. "It's a genuine gift. We're so proud of your progress."

"I don't doubt it from you, Odessa, but . . ." I shook my head, leveling a glare at Alexei. "Vamps don't give nothing without taking something."

"I suppose I'm different."

I paused, staring at him. "You went out of your way to get a silver weapon for a stranger? The same stranger you're training to kill your own kind?"

"You're a Saint, Jerusalem," he said. "You need a Saint's weapon."

"Well, supposing I just decided to up and use it on you?"

"You could."

"And yet?"

He shrugged with the lightest smile on his lips. "And yet."

We looked at each other a moment, and I felt a prick of something like gratitude in my gut. It felt odd to be grateful for something a vamp did for me. Part of me still wondered what his real motive was, what he meant by cashing in a favor for me of all people. And though it felt smarter to think the worst, the worst didn't make much sense in this scenario. The only thing that did make sense was what he and Dess had said—they wanted me to have a proper Saint weapon. And that they were . . . proud of me.

I looked away quickly—how long had I held his gaze? He could've hypnotized me with all that eye contact. Hell, maybe he did and talked me into thinking any sort of decent thought about him.

"Thank you," I murmured. "I love it."

"Now that you have a solid spear," Odessa said. "Tomorrow you can begin your real battle training."

"Tomorrow?" I said, making my way outside. "Hell naw."

"Jerusalem," Odessa said, frowning. "You've already overdone it for the day. Your body needs time to rest."

"If you wanted me to rest, you should've given it to me tomorrow," I said, unable to contain my smile. "I've been waiting forever for this moment, and I'm fittin' to take this thing out for a spin."

"I'm hungrier than a chicken in a coop," I said, chewing on a flower stem to ease the ache in my stomach . . . although all it did was make me wish I had me some real food. "We really ain't going to build a fire and cook something up?"

We'd found some nice ground to lay out our bags, surrounded by some good cover of bushes. The grass at the center was flattened, like an animal had been there first, but it was cold and there wasn't no signs it was coming back. Dess and me had taken off those annoying fake skirts, and we'd settled down for the night. There was some pretty wildflowers out here, and so Dess had started weaving a crown, even if it didn't make no sense. Didn't know who was going to wear a big old flower crown out on a secret mission in the middle of war.

Alexei had gone off to scout or something. At least that was what he said he was fittin' to do. I didn't want to think about what he was *actually* doing.

"We can't risk an open flame drawing attention to us," said Dess.

I groaned. "I can't stomach no more hardtack, Dess, for real."

At my words, Gael casually reached into one of his many pockets and pulled out a wrapped something or other and tossed it to me. I caught it, eyeing him skeptically as I opened it. Inside were little flat squares, maybe two inches on each side.

I sniffed it. It smelled like fruit, but it wasn't shaped like no fruit I'd ever seen. And when I bit into it, I found it was a little gummy, but sweet. Way better than a flower stem. It made my mouth water. It made me want more.

"Where you get this?" I asked.

"Made it," he said, lighting a cigarette.

"What in the hell—you been holding out on us? What in the hell?" I said again, 'cause I couldn't think of nothing that made sense to describe how good these squares was. So good they made me forget for a moment that I wasn't supposed to like Gael this much.

"Not too many," Dess said, in her stern mama voice. "You'll spoil your meal."

"Let her have them," Gael said gently, clearly trying to earn my good graces. He stood up and held his hands down to her. She smiled, taking his hands, and my stomach felt tied up in knots as he started singing something in Spanish and pulled her into a dance.

Well. We was back to not liking him.

Dess laughed as he spun her, and I wanted to yell at them to stop.

As if he heard my thought, Gael halted their spinning, gripping Dess's arms so she wouldn't fall over, and his eyes suddenly narrowed at the sky. "Querida," he murmured.

At the pet name—'cause I knew good and well it was that, as much as Dess denied it—she looked at him, and then up.

It was a flock of birds. A huge-ass flock of birds, like a black cloud, streaming through the sky.

Usually, I only saw so many birds at once when they was flying south for the winter, but not like *this*. Not frantic, like a swarm of bees. It was an omen, some people said. A sign multiple vamps was near, as if even all of nature couldn't stand the unnatural coldness of them.

I found myself smiling at them birds.

We was that much closer to our prey.

But when I looked back at Dess, her face looked distant . . . sad. And it didn't recover until she looked at me and smiled.

"I know it's early," she said, touching Gael's cheek before heading toward her pack. "But I'm exhausted."

"Come on, Dess," I said. "Don't go leaving me alone with these boys. I ain't got the patience for all that."

She chuckled, taking out her bed mat. "You'll survive."

I sighed and lay back in the grass, staring at the smoky gray sky. The sky was nice up North—in the South, you couldn't tell the storm clouds from the smoke, and it was dark all the time. Here, you could sort of tell what time of day it was, almost. Or at least you could tell day from night.

"Dess, what you think you going to do after we—?" *Kill them. When we kill them.* But Dess had sworn me to secrecy, to never talk about the mission out loud. Even if it was just the three of us out here. I rolled onto my stomach to look at her. "When the war's over, I mean?"

"Be with my family," Dess replied, placing the flower crown she had made on my head, and I couldn't help but grin at the small gift, forget what I said about war. "Of course."

"That's it? You ain't got no grand plans to do with all your war prestige?"

Odessa lay down on her mat. "To be frank, this war has been more excitement than I ever want to have again. There are far less vampire attacks to deal with in New York. We don't make them feel welcome there."

"Don't tell Alexei."

"I already told him I'm never going to see him again after this war," she said, smirking.

I laughed, hushing myself up as I saw Alexei drop down into camp from his crow form. For some reason, all I could think was I sure hoped he didn't hear what we was talking about, or me laugh about it, even though Dess had said it as a joke.

Wasn't nothing funny about not being wanted.

When Alexei walked up and saw me, he looked shocked for a second before his gaze shifted to something a little softer. Admiring? Naw. I was seeing it wrong.

"You look like a fae princess," he said.

"You the only fae princess around here," I muttered, and snatched the flower crown from my head, blushing hard.

He grinned. "Were you three beauties talking about me?"

"*Three* beauties?" I scoffed.

"You would say that with Gael standing *right there?*"

I looked up quickly, in time to catch Gael give Alexei a powerful side-eye before walking to the other side of our small camp. It was so well-deserved for all Alexei's ridiculousness that I applauded, nodding my head like we was in church. "Amen! Tell him!"

Dess sighed heavily. "Alexei, why do you enjoy irritating the people you like?"

"Because I'm starved for attention," he said with an exaggerated pout.

"Like hell," I muttered. "Quit acting like our lives revolve around you."

"Don't they?" he asked, and I could've smacked him.

"Arrogant, bloodsucking—"

"Did you find anything?" Dess cut in.

"Nothing but a nearby lake," he said, his joking air settling. "You can stay here and rest; I'll fill your canteens."

"Is it still water?" Dess asked. "That might not be safe to drink."

Alexei stared at her, then looked at me. "Humans still drink water, yes?"

"Yes, but the new plume might've already polluted it. We should boil the water," Dess said, and suddenly she was smirking as she sat up. "Why don't you take Jerusalem with you to collect some water and sticks?"

Alexei sent her a mild glare. "There's plenty of time for that *later*, Dess. Not *right now*."

"Y'all acting weird as hell," I said. "I done lived next to a plume for seventeen years and ain't never boiled no water to drink. Still alive and kicking. And besides, Dess, I know you just trying to get rid of us 'cause you want time with Gael."

Dess and Gael looked at each other quickly, and I knew good and well it was guilt that made him lower the brim of his hat . . . or so I thought till they both started laughing like foxes.

I felt myself blush in annoyance. "I ain't blind. The two of you, flirting like children. You know she got a husband back home, right, Gael?"

"My husband wouldn't mind, I'm sure," said Dess. "In fact, I'll tell him all about it when I see him." She handed me her canteen and gave me a gentle push, forcing me to get up. "Water. Now, please."

"How can you live with being a home-wrecker?" I snapped at Gael, and three heads turned to look at me.

"Jerusalem," Odessa chastised, her tone biting, and I felt shame rise up in me.

I didn't know why I was acting like this. It wasn't like my mama was cheating on my pa 'cause Dess wasn't my mama. But it *felt* like it, and that was the weird part.

"Sorry, Gael," I murmured, suddenly feeling exposed. I turned on my heel quickly and stormed through the high grass to make myself forget it.

"Jerusalem."

I sighed and stopped. I barely recognized Gael's voice with it above a whisper like that, I only knew it wasn't Alexei.

He stepped up to a polite distance—he was better at boundaries than Alexei ever was. "I knew Odessa long before the war. Our daughters grew up together. So believe me when I say, I have no ill intentions toward her."

Knew her . . . *before* the war? He didn't show up in the army not three months ago. No wonder they meshed so quickly. "Dess never mentioned all that."

"You know her," he said with the slightest smile. "Everything's on a need-to-know basis."

Hell, he had to be telling the truth—this was the most words I ever heard him string together at once since I known him.

Still, that didn't make me like him no better. If anything, that made it all so much worse.

"You love her?"

"Yes," he said easily.

"For how long?"

It was a test, that question. 'Cause if he said something like *at first sight*, I'd know he only let their babies play together to get to her despite her husband in the picture.

But he said, "I don't know," with a shrug. "Love is a creeping thing, sometimes."

And that answer made me stop and gape at him. It made me mad, but not for the reason I thought I'd be mad. Not 'cause of Dess and her husband, but 'cause of something deep inside me I didn't understand.

I shook it off quickly.

"If you been knowing her," I said, "then you been knowing her husband, too. And as soon as he got his back turned, you pouncing? That ain't right."

He sighed and removed his hat, wiping sweat from his brow. "I know that's what it looks like. That's not what this is."

"Then what is it?"

He replaced his hat and tipped it at me. "If you want the answer to that, ask Odessa."

I scowled as he walked away. Had he been trying to make me feel better? 'Cause all I felt was more frustrated . . . and confused. So I huffed off in the direction I'd been headed.

"Are you okay, Jerusalem?" Alexei asked—silent as the daggone grave as he followed. I would've stabbed him if he'd startled me any more.

"Why you boys keep walking up on me?"

"You seemed really upset back there. But, you know, a lot of innocent flirtation happens during war," Alexei reassured me. "And also . . . less innocent."

"Oh, thanks," I said sarcastically. "I feel so much better."

"All I'm saying is that if the two of them say it's fine, it's fine. They're grown adults."

"Ain't our business no how," I grumbled, even if it still bothered me.

"Right." Alexei was quiet for a moment before saying, "But I know you feel protective of Dess, and that's okay."

"Let's just drop it," I growled, and pressed on.

Was only a bit of a hike to get where we was heading, but it felt like a stroll compared to how far we'd traveled. And it was a big old lake, with rock formations and cliffs along one end. It was evening, but the days was still long with summertime even if they was dark and hazy with smoke. But the way the sun filtered through was like looking through a screen. Gray twilight. Kind of soothing.

"Oh, I done drank water dirtier than this before," I said, bending down to fill my canteen. "Ain't no good reason to waste time boiling it."

"Dess is a city girl," said Alexei, his tone teasing.

I raised a brow. "Ain't *you* a city boy?"

"I like nice things, if that's what you mean." He knelt beside me, filling Dess's canteen for her. "But no, I was born in a rural village."

I paused. "You ain't never talked about your childhood before."

Alexei seemed a bit caught off guard by me bringing it up. "I don't remember much of it, to be honest. Vague images. Ice fishing." He shrugged. "It seems pointless to relive. I couldn't keep the family I was born to when I became a vampire."

"'Cause your parents wouldn't accept you?"

"I don't even know how they would have reacted. Because I—" He seemed frozen in memory, and I wished to high hell I hadn't said nothing—he looked like someone who'd woken up from a bad dream, one of them dreams that felt more real than it should've.

"I left," he finished, finally. "And outlived them, obviously. My coven is the only family that matters. And you, and Dess, and Gael." He grinned, and the nightmare was over. Part of me was sure I'd imagined the whole thing. I ain't never met a vamp who regretted being a vamp, and I wasn't about to.

Still, something told me to leave it there.

"Okay, enough of this." I got up and stabbed my spear into the dirt so it stood upright. "Time for a swim."

He smirked like the brat he was. "You don't swim."

"Don't make me gut you for that vile stereotype."

"You haven't been swimming since I taught you that *one time* at Chesapeake Bay." He dragged his shirt off over his head. "So it's not a stereotype when I say you should hold on to me so you don't drown."

"Okay, Arms. Watch yourself." I took off my cowl and hung it off my spear, hoping he wouldn't notice I still had on the oversized undershirt I'd stolen from him.

"Speaking of arms . . ." he said, skimming his cold fingers along my bicep.

"Why you got to sound so shocked about it?" I asked, even though inside my heart was skipping. Alexei's body was perfect, and he thought *I* looked good?

"It's a nice surprise, that's all," he said, with a small shrug. "I clearly haven't seen you sleeveless in a while."

"You think *that's* impressive?" I turned to show him my back.

I felt a shiver go through me as his thumbs slid against the exposed skin along my shoulder blades, against the raised scars of too many whuppings, but mostly one severe one gone untended. His touch was gentle, but even still I could feel each streak his cold fingers left on my hot skin, like spreading salve on a wound.

Alexei gave a long whistle. "Murder me."

I barely held in a laugh. "Boy, you stupid."

"How many times have you trained without me, exactly?"

"Only, like, twice."

"Twice too many."

"Just trying to keep up."

Alexei flexed. "With me?"

"All right, all right," I said, rolling my eyes. I took off the rest of my clothes quickly and hung them with my cowl. "Your vain ass." I shook my head and smirked at him going on and on. "Don't get excited, now."

Alexei immediately looked down to make sure nothing was growing between his legs—thankfully he wasn't *that* vain. "You're ready to tear heads off with your bare hands, I'll bet."

"I don't know about all that."

"Have you tried it?"

"Boy, don't be weird," I said with a small laugh. "Course I ain't tried it."

"It's the same as doing it with a blade, only much more exhilarating." He dropped his trousers and kicked them away, leaving him in nothing but what God intended. I mean, Alexei always said naked bodies were normal, but his wasn't. Ain't nobody looked like *that*. "I'll show you how sometime."

"I'd rather not get that close to my enemies," I said. "That's why I picked a spear."

"Well, then, you stake; I'll behead."

"Deal. I love staking vamps."

"You love killing in general. You know you smile almost every time you do it?"

"You might've mentioned that once or twice."

"I love it," he murmured, so low I nearly missed it.

I raised my brows at him. "That I smile when I kill?"

"No, just ..." He shrugged, almost sheepish. "When you smile."

I turned away from him quickly, suddenly feeling strange ... not in a bad way, but part of me didn't want to think too hard and find out what it meant. "Hot as a clam bake at high noon out here. Let's swim."

"Hold on a second," he said quietly, and I froze. "Were you ... wearing my shirt this whole time?"

My heart raced like a scared chicken. "Last one in's a cow pie!" I shouted, and leapt in the water without waiting for him. It was nice and cool, murky but not the kind that made you feel like you had a film all over.

When I surfaced, he was sitting on the edge, soaking his legs.

"Come in," I demanded, ignoring the weird look on his face, and pulled his arm. "Ain't nobody out here to admire your pretty ass, so you might as well."

"Nobody but you," he said, breaking into a grin.

He might've been vain as hell, but he earned it, no mistake. And that was coming from me, a girl who'd never thought twice about white folks' looks in her life. I didn't know if he was born that way or if being turned multiplied everything, looks included, but the boy was beautiful. And it didn't feel weird to say it, even though he was a white boy ... even though he was a vampire.

I knew I wasn't nothing great to look at. Not like Mama or Lila or Dess, but I was pretty enough. Lean muscles, healthy hair. My body wasn't what men usually admired—no child-bearing hips, no pretty, smooth skin—and that suited me fine. I was scarred all over, which, since joining the army, had gotten me a lot of horrified, piteous looks. Up North, they was sensitive about slavery, but that didn't mean they had to be annoying about it.

But Alexei had scars, too. I'd seen them a couple times when he was changing, like I could see them now—a long one that curved beneath his shoulder blade, a few stab wounds in his side and stomach. They was white and not so visible against his fair skin as my dark raised ones were on mine, but definitely there. So we could've related on that, maybe, talked about how we got them, crushed this suffocating tension between us. I wouldn't even have to admit then that I admired his strong hands—what they could do—more than I probably should.

Instead I reached up, grabbed a handful of hair, and tugged hard. Vindictive and childish—and nonsense since he didn't actually do nothing wrong. It was just my mind making things that wasn't there.

His hands are good for killing things, Jer. No more than that.

He gasped, moving with me, and the look in his eyes was shock and something wild that sent heat shooting up my neck. And the smile that slipped to his face afterward made it so much worse.

"Do that again," he said.

And I did it again, but made sure he wouldn't like it.

"*Ow,*" he hissed, pressing his hand to his roots, like he was afraid I'd tear his hair out.

I shoved away from him in the water. "Pervert."

"I didn't mean it. Well, I did, but—" He checked for any lost hair, running his fingers through it. "What did I do to deserve the first tug?"

I suddenly felt stupid. The tension I'd felt before was one-sided, all me. He didn't want to touch me in any way but to examine muscle. Even the sensation he'd felt when I'd pulled his hair wasn't about me.

Besides, he was a vampire . . . so why would I ever want him to?

Why you even thinking all this foolishness about your friend?

Instead of answering, I sank down under the water.

ALEXEI

"Oh no you don't," I muttered.

Now would have been a good time to confess that I'd smelled a vampire and a few humans within a mile radius since the moment we reached the lake. But I didn't want Jerusalem upset or on her guard—as much as she enjoyed killing, I needed her to be able to relax in ways other than war. And I'd be able to keep my nose to it in the meantime.

So instead, I slid into the water and reached down to where she had submerged, gripping her upper arms to drag up back up. She protested, but her insults were cut off by an adorable giggle as I lifted her over my head. Water from her body poured onto me, and I blinked it away without releasing my hold. Despite her impressive muscles, my hands gripped cleanly around her biceps.

"Alexei!" She was back to scowling, though the warmth in her skin remained from her laughter, and when I shook her, a grin broke free again. "I'm about to shatter that pretty face of yours with my knee."

"Tell me what's wrong, or I'm throwing you clear across this lake."

"You don't get to demand nothing from me."

"Have it your way." When I smiled, hers dropped, hot blood

rushing through her. My grip tightened the slightest bit as I pressed down my need, a need I swore her own body was voicing to mine. Or maybe it wasn't, and I was simply justifying my own savage urge to taste every inch of her . . . blood included.

You despicable monster.

I threw her, barely able to enjoy her excited yell as she crashed into the water nearly on the other side of the lake. I had to get myself together before she surfaced. The last thing I wanted was to show her that side of me, to prove to her that I was the very monster she hated.

Hungry or horny, she smelled amazing.

I needed to feed, and soon.

I felt Tiny's small hands reach up my back, and I ducked down a little to make it easier for her to get her footing as she grabbed my shoulders and pulled herself up.

"You big-ass tree," she accused.

"You can't swim *or* climb, Tiny Saint," I teased.

"I can, too!"

"It's a miracle you've survived this long."

"The miracle is I ain't killed you yet." She wrapped her arm around my neck, and I sank down into the water to keep from being choked. The admirable but deadly thing about Jerusalem was that she knew I could take it, and so play wrestling was never play to her. She had never pulled a punch since I'd known her, never attacked without the intent of hitting her target.

So, in a way, it *was* a miracle she hadn't killed me by now. And, the scary part was, I wouldn't have it any other way.

We splashed and wrestled until she was laughing and panting and begging for a break. I leaned my arms on the bank and laid my head on them, grinning as I felt Jerusalem take that same position on the portion of my back that was surfaced.

"Should we head back?" I asked.

"I just want to be a turtle on a rock for a while."

I chuckled. "My back is all yours."

She sighed and snuggled against me, and I'd never experienced anything so perfect in my life. Still, part of me couldn't help but think about what Dess had said about telling her how I felt. Was now a good time, when she was in an amazing, agreeable mood? Perhaps my confession would go over well, but the other part . . . ?

The part about practically salivating over consuming her blood? Yes, jackass. Keep that to yourself.

"So, Tiny . . ."

"Hmm?"

"Would you consider us to be friends?"

"Sure, Lex," she said, her voice sweet and lazy.

Now was the time.

I cleared my throat. "Because I want to tell you something about my . . . uh . . . my feelings. Which is to say—"

I paused. Sighed. The intruders were close, approaching closer. Most vampires I'd met never attacked me without reason but were also pretty diligent about staying out of others' hunting grounds. But this one was coming straight for us, with three humans and possibly a horse, which left one of two possibilities—either they smelled me and assumed I was an ally, or they recognized me as the White Wolf and knew me as the enemy. The latter seemed less likely since we were in Northern territory, and four soldiers and a horse were too obvious a party to be spies.

Still, it wasn't the safest idea in the world to give away our position.

"What you saying about feelings?" Tiny prompted, lifting her head.

I shifted her from my back to in front of me as I moved us under and behind a section of the rock, the ceiling so low my shoulders could barely clear the surface of the water. Her pulse slammed quick and hot through her as I rested my hand on her stomach to keep her still against the stone.

"Lex," she protested, grabbing my fingers to pry me off, "what—?"

I shushed her. "There's a group of travelers approaching."

Her brows lowered. "Travelers? How many?"

"Three humans, a horse, I think, and a vampire."

"Too big a group to be scouts."

"Yes, they could just be passing through."

"A vamp with three familiars? They ain't that obvious with it here up North." She suddenly gaped and hit me in the chest, nearly knocking the wind from me. "Wait a second. You can smell things from a mile off. When was you going to say some-thi—?"

I pressed my hand over her mouth. "Keep your voice down. Let's wait and see who they are before we make ourselves known—" I tightened my lips against a swear as she sunk her teeth into my hand.

She let go almost immediately, snarling at me. "Don't ever silence me."

She hadn't broken the skin, and the red mark in the vague shape of her teeth would go away any minute. Still, it wasn't called for, and didn't hurt any less. "I wasn't silencing you; I was shutting you up, you tiny warmonger."

"I ain't afraid of three men and a vamp—"

I grabbed her chin, leaning closer to whisper, "You can't kill just anyone, Tiny. We don't know if they're the enemy yet. Hush your beautiful mouth and *wait*."

Her jaw tightened in my grasp, her breath traveling heavy and agitated through her nose as she glared at me. But she didn't say anything more.

The irrational urge to kiss her rose within me, but I tamped it down quickly.

Not the time or place, Alexei. Plus, as annoyed as she is now, she may bite again.

I looked at my hand. Signs of her bite had vanished, but I leaned my forearm on the stone ceiling, my hand safely away from her mouth. "Let the record show," I whispered harshly, "that I—a vampire—have never once bitten you, and you—a human—have bitten me no fewer than thirty times since we've met."

"And you deserved every last one." She whispered it, though, which meant she took my warning seriously, even if she didn't like it.

JERUSALEM

When Alexei looked over at the shore and muttered a swear, my heart dropped. He didn't even need to explain—my spear was still stuck into the ground, with my clothes hanging from it, and Alexei's clothes spread across the bank. And there wasn't no time to fetch them 'cause a moment later, the vampire on horseback rode out of the tree line.

She had long wavy brown hair and looked somewhere in between the ages of Dess and the colonel, but in an abnormally youthful, active way that immediately tipped me off she was a vamp, even if Alexei hadn't smelled her first. Alexei pressed closer to me, and I was suddenly all too aware of his big, strong hand against my stomach, grateful for the safety of his cool body so I could think what to do. 'Cause the men who stepped out of the trees with her was sure enough graybacks, toting their rifles and lots of packs.

There was no way they could be all the way out here. No way. Not unless . . .

Not unless the army was right behind them.

The birds we seen made sense now.

They was looking at our clothes, laughing until they revealed my spear. Then they was scared, on guard, especially the vamp, who looked around slowly from on top of her horse. She gestured to the spear, and a soldier grabbed the shaft. I wasn't worried—he'd never be able to pull it out, and I held in a scoff as he struggled to yank it from the ground before summoning a friend to help. The last of the three gathered up our clothes.

Dagnabbit.

"I know you're there, Demon Saint," the vamp called, which would have carried much more presence if the soldiers hadn't finally tugged my spear loose and practically stumbled over from it. "We got your weapon. Allow my horse some water and we'll be on our merry way in peace."

On their way in peace my ass. Tell the whole Southern army, more like. I turned to Lex, my lips nearly brushing his. I blushed from our closeness, but also somehow . . . I felt stronger this close to him. 'Cause we was always together when it came to a fight. "Now can we kill them?"

I wasn't asking; my tone said *I told you so* without saying it. He caught on right away and smirked.

"I'll save you some," he said with a wink. And then he shifted into a crow and darted off, leaving me splashing in his wake.

ALEXEI

I shifted back, landing in front of them, and as soon as the soldiers whipped their heads in my direction, I caught them in hypnosis.

The vampire looked oddly surprised to see me.

"You're outnumbered, White Wolf," she said, though she was clearly thrown off by my nakedness despite her lackies holding my clothes. "Stand down and let us pass."

I smirked. I was no longer concerned about her, if I ever had been. She had a Southern accent, which no Ancient had. She hadn't smelled my presence, only threatening us at all because she'd seen Tiny's spear. On top of that, she didn't recognize the slack posture shift of hypnotized prey. A New Blood. And a very recent one at that.

"Kill the horse," I commanded the soldiers.

They did as they were told with whatever means necessary, and the vampire leapt off the animal before it collapsed, stumbling away as she gaped at the scene. I grabbed her arm before she could run, quickly and easily pinning her to a tree.

"You're a New Blood," I confirmed, and fear was written all over her expression. "Let me guess—former familiar?"

She nodded quickly, her confidence from earlier depleted.

I could see Tiny using the advantage of the soldiers' hypnosis to get dressed—she stayed behind them, knowing any sudden movement could knock them out of it since I was no longer looking at them. "My Saint friend isn't as merciful as I, so you may want to cooperate before she makes it over here. Now, how many more vampires are with the army?"

"Seven. My mistress finally turned me 'cause she was worried I wouldn't survive the war." She smirked. "As if I'd go back to serving her afterward."

Seven? Definitely off from the number Odessa had quoted.

"I got away as soon as I gathered my resources," she added. "I only used the soldiers to carry my things. I'm trying to go North, to Canada. Please, believe me."

"You used *Southern* soldiers to try and sneak *North?*" Tiny scoffed, tapping the soldiers to wake them up. "Like you thought you wasn't going to get stopped for it."

The New Blood winced as Tiny proceeded to beat the men up without using her spear—and I only had that small window to get what we needed and let her go unless I wanted Tiny to end up killing her like the last one.

"I believe you," I said. "Answer our questions, and I'll let you go. How far behind is the Southern army?"

"I don't know." She sounded panicked, glancing at Tiny's violent pastime. "A few miles, maybe? I don't know."

A few miles could mean almost anything. I sighed.

Perhaps her information was useless, but we were on track, regardless.

Still, better to tell Odessa we needed to move on a bit before making camp.

Jerusalem had finished beating the men unconscious, so it was time to let this vampire go.

"You're free to leave," I said, realizing I was still naked and releasing her. I put on my pants quickly. As beautiful as my body was, I could see how it might be distressing for a woman traveling alone.

"Where do I go?" she asked. "H-how do I get there?"

"We could kill you and save you from wondering," Jerusalem said with a sarcastically polite grin before letting it drop and walking away.

"Head that way," I said quickly, pointing. "There's a town about ten miles northeast."

"Thank you," she said, defeated.

I sighed, shaking my head at her. "No one's going to fear you just for being a vampire if you cave when confronted. Don't be so nervous."

"I'll try. It's just that . . . being a vampire is different than I'd always envisioned."

That was the trouble, wasn't it. Too many people equated being a vampire with being some sort of god . . . and the truth of it was, vampires lost a great many things in exchange for any benefits the lifestyle afforded. But she'd chosen, and there was no sense now in telling her why she shouldn't have. "Please feed sooner rather than later."

She hesitated. "You're not like what they say about you at all," she said, almost in awe.

She looked like she wanted to say something else, but instead glanced once more at Tiny before running off. She was so freshly turned she hadn't even mastered another, more efficient form yet. I tried not to think of how she most likely had no idea how to hunt safely and correctly. I felt sorry for her, but there was nothing more I could do for her now.

"You and your New Bloods." Tiny shook her head. "You can't just be letting vamps go during wartime."

"You allowed me to let her go," I said, with the slightest smile.

Jerusalem paused, then looked away. "Yeah, well. They wasn't carrying war supplies. Her story checked out. But that's the last one, you hear? I ain't sparing no more vamps for you."

"Thank you, Tiny," I said, overly sweet.

I could sense her starting to blush before she turned around and went back to the soldiers' packs. "Don't ever want to hear you say we ain't friends."

"I would never say that." I joined her in the rifling. "*You've* said that."

She pushed me with her shoulder, an apology in her own way.

But suddenly a wall of scents hit me.

I froze.

No. There's no way . . .

No way in hell she'd found me.

"Alexei?" Jerusalem shook my shoulder. "What is it?"

It wasn't just her. A mass of humans, but those scents weren't as potent as the vampires with them. I recognized Zamir, and . . . her. I didn't know any of the others, but there were five more. Seven, like the New Blood had said. She'd been truthful in that, even if she had been a poor judge of distance.

"The army is here," I said.

If I can smell her, she can smell me.

"Really?" Tiny got to her feet, throwing one of the consolidated packs over her shoulder. "That's great!"

"*Great?*" I snapped.

She found me. She's here.

We had to get out of there. Immediately.

"We'd better tell Odessa," I said.

Tell her was an understatement. Demand answers, more like. Odessa was one of the best spies I'd ever met, and she'd never delivered faulty intel from a mission before.

I didn't want to think ill of my friend, but I wasn't born yesterday. There was no way this was an accident.

She smells me. She's coming for me.

When we reached camp, Gael sat cross-legged at the head of Odessa's mat reading a book while Odessa dozed with her head in his lap. If I hadn't been so enraged and panicked, I would have left them to their peace. But Gael looking not at all shocked to see me angry was the last straw.

"They're here!" Jerusalem said excitedly.

At her words, Odessa opened her eyes. "We figured they were close, judging by the flock of birds earlier."

My tone was merciless when I said, "You *figured* they were close but didn't think to say anything? Why are they so far North?"

Jerusalem raised her brows at me. "Come on, Lex, you don't got to fake it now that they here."

"Fake . . . what?" I watched my travel companions making no efforts to pack up camp, instead putting away their leisure activities and readying their weapons as if for battle. "What is going on?"

"The plan," said Tiny, slightly annoyed, as if I should have known.

"The plan is to overtake the stronghold."

Now Tiny looked more concerned for my confusion than annoyed. She looked at Dess. "You didn't tell him?"

"Tell me *what?*" I snapped.

Odessa leveled a warning look at me. "I would have. I planned on telling you even before I told Jerusalem. And then I saw your reaction to seeing Zamir's name on the list, and I knew you wouldn't have come along willingly."

"Naw, Dess, Alexei would've come either way," said Jerusalem with a conviction that almost made me feel ashamed. "He would've never made us do this without him."

I felt my hands trembling and quickly crossed my arms across my chest to hide it as I looked to Gael for help. "Did you know about this, too?"

"Know about it?" Odessa looked at Gael proudly. "He's the one who helped me track them down, used his military contacts to help prepare the phony correspondence to get them all in the same battalion. We wouldn't even be here right now if it wasn't for Gael."

"It was your plan," he said, blushing a little. "I just helped execute it."

"But there are more vampires than you reported to the colonel." My voice sounded like a crisp growl, my anger hiding my panic. "We're outnumbered."

Odessa paused, then shrugged, her jaw tight. "I can admit it now that we're here: I fed the colonel some false information. The true position of the Southern army, the true number of vamps traveling with them. If I'd told him the truth, he would've marched immediately, and no one wants their kills stolen out from under them. Jerusalem isn't the only one of us out for blood."

"It's a suicide mission."

"And what if it is?"

The quiet that overtook us was heavy. Crushing. Frightening. Because I suddenly realized I'd been wrong about Odessa for two years.

She'd been lying to me. The entire time.

"What if it is?" Odessa repeated. "Would that be so awful? To be with the ones you love again? Be with the ones who were taken from you?"

"Wait . . . your kids," Jerusalem said, her voice uncertain, sounding as small as she was. "And husband, too?"

"Murdered," Odessa said, pain mixing with coldness. "And Gael's daughter with them. All three of the monsters who killed them are in that camp."

She looked heartbroken, my poor, sweet girl. She had trusted Odessa, too, a woman who it was clear had no interest in any of our safety.

"That's not a fair move, Odessa," I said. "You don't get to use your loss against us like blackmail. You're not going to drag Jerusalem to her death."

"Why do you think you're here, Alexei?" Odessa asked, a strange calm in her expression. "If she survives, someone has to take care of her when I'm gone."

"You ain't going nowhere," Jerusalem said firmly, grabbing her arm. "We can do this without losing none of us. We all cover each other while we kill our targets. That ain't so hard."

"Three Saints and a vampire against an entire army?" I asked. "Please, I beg of you to *think*. We're sorely outnumbered."

As the words left my mouth, I knew they were fruitless. Jerusalem didn't *think*. She acted. She laughed in the face of death.

"The three *best* Saints in all the Union army and one hella skilled vamp. We can kill four monsters, no problem. And then we hightail it and leave the rest of the fighting to the battalion."

"Jerusalem." I grabbed her shoulders and leaned down closer to her level. "Odessa doesn't *want* to survive this. And you won't, either, even though I know you think you can."

She pulled away from my grasp, looking me up and down. "I ain't never seen you run scared, Alexei. Maybe there's a secret *you* want to share?"

The vampire who turned me and tortured me for five terrifying months is with the Confederate army . . .

But fear had never stopped Jerusalem before, and today wouldn't be any different. Frankly, I wouldn't have been surprised if she volunteered to slay my enemy for me. But she didn't know any better. She didn't know the evil she was dealing with. I had to protect her how I could.

You're a liar, Alexei. You just don't want her to know how scared you are.

"Look, Alexei," said Odessa. She was coating her arrows in holy water. I took a few steps back. "We're not going to charge in, metaphorical guns blazing. We'll sneak and find the best opening. Does that make you feel better about it?"

"What would make me feel better is if you took more than a minute to think about it," I said, tugging my hair.

"We've thought of it for years," said Gael, uncharacteristically harsh. "Before the war even began, we were seeking catharsis. It took years of searching and planning to get here today."

"But our battalion won't be even a day behind us," I said. "It would be safer to wait. If we fail fighting the South and they reach the stronghold before we do, there will be no hope in defeating them."

"We here to kill some vamps," said Jerusalem. "And that'll help the battalion out in the long run, right? Less vamps for them to deal with."

"We were assigned a mission."

"*This* was the mission, Alexei," she snapped. "I been waiting a whole-ass year to kill the monster who kept me and my family enslaved and then killed them, and now she's right where I want her, and you say we should just move along? Not to mention, if Granny Lee gets caught in the crosshairs, we could just about end the war. Naw. You out of your ever-loving mind if you think I'm fittin' to pass this up."

"There are too many of them. It's better to be wise about it and wait for the battalion."

"You ain't never missed a fight before," Jerusalem said, genuine confusion in her brows. "Why you acting like a coward?" She bent down to fish the small bottle of holy water from her pack, and I used the distraction to rush over to Odessa.

There was no more room for reasoning. If Odessa said no, Jerusalem respected her too much not to follow.

So . . . I would make her say no.

"Odessa," I said as she strapped her quiver around her waist.

"Are you coming or not?" she demanded, glancing up to see if I was ready.

That glance was enough to ensnare her.

She looked at me as if in a dream, a daze. There was an uncertainty in her expression that would only clear up after I'd given her something to be certain of. She was ready for my suggestions.

For my command.

We should press on toward the stronghold and allow the battalion to catch up. There will be plenty of time for revenge when we have more assistance.

The words were at the tip of my tongue, and yet I felt sick to my stomach. Hypnotism was a part of life for me, but Odessa wasn't prey, wasn't my enemy, wasn't some random human I didn't care about. She was my friend, and here I was manipulating her like some . . . monster.

I took a moment, battling with myself, then laid the backs of my fingers against her cheek to turn her gaze away from me. She blinked a few times, her eyes going wide when she realized what had happened. I hadn't told her anything under trance, so there was nothing for her to forget.

She turned to me slowly with a bitter glare, a look that felt more like an ending to everything we had for the past two years than a warning. Her voice was dark, perhaps not even loud enough for Tiny to hear, when she said, "Don't you ever do that again."

I closed my eyes against regret, but there was no time to apologize. She stormed off toward Gael already waiting for her on the edge of camp, calling, "You coming, Jerusalem?"

"Wait for me!" Jerusalem said, dropping her holy water back into her bag. "Lex, grab your sword—what you doing?"

I couldn't physically hold her back now without being burned by her spear. And if I moved to fetch my gloves from my pack, I couldn't block her exit. So I stayed put. She'd be forced to walk through the high grass and bushes, and I could at least slow her down while I thought of a better excuse she would actually heed.

I love you, and don't want you to get killed.

She will take me back if she catches me.

I'm afraid . . .

"Don't go," I said, a pathetic, childish plea.

"What's wrong with you, Alexei?" The look in Jerusalem's eyes shifted quickly from annoyance to confusion to concern to . . . heartbreak. "You really ain't going to fight with us?"

"I—I—" I was right in my thinking—going up against an army and seven vampires was foolhardy. But the longer I looked at her, the more of a coward I felt. The truth was, it wasn't about doubting her strength.

It was about the panic pounding in my head the longer we talked about it.

I didn't want to go back.

I would not go back.

"I'll watch our packs," I said stupidly.

Jerusalem's brows lowered, her lips pressing tight in pent-up emotions, words left unsaid. She raced by me to catch up with our companions.

And I, the idiot, let her go.

7

ALEXEI

Moscow
Late 1500s

$\mathcal{I}$ slouched against the stone wall of an alleyway, forcing my gaze to remain on the opposite wall. I blinked at the frost wanting to form on my lashes, finally swiping my eyes on the large fur coat I had bundled in my arms. The warmth of it had been soothing while it lasted. Now it was as cold as our surroundings but still smelled of the man we'd stripped it from. I huffed through my nostrils, trying to get rid of the distasteful scent. He'd smelled much better paired with a beating heart.

It was a true Moscow winter, so bitterly cold and wet that no clear-headed person would be out after sundown unless they wished to freeze to death. But vampires didn't have to worry about the cold, and it was the perfect opportunity to hunt down the last few stragglers headed home. Hunt, or . . . whatever it was Zamir was currently doing.

"It's missing something," he said, rubbing his chin, his skin nearly as pale as the soft snow beneath our feet. The snow that *wasn't* covered in blood, that was. "What do you think of this, Alexei?"

"It's gross," I murmured, and he looked up at me quickly before waving me off.

"You wouldn't know good art if it bit you," he muttered, though his tone was affectionate as he crouched down to appraise his work.

It was the man we'd just fed on, stripped of his valuables and positioned in . . . artistic fashion, as Zamir would call it. But instead of being manipulated by the joints already present on the human body, Zamir had chosen to crush places that weren't supposed to bend and turn them in unsettling directions until the man lay in a deranged tangle of broken limbs. The only thing that had truly remained intact was the man's head, green eyes staring toward the sky. Green eyes, Zamir had said before he'd begun to crush bone, had been inspiring him of late.

I sighed, scooped up some bloodied snow, and threw it at the opposite wall.

"Don't draw attention to us, boy." Zamir sighed. "I promised my hobby wouldn't force us to relocate, and you're not helping."

He tilted his head at his art, breaking up the frost that had formed in his dark hair as he ran his fingers through it. His hair was so raven that the bit of moonlight catching on it gave it blue highlights. His was the midnight sky to my silver moon. Some nights, I thought of it that way. Tonight I wished my hair wasn't so pale. Sometimes, when candlelight hit it a certain way, I thought it looked like urine in snow, like the color a small child would have before it eventually shifted to dark blond or brown as he grew.

Maybe that was why Zamir treated me like a child. My hair would never darken, I was nervous from living with Red Mask, and I didn't know anything about art.

I would never be anything like him.

"I know I'm younger than you, Zamir," I said. "But I'm still a man, you know."

"Yes, my *misiu*," he said gently but absently as he broke his artwork's fingers into the positions he wanted them.

That didn't help. Him calling me a sweet Polish pet name like that. Even if it did make me feel special to hear it.

"Then why do you treat me like a child?"

"I've missed having one," he said, his tone more matter of fact than sentimental. He nodded at his art and stood.

"But I'm not much younger than you."

Zamir smirked. "You are eighteen human years, my *misiu*. I have been twenty-four for seven hundred."

I faltered. "But we're both vampires. Why can't I be your equal?"

Zamir paused, like a panther hunting in the snow. I couldn't read his expression, and it scared me that perhaps I had said the wrong thing.

But he grinned at me. "I think it's time you learned a little about your new culture."

"My culture?"

"Vampires live their lives differently than mortals do. We have our own rules. We need to if we want to survive in a world that wasn't designed for us." He stepped near, and I slid down the wall a bit, making our gazes level. "The longer vampires survive, the stronger they become. The stronger they become, the more . . . let us say, out of touch they are. And so when they take on lovers, they become jealous easily of anyone who might be considered a rival, even if none such exist. More often than not, they will punish both parties involved. Because neither the lover nor the imagined rival is strong enough to challenge them. And who would dare tell them what they can and cannot do?"

I felt dread fill my stomach. "So I can't be your equal because she'd get jealous over nothing but my existence—?"

He shushed me quietly, giving me a subtle shake of his head, and I immediately fell silent. As if Red Mask could hear every word we said on the wind and would come after us. I hugged the fur coat, but it did nothing to relieve the chill I was feeling, nothing to comfort me. There was a tension in the air, and I watched Zamir as he listened, waited, as if the entire sky might drop on our heads at any moment.

And then he suddenly smiled at me and patted my cheek. "Come, Alexei, it's getting late. We should go home."

JERUSALEM

Dirty white tents and lean-tos stretched for a mile or more like an ugly field of cotton. There had to be tens of thousands of soldiers, even if *soldiers* was barely the word to call them—half of them was boys and men with no business being out here fighting. Most was sleeping, completely oblivious that we was camped just over the ridge, that we was hiding in the trees, spying. They'd stolen them tents from Union soldiers, which annoyed me, but I had bigger fish to fry.

Naw, they was nothing to worry about.

If vamps traveled in packs, they rarely left each other—the smallest they split was in pairs. And most vamps wasn't friends with humans like Alexei, seeing as humans was food. So there was more than good chance that all our prey would be together. It was just a matter of *where*. 'Cause if they was all at the center of the army, we could still do it, but it'd be a nuisance and a waste of time to get through all them silly soldiers.

Luckily, the distant sound of a lute and a voice gave away their position.

They was close to the front of camp, only about a hundred or so soldiers on all sides in my way. Most of those soldiers— the smart ones, anyways—was going to get right the hell out of my way as soon as they spotted my Saint weapon. After all, everyone knew of The Demon Saint, even if they never laid eyes on me till today. The arrogant ones who thought they stood a chance would be easy enough to cut through.

Silas Barton, silly little bard playing the lute.

Katrina, or something like that, who I'd heard of but only recognized from Odessa's description of dark tattoos on her fingers.

Betsy Mint, who I *hadn't*, but was the only woman other than . . .

Adelaide Troy. My prize.

The other three didn't matter. Let the colonel deal with them.

There they was. Minding their evil business, enjoying their music and games, totally unaware they was about to die.

All except Adelaide. She looked all too aware, looking around carefully. And I suddenly realized that maybe she could recognize my smell. Dess and Gael was just another human in the crowd, but it had only been a year since I last saw her. I didn't think she even really knew who I was before that day, let alone thought of me.

All I knew now was we couldn't let her find me first.

Gael nudged me, and when I looked at him, he held out another fruit square. I took it, if only to distract myself from all the waiting, shoving the whole thing in my mouth. For once, he wasn't smoking—maybe that was why he looked a little jittery, his hands shaking a little.

"You going to be okay?" I whispered.

"I kill better when I'm irritated," he replied, gripping his machete.

You'd think avenging his daughter's murder would put him in enough of a mood to kill without all that. But, as Dess had tried to explain to me multiple times since I met her, only a small percentage of people on this earth was coldblooded killers.

Bless her heart. She'd have known there wasn't a speck of truth to that if she'd lived a day in the South.

"I didn't know you lost a daughter," I said. "If I did—" *Maybe I wouldn't have disliked you so much. Maybe I would've been nicer. Maybe I would've understood why you and Dess's bond was so strong.* But that was sort of the worst thing to say at a time like this.

He nodded with a sad smile. "She would have been nearly your age."

"Oh." I didn't know what else to say other than, "Sorry."

He spun his machete in his hand once, abrupt and lethal. "Soon it will be okay."

I nodded at his words. Soon.

As soon as these vamps was dead.

"Ready, Dess?" I whispered.

But when I looked over, she was chewing on her lip. Her mouth twitched like she could've smiled but didn't. I didn't know what she was thinking, but she sure as hell didn't look ready.

"Charging into certain death is easier said in planning than in practice," she said, her voice hard but quiet.

Dess had never charged since I'd known her—she fired arrows, and always hit her targets. So I wasn't sure what she was worried about. If we acted quickly, we'd all be fine. For Dess, stay within the trees and shoot. For me, focus on Adelaide and get out. For Gael, Betsy. And with the cover of dark? It was foolproof.

I waited for her next orders. A few seconds passed without a word, without a movement except for Gael rubbing her back. In those few seconds, I prayed she wouldn't second guess the plan. Prayed she wouldn't leave me to fight alone.

'Cause I wasn't going to let that monster get away now, not when I had her right where I wanted her.

But we both blew out a breath when she carefully drew an arrow. "I have a clear shot on Barton," she whispered. "I'll give you two thirty seconds."

Instead of moving, Gael leaned over and kissed her, and for once, there was no shred of anger in me for him as she kissed him back.

"Te amo, querida," he whispered.

"Why did you kiss me?" Dess huffed, pressing her sleeve against her eyes to sop up any budding tears. "I was fine before you kissed me . . ."

I gaped at her. Not 'cause of the kiss, but 'cause . . . I ain't never seen her this emotional before a battle. Never.

She kissed him again before remembering where we was and forcing herself to stop with a small cuss. "Right." She moved back into position quickly, wiping her eyes dry. "Let's kill some monsters."

He tipped his hat with a wicked grin. "See you on the side-lines."

Well, hell. I was starting to really like Gael.

He slipped away from her, with me following, quick but silent. If Dess shot one of them, the rest would be on high alert, and the soldiers would stir up chaos, and then our surprise attack wouldn't be much of a surprise. We needed four vamps dead, not one. So we needed to get closer to be ready for that opening.

My heart was pounding in excitement . . . but also with nerves. I'd never fought a battle without Alexei fighting along-side me, and part of me wondered if all that courage in previous battles was just 'cause I had him to back me up when I'd needed it.

You strong enough on your own, Jerusalem. You don't need him.

Besides, I ain't never fought closely with Gael, but he knew what he was doing, and that was enough. I swallowed down my fear, turning it into adrenaline. 'Cause in the next moment, as soon as I got to the end of the high grass near the edge of the army, I saw an arrow quick as lightning go through the chest of the bard and three more soldiers who'd had the ill luck to be on the other side of him, just as another arrow took his head clean off from the neck.

"Specter!" a soldier cried. "We're under attack!"

And I countered his scream with my own war cry and charged forward.

ALEXEI

I sat in the middle of camp feeling . . . beyond stupid. *I'll watch our packs*, I'd said. As if there was anyone around to try and steal them with a battle about to rage. While I was ready and able to fight. While my friends needed me. While Jerusalem hated the ground I walked on for staying behind.

But . . . the bitter smell of my captor brought too many terrifying memories flooding in.

The searing pain of penetrating fangs . . .

The cramping, ache, and anger for days in a row of dehydration . . .

The threat of a violent death if I was too tired to fight back.

It had been hundreds of years since I'd seen, heard from, *smelled* my captor, and the fear was just as debilitating as the very first day.

The love of your life could die out there all because you're a coward.

Jerusalem was mortal, but the part of her brain that focused on self-preservation was evidently non-existent. I'd never seen her back out of a fight. The stronger her opponent, the more eager she was to kill them. She was facing down the enemy who had kept her enslaved since birth, who had mistreated her for far longer than I'd ever been a captive. But I, an immortal vampire, was afraid?

"Maintain a shred of dignity, Alexei," I murmured.

I didn't think about it anymore. I shifted to a crow and flew toward the ridge . . . changing my mind last minute to go around through the trees. Okay, so maybe I did think about it just a little, and that was the problem. I couldn't bear to face my captor again, but I could help them from a distance . . . right? I could clear out some of the army on the opposite end of where my enemy fought . . . and just hope she didn't recognize my scent.

There were tens of thousands of humans spread across the open land. Child's play. Most of the Confederate camp's far side had barely risen yet from the commotion my Saints were causing. The smell of blood and sweat ignited my killer instinct.

I dove at the ranks, shifting just overhead of the soldiers so I could whip out my shashka, dropping three, four soldiers at a time, severed parts flying.

And all at once, I was myself again.

JERUSALEM

I cut my way through the ranks, the ones with a shred of sense stumbling out of my way.

"Demon Saint!" someone shouted as soon as he saw me. "It's the Demon Saint!" and I laughed, the high of battle already racing through me.

That's right, worms. Hell has arrived.

Gael caught his prey quick, chopping off the vamp's arm in one stroke to the shoulder and giving her just enough time to beg before slicing her head clean off.

"The Butcher, too!" that same soldier cried, "There's three—!"Gael hacked him in half, shoulder to hip, before he could say another word.

The vamps that remained scattered like cockroaches into pairs, heading off in different directions. Usually, there wasn't that many to deal with at once, so it wasn't no big deal. But not one of the monsters we wanted to kill had paired together, like they knew we was after them. Adelaide took off with a dark-haired man—I wasn't sure which vamp he was—and I didn't much care. The camp was so big, it was going to be too easy to lose them in the crowd of tents and soldiers if I didn't act quickly.

I hesitated, thinking of Dess for only a second, before taking off after Adelaide. I couldn't afford to lose sight of her, not now. And Dess had plenty of arrows and a vantage point to handle her kills. It wasn't exactly as planned, but she was capable enough to handle her business.

"Mijita!" Gael caught up, covered a good bit in blood, and we'd only just started—all that hacking was messy. "Did you get yours?"

"She went that way!" I shouted over the ruckus, pointing toward the center of camp.

Gael hesitated, looking off toward the sidelines where Dess hid, but only for a split second. "Go. I'll cover you."

I raced off. I saw my prey rise out of the crown of soldiers and tents as bats to fly above everything, and I tried my best to follow while fighting. I didn't think they was running from me—Adelaide wasn't the running type. She wasn't no coward, even if the one with her was. Naw, they was heading to something important . . . or some*one*.

Wouldn't it be something if I snagged both Adelaide and General Lee in one day?

The colonel would have to eat his words, then.

The bats dropped back down to earth, and I pushed myself faster so I wouldn't lose them in the crowd and— *What in the hell?* I skidded to a stop. There was about a hundred soldiers at the ready guarding the tent. I scowled as an older man stepped out. It was Lee all right, with his beard and his daggone bowtie.

I released a war cry and ran forward—them soldiers was

really trying to surround me, overwhelm me, but it just got them within cutting range of my spear. I deflected bullets from the ones with guns, looking at where Adelaide stood grinning while the other vamp frowned at me like a disapproving father.

"Clear out!" Adelaide shouted suddenly and walked forward without any care of the soldiers around her.

Good. Serve your evil ass up on a platter.

I didn't even wait for all the soldiers to get out the way, just charged forward to strike. But, faster than I could think, Adelaide caught my spear shaft in her bare hand, redirecting it from her form and holding it steady.

What in the blazing hell—?

"Oh dear," she said with a mock concern, gasping into her free hand. "You didn't think that was actually going to work, did you?"

But a real concern was building at the back of my mind 'cause I sure as hell had spread holy water all over this shaft before we came out here. And this vamp was touching it. With her bare hand. Without being burned.

Don't lose your head, Jerusalem.

I maneuvered away and attacked again and again. She blocked each one, and I got madder and madder each time.

"Attack, you coward!" I shouted.

But before she could, I saw a flash of silver, Gael's blade, but this time Adelaide caught both my next attack and his, the flat of his silver blade against her palm.

"Oh bother, not another one." She clicked her tongue, shaking her head at us. "Saints are getting stupider these days, I swear."

While she spoke, me and Gael glanced at each other, and I saw a wild fear in his eyes. Something was sure enough wrong— silver should've good and burned her—but there wasn't no time to dwell. And it sure as hell wasn't no time to be running scared.

"Let's go," he mouthed.

Hell yes, let's go!

And I launched into an attack.

I barely heard him shout, "No!" over the pulse and breath, the panic and rage going on around us.

And maybe I dreamt it 'cause he stuck by me. We didn't have the same rhythm of fighting I had with Lex, but it should've been enough that there was two of us, that we was Saints, that she had a sword on her hip she'd had yet to wield.

But holy hell, there was *two* of us, we was *Saints*, and she had a sword on her hip *she'd had yet to wield*, instead blocking and redirecting our attacks with her bare hands like silver didn't mean nothing to her.

"All right, enough fun and games." She whipped out her sword. I felt the world stop at the impact of our weapons, or at least my breath. I glanced over to see she'd blocked both my spear and Gael's machete at once. What in the hell? . . . *How* in the hell—? "Which of you hideous creatures would like to die first?"

I laughed, and she raised her brows at me. And that was it, all doubts gone. This cocky-ass monster was fittin' to die today.

"Why do you look familiar?" she muttered, but I didn't answer or give her time to think before I screamed in rage and—

Gael tackled me, knocking the wind out of me, and rolled as we hit the ground to break our fall before he leapt back to his feet, practically dragging me away.

"What you doing, Gael?" I demanded, looking back to see that Adelaide hadn't bothered to pursue us, just stood with a smug smile on her face before looking away.

"We can't beat that thing with just us," he said. "She's too powerful."

"Get off me!" I jerked away from his grasp. "I been waiting a year to kill this monster, and I ain't letting her slip away now."

"Jerusalem, wait!"

I left him behind and raced toward Adelaide, who was already walking back to her companion as if I was nothing to worry about.

I leapt at her, but she quickly turned and held my spear with her sword.

"You try my patience, girl," she growled.

I knew she wasn't having fun no more 'cause she was mad as a bull, all her arrogance and ego died down to a simmer. I'd forced her to become desperate, resort to her sword. Oh, I had her now.

I attacked, she parried twice, then I attacked low quickly—a trick move I'd learned from Alexei a long time ago—but the monster stepped on my spear, and I let it slap to the ground so she wouldn't break it. She was faster than I thought—she ain't never moved like this at the plantation. I'd barely thought of my next move when she lifted her sword. In the next second, a giant knife blocked it. In the next, I thought about how glad I was that Gael came back. In the next—

The monster grabbed Gael's arm, a grip that made him cry out and drop his machete. "Gentlemen die first."

"Gael!" I cried.

"Jerusalem, ru—!" Gael's warning was cut off as the monster flung him away from us, with the height and force of an otherworldly catapult.

"No!" I cried, and snatched up his machete, but the monster was already gone by the time I turned around. I swore and threw the knife straight into the ground, then snatched up my spear. She hadn't broken it, thank the good Lord.

I raced forward, looking for her, but the graybacks started crowding.

"Get out of my way!" I shouted at them, scaring a few away. "You weak-ass, racist worms!"

And suddenly, multiple graybacks went down at once as arrows shot through them. I whooped as Dess rode up on a horse, reaching her arm out to me, grabbing onto my forearm to help me up to sit behind her.

"The battalion made it," she said quickly. "There's no reason for you to die out here." And she kicked the horse to turn around *away* from my target.

What? I thought she had come to help me. "Dess, I can't! Adelaide is—"

The horse screamed and fell hard, and I was flung off and away from it. I landed as best I could, rolling to a stop. When I looked up, the horse's leg had been broken strangely, and it lay kicking and fussing—oh Lord—on top of Dess's leg.

Before I could get up, a heavy hand pressed on my back, pushing me into the dirt.

"No, no, little girl," said a deep voice, close and over the sounds of war, his words thick with some sort of Eastern European accent. "Go back to Alexei."

Alexei? How does he know—?

His voice was so gentle, like how Pa used to explain things, that it took me a second too long to realize what this was. 'Cause even though he spoke sweet, the intense pressure of his hand could never have been human, could never have meant me any good. A vampire. I wasn't looking his way, so it wasn't hypnosis, but he was trying to manipulate me, all right. Keep me from saving Dess. Keep me from killing Adelaide.

But he hadn't killed me, and that was his mistake.

I threw my arm back, and since I was holding my spear, he got right up off me—it was either that or be burned by holy water—and I used the space to scramble up to my feet.

I rushed over to Dess, but I felt too slow, far too slow. 'Cause I saw Adelaide step on top of the horse's side, pressing the massive animal's body onto Dess harder. Too slow as I threw my spear, and the other vamp stepped in front at lightning speed, batting it away with one of his two swords like it was a toothpick instead of a spear. Too slow, as Adelaide used the time he'd bought her to bring her own sword down, breaking Dess's bow as she blocked it . . . as the blade went through Dess's stomach.

My insides scrambled as I screamed. I dodged around the other vamp, ran and snatched up my spear, lunging at Adelaide before she could attack again.

Adelaide caught the shaft of the spear in her fist, finally looked me in the eye . . . and a smile, slow and wicked with recognition, crawled wide across her face.

"Hello, Dido," she said, and her voice made my skin crawl. "Your brother is dying to see you."

"Zostaw dziecko," the dark-haired vamp said—and even though I didn't have no clue in hell what he was saying, his deep voice sounded rational in the midst of war. "Mamy teraz ważniejsze rzeczy do zrobienia."

Whatever he said made Adelaide turn and follow him as he threw Lee over his shoulder and rushed off.

They was going to escape with the general—the one person whose death could end the war, but who the hell cared about that? *Adelaide* was going to escape, right when I had her. I *had* her . . . and since they was traveling with a human, I could catch her easy if I took off now. But I tripped to a stop before I barely got started, looking back at Dess still under that horse—if the horse was still crushing her, it meant she couldn't move, that she was dying, that she was—

I cut down two idiot soldiers that ran at me. My gut twisted with anger at myself for letting my enemy get away, but I couldn't let Dess lie there injured on the battlefield, neither.

I ran to her, dragged the dead horse off her. She was shaking something terrible as she pressed her hand into her wound. But her eyes were open and alert. She was alive.

And I was determined to make sure she stayed that way.

ALEXEI

I saw Gael streak through the sky and left the soldiers I'd been slaughtering, racing over to him. I caught him just before he hit the ground, and thankfully was close enough to the edge of the Confederate camp that I decided it was better to get him to safety first.

But it only took me leaving the mass of pulses for me to realize I didn't feel one in him.

"Gael?" I said, even if I knew it was pointless. He was covered in blood, so it was hard to tell what was his . . . but the blood trickling from his ears and nose certainly was, and he had multiple bones broken, including his neck.

He'd been dead before I'd even caught him.

I only knew one vampire who could throw with that sort of force.

Idiot. Why did you let your friends go out there?

I laid Gael's body safely within the trees and went back for a Confederate tent, tearing away the cloth. Quickly, I wrapped my friend's body in it as tightly as I could.

What stupid thing had I said to him before he left for battle? Not goodbye. Nothing meaningful. And well . . . he had been one of my first real male friends in a long time.

Suddenly, all I could think about was Jerusalem and Odessa still out there, and something like this could easily happen to either of them. If something happened to Jerusalem . . . I could never forgive myself. Never.

But . . . Red Mask was still out there, too.

For a moment, I felt paralyzed. I was a coward, and there was nothing I could do about it.

I squeezed my eyes shut and pressed my hands to Gael's wrapped body, still warm. I'd been too late to protect him . . . I couldn't make that mistake again.

I took a deep breath and took off as a crow, praying I wasn't too late.

JERUSALEM

The battle raging in full force behind me was just irritating background noise as I pushed a stolen horse to the limit toward our tent, Dess over my shoulder. Alexei dropped out of the sky from his crow form—he must've seen us coming.

"Alexei, help!" It wasn't till I heard myself, high-pitched and frightened, that I realized the adrenaline had worn off. He ran up to us before I'd even halted, taking Odessa in his arms. I leapt off after her, not bothering to tie up the agitated animal.

He laid her on the ground, just outside the tent, tearing her clothing away from the injury on her stomach. I froze, seeing it, my baby sister's torn body flashing through my mind. It was a messy wound, jagged and deep and bruised all around, like she done got hacked by a dull ax swung by an unskilled hand. It was clear not even sewing it up would help.

But I wasn't about to accept that.

"Alexei," Odessa said with a grimace. "Remember our arrangement."

"We don't have to resort to that," Alexei said, lifting her upper body so her cheek rested against his shoulder. "If you let me turn you—"

"Don't you dare," I snapped, shooting daggers and fire at him with my eyes. "You ain't turning her into no soulless monster."

Odessa shook her head. "Not necessary. I got what I wanted . . . I know where I'm going." She gripped my hand, what she always did to shut me up, and I clenched my jaw. "I thought I'd only have five children until I met you, Jerusalem. My dear girl . . . I love you more than you know."

"Dess—" She squeezed my hand again, and I shoved back a sob.

She took Alexei's hand and held our hands together against her stomach. "Promise me you'll stick together. Take care of each other."

"We promise," I said quickly, just as Alexei said, "Of course, Odessa."

"Don't separate me from Gael," she begged, and I nearly broke.

"Odessa." I swallowed. "Gael is—"

"Don't separate us, Alexei."

Alexei nodded, squeezing her hand. "I won't."

She sighed, as if her relief at hearing that finally allowed her to relax. "Ya voy, mi vida . . ."

"You have him?" I whispered to Lex.

He nodded again, his expression sick. "Better she doesn't see him."

"This is the last time I get to hear your voices," Dess said, as if she hadn't heard either of us, her own voice fading. "So, I don't want to hear any arguing. I want you to say sweet things to each other . . . I want you both to admit that you love each other."

"She done lost her mind," I murmured to Alexei, my voice shaking. "What do we do? Ain't you got wound training?"

"There's nothing to be done now. Her organs have been torn up; she's lost too much blood," Alexei said, and then, desperately, "Odessa, *please*. Give me permission to turn you. You won't survive otherwise."

I shoved him in the chest, but not as hard as I could've since he was still holding on to Odessa. "Don't suggest that again! She won't never go to heaven."

But I bit the inside of my cheek. Won't go to heaven *one day*. I didn't say *one day*. Like she was going to heaven right now, and suddenly I couldn't breathe right. First my sister . . . then Mama and Pa . . . now this sweet woman who was a second mama in every way that mattered. I couldn't lose her, too. I couldn't.

"Lex," I begged, building tears burning at my throat. "What do we do?"

He'd been studying Odessa's face, but suddenly looked at me. He knew it as much as I did that it was all over, but for a moment we said nothing. And then . . . "I love you, Jerusalem," he said, and my heart raced like a wild horse. "But you must know that, surely, the way I contrive reasons to be near you."

I hadn't meant to gasp, but . . . had Dess been right? Hell, she was always right, but about this? About . . . someone loving me, not in the way of a father or brother, but as someone who might want a life with me?

I shook the thought from my hazy head. Alexei didn't love me, not like that. Dess had asked him to say it, so he'd said it. But, even if it wasn't real, the words had sounded so beautiful, so true coming from his lips.

And, if I truly cared for what Dess wanted, they would have to sound true coming from mine.

Still, I took a trembling breath as I stroked Odessa's cheek, the words stuck in my throat even though I wanted to say them for her.

"I love you, too, Alexei," I finally whispered, and suddenly felt sick to my stomach with emotion. "Even if you is an arrogant pain in the ass."

Alexei managed a small chuckle, but I could tell he was holding back tears. He looked human, almost, his eyes glistening like that. But he was too pretty to be human. Too unreal.

"I'd rather argue with you every day," he said, "than live a day without you."

"I don't want to argue," I said before I really knew what I was saying, "I'm just scared of what will happen if I let myself—"

I bit my lip to shut myself up.

You confess one truth, and the rest comes pouring out . . .

Dess was right about this, too—saying things out loud forced you to feel things, forced you to admit things . . . forced you to face the truth. The truth being, I didn't feel . . . entirely *wrong* confessing that I loved Alexei. You could love a friend, couldn't you? Love didn't have to be romantic.

Except I didn't want to love Alexei. I couldn't bear to—he didn't deserve it after what he done. I wanted to hate him for letting this happen. For letting Odessa—

"I love you," I whimpered. "I love you too much, and it scares me . . ." I squeezed Odessa's hand, even though I could tell she wasn't squeezing back. "I love you, I love you, I love you . . ."

I felt tears run down my cheeks. It wasn't just Dess I felt. It was Lila, Mama, Pa. Matthew, who might not have much time left. Everyone I ever loved, I lost. So maybe that was why I could think. 'Cause I'd faced death enough times that my mind didn't give in to a full cry. There was no time, not now. 'Cause my anger was simmering, not allowing my body to rest. Alexei was all roughed up, dirty and blood splattered, as if he'd been out there fighting. But he hadn't 'cause he said he wouldn't. And if he had, he would've fought alongside us like he was supposed to.

He would've protected us.

But I wasn't fittin' to disrespect Odessa's last request, so I kept my mouth shut.

We sat there, in the quiet. Quiet except for war off in the distance, gunshots and shouts and dying men—and, for once, I didn't want no part in that. Alexei didn't lay Dess down until it was clear she was gone.

And by then, I'd made up my mind that love was the farthest thing I felt for him.

"You did this," I said finally, the words tumbling out from holding them in so long.

Alexei looked at me, his brows creased. "Odessa didn't want to be saved, Jerusalem. From the moment she gathered the intel for Mills, she knew what she was going to do."

"Odessa was well and safe from the battle, on the sidelines shooting—she only came out on the field to get me 'cause you wasn't there to help. And Gael killed his vamp early on—he only died doing what you was supposed to be doing."

"They both wanted this," he said again, and that answer infuriated me—it was all an excuse. "Odessa lied to us to make it happen. Even if I'd been there fighting with you, they would've found a way."

"You wrong!" I snapped. "Before we went out there, Gael kissed her, and I saw it in her eyes. She didn't want to die no more. She wanted to be with him."

"But don't you understand; it was too late by then. She'd been planning this before the war even began. She made you believe it was possible, knowing from the beginning we would never survive. From the moment I met her, she lied—"

"What's that got to do with anything?" I snatched up my spear and stood quickly, and Alexei had the good sense to stand and back away. My spear was still coated with enough holy water to burn his fingers off. "She and Gael fell in love while seeking revenge . . . they would've been so happy together. And you just sat back and let that monster kill them."

"They used us, Jerusalem." He raised his voice, and it just made me angrier. "They wanted to die and would've let us die with them—"

"I don't care what you think they did!" I yelled, my chest hurting. "I care that you left us! I care that you let them die! I care that you don't think about anyone but yourself!"

I thrust my spear at him, forcing him sideways and back as I swung my weapon to follow him. He sped around, kicking up grass and dirt.

"You're upset," he said, behind me a few feet now, like he didn't think I could attack him from there. "You're not thinking straight."

The boy had the nerve to try and blame *me* for this. But the very fact that he ran gave me all the confidence I needed.

"And you're a coward." I turned and charged at him. He blocked my next attack with his sword, and the next, even when

I spun it. But I'd trained every day, and there was only so much he could do with one sword without touching my spear. Only a matter of time 'cause the dumbass had taught me to kill his kind.

And now I was fittin' to use that knowledge against him.

He blocked a few more attacks.

"Coward!" I accused, pushing against his sword.

"I don't want to hurt you."

I laughed, his fears granting me strength. He should've been aware by now that pain meant nothing to me. Life had hurt me more than enough to ever fear that.

His shirt sleeve was fitted, making it obvious when I hit him, even if I hadn't felt the pressure of his body run through the length of my spearhead—but he moved too quickly, leaving only a flesh wound. Still, I saw Alexei's eyes go slightly wide—that silver was burning, all right. But I didn't give him time to check it before attacking again, and finally, he gave me what I wanted and attacked right back.

My blood sprinted through my veins. Each blow that collided could've meant death for one or both of us if I cared about that. I didn't. I wasn't concerned with death, only killing.

Even Alexei?

If he deserved it.

But you love—

"No!" I shouted to get rid of it and any other thought that would stop me.

I was out of my mind, maybe . . . but I wasn't concerned with that, neither.

Suddenly the wind was knocked out of me as my back hit the ground, and Alexei used that brief second of human weakness to shift my spear above my head with his foot. His boot stepped down on the shaft, pressing my hands underneath it into the hard ground. I cried out and kicked at him, but his foot was more effective than mine, and he broke my grip and kicked my spear out of my grasp.

But that left him off balance, so I tripped him with my legs—not to his back, but enough of a stumble for me to shoot to a crouch and leap at him, tackling him the rest of the way.

I grabbed his hair with one hand much rougher than he liked so I could strike him with the other, but he caught both my wrists and rolled so I was forced onto my back. I wasn't going to break his grip, so I slammed my knee into his stomach over and over, never letting go of his hair, screaming at his oversensitive ears—he would feel my anger one way or another, even if it was mostly desperation by then. Nothing was thought anymore, only action.

Only anguish turned to rage.

He risked his beloved hair against my wrath by letting go of that wrist, grappling with my legs before shoving them sideways to pin them. Despite my struggling, he still managed to get to his feet.

He pulled me in, my back against his chest, and a brief flashback of a year ago when another vamp had done the same thing froze up my muscles for an instant. It was an instant too long.

I hated Alexei for taking advantage of our size difference. He could easily hug both my bent knees with one arm, and when I let go of his hair to drive my elbow into him, he—quick as anything—pinned my one free hand against my chest to join the other. I pushed my back against him to gain some leverage and shove my knees out, but he was stronger than I ever remembered him being.

There was no way . . . I'd been fooling myself this whole year I'd known him, and he'd been holding back the whole time.

No. I was just tired, human. I'd fought too long in a battle that raged even now, and against Alexei I was forced to fight harder.

"I hate you!" I screamed.

"No more fighting, Tiny Saint," he said, close to my ear. "You'll hurt yourself trying to break my grip."

I fought to straighten my legs, to pull my wrists from his hand. The more I fought, the more panicked my heart sprinted, the more my chest hurt from effort and trapped feelings crushing me. I screamed out my frustration. "Get off me, Alexei!"

"I'm not letting you go. Not until I know you're all right. Not until you stop fighting me."

"You don't own me," I choked on a sob, my vision blurring, *burning*. "You don't get to tell me when to stop."

"I love you, Jerusalem," he whispered, and I felt my breath tremble. "I'm not letting you go.

His voice was so comforting . . . but it had to be a trick—like the way that vamp had spoken to me on the battlefield. I couldn't fall for it. I couldn't give in to whatever this was—hypnosis or feelings or . . . helplessness.

But still, what he said meant something to me, even if I'd never say that aloud. Tears crashed down on me, like my brain finally had caught on to what was happening. I couldn't breathe, my sobs stopping up my throat, shaking my body in a way I couldn't control.

"I'm sorry," I whimpered.

He shushed me all sweet-like, like Mama used to do when I wouldn't settle in bed. "It's all right."

"But I hurt you."

He shushed me again, let go of my wrists, and I pressed the heels of my hands into my eyes to hold back the burning. And maybe it was the memory he'd just pulled out of me but, "I want my mama," slipped out, like a stupid, needy little kid.

I hadn't cried for her in . . . hell if I knew. 'Cause Dess had been there as a substitute in a way. No one could replace my mama, but . . . I thought I'd be fine. That I'd always have Dess and maybe be able to hold on.

But now all my walled defenses were caving in.

Alexei shifted me in his arms so that one arm hugged the backs of my knees and the other my shoulders, and I threw my arms around his neck and wept against his cheek. He pressed me close against him, his body cold and familiar, my nose filling with the scents of blood and battle and shortbread. And he murmured things I couldn't hear through my loud sobbing but felt the tone of right enough . . . his words was as sweet as his hands was cool against my overheated body. Comforting. They felt like . . . love.

And so undeserved after I'd just tried to kill him.

But you'd've thought he forgot all that, the way he let me snuggle up against him. The way he carried me into the tent and laid me on my back. The way he pressed his cool lips to my forehead. I squeezed my arms tighter around his neck.

"Don't go nowhere," I begged, through sobs and staggered breaths.

"I'll be right here." he whispered. "Try to sleep."

He tried to get up, but I was strong enough to hold him, keep him close. After a moment, he gave in, settling instead of holding his weight away from me. He was heavier than I thought he'd be, but it didn't hurt none, not yet anyway . . . it calmed me a little, even. I'd seen gentle pressure work on putting babies to bed but never thought it'd work on me, a whole-ass eighteen year old.

"I feel like I'm crushing you, Tiny," he said, positioning his hands on the ground to lift himself away.

"Stay," I whispered, my voice trembling.

He settled again, resting his forehead on the ground beside my head. I relaxed my grip at his neck and rested my wet cheek against him, his cool body and my exhaustion lulling me into a deep sleep.

8

ALEXEI

I no longer smelled Red Mask and Zamir in the vicinity, so I didn't dare move until Tiny's grip was limp, until her pulse eased, her sniffling silenced. I lifted my head and removed her arms from around me, laying them on her stomach. Her thick lashes sent shadows across her soft cheeks, her mouth open the slightest bit. Seeing her untroubled was a relief. I forced myself to my feet, the only way I could stop myself from kissing that sweet face. Not to mention... Odessa was still outside.

And Gael. His body was still lying in the woods.

I felt raw and sick for leaving their bodies out there for so long unattended, but now that my girl was taken care of, I could turn my attention to the others.

We'd discussed the plan about two years ago, Odessa and I. She'd been the only Saint in camp who wasn't intimidated by me, so we'd hit it off almost immediately. A month later, she'd made her request—that if she died, I was to cremate her and deliver the urn to her husband along with a letter she'd prepared.

Which, I realized now, would be a grave.

Did she only befriend me so she'd have a strong ally when it came down to this fight she'd orchestrated?

Maybe. But none of that was important anymore.

I touched the thin slice on my shoulder gingerly. It was only a surface wound, but a silver burn was a silver burn—it didn't burn too badly, more like the annoyance of a paper cut. Still, that sensation was never going to go away. My gut might've hurt worse, to be honest, where her knee had slammed multiple times. If the organs beneath had been of any use to me, they certainly wouldn't have been anymore. Luckily, that horrible aching would go away soon enough.

Served me right for training someone so well who hated vampires that much. She was never going to be stronger than me, based simply on her size, her need for oxygen, muscle fatigue, and the fact that we both trained regularly. But skill and strength were two different beasts, not to mention a lack of self-preservation. That might've been the main difference between us—I was afraid of hurting her, but she wasn't afraid of getting hurt.

It was an equally frustrating and attractive trait to possess.

But I needed to get back on task. My wound wasn't going anywhere for the rest of eternity, and it wasn't anywhere noticeable that would affect my appearance. It didn't deserve any more attention.

My friends, however, did.

Carefully, I fished Odessa's match safe from her pack. Flipping open the small metal container revealed two matches. I didn't have much experience with fire other than avoiding it, so would just have to hope it was enough. It had to be, because Jerusalem never slept more than four hours at a time, not nearly enough to wake up rested and ready to forgive me. When she awoke, she'd need my attention.

I walked outside. Calamity vultures were already starting to circle high above the battlefield, the massive beasts searching for openings to swoop down and collect their meals. They were big enough for Tiny to ride on, and getting rid of them ranged from a nuisance to borderline deadly, so I was grateful there were enough corpses over the ridge to take up their attention. I picked up one of the massive false skirts Dess and Jerusalem wore and tore the fabric from the framing. I didn't know how cremation ceremonies worked, but it felt far more respectful to cover her than to burn her out in the open. Again, I didn't know what was right.

I retrieved Gael's already wrapped body and brought him next to Odessa—she'd requested they not be separated, and I wanted to honor every last wish she'd had. I knelt beside Odessa slowly, as if I would disturb her peace if I didn't. Placing my hand on her still warm and creased brow, one would think she were amid a dream. But her chest and stomach were breathless, and I was so used to that movement of life in her that I instantly felt sick.

I was a warrior, used to battles and killing, used to losing soldiers on my side. But a sob escaped before I knew what was happening. Tears fell, choking me. I covered her with the fabric, tucking it around her, underneath, but hiding her didn't change what I knew. The more I fought to keep myself quiet, to not wake Jerusalem, the worse the tears burned.

I shifted to my wolf form and raced toward the woods. It was only a short distance from our tent, but with the rage of battle going on not far from us, it was enough to hide my sound when I shifted back and leaned my arms against the nearest tree to openly weep into them.

Jerusalem's words ground into my bones. If I had just swallowed my fear, been there to protect them . . . But Odessa would've found a way. I could say that with certainty. She was smarter than me, despite my centuries on her. Smarter, more skilled, more careful. And this plan had been three years in the making.

She would've found a way, regardless of whether I'd been there to protect her.

I lifted the hem of my shirt to press away more tears, then dragged it over my head and threw it away from me and tied my long hair up and out of the way.

I couldn't leave my friends out in the heat any longer.

There was no place to build a pyre that *wasn't* obvious, but the Southern army was a bit distracted, anyway, so I started a pile of broken tree pieces on top of the ridge. No ax, and my sword was in the tent, so I tore them apart by hand. It helped with the anxiety, and soon I worked without thinking.

From the ridge, I could watch the battle, the stark difference in uniforms making it easy to tell what was going on. Normally, I'd be chomping at the bit to join them. Today, there was no fight left in me.

I hurried back to my friends and set aside Odessa's broken bow and arrows. The urn had been built into the bottom of the quiver, a compartment beneath where the arrows sat. The quiver was too narrow for my hand to fit inside, so I tore it down the seam and twisted the lid at the bottom.

A single letter was inside, sealed with wax. I tore the remainder of the quiver away and removed the letter, hesitating.

For Alexei, it said.

Inside were addresses, for her parents, for the cemetery, and separate letters for each location. There was also an address for Gael's cemetery, but I think this was truly what Odessa meant when she said not to separate them, so I discarded it. I put the papers in my pocket and hung her bow and supplies over my shoulder. Then I lifted Odessa's body and carried her to the pyre.

I laid her on the bed of wood, thankful I'd covered her in cloth. It would burn away, but by then I wouldn't have to look. And besides, to take my mind off everything, I could stress myself out with the thought of striking this match without destroying myself.

Don't be foolish, Alexei.

The match was long enough that my fingers wouldn't even be close when I struck it.

I went back for Gael and laid him beside Odessa. I didn't know where Gael's machete had gone, so I simply positioned Odessa's bow and arrows with her, then struck the match before I could think about it too hard and lit the wood.

All at once, I wanted to snatch their bodies back, forget any of this was happening. But they were dead, and there was no point in pretending.

I walked away from the flame—far enough not to see *it* happen, close enough to keep the flame from burning out of control. Already the smells were unpleasant, so I rushed back to the tent to get Odessa's plague mask. The herbs were strong, on the border of stinging . . . but anything was better than burning flesh.

Jerusalem was still sleeping, which seemed a small victory.

When I exited the tent, I saw a Union soldier approaching on horseback. It wasn't completely unexpected, what with the beacon I'd created, but it was certainly annoying.

The boy—he was sixteen at the most—leapt from the horse and raced over to me.

"We're hurting for soldiers, sir," he panted. "Colonel Mills requests your assistance."

"You're hurting for soldiers, but they could spare you?"

He looked flustered, hot blood climbing to the surface. He didn't smell very appetizing, but I probably needed to feed before Jerusalem awoke.

I considered his pulse for a few seconds before moving on—I'd drink a Confederate when Odessa and Gael were safely sharing an urn. "Well?"

"We need your help, sir."

"Don't you have plenty of Saints fighting alongside you? Saints Jerusalem, Odessa, and Gael disposed of multiple vampires ahead of you. You should be making quick work of that army."

"Yes sir, but u-um—" The boy chewed on his lip, dropping his gaze. He was sweating. Terrified. I couldn't tell if it was because of me or because he realized he was going to have to ride back empty-handed. "I'm sorry, sir. The colonel insists."

"The colonel *insists*? Am I some dog to be commanded?"

"No, sir. Of course not, sir."

I smirked. I'd needed this odd moment of fun in my anguish, but I didn't have any more time to waste on torturing this boy.

"I won't be joining you. But do relay a message to Colonel Mills." The boy looked up at me, ready to take in my words. But I looked over at the tent, where Jerusalem was hopefully still sleeping. "Tell him, 'Waiting is what happens when you give away my mission.'"

9

JERUSALEM

*M*ama and Pa knew how to avoid trouble. They knew when to smile, when to keep they head down, when to ask for things, *how* to ask for things. They had a way about them in that they could make themselves valuable without drawing dangerous attention. It was one of the reasons, other than perfecting a skill, that they'd snagged themselves jobs in the big house—Mama cooked all the meals and Pa ran important errands and deliveries, and so rarely had to be around to get tortured. They was subtle. The best manipulators I ever met. Matthew and Lila had been blessed with them good genes.

As the middle child, must've skipped me right the hell over. 'Cause I sure enough was real good at giving lip at all the wrong times.

It was a week before I ran that all the trouble started. 'Cause I was downright sick of taking orders from people who hated who and what I was, who I could easily kill if I had the mind to—and I had the mind to, believe that. To be fair, it'd been bubbling up for years. It was only the thought of protecting my family that kept me obedient. And my respect for Pa, who always told me to keep my head down.

The hot months was always gross and sticky, and the smoke graying the sky didn't keep the heat back none—made it worse, somehow, like trapping us all in a big old oven. And that day, it was enough to make a cow pass out. But the big old oak blocked a bit of the hot air blowing my way, and weeding the mistress's flower garden wasn't what I'd call hard work when I was used to the field.

Lila had meant well, tricking Millie into handing me this easy job. In the field, I could keep my head down and stay out of trouble, mostly, but my big-ass mouth? In constant view of the house? That was where the plan had gone south.

Not that I ever worried, else I'd've shut up. I worked hard enough that the master wasn't going to get rid of me. Naw, I made him too much money while taking up less room and food than buying three slaves to replace me would.

That day, the master and Garfield was sitting on the porch cleaning rifles with Matthew's help, the weapons taken apart like a jigsaw, while I thought about how easy it'd be to kill both them white men in that moment. Then the youngest son came riding up on his bike. Adelaide had sent him to boarding school, so he only came home for Christmas and summer, and even then he was mostly off seeing friends. But he'd recently turned fifteen, had shot up an extra foot, and had found one stray hair on his chin, so he thought he was grown and should start acting like his pa.

He dropped his bike off at the little picket fence that separated the house from the rest of the property and jogged up the walkway. As he passed by, he slowed, and I knew in my heart I would kill this boy. If not that day, someday. 'Cause he veered off toward me, and next thing I knew, his boot had stomped down on my hand.

I kept quiet. It hurt, sure enough, but it wasn't horrible. I'd had worse, could take more than he could dish out, but he would never understand that.

"You're smaller than the squirrels I hunt, Dido," Donald had said.

He was one to talk, voice sounding like a whistling pot every time it cracked, like his body still wasn't sure it wanted him anywhere near manhood yet. But he was taller than me, even though I was seventeen, and I was pretty sure in his head that meant power. He didn't know I could probably press my thumb against his temple and poke a hole in his skull, but sure, it was the height that mattered.

"Still only squirrels?" I asked, and Lord knew I wasn't thinking about my poor brother sitting over there when I said it till I saw him glance up and lean over to say something to Garfield.

"What'd you say?" Donald asked, raising his voice in an over-the-top offended tone.

His foot was still on my hand, pressing it into the dirt, and I was sure my fingers was going to pop from the pressure any second. If he didn't get off soon I was fittin' to break his ankle and make it look like an accident.

Apologize, Jerusalem. Say it was nothing. But whatever you do, don't say—

"That ain't real game."

Donald's face went beet red. "You sass mouthing me, you little monkey?"

"Come on now, Donny," called Garfield, though he didn't get up from where he sat with his lemonade—Matthew's doing, I'll bet, since Garfield rarely interfered. "Now you know we can't have her out here being seen when the Stevensons arrive. Go on and get yourself cleaned up for dinner."

"Don't forget to wash your neck," his pa added, barely interested, a pipe hanging from his mouth.

I really could've killed that man. Hacked his head in half with this little hoe. Neither one of his stupid sons could've stopped me, and the one who could've was out acting a fool and playing God up in the fields. Lila's baby by him was due in about a week, so his death was way overdue.

"Yes, sir," Donald said sweetly. To spite his sweetness, he kicked me in the ribs—I winced, huffing air out slowly through my nose to keep myself from killing the boy—then he glared down at me and hissed, "You better stay out of my way, monkey girl. Next time, you won't get off without a beating."

"Neither will you," I muttered.

"What'd you just say to me?"

I was feeling more violent than usual. Couldn't hit the boy right in full view. *Someday. Not today.* Instead, I looked up into his face and said slowly, "Neither. Will. You."

Didn't rightly know what was in my gaze or tone, but he gaped for a moment, as if my threat had affected him, his expression slowly dropping into something like horror. He stammered a second before calling, "Pa! Did you hear what she said!" He ran to the porch, practically crying, and I couldn't help but snicker as I got back to weeding.

I'd probably doomed myself, to be honest. But at least I'd gotten a good laugh out of it.

And I didn't care . . . until Garfield got up and approached with Mathew on his heels, until Donald ran off toward the shed where I knew they kept a whip or two. And suddenly all

I could think was, *Will they take this out on Mama and Pa, too? On Lila, for suggesting me for the job? On Matthew 'cause he was right there anyway?*

"Children that age don't mean much of what they say, Mr. Garfield," I heard my brother say as they got closer, shooting me a glance that begged me to keep my mouth shut. "And there really ain't much time before the Stevensons arrive; we ought to be finishing up these rifles and getting you dressed."

"I know, Toby," said Garfield. "But if I don't, Donald will, and who knows if there'll be anything left of her, rotten boy. Pa already said we can't afford to replace the ones Walter killed." He took me by the elbow to stand me up. "You know you earned this, Dido. Don't fight it; we need to get it over with quickly."

As if that was some kind of mercy. Still, if anyone was going to whup me, I'd rather Garfield, with his weak-ass arm. The soft strikes was on purpose. Violence brought a sick look to his face, and he was always wincing at the crack of the whip, like he had something to be afraid of.

Part of me wondered why he still insisted on doing it.

As he drug me past Matthew, we locked eyes, apologies in his, assurances in mine, before he headed back to the porch. He'd done all he could, and we both knew it. Getting in the way now would get him whupped, too, and that wasn't helpful for nobody.

Meanwhile, Garfield made me hug the wide trunk of the big oak tree and tied my wrists together on the other side. I could tear those ropes easy. I could even whup them all with they own weapon, I bet. Instead, I rested my cheek against the trunk, listening to a spoiled brat argue with his grown-ass brother about who was going to whup me, how many lashings I should get.

Just get it over with so you can go back to leaving me alone.

I saw Matthew walk off with the rifles, toward where they

stored them. We had a system for this, Mathew and me—if it was clear I was going to get it and there wasn't nothing more he could do, he found some way to leave so he didn't have to watch. Wasn't no bitter feelings about it between us. I could take it, no problem, heal faster afterward, so I took all the whuppings I could for my family to spare them. They hated it, so I let them leave so all they knew was when I was feeling just fine later.

But I was mad this time. Matt had put them rifles together real quick—he had to've known a thing or two about using them. I started wishing he was more like me than our parents. I'd have turned them rifles on them white folks in two seconds.

But for the safety of my family, I pushed that bitterness away. I knew good and well he couldn't risk that. He was just a regular person, and I was . . .

Well, back then, I didn't rightly know.

But I felt invincible.

"What is this?" said a dark voice, scary in its calmness. "Why is this sorry little beast tied to this tree and no punishment being carried out?"

Adelaide.

I couldn't lie; my heart started to pound with the edge of nerves. The master was one thing, but I ain't never dealt with the mistress before. To me, she was like the boogeyman. Heard tell of her wickedness. Seen her from afar, like a shadow. But ain't never been close enough to experience her for myself, and didn't rightly know if I wanted to.

I heard her heeled boots walk down the wooden stairs as she said, "You might as well hand her a glass of lemonade."

I snickered, just barely.

The footfalls landed on the grass, and then I couldn't hear them no more. Adelaide's skirt came into view, and she crouched to look at me. She removed her wide-brimmed hat, dark hair falling across her pale forehead. Her eyes could've been brown, but they looked more red to me. Like rust. Dried blood. Unnatural.

"You think that's amusing, girl?"

No human would've heard that tiny sound I made. Cursed vamps . . . "No, mistress," I said, even though it was.

"You think a lot of things are funny around here, don't you? I hear you have a lot to say about how the boys treat you."

I ain't never said nothing like that, but white folks never did need a real reason to beat us. "No, mistress."

"So, I'm a liar now?"

Fouler than that. "No, mistress."

"You're quite the idiot, aren't you?"

Not as dumb as your stepsons.

Don't say it, Jer. Or you really will be that stupid.

"Yes, mistress," I said, trying to do what Mama and Pa would and not to sound hateful.

She laughed, a light, pretty sound that still managed to make me feel sick. "Come now, you don't believe that for a second." Her smile dropped, sudden-like. "You're far too arrogant and self-important for that."

She got up and walked away. "Donald, be a dear and bring me that leather box in my closet beside my hat box."

"Yes'm," the boy said, and I heard his steps jog off.

Adelaide had never gotten involved in punishments before. She oversaw the overseers sometimes but usually went about her vamp business. Didn't know what it was about me that got her attention. Flies buzzed near my sweaty head, bark digging into my arms through my thin sleeves, while that monster and her stepson talked of good horse-riding weather until the weakest of them returned.

"Watch carefully, boys," Adelaide said.

"What is that?" I heard Garfield ask, horrified.

"This, my boys," she said, and I could hear her steps coming closer, "is for silencing arrogant, sass-mouthing maggots who don't know their place."

And before I knew anything else, something hard forced its way into my mouth, metal straps surrounding my head. I tried to scream but only a panicked sound came out—the metal plate in my mouth pressed down on my tongue, the dull spines along it making it painfully impossible to even swallow. I felt the pressure on my head tighten, heard the click of Adelaide locking the metal straps into place.

"You see?" I heard her say, far too lightly against my panic. "Now she can't talk back, and you can get on with her punishment. Remember—time is money. She's more use to us out there working."

"So the punishment is the muzzle?" Garfield asked, sounding just as relieved as you'd expect of someone who'd clearly never had to wear one before, like it was doing me a favor.

"We don't get to whup her ass?" his brother demanded, like the spoiled child he was.

"Watch me, Donald," Adelaide said, "so you don't learn bad habits from the way Walter does it."

I heard the snap of the whip before it cracked against my back—a sting, but my body could take more damage than that, easy. I'd had whuppings worse than this for stupider reasons than mouthing off. The master's two younger sons found any reason to be cruel, and the oldest was too much a coward to stop them.

Only now I couldn't brace none, or the metal plate in my mouth would break my teeth for sure. And I couldn't breathe right, not even through my nose—but maybe it was just in my head 'cause I was already shaken from the muzzle pressing my tongue useless and my back about to be eaten up.

But maybe I didn't have to brace. 'Cause nothing else was—

Heard the whip again, and it felt doubly sharp from the first, the feeling of the two strikes burning together. I gasped, fought not to bite the metal. The whip had never felt like that before . . . like tiny metal splinters digging into my flesh, tearing as they went.

"Do you see how long I waited in between lashes?" Adelaide said. "If you whip too vigorously, the body doesn't have time to send pain signals. It's a punishment. Allow her to feel it."

Drool ran out my mouth around the metal bar at my jaw 'cause I couldn't swallow none. Even making a sound hurt too much to utter.

The sting of the whip came again, three times worse 'cause of the three lashes on me.

And this went on and on and on.

Four . . . seven . . . eleven . . . *Oh God, stop, please stop!*

Any sound of pain or stress made them spines press into my tongue, digging up more pain, more sounds, more *pain.* Tears burned and blinded. I tasted the tin bitterness of blood and let it run out of my mouth with my saliva so it wouldn't run the other way and choke me.

Monster! I wanted to scream but couldn't. The summer heat was too much, and I felt ready to pass out, and the tree was rough on my skin, and the metal muzzle dug in and hurt like hell, and the whip was tearing flesh away, and I was crying but couldn't sob, and I couldn't *take* no more.

I jerked my hands apart, tore the rope holding me to the tree and spun on her, letting out a sound that was the closest thing to a scream I could get to—a sound that forced the spine into my tongue like it would chop it in two, making more watery blood leak from my mouth. But I'd barely lifted a hand to hit her when she struck me across the head, and I was too weakened to stay on my feet.

I lay on the ground panting through my nose, my vision rocking bright and void like death come to take me.

"You boys need to learn how to properly secure ropes," she said, more bored than anything.

And she left me on the ground, seething with more pain and hate for her than my body could hold before I finally passed out.

I woke to the sounds of battle still raging, head aching and body spent dry from crying. I shifted to get up, but a cool hand pressed against my shoulder, and I felt my pulse rush with panic.

"You can sleep," Alexei whispered.

I let out a relieved breath. The past was still just a nightmare. "I'm thirsty," I croaked.

I felt his body leave me, his absence exposing me to the summer heat even inside our tent, and I suddenly felt stupid and embarrassed and disappointed and devastated. With his cool presence gone, all I could feel was sharp loss. Maybe I hadn't spent all my tears last night 'cause my view of Alexei approaching looked like a beautiful blur.

"How long did I sleep?" I asked, my dry throat barely letting my voice out.

"Six hours. More than usual."

Every muscle in me ached as he helped me sit up. I didn't shun his help—war wasn't easy on the body—and I had a feeling our fight didn't help none.

He handed me a canteen, and I drank. And after I replenished, I wasn't going to waste no more water on crying, I could tell you that. That bloodsucking monster stole the life of another person I love.

This time it would be the last.

I tipped my head back and poured some water on my face, scrubbing it with my hand and wiping down after with my sleeve. But maybe that was a bad idea 'cause it woke me up to how battered my body was . . . how broken my heart was.

This time when I went to stand, I shoved away Alexei's helping hand, only for him to catch me when my bruised and aching legs wouldn't hold me upright. I pushed him off anyway, collapsing to my hands and knees.

"I don't want your help," I said, my voice hoarse from . . . screaming, I guess. From pain.

"I know you don't," he said, and I winced as he grabbed my bruised arms and lifted me to my feet.

I jerked away, but he caught me again before I collapsed. I didn't want to think about the fact I was pretty sure his confession of love had been real 'cause even if Dess had asked us to say it, he'd gone and said it again when I'd needed to hear it most. I didn't want to get comfy in his arms like I was last night . . . didn't want to remember how *good* the weight of his body had felt against mine. He gave great hugs, and I needed one real bad.

But it was a stupid desire. Weak. Besides, he was only here for me *after* the fact. And he was a vampire, which canceled out anything else. He couldn't be trusted.

Still, if I lingered in his arms much longer, I might just give in. So I shoved away again, barely managing to stay on my feet, and walked slowly and stiffly out of the tent.

"Where's Dess?" I asked, horrified.

"I've taken care of her," he said gently. That would've made me feel somewhat better, except I was so pissed at him nothing was going to help.

I crossed my arms tight. It felt wrong, not being able to say a proper goodbye. But I understood—she couldn't stay out here, not with the heat and bugs. She deserved more respect than that.

I paused. "Gael, too?" Didn't know why I did—no human body, not even a Saint, could've survived the force of that throw. Alexei nodded, but I didn't need him to. I didn't need no reminder of how that man for sure deserved more respect than I ever gave him . . . that he'd done all he could to save my life in the end.

I cleared my throat. "They been fighting all this time?" I asked so I could think of something else.

"Nonstop," said Alexei, arms crossed, too, as he frowned into the distance.

He looked like he'd been fighting nonstop, his hair tied up in a messy bun, his posture a little hunched. Like he hadn't rested at all when I'd been sleeping.

"You ought to get some rest," I said.

"I did, a little. While you slept."

"You mean you ain't been helping the battalion this whole time? It'd be over by now if you was fighting."

He pushed stray hair out of his face, and I had a weird flash of that hand touching me instead, comforting me. "The battle's still going, so they must be holding their own without me."

His words made me remember why I was angry.

"Oh wait, why *would* you fight?" I asked bitterly. "You a coward now."

I glared at him before I stormed—well, staggered, more like—back into the tent.

I grabbed my pack, started stuffing my things into it. Odessa might've been dead, but Matthew was alive. He was my only family left. And now that Adelaide had seen me, it was a matter of time before she went back to get him. I had to get to the plantation before she did. And then, once my brother was in a safe place, I'd deal with her evil ass.

"Where are we headed?" I heard Alexei ask.

"I'm fittin' to go save my brother," I said, aggressively shoving my things into my pack. "You can go back to being a war hero. That's why you here, ain't it?"

"We promised Odessa we'd stick together."

"What she don't know won't hurt her."

I heard him sigh. "If you think I'm letting you travel alone, you don't know me at all."

"Then I don't know you," I snapped, turning on him. "'Cause you sure as hell left me high and dry yesterday."

"I know." He at least had the decency to look ashamed, which was something. "I'm trying to fix it."

"*Fix* it? The damage is done."

Alexei tore the ropes holding the tent up from their stakes and tossed the entire thing away from us.

"What'd you do that for?"

"I can't stand upright in there, it's too small—"

"You just too big," I snapped, even though his height was a silly thing to take my anger out on. But everything about him made me angry right then. His stupid strong hands, and his stupid long hair, and his stupid, stupid, *stupid* pretty face. I shoved him in the stomach, not hard enough to move him, not even hard enough to call it a shove. I was so weak and tired from everything, I couldn't even aggress my enemy right. "Nothing but a big old stupid tree . . ."

My hand didn't want to leave his stomach, cool and hard and relieving next to how hot and sweaty the rest of me felt. I wanted to wrap my arms around him, to get rid of this nauseous feeling in my throat and stomach. I wanted to cry some more.

But fighting was easier.

Alexei didn't say nothing for a second. Then he took my pack from me, but only 'cause my fingers didn't have the strength to keep grip on it. "Sit down, Jerusalem."

"You got some nerve telling me what to do after you—"

I reached for my pack, but he grabbed my upper arms in his hands and sat me down in the grass—didn't have to force me none, since it was a miracle my legs had carried me that long. The quick movement gave me a headache and built more sickness in my stomach, but as soon as I was sitting, I couldn't deny I'd needed it.

Inside, anyway.

"Backstabbing, bloodsucking, kiss-ass coward," I growled as he dug something out of his bag. "You don't get to force me to do nothing."

Alexei placed my half-finished basket of berries in my lap and handed me a big piece of jerky. "Eat."

"Die."

He grabbed the jerky before I could throw it at him. "You're not going anywhere until you eat something."

"I hate you."

"I don't care. I'm taking care of you, whether you hate me or not."

I didn't have the strength to fight back if he held me like he did yesterday. He ignored my desire to fight him completely, wiping his cool fingers across my sweaty brow and neck. He cupped my cheek with his hand, and I rested my head against it, wanting to close my eyes and sleep all over again, even though I had too much to do for something as self-indulgent as that.

"You make me so mad sometimes," I muttered, but I didn't sound convincing.

"And you try to kill me sometimes. We're even."

I couldn't even laugh, the little strength I had waning.

Alexei looked into my eyes, at my face, tracing every feature, and his brows lowered a little, as if searching for something. Like he was reading me, without me even saying a word.

"You look sick, Tiny," he said, his voice sounding more frustrated and concerned than annoyed and challenging. "Eat something. *Please.*"

Tears veiled my vision until I blinked them away. I bit into the jerky without another word.

He stroked my cheek gently. "That's my girl," he murmured, then got up.

I ate slowly, watching him pack for our journey. Every time I finished something, he'd hand me more food, as if knowing I didn't have strength enough to grab it on my own. It was . . . sweet. Sweet like when Dess had been on her spying mission and I'd spent my nights in his tent, lying beside his cool body to beat the summer heat. He was still bossy Alexei, always wanting things his way . . . but everything he wanted had to do with my welfare.

Why in the hell was he only sweet to me like this when Dess wasn't around to pick up his slack? *Lazy-ass donkey.*

By the time I was full, our supplies was all packed, the horses ready to go.

I really had been starving. The headache, shaking, nausea— that was all gone. The only thing left was enough sense to be sad instead of angry.

But I didn't have no more time to cry.

And I sure as hell didn't have no time to argue with this infuriating dumbass.

I did suck it up and let him put me on my horse, though, 'cause Lord knew I never would've gotten on otherwise. And I watched him tie my shoes for me. But that didn't mean I was going to let him touch me for the rest of the trip.

10

ALEXEI

One year earlier

I'd just finished feeding when, a mile outside of camp, an overwhelming aroma hit me like a drug. I nearly had to land on a branch to get my bearings. What was that? *Who* was that? I'd never smelled anything so incredible in my entire life.

I pushed myself to camp faster.

I shifted back at the edge of camp and strode directly toward the smell. I'd promised the colonel I wouldn't feed on his soldiers, but this person hadn't been here an hour ago, let alone a year ago at the start of the war. So . . . that didn't count, right? I could at least sneak a little taste—a little bit of dessert never hurt anyone. And who knew when I would ever get the chance to taste something so glorious ever again.

I felt jittery with anticipation at the prospect.

But as I followed the scent, I realized it was leading me directly to *my* tent. Someone was in there with Odessa, which was . . . odd, to say the least, and only not worrisome because I knew Dess would never plant anything inside my tent that could harm me.

Still, I stopped ten feet from the entrance and called her name. She came out quickly, holding the tent flap closed behind her. "You'll never believe who found her way to our camp," she said, approaching me so she didn't have to speak so loudly. "A runaway. From a plantation."

"A runaway?

Odessa's eyes sparkled in a way I'd never seen from her before. "She's a Saint, Alexei."

My eyes *didn't* sparkle. Not even close. I'd been looking to consume something, but an innocent woman who'd been enslaved . . . with a scent like *that*? That was the last thing I needed in this camp. The last thing *she* needed. "Hasn't she been through enough without going to war?"

"It's exactly what she wants. She told me there's a particular vampire she's after."

A *particular one* was a good sign. Unless she'd been owned by one, which was the most likely scenario in the Southern states. Or, rather, vampires took on familiars who owned property, goods, land, and ran the operation as if it was rightfully theirs. I'd never met a vampire who owned something they had actually paid for.

Still, that didn't change the fact that I could practically taste her blood, even standing outside of my tent, and had to swallow to keep my mouth from watering. "She couldn't have had much opportunity to learn how to fight."

"Neither have most of the soldiers here," Dess said with a shrug. "And anyway, that makes it all the better. We can train her and avoid her picking up any bad habits."

The prospect of spending any amount of time with that woman, in close contact, both excited and terrified me.

"Can I meet her?" I asked, forcing back my enthusiasm. This was the time to see her, if any, when I was already full and could more easily control my thirst. And besides . . . I was curious. So far, I had never met a Saint with her upbringing, and her situation reminded me of my past a little.

"She's sleeping," said Dess. "And I promised her that none of the men would come near this tent."

I let out an amused sound. "It's *my* tent."

"I know, but it was the best option—she was on edge and needed a bigger space; it was a wonder she fell asleep at all. Just stay away a few hours until she wakes up, and then I'll ease her in to meeting you. Remember, she was recently the property of a vampire, so she might not take kindly to another."

Well, there went any hope of civility between us—if that was her only reference for vampires, I was probably not her ideal candidate for friendship. But that could come with time. I was content to settle with Odessa's plan, to wait until this new Saint was ready to meet me.

But I could at least see who she was, cure this curiosity my senses had created. I'd never smelled someone so incredibly . . . alluring . . . intoxicating . . . appetizing. I had to at least see what mortal could possess my senses in this way. And then I would stay away as long as I had to, until she was comfortable enough to come to me.

After all, I was a vampire. I could slip in and out, and she wouldn't even know I was there.

"Anyway," said Odessa, swiping sweat from her neck. "I'm glad you're back, because I'm starving. Maybe you could watch the tent for a few minutes?"

No one would dare go into my tent, but . . . Dess being occupied for a few minutes could do nothing but benefit me. "Of course. Go for as long as you need."

She looked at me dubiously. "Don't wake her."

"I won't."

"I know you're going to look at her, at least."

I raised my brows. "Since when don't you trust me, Odessa?"

"I trust you, but I also *know* you. And you like to cross the line without a thought to see what happens."

Did I? I never thought about it.

I held my hands up by my head in surrender. "I swear I won't wake her. Enjoy your breakfast."

Dess shook her head, as if she still didn't believe me, but walked away.

I gave her a minute after disappearing from my view before entering.

Odessa had set her up in the middle of the tent on my bed mat and pillow with a nice blanket one of the boys had gifted me. The weather should have been too hot for a blanket, and yet she sounded as if she slept deeply, the blanket moving slightly with every gentle breath, her face buried underneath.

My steps made not a sound as I walked over and crouched beside her, lifting the blanket up with two fingers. Her aroma filled my nose, and for a moment, I closed my eyes and held my breath.

You can do this, Alexei. You just fed. You have self-control. Stop acting like a silly New Blood.

I took a calming breath and opened my eyes. She wasn't . . . what I'd been expecting at all. Small framed and much younger than I'd pictured, with a desperate, determined crease in her brow even in sleep. She was a Saint, so of course there was no question of her capability, but she was so tiny and gaunt and *scarred* that I had a sharp, unexpected desire—beyond comprehension—to protect her.

I suddenly thought of my wife.

I hadn't thought of her in . . . well, multiple lifetimes, if I'd still been human. Her name escaped me, and I had only a vague remembrance of what she might have looked like—brown hair, I think. Freckles. Wait. Unless I was thinking of the Scottish girl who'd taught me English?

I chuckled to myself, not even remotely sorry for the mix-up. I'd known her so long ago, I was glad I felt no sentimentality for her now—what could I do with those feelings, anyway, with her already being three hundred years in the grave? Perhaps we'd been in love, or at least liked each other, even if I was sure it had been an arranged marriage. But she was just a long-lost remnant of my former life with a title I understood must have meant something to me once.

I did, however, remember that she had been brave and capable, much like the girl sleeping before me.

And that neither trait had made any difference when I'd torn out her throat.

I cringed and shook away the memory.

The normal thing to do would have been to replace the blanket and leave. Instead, I left her half uncovered and sat down beside her to . . . *to what, Alexei? Watch her sleep?* Maybe. I hadn't slept in so long, sometimes just seeing others rest was calming.

But the longer I watched her, the worst my thirst became. I should've left immediately. Why was I doing this to myself?

Because there was something about her, something more than her intoxicating scent, that drew me to her.

Just admit to yourself that you want to feel needed by this girl so you can leave.

I sighed, feeling like an idiot. Later. I would meet her later. When she felt safe enough to come near me. When I had thoroughly gotten over her scent—if that was even possible. *Stick with the plan, Alexei.*

I reached out to replace the blanket over her head. She shivered, and I realized too late that my cold skin had brushed her. I jerked my hand away as she shifted and opened her eyes. She blinked a few times, slow and dreamy, and I froze to regard her. She was . . . absolutely beautiful. Like an angel.

And I was the demon, pining for her blood, thirsting for her, aching to destroy her . . . like I had my wife.

I felt sick, despite knowing I wasn't a New Blood anymore. I could control myself . . . I *would* control myself, for the sake of this girl, if no one else. I would protect her from myself at all costs.

I would not be a monster.

The girl looked at me, her eyes slightly wide in awe, and as she sat up, I decided it seemed too late to make my escape.

"Good morning, Saint," I said gently. "Can I bring you anything?"

"Bring me . . . ?" She gasped, as if still stuck in a dream world. She looked me over slowly, tentatively.

I grinned. I didn't know why, but it was all very cute. "Or I could take you—"

"You come to take me?" she asked, her voice small and worried, and I felt a twinge in my stomach for her. Did she think I would take her back to that vile plantation?

"Take you for a tour around camp," I finished, giving her a

reassuring smile. "You're safe, Tiny Saint. You can stay here for as long as you wish."

But as I spoke, the girl seemed to be waking up more and more . . . and as she did, her expression dropped from confusion to realization . . . to bitter rage.

And faster than I could have ever anticipated, she snatched something from under her mat and sprang at me. I grabbed her wrist, stopping her small knife from stabbing my shoulder. I bent her wrist down and jolted it quickly enough to break her grip, and when her hand released the knife, I knocked it away. But in that time, she used her free hand to strike me in the throat.

I gasped, my throat bruised by her fist but not crushed, although attempting to talk through the pain was ineffective. I was stunned, too slow to stop her from closing her jaws on my forearm. There was no blood drawn, only crushing pressure.

She was mortal. A Saint, but human. How was she this fast?

"I'm not going to hurt you—" But I barely got the words out before she slammed her knee into my stomach.

Disengage, Alexei. You're scaring her.

But as soon as I released one wrist, I had to divert her reach from snatching my shashka from its sheath.

She let out an angry, desperate scream. "Monster!"

"Alexei!" Odessa stormed into the tent, her voice just as desperate.

I managed to shove the girl away from me as gently as I could, backing away while Odessa got between us.

"You lied to me!" The girl stumbled back, snatching up the closest thing to her, and Odessa didn't aggravate her further by following. "You said this was the Union army."

"And it is, sweet girl," Odessa said gently.

"I ain't sweet, and y'all 'bout to find out real quick if y'all don't let me out of here," she snapped, shifting her gaze between us and the only exit.

Despite her efforts to sound brave, her heart was fluttering like a hummingbird. She was terrified, and I couldn't blame her. I looked at my bite mark. She hadn't drawn blood, but it was bright red, although already fading. I should've listened to Odessa. This was the worst way possible to have been introduced.

"I'm on your side," I assured her, and Dess glared at me for responding—though rightfully so because hateful anger quickly dominated the fear in the girl's eyes.

"Like hell, bloodsucker!" She shifted her glare from me to Dess. "You his familiar?"

"Alexei," Dess said firmly, waving me out. "Go."

To that, the girl's brows rose. "Guess not."

I laughed without thinking, and the girl shifted the glare back to me, fire and brimstone in her eyes. "You ain't the first vamp I ever killed, and you sure as hell won't be the last."

I slipped out of the tent without another word, her look still burning through me.

JERUSALEM

We stopped hours later, as soon as we came across a farm, so we could swap our rides out for some fresh ones. Mortal horses was weak. I didn't like vamps, but we could've used some bloodsucking horses that didn't get worn out so quick.

"How far do you think we are from the plantation?" Alexei asked as we quickly put our saddles and bridles on some stranger's horses. It was the first thing he'd said to me since we'd left the battlefield behind. Mostly 'cause I told him to shut up every time he tried to talk, but still.

Hours later, and I still hadn't cooled off.

"Too far," I said, chewing on my lip. "Vamps don't need sleep, and they don't need to change out horses. If we want to beat Adelaide, we have to take the Underground Railroad."

"A train?"

I hated myself for letting him see me smirk—didn't want him thinking we was on good terms again. But I couldn't help it. I liked knowing something he didn't—not that he *could* know. The ones who needed it and the ones who ran it knew about the Underground—if everyone else knew, there'd be no point.

"Ain't no train," I said. "It's the road to freedom."

Alexei still looked confused, but I didn't want to explain no more inside this barn where anybody and their mama could be outside listening. Instead, I mounted my new horse and road off. We had to get off this property and back in the woods, anyhow. No time to sit around.

The farther south we went, the more people would give us trouble, even just for traveling together. No doubt about it, the Underground was the only way to cover that much ground, no harassment, no needless stops. There was no way to get in without help, and it was too easy to get lost in the swamps—the only entry point I knew of—even if you'd been there before. But a Conductor would find me. They always found wandering Black people in need of saving and freedom. And maybe, if I could find the Conductor who'd led me before, she would better understand why I had to go back and wouldn't try to stop me.

Wasn't no need to tell Alexei all that, though.

"Why can't you just tell me where we're going?" Alexei asked, catching up to me.

"'Cause I don't trust you, that's why."

He grabbed my reins, halting the both of us. The horse jerked as I tried to pull away and couldn't.

"You slowing us up, Silver Fox."

"You do trust me," he said, ignoring what I'd said. "You're holding a grudge, but last night, you trusted me."

My stomach hurt just thinking of it. "I was emotional. I would've trusted a cougar at that point."

"You don't have to pretend you don't feel things, Jerusalem. There's nothing wrong with trusting people you normally wouldn't. There's nothing wrong with caring about people, with . . . loving people."

"I don't love you," I snapped, getting down from the horse to get away from him since he wouldn't let go. "Odessa asked us to say those things as she lay dying, so I said them for her sake. But love ain't even *close* to what I feel about you."

He sighed and dismounted. "Now you're just being spiteful—"

"You think I love you just 'cause you love me? Like you own my emotions, my heart, just 'cause you want it that way? Well, let me tell you something, you privileged-ass bloodsucker. You don't get to own not one piece of me."

He seemed thrown off by my words. Frustrated. "I don't want to own you, Jerusalem. I want to be with you because I love you—"

"Well, I sure as hell don't love you." My voice breaking at the end, I backed away as he reached for me. "Matter of fact, I hate you. There's your honesty. I *hate* you, Alexei. 'Cause you left us to fight alone. You let Odessa and Gael die."

Alexei paused, as if sorting through every insult I'd laid on him. "We both know they went into that fight *wanting* to die."

I screamed and threw my spear, my mind realizing what

I done too late. But Alexei sidestepped it easily, and it shot through no less than three trees before locking itself deep into a fourth, splintering the wood where it impacted.

My heart pounded, fear shifting quickly to relief.

Alexei rested his hand on the closest tree, redirecting it so it fell against the other two instead of on us. I winced as they crashed through the trees around them, the crushing of leaves and snapping and crunching of branches far too loud before they slammed onto the forest floor.

All around, nature protested the disturbance, but neither of us spoke. The look on Alexei's face said enough—he was hurt. Betrayed. But also pissed as hell, and who could blame him when someone he was supposed to trust had almost killed him. It made me want to cry, but I couldn't, even if it was only stubborn pride stopping me.

I should've said sorry, but I was mad as a dog. And anyway, he was fine. So I scowled and shoved past him to get my spear, his cool presence sending a shiver through me that I knew good and well had nothing to do with his temperature.

"That was the wrong thing for me to say," I heard him say.

"You think?" I growled. "I done told you already that at the last second, they had a change of heart."

"But that doesn't change the fact that Odessa's wounds were untreatable."

I knew it, I did . . . but I couldn't think about it too much or I was bound to cry, so I focused on my spear buried deep in the tree. I propped my foot on the trunk and tugged, once and hard, grateful I didn't stumble back all weak-like when it yanked free. "And what about Gael? He would've gone back to the sidelines to be with Odessa. Instead, he died standing in for you while you sat in camp like a pathetic coward."

We fell quiet again.

"You *would* equate rational thought to cowardice," Alexei said finally. "You, who runs into every situation with one thought in mind, never considering your safety or the safety of others—"

"We was strong enough; we was just outnumbered."

"Yes, three Saints *would* be outnumbered by *an entire battalion.*"

"Both me and Dess told you why it was a good idea to attack," I said, approaching him with my spear, "but all you had was excuses. It's like you said, the only reason you in America is this war. You should've been there fighting with us, if only 'cause of that." He was already resting against a tree, but I shoved him into it anyway. He didn't stop me. Didn't speak. His silence burned my throat like a sob. "We needed you, Alexei, and you left us."

He moved to touch me, but I aimed my spear at his throat, halting his hand.

"*I* needed you." For a second, I couldn't go on, shocked by my own devastation. I swallowed. "I needed you beside me, and you wasn't there."

The silence between us stretched. All I could hear was my own desperate breaths, my racing heart. Slowly, Alexei moved my spear aside with a gentle push of his fingers, and I had no will to fight him on it. He leaned down and wiped my tears just as gently. I hadn't known I was crying till he touched me, as if feeling didn't exist without him. And then he kissed my forehead like he'd done last night, and I felt like I might shatter.

"You hypnotizing me?" I gasped.

"No, sweet Saint," he whispered.

"I can't move."

"Yes, you can. I'm not holding you."

But I couldn't. 'Cause I didn't rightly know what I wanted . . . except I did, and that scared me worse than anything. Only I didn't want to take or lose it. If I stepped away from Alexei now, things could stay the same, or almost. But if I took what I wanted—and deep down, I knew what I wanted—what would that make me?

A girl who kisses monsters.

Dangerous, arrogant, annoying, strong . . . beautiful . . . gentle monsters.

I twisted my grip on my spear.

Naw. Never. How could I ever want that with Alexei after what he'd done?

And, more than that—and far less petty—he was still a vampire. A white one, at that. That was never going to change.

I stepped back from him quickly, blinking away any awe or warmth I felt a second ago. "You knew how important this was to me, to be rid of the horrible monster who slaughtered my family. You knew, and you abandoned me, left me to fight alone. Gael was scared, too, but he fought anyway, gave his life to save mine. And Odessa—" I choked. There wasn't no point in saying it. "I needed you *yesterday*—not today, in the afterbirth, when I already been torn open . . . like trying to sew scraps of me together."

I blinked, and my vision blurred. Hot tears started running down my face.

"She remembered me, Lex," I whispered. "If I don't get to my brother first, she'll—"

She'll kill him. But make him suffer for God knows how long first just to spite me.

I swallowed and swiped my eyes. But now I could see Alexei, which made it all worse, his beautiful, creased brow taunting me with its promise of comfort. He didn't step closer again, just gripped his fists at his sides, in and out.

"Abandoning you was never my intention," he said, his usual confidence thinned to something more painful. "Please, know that. But Odessa had lied about where we were headed, and I . . ." He took a moment, finding his words. "I had picked this mission because I thought it would lead us *away* from the army, because there was a vampire with them I didn't want to face."

"You, Alexei?" I forced myself to stop gaping, shook my head. "Scared of a fight?"

"I still have human emotions, Jerusalem."

"I know you do," I said quickly, feeling a bit of shame creep around my stomach.

"Do you? Or am I just another monster to you?"

His words stung fresh tears into my eyes. I looked away to wipe them with the back of my hand so I wouldn't have to see his face when they cleared—how hurt he was that I could think such a thing of him.

"Not all vampires begin as familiars or lovers who want to be turned," he said bitterly. "Not all of us had a choice."

"I didn't know." I sounded stupid and small and . . . it shamed me to admit, scared. Even knowing Alexei, I was still scared of that part of him that was a monster. Scared he'd be like the others . . . that he'd lose control.

Scared I'd be forced to hate him for it.

Forced to kill him.

"I don't want you to be afraid of me," he said, like reading my mind, and I looked him in the eye to prove him wrong.

"Nothing scary about your pretty ass," I said.

He burst into laughter, laughter that turned into a pained yell as he shoved a tree clean over, root and all.

I gripped my spear but didn't move none. I'd expected him to flirt with me, like he always did. To be honest, Alexei *not* flirting was scarier to me than any outburst. Worrisome. "Who is this vamp that's got you like this, Lex?" I asked, storming over to him. I grabbed his arm, looked up into his face. "Who did this to you?"

And what you going to do with that information, huh? Prance back to the battlefield and go after a monster the most powerful vampire you ever met is afraid of?

Alexei stood quietly, just staring at his tree. He didn't react to my hand against him. That was worrisome, too. "I don't know who it is by looks. Only by smell. There was a red mask. And during our encounters, I was usually . . . restrained in some way. Unable to fight back."

I felt sick, my stomach twisting painfully like I might vomit. All I could see was his pretty face, creased in distress and fear, as he was tied up and kneeling on the ground, his body at the mercy of a monster.

The image of my sister's willowy frame, her stomach torn wide, flashed through my mind before I could dampen it.

My parents' bodies, swaying side by side from the old oak.

Odessa's terrible wound, her last breath . . .

I ground my spear into the ground, sharpening my anger.

Zamir the Mangler. Had to be. He was the only Ancient I'd seen in the army that I was sure was older than Alexei, not to mention he was a literal serial killer. Wait—that dark-haired vamp had said Alexei's name. They knew each other. It had to be.

"Follow your nose and point him out," I said. "I'll take care of it."

"Ha!" Alexei released a heavy breath and gave me an unamused look. He paced a few times before sitting on the tree he felled. "Let's get back to you being angry with me while I repent."

"Oh, no, you don't." I sat beside him. "You ain't changing the subject now."

"You know how Ancients survive to be ancient? They avoid facing enemies they know can best them. Adapt to the century they're currently living in. Lie *low*. Until they've lived long enough to become so powerful, everything ceases to be a threat to them." He shook his head, running both hands through his hair. "And if I'm caught by . . . by my maker again, there will only be two possible fates—eternal torment if I amuse her or death if she gets bored."

I . . . never thought of that. I knew it, but never thought of it 'cause who could best Alexei? Powerful, immortal, beautiful Alexei, stronger and more skilled than any vampire I ever heard of. I would never say all that to his face, but it was true. No one could match him.

"We going to figure this out," was all I said. It came out angrier than I wanted it to, but that was better than the truth—that I'd never imagined losing him before and . . . it scared me.

To be without him scared me.

"Okay," I continued. "We can figure out who it is right now, narrow them down. There was seven vamps with the army, right? And not all of them was Ancient."

Alexei looked at me as if I done said the most genius thing he ever heard. "Which ones do you know?"

"Most of them. I don't know how it is in Russia, but over here in America, vamps visit each other *constantly*. Only three of them was Ancient, that I know for sure. That's John Carter, Silas Barton—who we killed already—and Zamir the Mangler."

"That can't be right." He tugged on his hair a little, shaking his head. "We're looking for a woman."

I chewed my lip. "Only three was women, and not one was over a hundred, I can tell you that. And two of them we killed."

We both froze at once, gaping at each other.

"Naw . . ." I shook my head. "Not Adelaide. She been here since before I was born, but she ain't no Ancient. You sure your vamp is a woman?"

"Positive."

"But she don't even sound European."

"I mean, neither do I, and I've been here for far less time than she has, apparently. She's probably mimicking some sort of American accent. It would make sense if she wants to blend in."

I pressed my tongue to my lip to stop up the blood from chewing it through. I shook my head over and over. Something wasn't right. It couldn't have been her, could it?

"I could smell her and Zamir heading northward before their scents got away from me," Alexei said.

"They had Lee. They was probably headed to the stronghold."

"Good. That buys us time to save your brother."

We fell into a silence thick and full of terror.

My hands was shaking. No way in hell Adelaide was an Ancient. A vampire who had survived hundreds—maybe thousands—of years before Alexei was born . . . the same vamp who had turned Alexei, abused and scared him enough to make him run from a fight.

I wanted her dead, but how in the living hell could I measure up to that?

Alexei looked down at me, and I felt . . . helpless. Weak, not like I did after a battle but like . . . like I wanted him to hold me.

But we was both in pain, both terrified, and what would become of us if neither of us was strong enough to drag up the other?

What would become of Matthew?

He turned his eyes down, like he didn't want me to see him cry, and I suddenly had a hungry urge to kiss them eyelids, to make his tears stop. Lord . . . right then, I couldn't tell if that was worse than feeling helpless.

"We got to kill her," I said, gathering my wits. "Together, we can do it."

"I don't think we can, Tiny," he said, almost distant.

"We ain't defeated yet. Don't talk like we is."

He laughed bitterly. "Why do you never see danger?"

"I see danger. I just run at it instead of away." I glared at him as he scoffed. "I got lots on the line, Alexei. More than you, I reckon. My brother's life. My life. I only been free a year, so that, too, if she don't kill me instead. Anything you been through, I been through longer." I dragged him to me, and he caught himself on the bark beside my thigh with his other hand, bringing us all the more closer. And Lord, if I didn't lose my wits all over again, Alexei's cool lips were just short of brushing mine.

I'd meant to give him a pep talk while shaming him for not pushing through his fear, but I suddenly felt desperate . . . for revenge, for love, for comfort, for too many things I couldn't understand 'cause I ain't never had none of them.

"I lost my sister, my parents, Gael . . . Odessa," I said, focusing on my words to push away all other distractions. "I ain't losing nobody else." I nearly broke again—*helpless*—when he touched my cheek. Despite his touch, I grabbed the back of his neck like he'd leave if I didn't, like I'd die if he left. "If I have to butcher the entire Southern army to protect you, I will. You hear me? That monster ain't taking you away from me."

"Heroic little Saint. You shame me with your courage."

"Good."

"As you should. Knock some sense into me."

"You leave me again, and I kill you."

He chuckled. "I'm not leaving. It's you and me, Tiny. Until the end of us."

I pressed my forehead to his. I wanted to rest, to disappear, to not have to deal with everything that was coming. I wanted it to all be taken care of with a snap of my fingers. And for just that moment, I imagined a life that wasn't so cruel, where I didn't have to fight for everything I wanted and needed. Where my brother was safe . . . where maybe Alexei and I could—

"Jerusalem," he murmured, his voice soothing me.

"Hmm?" I answered.

"I . . . I have to tell you something."

Something about the way he said it made me brace myself. Like he was fittin' to throw me away. But I didn't want to think about nothing too hard 'cause the truth of it all was much different than I wanted it to be.

I just wanted to rest here and think of nothing.

His hand hesitated at my cheek, and then he got up abruptly. It was strange how empty the space felt without him.

"Why you so nervous?" I asked, watching him pace in circles. "Not another secret."

He stopped a few yards in front of me and laced his fingers behind his neck. "This one's a little more difficult than the last."

I stared at him for a moment. "Alexei, what in the hell could be worse than everything we went through over the past day?"

"I'm a vampire," he said quickly. "And I drink human blood."

A grin pulled at the corner of my lips. But I figured that wasn't the point he was trying to make, so I stayed quiet.

"But it doesn't mean I would ever view you as a meal," he went on. "And not all blood smells or tastes the same to me."

There it was.

"Like how I don't like mushrooms," I said. "Some people is delicious and some ain't."

"Yes, exactly."

"So what you saying is I stink."

He laughed and then bent over, resting his hands on his thighs, head down, like he was trying to catch his breath. Like he was going to be sick.

Part of me hated this confession. I hated the idea of being somehow gross to him . . . 'cause I was unappealing to so many white people for other reasons, and it hurt that Alexei could like me in every way except this wild card. I wasn't real vain, wasn't real concerned with what people thought. But I had been so sure that when he said he loved me, he meant as more than a friend. But how could he if he couldn't even stand the smell of me?

Still . . . there was no changing the facts. And besides, it could've been worse.

"That ain't nothing to stress over, Lex." I got up and went to him, rubbed his back. "I know you drink blood. I appreciate you go off and do it where I can't see, but I know you got to drink it. And if I smell like rotten eggs and moldy meat to you, well, that can only be a good thing, can't it? At least you don't want to eat me or nothing."

He groaned, which worried me a little. I kept at rubbing his back. "You going to throw up?" I teased. "You ain't going to hurt my feelings, you know. And I can steal Millie's real expensive perfume when we get there to cover up my smell. Okay? Don't even worry about it."

Alexei huffed but stood upright again and nodded. "All right."

"Now come on," I said, walking toward my horse, "we got to save my brother before a pair of vamps get there first."

"You are human and need rest. Next town we come across, we're getting a room."

I curled my lip, and not even on purpose. Just the thought of having to enter a Southern town for the first time in a year, where everyone and they mama would sooner kick me than look my way, made me want to murder the world. "Rather sleep in the dirt."

"When's the last time you slept in a real bed?"

His question shocked me a little. Ain't nobody ever asked me that before; ain't nobody really cared about my comfort. "Depends on what you mean by 'real.'"

"That's it. We're finding an inn with a giant bed."

I scoffed. "You done lost your mind, Silver Fox. They ain't letting my Black ass use no bed meant for white folks."

"I'm white folks. And if you're with me, what business is it of theirs?"

I didn't know whether to smirk at his enthusiasm or punch him in the face for his stupidity. "You got inn money?"

"Vampires don't need money. We just have to hypnotize the right people."

"So you steal."

Alexei opened his mouth and hesitated, lowering his brows. "I never thought of it like that. I mean . . . I suppose. Technically."

I busted out laughing. "'Technically' my ass. You're a thief."

He grinned slowly. "Would you rather I didn't?"

"Naw, let's steal. Reparations." I headed off, and Alexei followed, catching up.

For a while, we rode in silence, but this time it wasn't full of anger. It was almost peaceful.

"I got a question, though," I finally said. "Odessa ... they didn't put her in no mass grave, did they?"

"She'd requested to be cremated ..." He looked like he wanted to say more, but gave a small, half-hearted shrug. "We'd worked out the arrangement nearly at the start of the war."

"Cremated?" It was a relief. Kept her body out of the heat and grubby hands from stealing valuables off her. But despite everything, I felt the slightest smile touch my lips. "You did that yourself?"

"Everyone else was busy," he said, gesturing behind us to the literal war.

"Ain't vamps scared of fire?"

"I don't want to talk about it."

I laughed full out, and he gave me a pretty scowl that slowly turned to a grin.

"It's nice to hear you laugh," he said.

It was my turn to scowl, and I kicked my horse forward so Alexei wouldn't see when it turned into a smile.

11

ALEXEI

Russia
Late 1500s

*P*erhaps I'll behave and stop at seven this time," I heard Zamir's voice say through the haze of my thirst.

"Seven?" asked Red Mask casually.

"Victims."

"Oh, Zamir, must you? Every time you indulge in serial killing, I worry we'll have to relocate."

"We live deep enough in the forest for it not to be an issue. And I'll keep to Moscow—they won't think to search the countryside if all the kills are city bound. You have your hobby; allow me mine."

"I select pets from small villages and leave no trace of their existence behind. You leave a trail of mangled bodies for the authorities to find."

"Yes, my love. That's what makes it fun."

I stood, chained to the wall, swaying on my feet as my mind shifted quickly in and out of consciousness. It was a wonder I'd heard their conversation at all with the senseless growl rumbling in my chest and head. I hadn't had blood in . . . three days? Four? My room was windowless, so I couldn't tell, and in my state, I'd ceased being able to process much of anything.

It was a hard thing for a New Blood, waiting to eat. But Red Mask liked me violent when she needed me to be, and keeping me thirsty ensured that. It was part of the grooming process . . . or the amusement, it seemed, sometimes. I was being used for something . . . or made into something. I still wasn't sure what.

But for the past ten minutes, I'd been smelling live blood, and it was close. A hallucination, surely, from such intense thirst. Movement, too, at the end of the room that could not possibly be real. Red Mask stayed out of my eyeline on purpose during these starvation sessions.

But there *was* movement, and it smelled *alive*, its scent practically stinging my nose, making my mouth water. I had to get to it. And suddenly, it looked like her. Red Mask. There was nothing satisfying about feeding on vampire blood—I knew because I'd tried to drink my own more than once. I needed it alive and beating. But my starvation had been taken too far, and my urge to kill wasn't backing down. After I spilled her blood, I would be free to find something else.

Maybe I couldn't break the chains, but I pulled against my shackles, dislocating and breaking bones in my hands until they were able to slip out. And I wasted no time in springing forward.

As if waking from a nightmare, sense suddenly returned to me . . . but with it a disgusting taste saturating my tongue and throat, and a roiling in my stomach. I dropped two bloody, torn halves of something furry on the ground, barely recognizing it as a rabbit before I gagged then vomited up a bucket's worth of blood.

Animal blood was vile, but somehow rabbits were one of the worst. Such a small creature to have such bitter and overly acidic tasting blood at the same time.

Somewhere behind me, Red Mask laughed.

That's why she gave it to you, I thought bitterly. *She hates you. She wants you to suffer.*

With most of what I'd just drunk coming back up, a bit of my thirst madness returned, my head throbbing and a growl growing at the back of my throat. Or maybe it wasn't madness . . . because I knew exactly what I was thinking as I gripped my blood-slicked fists. I had no clean hands to wipe my eyes, so I blinked at my tears until I could see. Then I glanced over, only moving my eyes so not to draw attention, at where Red Mask sat in her big bear-skin chair. She had ceased to find me amusing and was absorbed in a book, back facing me.

She was rarely in the same room as me when I wasn't chained. I doubted this opportunity would present itself again—her throat in my hands. The way she and Zamir talked, it seemed I should have enjoyed the idea of torturing her, but I had no desire to linger over it. I wanted to kill her quickly. I would tear her apart the way I'd torn that rabbit, bones and all. Head separated from her body so she would never be able to torture me again.

I blinked hard to press my vision clear and pushed myself away from the wall. But I didn't take more than three strides toward my prey before Zamir stepped in my way and in one swift movement took the back of my neck in hand and began wiping my bloody mouth with a cloth.

"Are you all right, Alexei?" he asked tenderly.

How can you ask me that?

But I didn't say anything because what could be done about it? He set to wiping my hands and fittin' my joints and bones back into place to better heal while I leaned my chin on his shoulder to watch my prey continue to read.

You can still do it, Alexei. When Zamir is no longer touching you, so he can't hold you back . . .

Zamir took my chin in his hand to look me over. "Come, you need fresh air. We'll hunt down some real prey, just you and I."

My prey is sitting in a bearskin chair. My prey chained me, starved me, and forced me to eat something vile.

But as Zamir led me away, I realized that wanting to kill someone and actually killing them were two different beasts. That the relief I felt at leaving the room she sat in was stronger than any urge to get close enough to kill her. I hated her, but she . . . terrified me. Getting close enough to kill her also meant I was close enough for her to hurt me.

I was grateful when we left the room, when we made it downstairs, when he swung the heavy front door wide open and a savage wind nearly blew it closed again. Snow had piled two feet high since the last time I'd been outside, and there was no sign of it stopping—the wind howled, swirling large, soft flakes across the dark sky. I wanted to lie in the snow and get lost, forget everything. But my stomach was too angry for that.

So I followed Zamir into the night, flying farther and farther from that wretched mansion into the only degree of freedom I'd ever known—hunting.

We flew until I followed him to a thick tree bough, shifting back into our human forms. He sat, and I followed his lead, as always.

"I don't smell anything," I said.

"They're coming," he assured me, and patted my back. "Your range will increase over time."

We sat in silence for a moment.

"What does she want with me?" I asked, as I had asked almost every night for the past two months since being turned.

Usually, I asked first thing in the morning and again late at night, only to be met by Red Mask's laughter or Zamir's silence. Usually, I didn't have sense enough through my thirst to ask while hunting. But that night, Zamir actually looked at me. His body appeared only a handful of years older than mine, but in his dark eyes were centuries of captured pain, of having seen the worst of humanity.

"Keep asking," he murmured, and if I had still been human, I would've never heard him over the howling snow. "Keep fighting. Your stubbornness to accept your fate is why you're still alive."

"But why?" I was nearly growling, my thirst combined with my frustration threatening to push me over the edge. "I'm a vampire, just like the both of you."

"Only to create more of a challenge. That is what she wants."

"Stop skirting my questions, Zamir. What does she really want with me?"

"People are always seeking a reason . . ." He fell silent for a moment. "It feels better to say we subjugate people because they are lesser, because they deserve it. The truth is, reasons are fabricated to bring law and order, justification. You either want to do something or don't. You like or dislike. Reasons are just excuses. Embellishments."

"We hunt at night for a reason," I countered. "So the sun doesn't irritate our skin."

"We could cover up and hunt during the day. We hunt at night because we like to."

I paused, staring at him. "So I'm being kept against my will—?"

"Against your will? You would leave me if given the chance, my *misiu?*"

"Not you, Zamir. Never." I felt my heart swell as he held my chin with a fond grin before looking back out into the swirling snow. "But do we have to stay here . . . with her?"

"She enjoys you."

"Enjoys *torturing* me."

"Not torturing. Subjugating."

"Why?"

"Because she wants to." He patted my cheek, a gesture I'd grown as used to as dread. "You smell your dinner?"

Whomever it was didn't smell overwhelmingly appetizing, but my body was on edge from thirst, and anything was better than that rabbit.

He stood up on the thick bough and pointed his chin toward the distance. "Go feed, boy. I'll be right behind you."

It was deep night by the time we made it to an inn. Dark enough not to make trouble for us—not that I couldn't easily dispatch trouble. But Jerusalem needed rest, and the last thing I wanted was to draw negative attention and prohibit that. Which was why I went in first and hypnotized the innkeeper while Tiny snatched the key to the biggest suite she could find and hurried up to hide in the darkness of the stairs.

"Don't look, Tiny," I said, before feeding on the innkeeper's wrist. I wasn't taking any risks tonight.

I caught up to her in the middle of the stairwell, looking at the hand she held behind her, reaching back toward me. I took her hand, wondering for an instant if that was what she meant, if she would shake me off . . . but she didn't. We held hands in the dark, a moment of forbidden magic, as I felt her pulse sprint through her fingers, warm and welcoming. But the magic was cut short when we reached the dim hall and she raced ahead of me to unlock the door to our room.

Still, my hands hummed with the sensation of her warm skin.

When I entered the room, she was sitting on the bed with her spear balanced across her lap.

"Didn't want nobody to spot me out there," she said as I locked the door. "I mean, after you went through the whole trouble of hypnotizing the innkeeper."

I could sense her warm pulse, just as quick as when we'd touched in the stairwell, and grinned. "Makes sense."

She raised a brow at me. "What you smiling about?"

"Nothing."

"There's a joke, and I missed it."

I knelt in front of her, unlacing her shoes. "You're cute, is all."

Her skin radiated heat, all that hot blood rushing close to the surface, as beautiful as it was unbearable. "How about I cave your head in? That won't be so cute."

"I have to say, you're not helping your case *at all*."

Her smile was like a sunrise. She looked away, thinking she could hide her blush, and I wanted to take that warm body into my arms so badly my muscles hurt from fighting back.

"How did I attract the craziest white boy in the Union army?" she mumbled.

"I wouldn't say crazy."

"I would."

"Obsessed, maybe."

"That ain't no better. You know that, right?" As she stood, I felt her slender fingers slide along my scalp through my hair. I closed my eyes, just barely holding in a sound of pleasure at the back of my throat. Her fingers stopped abruptly, tensing. "Think I'll draw a bath," she said, rushing away.

It took everything in me not to go after her.

"Take your time," I said instead, clearing my throat. I heard the door to the washroom shut and promptly pressed my face into the bed, gripping the comforter, and silently screamed. She'd slept in my tent before, plenty of times. I'd survived those nights. This would be no different. But . . . her fingers through my hair . . . my one true weakness. And was I going mad, or did she smell abnormally good tonight? Maybe it was because I wanted so badly to kiss her.

You want to do more than kiss her, Alexei.

"Down, boy," I murmured to the blanket. "Don't scare her away."

I went to the window and opened it to air out the room, then sat on the bed to remove my boots. Nudity in itself wasn't necessarily sexual, but I kept my clothes on so she wouldn't think I had any ideas. But I was probably the only one thinking that. I was paranoid—I'd shared a sleeping space with her before; this shouldn't have been any different. Either way . . . better safe than sorry.

I lay back on the bed, feet still planted on the floor, until I heard the door and leaned up on my elbows. She walked out in nothing but her undershirt . . . *my* undershirt. Did she always look that good in it, or were nerves making my stomach ache on top of my body's normal reaction to seeing the girl I loved?

Why are you nervous at all, Alexei?

"That soap's real nice," she said, using her spear like a walking staff and carrying the soap wrapped in a small towel. "Got flower petals in it."

"Smells like lavender." Repulsive. It covered her scent enough to annoy me. *It's better this way, Alexei.* "That should help you sleep."

But she didn't look tired as she leaned her beloved spear against the wall and stowed the soap in her pack before sitting and facing me on the bed. Everything about the entire sequence made me grin.

"We should leave early tomorrow," she said, "before too many people wake up."

"That's nice to see," I said instead of answering.

"What is?"

"Never mind." I shrugged. "If I say it, you'll stop."

"What is?" she snapped, throwing a pillow at me.

I caught it easily—it was clear she hadn't even tried—and shrugged. "I think I'll enjoy it for a little longer."

"Alexei!" She patted herself all over, as if checking to make sure her hair or clothes weren't embarrassing her. "You best spit it out before I send this bed post at you next."

"Your spear. No, don't go get it." I sighed, as she slid off the bed to do just that. "You usually have it right beside you, but this time, you put it all the way in the corner. Am I to take that as a gesture of trust?"

"Wishful thinking, Silver Fox." She sat on the bed again, setting her spear beside her. "You want to bathe now?"

"Should I?" I sniffed my armpit. "If you want me to."

"Not really. You smell like blood and outside."

"U-um—" I raised my brows. "That's a good thing?"

I might've sounded too shocked, because she dropped her gaze to her lap, embarrassed. "Like shortbread, too," she murmured. "Your skin always be smelling like shortbread cookies."

I felt my mouth twitch into a grin. "I've never had those. Are they good?"

"Real good. I ain't had one in a minute. Not since Mama sneaked some she baked at the big house a couple years ago."

The shift in her mood was palpable. Reflective. Sad. This poor girl . . . I knew this pain all too well. The pain of never being able to forget, never being able to rest because of it.

I wanted, more than anything, to ease that pain.

I reached my hand toward her. "Here, have a taste."

She laughed, smacking my hand away. "Lex!"

"You bite me all the time, anyway."

"Boy, you so stupid."

I *was* stupid, torturing myself like this. I had to grip the blanket again to keep from pulling her into my lap. *You smell good, too,* I wanted to say. *Like heaven.* But she was so content, so relaxed. The last thing I wanted was to ruin her peace.

There was time. When her brother was safe, when I helped her rid the world of her enemies. There would be plenty of time.

And perhaps by then, she wouldn't hate me quite so much for it like she would now.

"I'll let you sleep," I said, getting up. I couldn't take much more of her warm body so close to me before I lost all control of myself.

"I ain't really tired, yet," she said, hugging her pillow. "Maybe we could stay up and talk a while?"

I didn't have any body heat, yet my gut felt unusually warm. "All right, but lie down. That way I can talk you to sleep."

She didn't argue, just plopped down onto her side, hugging the pillow.

"Killed a man on a bed this big once," she said.

"Oh?" I sat down again. "Do tell."

"The man who used to own me," she said, a phrase that made me want to kill someone myself. "I woke him up in the middle of the night just to strangle his ass to death."

"Well deserved."

"Wasn't so good for my family, though. She curled up a bit in the fetal position. "I only fought Adelaide for a little bit back on the battlefield. You know much about her strengths? Weaknesses? All I know is silver don't seem to affect her."

At the mention of my captor, my muscles tightened uncomfortably, and I tried to force the feeling away with a laugh. "Do you know how to talk about something other than killing?"

She shrugged. "That's all I'm good at."

"Not true."

"I mean, maybe. But my mama told me to perfect a skill, and this is it." She paused, her eyes going distant as if thinking too deeply, and then she blinked and looked at me, determined. "And besides, we got to talk about our strategy sometime, might as well be now."

I swallowed, looked away. "Same as any other vampire, I imagine."

"Can't be. Or else how could she survive so long?"

"There are many ancient vampires all over the world; you just never see them." I didn't want to think about it too much, even though I didn't have much of a choice. "She's powerful and careful where it counts. And she has Zamir."

"Her hired muscle?"

"Her lover. That's what he claimed, anyway."

"Hmm. So we might have to take care of him first."

"We may not have to. He can be reasoned with."

Tiny raised her brows at me. "Right, they called him *the Mangler* 'cause he's so great at *talking things through*."

"He'll listen to me. He always did, back when—"

I hesitated, on the edge of words.

"He knew your name. On the battlefield." Jerusalem's small voice filled the silence, the threat of violence against anyone who might hurt me like a balm. "He was there with Adelaide back then, too, wasn't he."

"Yes. He would comfort me after . . ." I didn't even want to think about the horrifying moments, so I shook my head. "After. He was my friend, my mentor. He taught me how to be a proper vampire. And, in the end, he saved me."

"Saved you?"

"He arranged a carriage to sneak me from the house."

"But he abused you first?"

I cringed at her words. "No. Never."

"He let Adelaide do it, though. And now he's with her causing havoc, so clearly he ain't reformed none. One good act in the middle of all that evil don't mean nothing."

I paused, taking in her words, feeling more and more uncomfortable. "I'm not disregarding your experience, Tiny, but *evil's* a strong word. Nothing he did felt evil." *Oh no, Alexei? He mutilated people for fun.* "At least in regard to me," I added.

"Naw, it wouldn't next to what Adelaide was up to."

I felt my whole body freeze up. I must have known that . . . I *must have*, deep down, even if I'd never thought about it. "He was good to me. And . . . well, he'd tell me what to do, but not in a cruel way. I obeyed because I trusted him. None of it felt wrong."

"He was using you just as much as Adelaide. He made you believe he was your only escape from a monster. That maybe he wasn't perfect, but at least he wasn't *her*." She wrung her hands slowly, like trying to tear them apart. "That's what I thought with Garfield. He spoke gentle. Was never mean. Better working conditions in his house. My baby sister would be safe with him, right? Until she wasn't. She never was. Evil don't have to be outright to still be evil."

We were quiet for a long moment.

"The messenger you killed the other day," I said. "He's the one who killed your sister?"

She started to shake her head, then stopped abruptly. "Too much of an overcooked asparagus to do it himself. But he sure as hell stood by and let it happen in his home."

I reached out and caressed Tiny's cheek. I wanted to pull her into my arms, but there was a volatile energy in the way she glared at the bed. Killing that man hadn't healed her, would never bring her sister back, and she knew that all too well.

But her words didn't only stab me in the gut because of her pain.

It felt like a reflection of my own.

Because I finally understood. Zamir had always told me people did things because they wanted to, no reason required. Reasons were excuses. Not real.

So . . . so he had . . .

I swallowed. By his logic, he'd let Red Mask—Adelaide—hurt me because he wanted to.

He'd wanted me to rely on him, and him alone.

"Lex?" Tiny crawled closer to me. "You okay?"

"Are you?"

"I asked you first."

I smiled at her insistence. "Sorry, I just . . ." I paused to order my thoughts. "I feel really stupid."

"You ain't stupid."

"I idolized the man. And hundreds of years later, I'm just now putting together that our relationship was abuse. I am beyond stupid, Jerusalem."

She took my jaw in her hands and shushed me. "It's his fault, not yours. He was older and wiser. He knew what he was doing."

"I don't . . ." I didn't know what I was feeling, so couldn't find words to match. "I don't want to think about it anymore."

"Hoarding thoughts away is how you end up like me—bitter and vengeful."

I laughed—or at least I thought I did, but a second later, it felt more like a choking sob. Jerusalem moved my head to rest on her shoulder, wrapping her arms around me as best she could.

Why was I crying? Tiny had been enslaved her entire life. I'd only been captured for five months out of 3,600. And I hadn't even seen Zamir in that time of freedom . . . I should have been over it by now. This shouldn't have hurt as badly as it did.

"Pull it together," I muttered to myself. "You're three centuries old."

"You still eighteen, Lex," she whispered, and I pressed her warm body closer to me. "Go on and cry."

So I did. I could feel stupid about it later. Jerusalem ran her fingers over my scalp, through my hair, soothing away these unknown, unwanted feelings from the past.

This was a side of her I rarely saw. Nurturing. Openly loving. I didn't hold this side of her above any of the hate and temper because they all came together to form the girl I loved. But it was also a side of her I greedily savored . . . and maybe that was why she didn't show it as much as the rest. Maybe I was the one who scared her from it by returning it so ardently.

And I was doing it again. She was so beautiful, and her hands felt so good. She smelled like heaven, like sin. Like everything I could ever want. I cradled the back of her neck and leaned in close, inhaling, instantly light-headed. All I could hear was her heart, loud and rhythmic . . . pumping blood quickly, oh so quickly through the pulsing artery in her throat—

"Lex." She gasped with a small terror that made me immediately freeze.

I glanced down to where I'd grabbed both her wrists without even knowing it, preventing her from taking up her spear with one hand and possibly striking me with the other.

She trembled against me. Terrified. It made me sick to my stomach, and yet I had to actively force back the urge to give in to the hot thrum of her blood.

There was no denying it. As much as I swore I was in control of myself, I had almost bitten the girl I loved. Just like back in the war tent—as much as I wanted to deny what happened that day. To be bitten in the neck was nothing but crushing, sharp, digging pain, and I hadn't even thought twice about forcing that onto her. Even to bite gently was pain I never wanted to put her through. Hypnosis was the only way to avoid it, at least during the ordeal.

Get yourself together, Alexei.

But her blood flows like silk—

"What was *that*?" Tiny snapped, her fear shifting to justifiable anger.

"Sorry," I said quickly. I let go of her wrists, dropping my hands to grip the comforter—wrongly named in this moment—and moved my face away from her neck so all I could smell was that vile flower.

"You still thirsty after eating the innkeeper?"

"No." *That beautiful throat . . .* "Sorry."

"Then why—?" She swallowed the rest of that sentence as hot blood bloomed against her skin, singing to me, even with the lavender veiling it. Making my desire so much worse.

And I had never been more relieved than in that moment.

She's blushing. She thinks you were going to kiss her.

But I couldn't tell if she was embarrassed by that or wanted me to. She was normally so vocal about things—or, if not vocal, physical. But this silence . . . it was frightening.

"Thanks for letting me cry," I said because I was sure we *both* needed a change in subject, and I needed to think of anything other than her throat and her lips and her—

"How are you so wise, Pocket Saint, after only eighteen years on this earth?"

I could feel her heart racing against me, wild and electric, her lips close enough to kiss with only the slightest movement. I wanted to taste those lips so badly, it hurt, and not in the thirst kind of way. It almost seemed as though she'd let me, her breath unsteady and warm against my face.

"'Cause I don't trust nobody." She broke away, my need for her only increasing to unbridled proportions as she sat cross-legged to face me. "So I don't fall for nothing."

And suddenly, what she said felt like it could have been personal . . . could have been aimed at me. "You can trust me, you know. You can always trust me."

Can she, Alexei?

"I do, for the most part," she said, "But you can't really trust nobody all the way."

I wanted to take her into my arms and kiss away the hurt in her expression. Instead, I shrugged and ran my fingers through my hair, but really all it did was remind me I wasn't touching her. "I suppose it's a vast improvement from when we first met."

"Well, you're white and a vampire. What did you expect?"

"Not for you to try staking me at first sight."

"Not at first sight," she said, and I felt her pulse pump hot blood toward her face. "I didn't know you was a vamp at first. Thought maybe I was dying . . . that you was an angel come to take me."

It was so funny; I'd thought the same thing about her the first time I ever saw her. My angel come to earth.

But she avoided me, looking at her lap instead, and I felt my muscles tighten with an urge to hug her.

"But angels ain't even white," she muttered, "so don't know what I was thinking."

"Are you anxious about what just happened?" I asked.

"Ain't anxious."

"I can hear your heart, Jerusalem. And you bathed, yet I can smell you sweating."

"It's hot in here."

"Tell me what's wrong."

"Why don't you keep your nose to yourself?" she snapped.

I grabbed her muscular thighs and pulled her toward me still cross-legged, shocked to see her tug her shirt down and press the hem between her legs. I paused, watching. And suddenly *I* was the anxious one, shame of myself and fear for my tiny one warping my thoughts. "Did I do something between when we went swimming and now to make you feel ashamed of your body?"

"You know what you did," she said, her voice sounding at the edge of tears.

I paused, hands shaking. "Tell you I love you?"

We were quiet for a moment.

"It's different between us." She shifted awkwardly, looking away. "My body . . . means something different."

"Not to me." I lifted her chin gently, my body vibrating with the need to comfort her. "I don't think you realize how much of this past year I've spent loving you."

She looked at me, melting me with those razor brown eyes. "Dess said it, you know. She kept telling me. I never wanted to believe her."

"Why?"

"'Cause you annoying as all hell."

I gave her my most innocent smile. "Part of my charm?"

She pursed her lips and shoved my hand away from her chin. "Naw."

We laughed. It was a good sign. That at least she wasn't completely uncomfortable with me, even after what I'd done. That at least I could pass the night normally, knowing she didn't hate me, even if she . . . even if she didn't love me.

JERUSALEM

We *was* different. *I* was different.

But how could I tell him it wasn't his confession in front of Dess that had changed things?

It was all the looks and playful touches and shared laughs

and fights and tears. It was how he'd taken care of me after our brawl, how he'd cradled me . . . comforted me. It was his confession about Adelaide, and how protective I'd felt of him, a feeling I'd never had for nobody but my family. It was that I felt safe enough to sleep beside him, despite everything he was. That we knew every little quirk about each other, enough to push each other's buttons.

Gael had been right—love was a slow, creeping thing. And I could admit it even if I didn't know how long I'd been feeling it. My thoughts, my feelings . . . my *wants* had changed. I used to thrive off compliments from the great warrior Alexei, now I wanted him to see my body as more than just powerful. And, worst of all, I wanted his strong hands to touch me . . . to show their skill in something other than bloodshed.

But maybe all of this was stupid. He was a vampire. Nothing was going to come of these dizzy feelings, anyways.

I didn't want to bury them again . . . but maybe it was better if I did.

"Reckon I ought to sleep," I said, clearing my throat. "We got to leave early, and I don't want to slow us down."

Alexei nodded, pausing to look at the comforter thoughtfully before standing. "Time to put the weapon away, then."

"I got to have my spear," I said, gripping it to my chest.

He grabbed it, but I wasn't about to let go. He lifted me up with the spear, my hands still gripping it, my knees tucked up so I wasn't touching the bed. A shocked laugh poured out of me, and suddenly I was giggling. Like when I used to grab Pa's arm when I was little and he swung me, except not like that *at all*.

'Cause even though Alexei was hundreds of years old, I didn't think of no father when I looked at him.

His brows creased, as if he didn't know what to make of me.

And then, a slow grin pulled at his lips, as dangerous as it was beautiful.

Lord. That would've been enough, but his shoulders were strong as hell to hold me with an outstretched arm and no wavering. I probably weighed half what he did, and he had enhanced strength anyway, but *good God Almighty*. On top of his open confession a minute ago, this was too much. My body's reaction was visceral, my last brain cell evaporating into the night.

I ain't attracted to this. I ain't attracted to this. I ain't attracted to this—

Aw, hell. I was attracted to this.

Alexei lowered me toward the bed and lifted me up again, knocking another laugh from me.

"Lex!"

"Having fun?"

"Put me down You want them white folks to hear me laughing and find out you snuck me in here?"

"Let go of the spear, you tiny menace."

"I don't tire easy; you going be waiting around for me to let go till tomorrow."

He let out a breath of laughter. And then his blue eyes wandered over my face, drinking me in, and I felt my muscles tighten with each passing second. "Your joy is so beautiful," he finally murmured.

I dropped my knees to the bed almost too quick to land right, letting go of the shaft like it was made of fire. It wasn't so much what he said as much as *how*. Like the words came from deep inside him. Like it was the truest thing he could've ever said.

So when he begged, "Don't run," I felt a twinge in my stomach. That I could deny myself to someone who knew me so well, over and over, day after day. Who could be so sweet to me still, knowing I might never stop running like a fool.

He leaned down on the bed, his fist still holding my spear, his other hand stroking my chin like he was cradling a delicate petal before sliding it across my jaw, matching my usual deliberate energy as he grabbed the back of my neck. My heart slammed inside me, desperate to get to him. My whole body felt like an overpacked furnace, burning something wild.

I sat up on my knees, pulling him by his shirt the rest of the way to my lips . . . and *my* God, even then he wouldn't give me what I wanted, our lips brushing, flirting without satisfaction.

"If I could put you at ease like that every day of your life . . ." he murmured.

"Just kiss me," I said.

And when I tell you the boy could *kiss* . . .

He kissed me slowly, hungrily, till I felt tears prick at the backs of my eyes and my insides burn like a wildfire. His kiss was addictive. Dangerous. Exactly how one would think a vampire's kiss should feel, and yet fear was the last thing on my mind.

I grabbed his shirt, but he dragged it over his head before I could tear it off him. And then my back hit the mattress, and I wanted more of his weight on me than he was allowing.

"Squish me," I commanded, trying to drag his body down, and he burst out laughing, his reaction making me laugh, too. "Was that weird?"

"No, I loved it," he said, and he'd barely finished speaking before he was back to kissing me, letting his weight settle on me like I wanted. I didn't even think about the fact I was kissing a *vampire* with *fangs*, and wasn't that a hazard? Until—

I felt the chill of his lips against my neck. Earlier, he hadn't made contact, and I'd wrongly anticipated he'd bite me. But feeling him now, it should have felt good. Yet I froze in a cold panic, my mind racing through images of bony fingers stretching my neck, steel-cold nasty lips ready to violate my flesh, ready to sink in and take me alive—

"No!" I shoved Alexei in the chest and swung at him, but Alexei caught my hand and backed away. I went after him, shoving him, his back slamming into the headboard, but he caught my hands in his as I went to hit him again, and—

And suddenly, all I could see was red hair, glowing predator eyes, torn lips and fangs about to tear through me—

"You *was* going to bite me before," I whimpered, my breaths coming out in panicked huffs.

"Jerusalem, I would never—"

"Then don't go near my throat, you bloodsucking monster!"

Alexei let go of me, and as soon as my hand was free, I slammed him across the face with the heel of it, shame overtaking me the moment I did. He didn't move, his hands held up near his shoulders in surrender.

"Oh God, Alexei, I—" I trembled where I sat in his lap, my face burning hotter with shame with each passing second. "I'm sorry."

Alexei shushed me gently, shook his head. "It's all right."

"It ain't." He closed his eyes as I touched his cheekbone with trembling fingers. "What's wrong with me? I can't stop hurting you."

"You didn't even break anything. I swear I'm fine." He watched me, as if looking for signs that I was all right. Meanwhile, he was the one with a bruise growing, even if it would go away any minute. "Are *you*?"

"Yes," I said quickly. The room was dead quiet. Even the lantern knew good and well I was lying through my teeth.

"I'm sorry," he said.

"Don't keep saying that. You ain't the one in the wrong here."

"You were protecting yourself."

His insistence was annoying, even if it wasn't nothing new. "You ain't got to be right all the time, Silver Fox."

"But I am, usually," he said with a careless shrug.

"Quit being a pain in the ass and accept my apology."

He let out a breath of laughter. "Okay. I forgive you."

"Good. Okay. Um . . ." I needed to get off his lap, but the coolness of his body was helping my hot nerves. His hands were beside him, and I wish they was on me. *What in the hell you doing, Jerusalem?*

I'd just kissed Alexei. Lord. I sure enough did, and I couldn't begin to understand how I felt about it, so I picked anger. "You usually block my attacks."

"I thought touching you too deliberately would . . . frighten you."

"And I hit you anyway," I said curtly, feeling petty and awful when all I wanted was for him to kiss me again—*Lord, no! Not Alexei. How can you want a vampire kissing you? And a white boy, at that.* "Next time, block."

"Yes, ma'am," he said with an amused grin that made a vein in my temple tic.

"I'm fittin' to hit you again."

"Your wooing tactics are strange, indeed, Tiny Saint."

My face burned, his smile forcing my gaze away from his quickly. "I can't stand you."

I felt his cool hands play with the fabric at my waist and faked clearing my throat so I could hide that my breath didn't want to keep at a level pace.

"Why do you say things like that," he asked, "when you really want to say the opposite?"

"What makes you think I want to say the opposite?" I bit back, forgetting my face was blazing hot enough to give me a headache.

"Because you love me."

"Arrogant ass."

He held my chin so I'd look at him, and for some reason, I didn't fight it. "You love me, and you're afraid to admit it. Why?"

"You don't get to demand answers."

"I am *asking* you, Jerusalem."

I wasn't *trying* to be avoidant, but just then, I saw the small cut on Alexei's shoulder. It looked raw, as if it had just now been inflicted, the skin around it pink. Softly, I touched the pad of my finger against it, guilt filling my stomach painfully. I'd done that to him. It was small, but it wasn't never going to heal. I'd been so mad at him. Mad enough to *hurt* him. How could I hurt someone I cared about so much? How could I have been so swept up by my anger?

But that forever-wound reminded me of why I couldn't answer his question. Couldn't say I loved him, even if . . . even if I did feel things.

"Odessa said I should judge people by who they are, not what," I said quietly. "But all my life, vampires have been my enemies. My tormentors. It's hard to separate those traits from the person . . . see them as anything but monsters."

"Even me?" Alexei asked, and if you could hear a broken heart, it was his voice. "After everything we've been through, you still don't trust me?"

"I want to." I gasped and immediately bit my tongue, shutting myself up. Too vulnerable. Too needy. I couldn't show myself to him this way. I couldn't let him know my weakness like I knew his. Couldn't give him nothing to use against me.

He loves you, Jerusalem. He ain't your enemy.

I cleared my throat and looked away, shame burning. "It'd be nice, you know. Living how other people live. Not looking over my shoulder or thinking the worst of everyone. It ain't against you especially, Lex. I just can't trust vampires. I'm sorry, but I can't."

He was quiet for a moment, his cool hands at my waist still. "I would never hurt you, Jerusalem."

"See, you can't say that. 'Never.' Life ain't perfect. 'Never' ain't real. Just 'cause you wouldn't mean to hurt me don't mean—" I took an even breath. I wanted to get away, run like I always did—only now it was 'cause it didn't feel right to be in Alexei's arms, to show him love and comfort when I felt this way. "I almost got bitten by a vamp once. He looked at me like I wasn't nothing but cattle to slaughter. And you . . . you looked at me like that, too. In the war tent, before we left. In those few seconds—" I hugged myself, feeling tears burn the backs of my eyes. Feeling . . . lost. "I saw it in your eyes, Alexei. I wasn't nothing to you. You was one of them."

"Jerusalem . . ." Alexei caressed my cheek, his blue eyes liquid, bright with tears that made me want to be strong for him, forget I hated his kind. But it felt wrong to do that to him. Either way felt wrong. "I wish I could be different for you . . . I'm so sorry."

"Maybe we can't be no closer than this," I said, shaking my head. "Maybe it's stupid to even try. You can't change that you a vampire."

"No, I can't. But I didn't ask to be turned, just as you didn't ask to be born into slavery. And yet here we both are, defying what society says we should be."

"That ain't enough, though," I said, still shaking my head over and over. "I wish it was, but it ain't. And it ain't you in particular. Know that. It's . . . it's the nature of being a vampire that I can't bear."

He nodded a few times. "You've been traumatized. And I am everything that has ever caused you pain . . . I don't fault you for feeling the way you do." He hesitated before removing his hands from me. "Is this the end, then?"

"The end of what?" I asked, panic rising.

I felt him tremble as I put his arms back around me. It was the least confident I'd ever seen him, and I hated it. And here I thought his arrogance was a nuisance, but without it, I knew something was wrong. "I can't bear something wrong between us," I blurted. "Something that might make you leave."

"I would never leave you."

"You promise?"

"I would rather die, even without a soul." But still he looked away, removed his comforting touch from me again. "But I will not touch you while you view me as a predator."

To that, I laughed, as odd as it was. He looked at me quickly, his expression brimming with shock.

"I am a predator," I said. "I just hunt monsters."

"Like me," he murmured.

I shook my head. "Not like you."

I ran my fingers through his hair, and I could feel his muscles tighten as he held himself back from kissing me.

"Not if you're afraid of me," he whispered before I could meet his lips. He sounded like he might cry—and, Lord, I could've cried, too, from how much he cared about what I thought, what

I wanted, what I needed, what made me happy. My arrogant, gentle monster. He would put aside what he wanted . . . for *me*. I felt overcome, and all I wanted to do was comfort him.

Maybe I couldn't trust what he was, but maybe I didn't have to trust to feel something.

"I ain't afraid," I breathed.

I kissed him, thankful he didn't pull away. And suddenly I felt weak and powerful at once, held together by only his touch, like some unstoppable force. I wanted him to want me—need me—like I wanted and needed him. We kissed till there was no more walls between us, till he wrapped his arms around me with that fierce strength of his, driving me feral as hell with his tongue in my mouth. Till fear of the past, present, and future finally melted away, and I felt nothing but love in his touch.

"I have imagined kissing you more times than I can count," he murmured to my lips when we finally broke away.

"Don't lie." I gasped, feeling breathless and flustered. Elated.

"Nothing beats the real thing."

I laced my fingers through his. "What else have you imagined?"

He smirked. "I don't think I should say."

"That nasty, huh?"

"Yes."

My face burned. Part of me wanted to remove everything between us, secrets and clothes included. "Tell me."

He smiled at our fingers entwined, then kissed my hand. "A life with you. That's what I imagine. A life where I make you feel happy and safe and loved, always."

"That ain't so nasty," I murmured, unable to contain a grin.

"And I make you moan with pleasure at least five times a day."

"There it is."

"Trust me, Tiny, if you could read my mind, you would

consider that to be the incredibly tame version. For more specifics . . ." He pressed his lips to my jaw and inhaled, as if he needed to smell me to breathe right. "I'd rather show than tell."

A thrill went through me, as good as the chills I got during battle. "I ought to use that soap more often, looks like. Who knew smelling good would get me all this."

"No, I beg you, my love," he murmured, and kissed my lips, interrupting his own sentence. "Never use that soap again."

I didn't know what he meant—he'd told me himself I smelled like a fly's delight. But hell if I cared. I shoved out the dozens of thoughts, fears, and doubts trying to crowd my mind. What did thoughts have to do with the senses, anyhow?

'Cause the cool of his lips soothed me, like icing a long-neglected ache. He tasted like the high of battle, like that sweet moment of satisfaction when I knew for sure I'd landed a kill. I wanted to make my home in his arms, let his strong hands hold me steady forever. His hands . . . I'd spent hours over the past year staring at them, admiring them. And now they was all mine.

"My favorite," I sighed.

"Favorite?"

But my mind was still vacant of thought, only senses, only feelings, so I didn't even know how to answer that. Except I did, when I inhaled against his cheek and smelled everything I loved—shortbread and carnage and Alexei . . . Alexei . . . *Alexei*. And he wondered why I bit him so often.

For an instant, a thought broke through—*How have I gone so long without his lips against me like this?*

But now wasn't no time for philosophizing.

I took his hand, and he held it until he realized I was guiding it to my lap.

"You want to?" he asked—more like begged—his enthusiasm

obvious. And I wanted to say yes, more than anything, to all of it. But I didn't know if vampires could make babies, and I didn't even want to entertain nothing close to it, not after—

I kissed him—hard—to press the thought of my sister out.

"Just your hand," I whispered.

He muttered an excited swear against my lips . . . and his hand found where I could feel my pulse, like a current running through me.

I grabbed his wrist, but not with enough force to push his hand away, and so he kept *stroking* me, holy *Hell*—! "I knew it."

"Knew what?" he asked with a voice that could steal souls just from its beauty.

"That you'd be good at this."

He laughed, a sound that raised the hairs on my arms like adrenaline was running through me. "I suppose you'll want me to keep going?"

I pressed my forehead to his, feeling more happy, more content, more perfect than I could ever explain. "Stop, and I'll kill you."

And so, he didn't stop . . . and I melted at his touch, *helpless*, my nerves crumbling into chaos. I gripped him close, either kissing him like I didn't know what else there was or unable to kiss him 'cause it was all too much. A feral being lost to all sense . . . all sense but my Alexei.

"I love you, Jerusalem," he whispered in those moments where I couldn't kiss him, knowing *good and well* what his voice was doing to me. And we went on till I couldn't take no more, till I was crying from too many feelings I couldn't piece together—except I think I really did love him, and he loved me. No one had ever loved me before. Not like this.

I collapsed against him, panting and crying, feeling more

alive than I ever had before as he wrapped his arms around me. I stayed there for a while to catch my breath, till my brain started working again, while Alexei rubbed my back and kissed my head, all comfort and love in his touch.

"God, forgive me," I breathed when I finally could, even though I was a liar—I didn't want to be forgiven, not for loving Alexei.

"You're forgiven," I heard a murmured reply.

I pushed against Lex's chest to sit up and look at him. "What'd you say?"

"You asked for forgiveness."

"From God, you ass."

"Close enough."

I snatched up a pillow and pressed it to his face to smother him. "Why did I ever let you touch me, you arrogant, self-absorbed—"

He finally got the pillow away, shutting me up with a kiss.

"Jackass," I finished through his kisses.

"Admit it, you like me behaving badly," he replied, and then his tongue did that incredible thing in my mouth again, so I had to agree with him.

Finally, he broke away, holding my jaw to keep me from kissing him. "I love this more than anything, Tiny, but I can't be selfish. You need to rest."

"You horny as a rabbit at all hours, and now that you got me, you don't want to?"

Alexei laughed, and I felt my entire body pause to regard him. He was so pretty it hurt, and for once, I didn't want to hide my blush. But in that pause, he moved too quick without me even thinking to stop him, and suddenly my head was on my pillow. I missed the soothing touch of his body against my hot blush as he stood and covered me in the blanket. I kicked it off.

"I have you right where I want you," he said, leaning close enough to kiss me, yet *again* tormenting me by not. "Begging for me to pleasure you."

"Boy, get your ass out of here," I laughed, shoving him. "Begging. You wish."

"And yet, I'm about to let you sleep. I really am, as you say, a dumbass."

"Just figuring that out, huh?" I pulled him against me, and for a while, we kissed like we would never stop.

Until he gave me one last swift kiss and got up fast, as if he never would if he didn't force himself. He picked up my spear and looked at me. *Admired* me in the candlelight. "Will you let me be your spear tonight, Sweet Saint?"

I bit my lip instead of embarrassing myself with words and nodded. I watched Alexei walk it over to the wall and rest my spear in the corner before heading to the dresser.

"Goodnight, Tiny," he whispered from across the room.

I wasn't tired. I was high on whatever was in his touch, my whole body trembling to return to him. But he was right, even if I hated to admit it. I needed rest. I needed strength for what was coming. "Goodnight, Lex," I breathed.

And he turned out the oil lamp, bathing the room in calming night.

12

ALEXEI

Tiny had gotten up to relieve herself, and I had to coax her back into bed, fighting the urge to kiss her. I could tell she was exhausted, her movements sluggish, and getting her to sleep at all was challenging enough.

"See you tomorrow," I whispered, kissing her on the head as I lay her on her pillow.

"I don't want tomorrow to come," she murmured.

You and me both, Tiny.

I sat on the chest of drawers across from the bed, waiting for her to fall asleep. She turned in the sheets a bit before settling.

Finally, I sensed her pulse's steadiness, her relaxed breathing. She smelled twice as good when she was sleeping, as if all her stillness concentrated her scent. But tonight, she smelled even better because our scents were mingling. I smelled myself on her all the time—any time she'd come from my tent, or I picked her up, my scent lingered on her for a little while.

But tonight it smelled different . . . it smelled intentional. It smelled like love. I had to stifle a giddy laugh with my hand.

She was so beautiful and strong and perfect, and she'd let me please her, and somehow it was the most satisfying feeling in the world. I think if I died now, I'd go to heaven, no soul required. Or, more likely, hell.

And yet with her sleeping, and no tasks for me to perform or hunting to do, I suddenly felt a powerful dread settle in my stomach. We were getting closer to the plantation. I would help Jerusalem save her brother—that wasn't even a question. But if Red Mask recognized me . . .

I winced at the sound of cracking wood, covering my mouth with my hand as if I had made it, as if I could shut it up that way. When I looked at my other hand, I was gripping a chunk of the dresser, the broken end splintered. My hand trembled as I carefully placed it beside me.

"Hold it together, Alexei," I murmured, flexing my fist in and out, pressing out the tremors.

Logically, if she recognized my scent, she would have come after me already, right? She would have found me on the battlefield without any trouble, taken me right then and there. So, whether or not my body wanted to believe it, I was safe.

For now.

I wished I had thought of it sooner. If I had been with Jerusalem on the battlefield and kept behind Red Mask so she wouldn't see me, we could have easily killed her together. My scent would've drifted into the background of the many other vampires with her in the army—and even if she'd noticed a difference, by then it would've been too late. It would've been over. Instead, I abandoned Jerusalem out of fear. The girl I loved could have been killed because of my cowardice. My friends were already dead because of it.

I took a deep breath and slid off the dresser, making my

way silently to my pack in the corner. I brought it with me out the window and onto the roof—it'd been hard enough getting Tiny to sleep, better to keep the sounds inside the room to a minimum—and began sorting through the items I'd taken from Odessa and Gael. I'd cleared out their pockets without really looking, but now it seemed important to make sure there were valuables to be sent to their families and not just random trinkets.

It was an odd experience, sorting through friends' belongings . . . friends whose ashes I carried with me. But I forced myself not to bring sentimentality into it as I separated everything, all those good intentions as far out the window as I was when I saw Odessa's letters . . . and suddenly I felt too many things at once. This was why vampires didn't bother with friends. Not mortals, anyway. Death and the feelings that came with it. And maybe I just felt too much always—even the vampires in my coven could be friendly with humans one day and forget them the next. Or feed on them. Worst-case scenario, turn them into pets. Friendship between vampires and humans wasn't normal.

Let alone what I had with Jerusalem.

I moved on to organizing the other items. Gael's tobacco tin was a nice antique, but the matches could go. Tiny would love to finish off his fruit treats. There were a few random trinkets I couldn't make sense of, but it also seemed like Dess had kept the letter from those Confederate messengers. She'd clearly read it, the envelope was open, but I supposed she didn't deem it important since we weren't headed that way. I didn't care about that; couldn't have read it if I'd wanted to. But there was also a small velvet sack inside, and opening it revealed . . .

A silver bullet?

They were so rare that for a long time, they were believed to be more legend than a possibility. A story humans used in a futile attempt to scare both vampire and werewolf alike. They were constructed in such a way that they didn't go through the victim no matter where they hit but stayed lodged in flesh. It could slow down the victim significantly, and from what I'd heard, didn't require any special sort of gun to use.

"What did that letter say?" I murmured, glancing at it. I could only make out a few words, but *White Wolf* was all that mattered.

I smirked.

Clearly, Odessa and Gael had not only made sure the colonel thought the stronghold was our goal, but that the Southern army got wind of the plan, too, to keep them off our tracks. So, of course, the bullet had been intended for me.

For a powerful vampire . . .

I paused, staring at it. It was real, and the perfect size for a revolver. Making silver bullets was difficult enough without also making them fit for battle, but someone had pulled it off. Still, even if it were real and functional, one would have to get pretty close to a vampire for it to hit its mark—dodging would be almost too simple unless they were distracted. But it could be done . . . and afterward, there was no getting the bullet out except with tools or a familiar's help. Not unless the vampire wanted to lose use of their hand.

I pulled the pouch's drawstrings to keep the weapon away from me. That would be my task tonight. Locating a gun.

I returned everything to my pack and walked back across the roof and down the side of the inn to the window, peeking in long enough to lay my pack inside and make sure Tiny was still asleep before heading to the ground. It was late, only a small group of drunken men up ahead making its way home. The nights were darker here than up North. No sign of stars through the thick-layered clouds, not even the smallest beam of moonlight . . . like an impending violent storm. Other than lit streetlamps lining the street, there was no light.

I sighed. *Only one option to gather intel, then.* I flew off to the front of the inn, shifting back before entering the front door.

"We're all full up for the night." The innkeeper looked up with a tired nod, as if he hadn't seen me an hour ago. I couldn't even remember what I'd told him during hypnosis, but it must have been thorough. "Old Lady Henry runs a boardinghouse downtown; she may have a spare room."

"I don't need a room," I said. "I need a revolver."

He gave me a cautious look, like he was debating if he should have his own gun at the ready. "What for, son?"

The question annoyed me—it was none of his business, and the back-and-forth would take up precious time. So I caught him in hypnosis and said, "Do not talk to me unless it's an answer to my question," before asking, "Where can I get a revolver?"

"Ain't no place to buy artillery here," he said. "You have to go a town over."

I took an impatient breath. This was just as irritating as his back talk. "That's not what I asked you. Where is the closest revolver?"

"Probably Joe Hickery's. He lives above the tavern two doors down."

Okay. That was something.

I froze at the sound of a small, distressed whimper—even from a distance, I knew my girl's voice. The innkeeper, catching nothing with his unremarkable human hearing, continued to talk about his neighbor. I huffed and caught him in my gaze.

"You did not see or speak with anyone for the past hour," I murmured to him, then flew out the door and back to the window.

By the time I was on my feet in our room again and rushing to the bed, Jerusalem was gripping the sheets, crying. I felt my chest tighten.

"Okay, baby, it's okay." I shushed her, pulling her sweaty body against me as I lay down beside her. She half turned to me, burying her face into my cool chest.

"Lex," she whimpered, still half asleep, half panicked. "She's hurting me."

It was obvious who *she* was, but I didn't want to dwell on that. Instead, I shushed her again, gently pressing her against me until she began to calm. "It's only a bad dream, my love. No one is hurting you."

"Let's kill her," she replied, and I choked back a laugh. My same violent girl, even in her dreams.

After a moment she quieted, but when I tried to move my arm from beneath her, she stirred again. So I settled in beside her, not daring to move even when her body went slack against my arm. I needed to get that gun while she was calm, but she was such a light sleeper, my next movement might wake her up for good . . . and maybe I needed this as much as she did.

Vampires didn't need sleep, but I could do it if I put myself in the right frame of mind. Only, I hadn't done it in so long, I didn't know how to do it anymore. So I just rested beside Jerusalem, feeling her breathe. It was such a strange thing, breathing. The way a human's very cellular makeup needed it to function. The way bones and muscles moved in a sort of gentle rhythm. And Jerusalem's rhythm was soothing.

One last sleep for Jerusalem before we charged headfirst into death.

Hours might have passed, yet it seemed far too soon when my nose caught the scents of the last two vampires I wanted to see.

They were within a mile of us. Our head start was void.

I glanced at the clock. Tiny had only gotten three good hours of sleep. In another life, another time, I would have let her sleep for as long as her body wanted. But she would resent me forever if I was the one to let our enemy reach her brother first.

I woke Jerusalem gently, and she wrapped her arms around my neck without opening her eyes.

"More?" she asked hopefully.

I grinned. If only. "We have to leave. I caught the scents of Adelaide and Zamir."

"Son of a preacher man . . ." she grumbled but got up and threw on her clothes as quickly as her stumbling body would allow.

We rushed outside into the dark early morning.

"We definitely got to take the Underground," she said, more awake now. "It's the only way to be sure we going to catch them in time."

"How far is it?"

"A few miles south."

"Then let's not bother with horses," I said. "You should just ride me."

"You know exactly what you said," she said, and I could sense her blush.

"This time—and only this time—that wasn't an innuendo. My wolf form is large enough that you can sit on my back, and we need to travel at vampiric speed if we want to catch up to two vampires."

Tiny sighed. "Not really a fan of dogs."

"It'll still be me," I assured her. "Only a little furrier."

She hesitated, then nodded. "If that's the quickest way."

I shifted into a wolf, feeling Tiny stiffen at the change. She stood a few feet away and chewed on her lip before muttering, "Aw hell," and climbing onto my back. She was so light, her weight barely any pressure against me. I felt her hands stroke my thick fur before her fingers buried in it, and an unintentional shiver of pleasure ran through me.

She yanked my fur *hard*, and I yelped. "What did I do?" came out as a small, growly bark.

"Pervert," she murmured to my ear before gripping me securely around the neck.

I wanted to shift so I could kiss her for that, but there was no time. I ignored all my carnal instincts and took off.

Tiny buried her face in the fur of my neck, keeping her body close against my back. It was so perfect, and I wish I'd thought of suggesting sooner, just so I could keep her close.

"Are you sure it's here?"

The swamp smelled worse than I imagined it would. Well, to be frank, I never wasted my time imagining swamps, but still. With my enhanced senses, it was enough to make me want to vomit. And if there was anything to drink here, the stench blocked it out completely. But if someone wanted to hide out, this would certainly be the place to do it—unless I was smelling nothing because there was no one out here.

"So we just . . . stand around and wait?" I asked. "Because I don't smell any humans out here. We could be waiting a while."

That, and the bigger concern: I still didn't understand where they would fit a train, even underground.

"Naw, it might be you slowing us up," Tiny said, looking around. "They don't pick up white folks. Or vamps."

"Excuse me?"

"Yeah, so maybe duck behind a tree so I look like I'm alone and lost."

"Wait a second—"

Scents invade my nose out of nowhere, and I just had time to shift Jerusalem out of the way and whip out my shashka, blocking the descent of a hammerhead as big as my own. I used my weight to shove my smaller assailant away, waiting for the larger one behind her to make a move.

I took them in quickly, our attackers—the young, indigenous woman looked more like a debutante than a warrior, but the way she'd swung that sledgehammer clearly painted a contrary picture. A Saint, judging by her strength in handling her silver-headed weapon. Not to mention her trophies—she had sewn vampire fangs into leather as a spiked collar around her neck as well as along the backs of her fingers and knuckles of her elegantly formal fingerless gloves. Not as many trophies as Odessa, but she probably didn't see many vampires in the swamps. Though it was still enough to make me cringe.

Then there was . . . a giant ape-human thing? Like the yeti of the Himalayas, but not quite. A sasquatch? I'd heard of those, though anyone you asked on this continent would say they were just a legend. He wore a white shirt and vest, like a gentleman who'd removed his coat to play a game of cricket.

A few inches taller than me and covered in brown hair from what I could see of his exposed forearms and neck. The hair on his face was styled as a mustache and beard, braided and beaded, extending down to his chest.

I opened my mouth to question them, but the sasquatch beat me to it.

"Jerusalem!" his voice boomed.

JERUSALEM

At Gus's voice, Julia snapped out of attack mode. I winced as she screamed in delight, dropping her sledgehammer handle-up on the ground with a heavy thud. "I knew it!" She hugged me, squeezing unnecessarily tight, then held me at arm's length. "I knew the Union army wouldn't overlook you. Did I not say that, Augustus?"

"You did, dove," said Augustus, nodding his approval. "And the famous Demon Saint, no less."

"The papers did that," I said with a shrug. "Not the army."

The army sure as hell didn't care, but I couldn't have found two more caring people than Julia and Gus if I tried. Well, if *person* was what you'd call Gus? Wasn't sure what the preferred term for a sasquatch was. Anyways, even though it was their job to guide Black people to freedom, they really seemed like they truly believed in it, really and truly believed we was equal and human and worthy of love. Although, Julia was Seneca and Gus never even *used* to be human, so maybe that made the difference—white people and vamps was the ones owning people.

Except for Alexei. He was . . .

Well, I blushed too much thinking about what he was. Better not to.

But Lex wasn't Lex if he didn't make himself known, so he stepped up next to me and said, "This is all very lovely, catching up, but we really are on a tight schedule. Jerusalem said you'd allow us to use the Underground Railroad."

Julia and Augustus exchanged a look that told me this wasn't going to be no cheery reunion with an easy answer.

"My brother is in trouble at the old plantation," I piped in quickly. "We was hoping to travel by the Underground so we can get there before a pair of vamps do."

"You are more than welcome, my dear," Julia said. "Unfortunately, the White Wolf is not."

"Oh so you *do* know who I am," Alexei growled. "And yet you tried to kill me."

"Apologies, but you all look the same from a distance," Julia said, the innocent batting of her lashes tainted by a small smile. "And by the time we got close enough, I was already committed."

Alexei didn't look vamp-mad, the animalistic type that catered to tearing off heads, but something told me he could get there without too much trouble. "*'All look the same'?*"

"What Julia means to say," said Gus, resting his big hand on her shoulder, "is that knowing who you are is irrelevant. Vampires are not allowed in the Underground. And, as she is a responsible Conductor and I a responsible Stationmaster, we must refuse you."

"He's with me, Jules," I said, linking arms with her, if only to keep something bad from happening—she kept eyeing Lex something fierce. "Can't you let it slide this once? This is life or death."

"I'm sorry, my dear," she said, "but I can't put the Underground in jeopardy. It's life or death for everyone who needs to travel it. And it's bad enough a vamp knows about it at all."

"You're Ely Parker's youngest sister," Alexei said, as if just piecing it together. Julia had told me her brother was friends with a Union general and a hugely important figure as far as relations between her people and the government went, but that was all I knew. Badass family. "When I first met with him and General Grant at the start of the war, he mentioned his sister is a Saint."

Julia smirked. "Knowing my brother doesn't get you a ticket to the Underground. Nice try, though."

"Come on, Julia," I said. "What we got to do to get him in? It's going to take so much longer to go around, and we can't afford to lose time."

"I'm sorry, Jerusalem." She wrapped me in her arms. Every time she hugged me, she made little sounds like cooing at a baby. I'd be annoyed, except she did that to everyone, Gus included. "I wish we could help you."

"Let us at least feed you before you go," Augustus said.

"Not the Wolf," Julia said, raising her brows disapprovingly at Alexei.

"We ain't got time," I said, barely sounding friendly anymore, I was so impatient and desperate. "But thanks, anyways."

"You should go with them," Alexei said, and he was lucky I only glared at him for how bossy he sounded. I grabbed his hand and dragged him away. "It's been a while since you've eaten."

"I can eat when my brother's safe. We got a long ways to ride."

"Wait." Gus's voice came from where we left them. When I turned, he and Julia were whispering to each other, Julia's dainty hands gesturing passionately. They ended the discussion with Julia nodding as they squeezed each other's hands before looking over at us.

"There is a way that you both can take the Underground," said Gus. "If we bring it to a council of our fellows, we can vote on allowing him a ticket."

"Well, why didn't y'all say that before?" I asked. "Come on, let's do it."

The way Julia and Gus glanced at each other then made me pause.

Julia took my hand, rubbing it as if to soothe me. "If the majority vote nay, the White Wolf will not be allowed to leave alive."

Now it was mine and Alexei's turn to look at each other.

I pressed my hands to his stomach to back him away from my friends. "Give us a minute."

"I'm not concerned," Lex said with a small smirk when we'd gotten far enough. "I've been working with the Union army for two years. If that isn't enough to vouch for me, I don't know what is."

"And if it ain't?"

"Still not concerned."

"Well it ain't just about you now, dumbass. What about me?" Warmth rose up my cheeks as I realized my slip up. I gripped his shirt in my fist, threatening him as his smirk turned into a genuine smile. "Shut up. I need your help to save my brother."

"Are you scared I won't make it out alive, Tiny?"

"I ain't scared of nothing."

"You love me," he sang. "Admit it."

"I'd rather kill you and save them the trouble."

"All right, Tiny, all right." He rubbed my shoulders. "What do you want to do?"

I chewed on my lip. "It's way too far to ride and make it on time. A full day. Matthew ain't got a day."

"What if you took the Underground, and I flew to meet up with you?"

"I don't want to separate," I said, and felt myself shift closer as if to hold him still. I looked down at his hand instead of his face, knowing full well my expression would betray me. "And even that might be too long. Adelaide and Zamir are already ahead of us."

Alexei wrapped his arms around me, and I leaned into him. "We don't have another option if we want to reach your brother first."

"I know," I whispered. I felt myself trembling in his arms like an idiot and couldn't make it stop.

But I can't lose you, Lex.

I wanted to say it so badly, but I felt foolish for it. What was I scared of, anyways? Ain't no way Lex wasn't coming out of this alive.

Ain't no way.

"Underground?" he asked.

"Underground," I agreed. I took a deep breath before turning to my friends. "All right. What we got to do?"

Julia clapped her hands together and laced her fingers, beaming. "You don't have to do anything, my darling. Augustus will take you somewhere safe to get something to eat while the council takes place. These things don't take more than an hour normally, as long as we can gather them quickly."

"We'll be right back," Gus said, and when he took Jules's hand they both disappeared.

"This is unbelievable," Alexei muttered.

"You think Gus's abilities ain't believable?" I asked, raising a brow at him. "Like you ain't walking around turning into a bird at will."

"No, I mean—" He smirked, and I felt myself wanting to blush. "You're so cute. I meant me having to prove my innocence."

"Welcome to America," I said, maybe a little more harshly than I meant—but he really did have me blushing. "Good thing is you white, so they'll probably believe everything you say."

"And if not, that's what hypnosis is for." He shrugged when I glared at him. "Again, I'm not concerned. But I don't know these people, so have no qualms about succeeding by any means necessary."

"I only know Jules and Gus; ain't got no loyalty to the others. So I really don't care what you do." Lex bent down to tie my shoe, and I felt my nerves about to shatter. I fought off a wild urge to bury my fingers in his hair, to steady myself. I had to get it together before someone saw me like this. "Just come back."

He looked up at me, his expression so knowing, so sure, that it gave me courage. "I'm coming back, Tiny."

There was a tapping on a tree, and I knew it was Gus without him having to say nothing. He always did stuff like that for passengers rather than just start speaking, like it would make people less disturbed that he'd appeared out of nowhere.

"Julia is gathering the council," Gus said, stepping up to us. He nodded at Alexei. "You'll have to leave your weapon with me."

"I'll take it," I said before Lex could argue. He sighed and handed me his sword—dang, I ain't never held it before. It was heavier than I thought.

"Speaking of weapons," said Alexei. "We need to borrow a gun when this is all over. Do you have anything that can fire this?"

He tossed Gus the small velvet pouch.

"What's that?" I asked, feeling a little put out Alexei had been hiding something from me.

"Remember that envelope we took from the Confederate messengers? There was more than just a note inside."

Gus let out an impressed whistle as he peered inside the pouch, and I pulled his arm down to see. A bullet. Silver. Looked not much bigger than the sorry-excuse-for-bullets Donald had used to kill squirrels.

I scowled at Alexei. "When was you going to tell me?"

"I found it last night. And, you know, we were in a bit of a rush."

"Incredible . . ." Gus mused. "Smaller than I imagined, but . . ." He poured it out onto his big palm to study it, and it looked a hell of a lot smaller than in the bag. "I'm not sure we have any extra revolvers lying around, but we can check."

"Don't tell me we fittin' to use it against Adelaide," I said, throwing my arms up with an annoyed sigh. "You crazy if you think that'll stop her."

"It won't stop her," said Alexei, "but it'll slow her down enough to land a killing blow."

"One: she so fast, you'd have to be right up on her to even land the hit, which kind of defeats the purpose of a gun. And two: silver don't do nothing to her—I saw it for myself on the battlefield."

"It will work," Alexei said, his insistence as annoying as a hungry gull. "Her insides are vulnerable to it, I promise you."

"Fine." I sighed. "I don't see how you'd ever get an opening to do it, but if you think it'll work, go on and handle your business."

"Thank you, Tiny," he cooed, and I blushed. Why did I always fall for this giant-ass ancient warrior teasing me like that?

"There might be some proper guns in our lost and found," said Gus. "We can check after the trial."

I smirked at the familiar term. By "lost," he meant *taken* when someone was "found" dead after a Conductor killed them. I'd gotten my first little knife from there—the same knife I'd tried to kill Alexei with the day we met.

I'd hated why I'd needed the Underground, but the place itself was full of nice memories. Of the people, of what they'd done for me. The feeling that someone, somewhere, finally wanted me to be safe. Even the food left a warm memory in my belly.

But I didn't say all that. I just said, "Thanks, Gus," and took the pouch when he handed it to me. Guess that counted as a weapon, too, even without the gun.

"You'll be placed in holding until it's time," Gus said to Lex. Then he smiled at me, and I immediately grabbed his hairy forearm without him having to say nothing. "Hungry?" he asked anyway.

"You got to ask?"

I blinked, and the ground shifted. I let go of Gus's arm inside a kitchen area with a huge table in the middle laid out with food—a pot of stew, cornbread, and some kind of cakes or muffins, not that it mattered since I knew it was all going to taste great.

There was a rescued mama and her little girl sitting at the table eating, and when I turned around to grab a cake, their expressions were so familiar. Shocked, a little nervous. Trying to settle in to being free but not knowing how. I didn't believe it till I reached the North, neither. Till I was with Dess and Lex in the army. Not that I didn't trust the people in the Underground—

but they was all so sweet and helpful that they felt like a dream I could suddenly wake from.

But they wasn't a dream. *This* wasn't a dream. I wished I could be like them, helping people like me find their way to safety. To freedom. Somewhere they could call home.

But their task required secrecy, and I was never one to hide in the shadows.

"You really like him," Gus said. It wasn't a question.

More than like him. But suddenly, all I could think about was Alexei's hand last night, so I turned away toward the table and shrugged to hide my blush. "Yeah, he's all right."

"And it's not a problem that he's a vampire and you're a human." Again, not a question.

I laid mine and Alexei's weapons on the table and turned to face him, leaning against the edge. "I don't know, to be honest. If I think about it, it don't make a lick of sense. So . . . I ain't thought about it."

He made a small sound of understanding. Hesitated. "I'll be back for you in an hour or so. Try not to worry." And he disappeared.

"Whoa," whispered the little girl. I grinned. That'd been me, too, a year ago.

The stew was lamb with lots of vegetables in it. Real healthy and hearty, and I scooped myself an extra-large bowl.

I'd been in this room before, but it looked different to me with free eyes. So many things I didn't notice before, like the clay pottery decorating the room and the mural on the wall— naw, not mural. The thing with the little tiles, what was the name of it? . . . A mosaic. It was of a chimera, its different animal parts flying wild surrounded by the woods. Real pretty, but I wasn't about to stare at art for an hour.

I sighed and sat at the table, turning my attention to the stew instead.

ALEXEI

There was a rush of movement that rocked my stomach, and then the swamp was gone. Ill memories plagued my mind. Perhaps it was an overreaction, but the last time I woke up in a strange place without the knowledge of how I got there— *Don't be stupid, Alexei.*

My insides felt tight and tingly in a bad way, like ants walking all over the inside of my skin. "What *was* that?"

"The tingling will go away momentarily," said Augustus, as if reading my mind. His deep voice, the few inches he had on me, and his lack of disorientation felt like a blatant challenge of dominance.

I glanced around. We were . . . in a cave? But I was unbound, and my senses worked. In the dark, I smelled and saw the bones of decaying bodies. So the part about potential death hadn't been a bluff. A bit disconcerting. Also disconcerting that I could smell how we weren't the only two here. There was someone else, close and alive . . . and massive.

"Tingling?" I asked, as if I didn't feel it, let alone cared. "I meant what you just did."

"Instant transportation." I couldn't see his mouth, but his mustache and braided beard shifted as he grinned. "It's why my kind are known as legends around here. We always seem to disappear before humans can get a good look at us."

"Why can't you just transport us to the plantation, then?" I demanded.

"Because I've never been there before. I have to be able to visualize where I'm going, otherwise I'll end up materializing into a wall or something." He cleared his throat. "A couple of my fellows have died that way." There was an uncomfortable pause before he said, "Would you like a lantern, or are you content to use your night vision?"

"Where exactly did you take Jerusalem?"

"Somewhere safe, I assure you."

"I asked you *where*."

"I cannot disclose that." He sighed. "The Underground is the safest place someone like her can be. Nothing will happen to her, I promise you. In the meantime, Julia and I will try to urge our fellows to vote quickly and in your favor."

"You'd better," I said. "I'd hate to kill any of your Conductors who try to kill me."

Augustus chuckled. "Oh, we don't risk the lives of any Conductors for that—your executioner will be someone a little less prone to death. But, for Jerusalem's sake, let's hope it doesn't come to that." He squinted at a pocket watch. "By the way, I'd stay away from those bars if I were you. I'll be back soon to fetch you for your testimony."

"Wait, what—?" I growled. He'd disappeared again in a warp of air. What a frustratingly enviable ability.

I sighed and stared at the bars in question. Metal bars set in stone, spanning the entire wall.

"Stay away from the bars," I muttered. As if I should be afraid of what was behind them.

Who did he think he was, *warning* me? Better yet, who did he think *I* was?

I approached the bars, but they weren't quite large enough for me to fit my head through to look down. But there was a large opening, like a massive fox hole. The other presence I'd smelled was definitely down there.

A low growl echoed up the chasm, and along with it I saw . . . tentacles? Like those of an octopus, they crept up from the darkness. I didn't hear any water that would allow for such a creature, but I heard the ruffle of large wings, like a bird stretching. A giant bird with tentacles. And glowing red eyes, which I could now see were set in a reptilian face like a sharp-beaked dragon.

A chimera.

I backed away from the bars and waited quietly to not draw attention to myself as the tentacles ran over the bars, blessedly too thick to get through. I'd once had a run-in with such a beast in Egypt and had only survived because I was faster than the rest of my group and could escape while it was distracted. The one true predator of vampires other than Saints.

"That's Molly," I heard Augustus say. If I hadn't smelled him appear, I probably would have killed him for sneaking up on me while I was agitated. "She's a snallygaster. Probably the most un-killable creature in North America."

That word meant nothing to me, but I had put enough together to say, "The executioner."

"To be fair, she's really just minding her beastly business and eating what's put before her."

"Perhaps. But you lot aren't if you're deliberately feeding her vampires."

He gave me a sheepish shrug, but that was all. My own concern for New Bloods seemed to be a personal struggle that no one was ever going to understand.

But I had something more immediate to be concerned about.

"So what was the verdict?" I asked.

Augustus folded his hands behind his back, clearing his throat. He didn't even need to speak.

"It's a no," I confirmed.

"They don't believe you're the White Wolf—most vampires choose swords as their weapon, so even the articles in the paper praising you won't be of much help. There will be no official vote until after your testimony, but as of now, it's not looking favorable."

"How many votes do I need?"

"Six will make a majority."

"So all I need is four since I already have you and Julia."

"Um, well . . ." He rubbed the back of his neck. "You have mine, anyway."

I raised my brows. *That backstabbing, underhanded little—* "Wonderful."

"Do you know what you'll say?"

"I was going to rely on my Union service to speak for me, but since that's off the table . . ." I shook my head and shrugged.

"That's rough, buddy." He patted my shoulder. "Ready?"

"Like hell," I muttered. Tiny was rubbing off on me.

Augustus transported us, and we arrived in an empty room, standing in the middle of a circle etched into the ground. As I recovered from my nausea, I realized we were no longer near the swamp—I could smell everything perfectly here. I glanced out the window, and the trees were thick enough that I half expected a bear to walk by. We were somewhere deep in the woods, away from civilization.

Augustus walked forward and opened the door before us, holding it wide for me. Without hesitation, I walked through into a fully furnished living room. It seemed to be a very informal council because some were standing, some sitting, and one was eating a bowl of stew. There was a sasquatch for every human, ten in all—so a Stationmaster for every Conductor. A surprising mix of races among the humans, too—mostly Black, a few indigenous, and one white woman. One of the humans in here, however, was a charlatan—the odd, gross scent of a werewolf invaded my nose. Like strong urine. Ugh. They let werewolves near the Underground but not vampires? It seemed a misinformed bias to have.

Everyone in the room wore dark glasses, which made it impossible to see their eyes. Well, hypnosis was out of the question now, not that I thought I'd have to resort to it.

"What do you have to say for yourself, vamp?" asked a middle-aged Black man. He held no Saint weapon, only a normal rifle across his shoulder. None of the humans except Julia were Saints, which strengthened my odds if things turned south. Still, they all had some sort of silver blade on them.

"That I'm not sure why you doubt my good intentions," I said, "seeing as I came here with a girl you yourselves led to freedom."

"Vampires keep familiars," he said. "And humans as playthings."

"And perhaps," said a woman, "she felt she couldn't say no to you out of fear for her life."

"It's not like that," I said, trying to force back my annoyance at their assumptions. "We were in the Union army together—"

"Where are your uniforms?" asked a Stationmaster, older than Augustus and with a much longer beard. "What are your orders? Why would you be down here by yourselves?"

"Vamps don't do spy work out of pure ego," said the werewolf. His Scottish accent, as tame as it was, might have sounded comforting if I didn't want so badly to tear out his throat.

"Are any of you actually going to let me plead my case?" I snapped. "Or are you just going to keep interrupting with your stereotypes?"

"Let's hear his testimony," said Augustus, and I could've kissed him, even if he was holding the hand of a traitor.

"I already know," I said, "that you don't believe I've served with the Union army for two years. So I won't talk about that. I'll talk about Jerusalem."

I swallowed. *Here goes nothing.*

"Jerusalem—did you see her? The fiercest, most beautiful girl on this earth. She's tiny—like, so short." I gestured with my hand to show them. "She handles a spear that's twice her height. You might know her as the Demon Saint from the newspapers." I paused, but none of them said a word. That annoyed me, but I went on. "I know you know her because she used your Underground Railroad to travel North to freedom a year ago. And—" I paused and glared at the werewolf before it could interrupt. "You're probably going to say something about how you help hundreds and thousands of slaves, so how would you remember this one girl? Because she's a flame, that's why. A wildfire that burns everything she touches on purpose. You can never forget a girl like her. I know I can't."

They were silent. I had a point . . . I hoped.

I took a deep breath. "Well, her brother is in danger—two Ancient vampires will kill him out of pure spite if we don't get to him first. He's her only living family, and if you don't let us use the Underground, we'll never make it there in time to save him."

"So we should endanger the lives of tens of thousands," said the first Conductor, "for the sake of one *supposed* brother?"

"Her brother died, I thought," said another.

"He's alive," I snapped. "Why on earth would I lie about that?"

"Quite the temper on this one."

Another Conductor waved his hand. "I think we've heard enough—"

"It's my fault," I said, the words falling out of me, the next ones choking me for a moment. Jerusalem. All I could think of was Jerusalem. How if I didn't say the right thing, I would leave her alone with no brother, no Dess, no . . . me.

I couldn't leave her alone.

"It's my fault," I repeated, my throat tightening. "She needed my help killing her enemy, and I didn't help her. And now they'll kill her brother if we can't get there in time. I love her too much to let that happen." Tears broke through, and I felt exposed as they ran down my face. As frightened and stupid as I did the night I was turned . . . except the fear wasn't for myself. "You say you value Black lives. Enough to lead them from slavery, but what about afterward? Are they considered 'no longer your problem?' If a skilled Saint such as Jerusalem can be thrown by the wayside, left to fend for herself while her only family and the man who loves her are murdered—yes, *murdered*, you cowards, because I haven't done a thing to you—I'd hate to see what you do with the average human.

"I'm going after two of my own kind all for the love of a girl. Because I love her, and she loves her brother. And I will not let her fight alone." I swiped my eyes, blinking away more tears. "If love doesn't matter to you, or the well-being of a girl you helped free, or the life of an enslaved boy whom we could very well save . . . well, then, what is this whole operation even for?"

I was met by silence.

"You love her?" asked a small, shaking voice. And when I

looked over, I saw Julia had taken off her dark glasses, her eyes brimming with tears.

"With everything," I said, the truth of it pushing courage through my words. "All of me."

I looked at the rest of the council. A few of them were whispering to each other.

He's helping this one girl. But after?

He must have a coven; how do we know he won't tell them about us?

Even if he won't attack, they will.

Immortals can't truly love.

It was almost as if nothing I'd said mattered.

They had made their minds up about me before I'd even entered the room.

"All in favor of allowing this particular vampire onto the Underground," said the first man, "raise your hand."

My heart dropped as four members of the council lifted their hands—including Augustus—but not Julia, the spiteful harpy. The fact that Jerusalem considered her a friend was the worst part.

"All opposed to allowing—"

I didn't even need to hear him finish. I was already trying to get over my emotions, trying to mentally prepare myself to face . . . whatever that beast had been back in the cave. And then I saw five hands go up . . . wait, wasn't six the majority?

"Who didn't vote?" demanded the werewolf. I hated him, even if it was irrational. I wish he'd stop existing. "We have to get this done and return to our posts."

"Five is more than four, anyway," said a woman.

"It's invalid," said the leader. "Everyone present must vote."

"I needed more time to think," said Julia.

She didn't vote. She was . . . conflicted. I could see it in her face, even if she hadn't revealed herself.

Now she would vote in my favor. They'd need a tiebreaker, then, but I could only handle one stress at a time.

Augustus squeezed around her shoulders and whispered something to her as the moderator asked for a vote for those in favor. Four hands went up as before. Still not including Julia.

She seemed to have been moved by my declaration of love for Jerusalem. There was no way she would—

Six hands went up, opposing me. Including Julia's. If my heart could beat it would've stopped.

"Let the sentence be carried out," said the leader.

"You're supposed to be Jerusalem's friend," I growled, but I'd barely taken two steps to approach her when I felt a heavy hand on my shoulder from behind.

I stumbled forward on stone in the dark, my stomach reeling. I looked up in time to see the Stationmaster who'd grabbed me disappear . . . and in his place, a rumbling through the ground, the air.

And glowing red eyes slowly opening in the darkness.

JERUSALEM

By my second bowl of stew, I was about ready to kill something. Why was it taking so daggone long? The mama and little girl had been escorted to the next section, and I'd been left alone, for . . . well, I didn't rightly know. There wasn't no clock in here.

But it felt too long. It shouldn't have taken them so long to decide. Alexei was with the Union army—ain't no way they could refuse him with all that going for him. And we had two guaranteed votes in Julia and Gus.

But I knew from experience that if something didn't feel right, it wasn't.

I paced around the long table, getting angrier the longer I waited.

"Alexei's in trouble," Gus said, his voice making me jump. He was lucky I wasn't holding my spear, else it'd be in him.

My gut dropped into my feet, even though I'd known even before Gus and Jules had shown up. I snatched up my spear and Lex's sword. "Where we going?"

"We have to grab him and get out," he said quickly.

"Augustus!" Julia chastised, disbelief written across her face.

"Listen to me, Jerusalem," he said, kneeling to be closer to my level. "We get Alexei and get out. We cannot survive what's down there."

"What's down where?" I asked on edge. But he didn't have to say nothing as my gaze fell on the mosaic again . . . of the mashed-up monster among the trees.

"It's a death sentence," said Julia. "*Literally*. I won't let you risk it."

"This trial was you and Gus's idea," I snapped. "And you failed to tell us there was a giant-ass monster involved. Oh, you getting us out of this, risk or no risk."

Gus lit a lantern, and I grabbed his arm.

"I can come back for you, Julia," he said.

She disregarded his suggestion and grabbed his other arm but didn't look happy about it.

In the blink of an eye, we was off.

ALEXEI

My heart dropped as I felt for my sword and found nothing. Immediately, I shifted to a crow and flew into the shadows. As a being of the hunt, I knew with certainty it was a pointless move, hiding. Even if it couldn't smell as well as I, there was no doubt those hawk eyes could see me. My only saving grace was that I held no body heat to detect. All I had to do was buy myself enough time to think of a better plan.

But the beast screeched in my direction, flinging a massive tentacle, forcing me to move. I shifted to a wolf so I could run. All I had to do was get to the metal bars. Once I got closer, my crow form could fit through—

A tentacle blindsided me, sending me quite literally into the stone wall. My head spun. I tasted my own blood as it leaked from my nose. *Get up, Alexei.* I pulled myself out of the crater I'd made in the wall, sharp pain in my sides alerting to me several broken ribs.

I was lucky it was only ribs. Another hit like that, though, and I'd have more to worry about.

I changed direction and headed behind it instead, dodging tentacles and giant wings. Its limbs weren't much safer there, but at least it couldn't see me. It was fast but couldn't possibly turn around fast enough in this small space. If I could just stay behind it long enough, maybe I could fatigue it into disinterest. Anything was worth a try.

Except with something as vicious and ancient as a chimera.

It blocked my way with each attempt, wings, beaked jaw, tentacles all working to stop me, to kill me.

I shifted to my human form and took hold of the next tentacle that came at me, tearing it open. The beast roared in pain, and I managed to dodge before it could knock me away. Chimera scales were too hard, and attacking the wings or face was too risky, and so the tentacles were my only option to try and slow it down. They would regenerate eventually, but not quickly enough to affect my plan.

I tore at another tentacle, ripping it in half, but the creature had caught on to my method. There was no time to run—I just managed to catch its eagle-like talon before it could stomp me into the ground, its massive claws digging into the stone like a bony cage, trying to pin me with a crushing weight. I managed to stay on my feet and pushed right back, leaning my entire shoulder into the action. The beast screeched angrily and tore its talons through the stone, but I bolted out of its grasp before they could close around me fully.

I tried to fly off but, only one wing flapped, taking me nowhere. My muscles tightened in panic as I shifted back.

It tore my arm off. But when I looked, my arm was still there, although mangled and dangling by sinews away from my shoulder. Only then did the pain flood me, delayed and cruel. It felt all too familiar, but the memories it conjured were far worse—of broken bones and stab wounds and a red-masked demon watching me weep.

But I couldn't just sit there and let this creature kill me, no matter how much my common sense reminded me how impossible it was to defeat a chimera. Reality didn't matter. Not when I'd promised Tiny I would come back.

One way or another, I had to find my way out of this.

The beast suddenly screeched again, a cry of pain, and when I looked up, a long stick stuck out from the creature's shoulder. I swiped my vision clear and saw Augustus appear out of thin air, yank the weapon out of the chimera, and vanish. In the next moment, Jerusalem was running toward me. The impact of one of those limbs would kill her. She couldn't be here. What was she doing?

Saving you, dumbass, I could hear Tiny say in my head.

My fearless little Saint.

Augustus snatched her up, transporting in time to dodge a swiping tentacle.

I felt a warm body beside me, and suddenly Julia was half-guiding, mostly pushing me into a corner. Tiny and Augustus distracted the chimera, and it didn't look our way.

"I hate you for putting my husband in danger," Julia said, shoving me against the wall. My head ached a little, more from my injury than anything, but *that* certainly didn't help. "You'd be dead now if not for his merciful heart. Count yourself lucky, bloodsucker."

And then a familiar arm wrapped around my waist, while another hand grabbed hold of my good arm before the darkness disappeared.

JERUSALEM

As soon as I saw we was somewhere other than that cave, I shoved away from Lex, backing away so I could get farther. 'Cause I couldn't breathe, my lungs burning, my head throbbing.

Oh my God . . . I almost lost him.

"You dumbass." I gasped, grasping at my throat, my chest. I couldn't get no air . . . "You said you wasn't concerned. No!" I moved away as he reached for me. "Get in killing range of me and see what happens, you giant idiot."

"I promised I'd come back to you, didn't I? Look at me, Tiny." I swung at him, but he snatched my wrist and pulled me close, and his touch tempered my will to fight him. "Everything's all right."

"A giant bird lizard sea beast thing crushed your arm," I said, staring at the remains of his arm dangling at his side. "That ain't all right."

"It'll heal." He grimaced, clearly in terrible pain, and yet he stroked my cheek with his working hand and shushed me gently. "It's healing as we speak."

"Looks like it hurts, though."

He shushed me again. "I'm all right."

"Don't hypnotize me."

"You know me better than that."

He was right. I knew good and well he wouldn't. But if I didn't know myself, if I didn't know how I felt, how else could I ever explain what his touch and gaze did to me? How I didn't want to move away. 'Cause it wasn't that I felt captured by him in the way hypnosis worked.

I felt . . . safe.

"Don't ever scare me again." I laced my fingers behind his neck and pulled him close, pressing my forehead to his. "For crying out loud, Lex. Can't let you out of my sight for nothing."

"Brilliant. My plan is working."

"Dumbass." I laughed and shoved away from him, joy and relief flooding me . . . but the tears hit me hard, too, and I ran to throw my arms back around his neck and pull him close.

It was one thing to feel safe with him. It was another to realize that not even a minute ago my safe place, my home, was almost crushed and eaten by a big-ass beasty.

That the threat of Adelaide recognizing him and taking him from me was more real than I ever wanted to admit.

Don't think like that, Jer. That monster ain't taking nobody else away from you. Kill her before she gets the chance.

Suddenly, I remembered Julia and Gus and shoved away from Lex—not that they didn't just see me blubbering like a baby out of milk. I wiped at my tears quickly and made him sit in a nearby chair. "You said you wasn't concerned, Lex. So what happened in there?"

"Ask her," he said, glaring at Julia.

I glared at her, too. If it was choosing between her and Lex, he was the one I knew better than anyone. He wouldn't accuse nobody unless they'd earned it.

"It would have been a tie without my vote, anyway," she said shamelessly, without me even having to ask. "And a tie breaker would have likely landed him in the same predicament. I'm not the only one who doesn't trust an Ancient vampire escorting a young woman around as a pet or—"

"I ain't his pet," I snapped, throwing up my hands. "What in the hell gave you that idea?"

"Well, that's what it looks like, Jerusalem—you must see how wrong it looks from the outside."

Okay, well . . . I paused at that. 'Cause she wasn't wrong, even if she should've known better.

"I been fighting alongside him for *a year*; he left the army and came all this way to help save my brother, and you think it's cause I'm his *pet?* What vamp would do half that much?"

Julia didn't look convinced. "I made my choice to protect you and every other soul in need who passes through here."

"My brother's a soul in need," I growled and snatched up my spear, storming up to her. "What about him?"

Gus stepped between us. "Peace, Jerusalem. Why do you think we're here now?"

"For my brother, I hope." As much as I was itching to kill something, I probably *would* regret making it Julia. But that was beside the point. "Which way'd you vote?"

"For you and Alexei. I would never have suggested the trial if I didn't plan to help you succeed."

"You don't see me as his pet?"

"If I didn't follow the papers so closely, maybe I would. If I'd never seen the way the two of you look at each other . . . you're in love; that much is clear."

I huffed, giving a sharp nod.

"It's an act, Augustus," Julia cut in. "Jerusalem, when we first met, you hated vampires. You wanted nothing to do with them except revenge. Now you expect us to believe you're willfully with this vampire, no manipulation involved? I don't believe it."

"Well, who cares what you believe?" I snapped. "It ain't your business who I love."

"Who *you* love—?"

"Yeah, that's right. I love him. Now what you got to say about it?"

Holy hell, Jerusalem. I couldn't look at Alexei. Whatever his expression said, it would put more meaning to such simple words than I was ready for. 'Cause the truth was, I'd poured my heart into them words without even trying.

And they felt as real as when Dess had asked me to say them.

But it didn't look like nothing I could say would make Julia stop scowling. "That doesn't make me any less concerned for you. He's not human, Jerusalem."

"Well, you ain't with a human, neither," I said.

Gus cringed. "She has a point."

"Oh, stop that." She took his hands, looking up at him earnestly. "You are a sweet, kind, gentle soul. The complete opposite of a vampire."

"Will your parents see beyond what I am to learn that?"

She sighed. "Can we not worry about my parents until after the war, please?"

"Just because someone isn't human doesn't mean they are incapable of true emotions. They love each other, Julia. You must concede."

Julia scowled at Lex with a clear pent-up urge to scream at him. I knew the feeling well. "I want you to know that I had nothing to do with your rescue, and if you do not bring Jerusalem and her brother back to the Underground alive and well, I will hunt you down and burn a hole through your chest with my hammer."

"And then I'll chop *you* in half with my spear," I said, more annoyed than hateful. "And poor Gus won't have nobody to love."

"Ladies," Gus chided.

"Mind your business, Jules. Swear to God." I looked at Lex sitting at the table all pretty and quiet, and my anger dipped down to a simmer. His arm was in one piece now, no more sinews or bones hanging out. But it did look a little rough, like something being sculpted out of clay. "You doing okay? Your arm looks like an arm again."

"Just a little more internal work," he said with a wince.

I combed my fingers through his tousled hair. "We got the time."

We really did—we'd gained *hours* with Gus and Julia's help, even with the chimera incident, and I'd be forever grateful. If all went well from here, we was sure to arrive at the same time, if not earlier. Either would do for me, so long as I got to Matthew before that monster did.

So I finally took a breath and a moment to look around. We was in a one-room house. Instead of a bed, there was a big hammock hanging from the ceiling in one corner, a small kitchen, a wardrobe, and drawers. Nothing fancy, but somewhere safe to call home.

"This where you live?" I asked Julia and Gus, who had given us space, as little as they could in the cozy-sized house.

"Just for now, during the war," said Julia. She'd cooled off, which made me glad. I didn't want to actually have to kill her. "We'll eventually move up to New York, closer to my family."

"Looks like a great place to get away."

Julia looked pleased. "I'm so glad I decided to tidy up last night. You might be our first-ever visitors."

"It was too risky," Gus added, "to take you anywhere other Stationmasters may travel."

"Speaking of, how's this going to work?" I asked, hugging Lex's head and resting my chin on it. "Like, how we supposed to get through the Underground if we can't *use* the Underground?"

"It'll be no different than any other day," Gus said, like he was spouting some great plan. "We escort people who need help, and that's what we'll be doing."

Julia looked like she was fittin' to snarl like a wolf. "He doesn't exactly match our usual passengers. And he's practically your height; there'll be no hiding him."

"We'll find a way," Gus said, reassuringly.

Julia twisted her hammer nervously in her hands. "I hate this. We don't know what will happen to us if we're caught."

Alexei scoffed. "I've never been caught by anyone in my entire vampiric life."

"Well, you've never been in an environment," Julia cut back, her tone irritated, "where everyone is trained and experienced at dealing with vampires. Not to mention, we're so covert, only the people who need to know about us know we exist. So I wouldn't sound so haughty if I were you." She looked around quickly, snatching up some blankets, a cloak, and a mask, holding them out to me. "I don't care how great your vampire friend thinks he is, the best way to use the Underground is to not draw attention to ourselves. Take these."

I side-eyed her but took the supplies from her, anyways. "You helping us, Jules? After all that protest?"

"Augustus had been working with the Underground years before the war even started, before I'd even met him. He's going to help you whether or not I go with him. And given the choice, I'll always choose to go with him."

Gus held an arm out to her, and she went to sit in his lap. "You're a better woman than I'll ever deserve."

"Oh, stop it. You deserve the world."

"I love you."

"I love *you*."

They talked in sweet whispers while I handed Lex the mask and blanket—couldn't have his pale face giving us away—and put on the cloak myself.

"Hunch over," I said, trying to pull him down. "You can't be looking like a walking tree in the Underground."

"You know," said Lex, "I think it's time you knew the truth, Tiny—I am not a giant. You're just short."

"You asking to get punched, Silver Fox."

"Couples shouldn't argue as much as you do," Julia said from her cuddly spot.

"Go on and hush, will you?" I asked. "We working it out."

I tilted my head at Lex's outfit. "Come to think of it, might be better if you go as a crow. Easier to hide you."

"Only problem with that plan," said Lex, "is that crows aren't exactly commonplace underground."

"Most of the stops ain't actually underground, dumbass." I smirked, opening my cloak. "I'll hold you, then."

Alexei beamed like a kid getting candy. "That's adorable, and I'm going to accept before you change your mind."

"Fittin' to change it right now," I muttered, but by the time I finished my sentence, his black, feathery self was all nestled in my arms like a snuggly duck. I had to admit it was cute as hell. I held him close under the cloak, his cool feathers against my chest easing my nerves.

I looked at Julia and Gus. "You two done cuddling over there? We got some vamps to kill."

ALEXEI

Augustus gave us two words of warning before we left: keep quiet and be prepared to transport at any time.

Already I knew this was going to be an unpleasant morning.

Tiny's demeanor remained calm, but her heart was pounding nervously against me as Augustus transported us to the first stop. In this smaller form, I didn't feel the nausea as much, but I worried for my girl and leaned closer to comfort her. It was all I could do, hidden this way. And she seemed to respond to it, because she scrunched her fingers in the ruff of my neck, petting me as if she'd forgotten I wasn't an actual crow.

But if that was all I could do to help her, it was enough.

I peeked through the small sliver of light Tiny's cloak allowed in. Perhaps most of the stops weren't underground, but this one looked it. A cavern with a few stone halls branching off from it. Like in the house where my trial had taken place, we had landed on a designated circle, and I finally understood its significance as another Conductor and Stationmaster appeared in their own circle a few feet from us. It could have easily been a disaster if they hadn't known where to land.

Julia had to come with us, the witch—it made everything seem more natural, I supposed, a Conductor and Stationmaster together with someone they'd just rescued. No one would look our way. But still, it annoyed me. I had a small, awful feeling she might very well betray us and give me away—after all, she'd already done it once.

"Let's not linger at this stop for too long," she said before striding forward, her hammer resting on her shoulder. It didn't elude me that the silver head faced in my direction.

We walked down one of the torch-lit halls, Jerusalem tucked between Julia and Augustus, and me tucked to her chest. But before I could figure out where the hall led, we transported again into a large room, this one most certainly a building above ground, judging by the wooden walls and floors. It was organized in sections, like an enormous shop or a well-stocked pantry. There was plenty of clothing in all sizes, travel supplies, even cooking utensils. I was certain most of it hadn't been *lost*, and knowing they conducted business the same way I did made me like this place even more.

But the thing that stole my attention was the immediate reek of a dirty shifter. I peeked through a slit in the cloak and saw him across the room with his Stationmaster looking in our direction. His features might have been an ambiguous mix of races, but his horrid scent and the stretch marks that ran across his cheeks like animal whiskers were distinctly werewolf.

Of course.

Julia took her beau's hand, leaning close to whisper. "Take us back home."

"The weapons are just on the other side, dove," he said.

"I know. I'll tell you why when we get there."

He nodded without questioning her and did as he was told. I leaned against Tiny and closed my eyes. The first time had been nothing, but being transported that many times in a row had me beginning to feel the nausea despite my size.

Tiny looked around, and I could tell she was stressed. "Wait, why'd we come back—Lex!" She let out a yelp as I shifted and then shoved me as retaliation. I pulled her into a hug, resting my head against her to ease the travel sickness, and I could feel her heart beating rapidly. I had startled her, poor girl. "Don't do that, dumbass," she commanded, but affection bloomed in my gut at the fact she rested in my arms instead of squirming away.

"Ewan suspects something," said Julia, pacing. "Glancing to see who's there is normal. *Staring* as soon as we arrive and even after is not."

"Who's Ewan?" said Tiny, a bit dismissively, a tone that meant she knew she could kill him so wasn't worried.

"As far as he's concerned, we aren't doing anything out of the ordinary," said Augustus. "I don't see why he would suspect anything."

But *I* did.

Werewolves couldn't distinguish human scents from vampires, but he probably *could* pick out a scent he'd experienced in an enclosed room less than two hours ago. Still, we needed that gun. And if all I had to do was outsmart a stupid dog to do it, well that was no task at all.

"Tiny," I said, "I need you to wash me in that lavender soap you brought."

She turned her head slightly to look at me. "Why?"

"To get rid of Ewan."

Julia lifted her chin slightly, giving me a look that bordered on respect, but said nothing. Perhaps she wouldn't give us away, after all. Tiny fished out her soap while Augustus prepared a small bowl of water. I shifted back into a crow and stood in the bowl while she washed me. Unfortunately, birds could not pinch their nose against disgusting smells, but I supposed it was better than smelling that werewolf. And certainly better than getting caught.

And it felt *nice*, Tiny rubbing the suds down my sleek feathers. Even if it did smell like a wretched garden.

When I was clean and mostly dry, she took me into her arms. The smell was even more atrocious from within the cloak, and I fought not to cough. I would hold my breath the entire time in the Underground if I had to.

Again, we transported to the lost and found, and Ewan and his Stationmaster were there waiting for us. They were escorting three people who were still sorting through clothing that might fit them, but it seemed like an excessive amount of time to stay in one place, and I wondered if they'd encouraged the people to take their time. He looked at us, his nose twitching, as Gus went to a locked cabinet full of weapons.

"Welcome back," Ewan teased. "Did you forget something?"

"Our passenger is sensitive to smells, so I gave her a little of my essential oil." Julia held up a hand, keeping the dog from approaching. "She is also uncomfortable with men, if you'd keep your distance."

I had to admit, my respect for Julia increased the smallest bit. Having experienced both sides, she was definitely someone I preferred as my ally than an enemy.

The werewolf respected that boundary, halting immediately. He gave Jerusalem a reassuring smile, but I could tell he was trying still to solve the riddle that was my scent, now veiled by lavender. "You have nothing to worry about from anyone here, dear heart. I promise you."

I pressed myself closer to Tiny so I wouldn't launch myself at him for calling my girl any sort of pet name. But with her being covered in a cloak and her height, he most likely thought she was a little child.

"Go on and look through the clothing, my dear," Julia said to Tiny, gently prompting her toward the children's clothing. It put further space between us and the werewolf, which seemed to be the point.

"That was a wild trial today, wasn't it?" he went on, confirming what I already knew—he had recognized my scent. Gus was sorting through the cabinet. I'm sure he wasn't rushing to maintain an air of innocence, but I wished he'd hurry. "I don't know what your husband was thinking, bringing that vamp here."

"This isn't a proper topic to discuss in front of passengers," said Julia, and I wasn't sure if her sigh was real or if she was simply playing along.

"How did she take the verdict?" he asked, ignoring her statement, though lowering his voice the slightest bit. "Not well, I imagine."

"You could sound a little less chuffed about it."

"I'm not, honest," he said, his small chuckle betraying him. Jerusalem, knowing me too well, covered my head with her hand, holding my beak shut. "But I am a little concerned . . . usually Molly's pretty content after a meal, but I heard she's agitated."

"Augustus, my darling," Julia beckoned, just as he was making his way over anyway. She turned back to the werewolf. "It's frankly insulting to Molly that you would ever feel concerned for her, as if chimera aren't the most powerful beings on earth."

"All I'm saying is Molly's hungry, so it must mean the vampire escaped. Don't you agree, Gus?" Ewan tried with Augustus as Julia came and retrieved a very agitated Tiny—the cloak had ultimately been an excellent idea.

"Escaped?" Augustus replied. "From Molly? Impossible." He gave the werewolf a polite nod. "Enjoy your day, Ewan."

I blinked, and the werewolf and his dissatisfied expression were gone.

13

JERUSALEM

Finally, we was on the other side of the swamp, and this time I put Alexei down and backed up a step before he shifted. We'd made record time and was pretty close to where the swamp met the woods . . . the same woods where I'd killed my first vamp.

I was so close to seeing my brother I could've cried.

Later, when there ain't no more killing to be done.

"You were right, dove, as usual," Gus said, concerned as he looked back toward the swamp, like we was being followed. "He knows something."

"He ain't going to report you, is he?" I asked.

"Thankfully, he doesn't have any proof," said Julia, hands on her hips. "But we will need to do a bit of damage control to make people forget about it."

"Don't worry about us." Gus took the gun from his pocket and handed it to Alexei. "Our job is easy compared to what you'll be facing. Good luck."

Julia made a mournful sound. "This is where we leave you, my darling."

"Thanks for everything, Jules. Gus," I said.

She took my hands in hers and pouted like a disappointed kid. "It was so wonderful seeing you. You *must* visit again and bring your brother, and we'll have a proper meal prepared."

"After we lay our friends to rest up north," I said. "Promise."

"Maybe by then, the war will be over," Gus said.

"Wouldn't that be something," I said, grabbing Alexei's hand. "Okay, y'all, see you—"

"Zamir," Lex warned us, low, and we all drew our weapons without questioning it.

The Ancient vampire stood a few yards away. Unconcerned, leaning against a tree. It was the same one who had been with Adelaide on the battlefield—not as tall as Lex but bulkier, with dark, shoulder-length hair and a resting face that looked like he wanted to kill you even if his posture said otherwise.

Although, he did probably want to kill us.

Alexei hadn't smelled him 'cause we was still in the swamp. But as long as we kept an eye on him, that didn't matter. Silently, he moved away from the tree and walked toward us, almost casual. It was . . . strange. What was he doing, trying to get killed?

We moved slowly, too, until we had him surrounded. He stopped walking and put his hands into his pockets, like he was standing in a park instead of a circle of weapons.

This was too easy—no way did this Ancient vampire let us *surround* him without a fight. Something was wrong, but we'd take care of it after we killed him. Ancient warrior or no, there was a hell of a death waiting for him if I had anything to say about it.

And it had to be quick, too, 'cause Adelaide not being here meant she was on her way to the plantation . . . she might've already gotten there.

"Zamirek," said Alexei. "Nie rób tego. Nie możesz wygrać."

I knew he knew the monster, but I still felt as surprised as Julia and Gus lookedwhen we glanced at him, before locking back on our target. I didn't like I couldn't read his expression beyond being reserved.

Zamir tilted his head and said, "Muszę porozmawiać z tobą na osobności."

"He just wants to speak with me," Alexei said in English. He didn't bother to whisper. Zamir'd spoken a little English on the battlefield, but I guess he didn't understand us too much better than we understood him.

"Like hell," I growled.

"You two go ahead," said Julia. "Augustus and I will take care of him."

"No," Lex said, far too quick for comfort. I knew good and well how Lex felt about him, and the last thing we needed was his emotions getting in the way. "He's not to be underestimated."

"Well, look, y'all can sit here and talk it over," I said, cracking my neck. "But if he wants us distracted, it's working. So let's cut the chitchat and send his ass to hell."

"Agreed," said Gus before glancing at Julia, "Ready?"

She nodded at him with an admiring grin. "Go."

Gus vanished just as Julia charged forward.

Clearly, they done this plenty of times before.

I didn't have to get as close with my weapon, so me and Julia attacked at once—and the monster blocked us both, one sword for each of us. With her heavy hammer, her attacks were a little slower than mine, but we found a good rhythm that was hard to break. We kept at it, and he kept defending, but we didn't give him no opening to attack until he was forced to leap straight up into the air—*running scared!* But Gus dropped out a tree and knocked him down like dead weight, knocking one of his swords out of the fight.

I laughed, adrenaline rushing through me. "Hell yeah!" I whooped, racing to block Zamir's descent to the ground with my spear, but, clever as a cat, he stepped his boot off the spear's shaft and moved off sideways—where Gus appeared and slammed into him. But his right arm hung useless as he moved, like it was broken.

We had him.

What happened next was too quick, but suddenly Alexei had Zamir pinned on the ground, his hand around the monster's throat—he hadn't had the opening, since there was too much silver in the fray, but I was happy to give my boy his turn.

"Nie rób tego," Alexei growled at him, but whatever he said, Zamir didn't listen. Instead, he broke Lex's grip, and then they was up, quick as lightning, clashing swords. Julia and I swooped in on either side.

"Alexei, watch out!" I shouted. Zamir could only defend with one arm, so either he'd have to step it up and try to kill us or he was about to die quick and brutal.

And *oh*, my blood raced with a feral desire to see that.

I swung my spear down at him, and he caught it with his sword, pushing up as I pushed down, locking him there so he couldn't defend himself against Julia without risking me slashing him in two. And as if Julia read my mind, she cocked back her hammer for a crushing blow.

ALEXEI

I'd eventually found out Red Mask had two other playthings like me, both captive in different houses. Sometimes, she would be away for days at a time to torture them, leaving me a stretch of peace to do normal activities. Of course, those days were also miserable, seeing as I was recovering from injuries and couldn't heal as quickly as an Ancient yet. But still, Zamir and I would have fun for a change—go on walks unrelated to hunting, play games, or just lie around for hours and talk about things that didn't chill my blood. Or, if he was busy, I would do nothing but lie in bed and close my eyes. Because I could, safely, when she was gone. Because it was soft and cushioned and not threatening. The window latches were all silver, in a vampire's mansion of all places. Red Mask and Zamir had a way of opening them, but, in general, they didn't. They just used the front door. So I couldn't leave, but even if I could, there was nowhere else to go since I wasn't allowed to hunt until she returned.

Until one day.

"Come, Alexei," Zamir said, peeking his head in my room. "Let's go hunt."

"Red Mask won't like it," I said.

He shrugged. "She won't be back until tonight."

"Tonight?" I leapt from bed, snatching up my boots. "What time is it?"

"Sunrise begins in an hour. Come."

I followed him down the grand staircase, and when he

opened the door, he put his hand on my chest and looked up at me sternly. "Leave no signs in the snow."

I nodded. He exited in his bat form—a very Ancient tradition that was a little too on the nose for my taste—and I followed him as a crow. We flew through the surrounding woods, fast and silent. There were no humans living around for miles, but I smelled some after only a mile of flight—perhaps that was why he'd wanted to hunt. Easy prey.

I spotted a horse-drawn cart with massive beasts at its head and four men tending to whatever was in the cart. Usually, we waited in the trees, but Zamir headed straight for it. My mouth was watering as I dove down behind him. But as soon as I shifted into a human, I was yanked by the collar and found myself sitting on the cart with Zamir holding the back of my neck as he crouched in front of me.

"Listen to me, Alexei," he said, his voice as quiet as always but with an edge to it that was unfamiliar enough to set my nerves razor sharp. "These men are going to seal you into this box and take you somewhere—"

Perhaps it was instinct, but I swung at him. His hand clamped tighter on my neck as he grabbed my fist with his other, halting me. "Somewhere *safe*," he said, only a bit louder, and my muscles froze. "Somewhere she won't find you."

My body trembled as if from cold—but I couldn't feel the cold, not anymore—and when he released my wrist, my hand lowered aimlessly, uselessly. "Where she won't find me?" I repeated dumbly.

"The travel will be long," he continued, and it was a wonder I could process his words, "and you will not be able to leave this box until you arrive. But I have a lover who will help you on the other end. You will be quite safe."

"This . . . this is a trick," I gasped.

"No trick," he said with the slightest smile at the corner of his lips. "You are leaving me, my *misiu*. Now get in the box. I need to be home before the sun rises."

"I don't want to go without you."

"You must."

There were the edges of light along the rim of the horizon. I hadn't seen the sun in months . . . since I'd been human. I swallowed, my throat burning with a sob. Every sensation, every thought, was almost too much . . . overwhelming, like the moment I'd become a vampire.

"Come now, boy." Zamir sighed heavily. He shushed me harshly, and I fought to hold back my tears. When I couldn't, he patted my cheek, hard enough that it would've felt like a slap if I'd still been human. "None of that."

"Why are you doing this?"

"Always with *why*." For a moment, he looked at me. Then he grinned, an almost melancholy twist of his lips, and rubbed small circles on my scalp until I calmed . . . the last small comfort I'd ever feel from him. "Get in the box, Alexei. I won't tell you again."

He didn't have to. The box wasn't long enough for me but deep enough that I could at least bend my knees. It wouldn't be comfortable for as long as I'd have to be inside, but I didn't care.

It wasn't until the cart started moving that I thought to panic. What if . . . what if this *was* a trick? What if Red Mask had decided I was no longer entertaining, and this was her way to get rid of me? For all I knew, they were taking the box away somewhere to set on fire.

No. Zamir wouldn't do that to me. He cared about me. He was saving my life.

Someday, I would repay him for that.

My shashka clashed with Julia's hammer as it came down, and Zamir used the brief delay in potentially having his head crushed in to shift into a bat and fly off—slower than usual with his injured shoulder, but faster than any living bat.

"It's over," I said. "Leave him to me."

I followed him as a crow. We flew for a while, far enough and high enough that we couldn't have been chased on foot. Until finally, Zamir landed on a suitably large branch. I leaned against the trunk, watching him crouch and grip his shoulder with a small sound of discomfort. It would heal soon enough if it was left to do so. The look of betrayal in his eyes . . . that would be harder to fix.

But after everything, maybe that didn't even matter.

"What are you doing, Alexei?" he said, careful not to yell and give away our position—though I'd never heard him yell, anyway.

But a lot could change in three hundred years.

"What does it look like?" I asked. "Saving your life."

"'Saving,'" he scoffed. "You simply changed your mind."

"So did you!" I snapped. "You let that monster torture me for months and then changed your mind. I don't see the difference."

He shoved disheveled hair away from his face but said nothing.

"I could've let that Saint smash in your skull," I said. "In-

stead, I'm buying you time to heal. And *when* you heal, I expect
you to get away from here, not charge into another fight."

His brows raised as he stood. "Ah, I see. You don't want me
to kill them. Familiars or pets?"

My jaw clenched, and I just barely held back the desire to kill
him right there in the trees. "Friends."

He smirked. "Come now, Alexei, I smelled you all over the
little one back on the battlefield. She is a pet, clearly."

If muscles could feel panic and relief at once, the pain in my
gut was that. "What did you do to her?"

"You sound so concerned." He tested his shoulder with a
wince. "I only tried to make her return to you, but she could not
be reasoned with. Fearless little thing. Incredibly foolhardy, but
I can see why you're fond of her."

"I'm more than fond of her. I love her."

"You see, a pet. As humans love their horses."

"No."

Zamir paused, his expression balanced between confusion
and disgust. There was a time when I would've understood that
emotion completely—humans were food to us. Things to use
and consume, not to love. An Ancient of a thousand years could
never understand the feelings Jerusalem raised in me. Though,
to be fair, as a serial killer, he probably hadn't had a very high
opinion of most humans when he'd been one.

"Whether or not you believe me, Alexei, I am trying to protect you," he said with a heavy sigh. "She does not recognize
your scent. Use that to your advantage and get away now."

It was a tempting suggestion. But impossible. "I won't abandon Jerusalem."

"Then you will die together."

As usual, he was on the side of evil . . . but in the most confusing way possible. "If you're trying to ruin her plans so badly, why don't you join us? Two vampires and a Saint should be more than sufficient odds to defeat her."

"*Sufficient odds?*" It was the closest thing to fear I'd ever heard in his voice. "She's five thousand years old."

His response sent a chill down my spine. "No vampire is invincible. She can be killed."

"In theory. But you will never be faster or stronger than her. And it takes at least a minute of constant contact for silver to even begin to affect her."

"But staking her in the heart *will* work."

"Yes, if by some miracle you get the chance." He shook his head. "You will not get that chance, Alexei."

I sighed, fisting my hair in my hands. I couldn't linger here much longer, but his words were worrying. Not that the fear hadn't always been at the back of my mind—I was more powerful than when I'd been turned, but so was she, and I was never going to catch up to her. And if I couldn't match her, Jerusalem certainly didn't stand a chance.

"That's still your comfort spot," Zamir said, and when I looked up, he was grinning. He gestured to his head. "Your scalp."

I dropped my hands immediately. "Do you still love her?" I had to get away from anything that would make me feel too much.

His only response was a scoff.

"Then help us. You know she deserves it."

"We don't all get what we deserve."

"Exactly right," I growled. "Me sparing you, for example."

He gave a slow grin. "We haven't seen each other for centuries, my *misiu*. What have I done to deserve your wrath?"

His smile brought back memories . . . not all of them horrifying, even if now I knew none of it was right. Jerusalem had spoken the truth, and yet contrary emotions still battled each other for dominance somehow.

"You manipulated me," I said bitterly. "You used kindness and affection as a tool to control me."

As I spoke, his smile dropped down to an expression far more self-aware. "I loved you very much by the end, Alexei."

My gut twisted, and I felt a childish hope . . . that same hope that sustained me, for five months those three hundred years ago, that Zamir truly cared enough about me and would take me away.

Thankfully, it was fleeting.

"And before that?" I demanded. "When you did everything in your power to keep me reliant on you so I wouldn't run?" I waited for Zamir to speak. When he remained silent, my frustration grew. "I worshipped you, you know."

"I know," he said, his tone bordering something close to remorse, if he could feel that anymore. If he had *ever* felt that.

Time was ticking by all too quickly. I wanted him to explain himself. Apologize. *Something.* I was never going to see him again. Instead, I said, "They'll be looking for me. You have to go."

He nodded, testing his shoulder again. Augustus must have really crushed the bone to dust. "I suppose we're even."

"Not even close."

He smirked as if I were joking. "Then I will allow you the option to write if ever you need a favor—"

"No." I shook my head to emphasize it. "No, I don't want to have anything to do with you ever again."

Zamir looked disturbed. "Come now, it can't be that serious."

"You have to go."

"Alexei." He sighed. "My *misiu*—"

"Don't call me that." I felt like a tattered rope holding on by its very last fiber, ready to snap. "And don't say my name like you actually care about me."

"I do care—"

"Stop it," I snapped, like I was shutting out a siren's song. I closed my eyes briefly, remembering I had people waiting for me who might hear us and judge what I was doing. "It's too late, Zamir. *Leave.* If I see you again, I'll kill you myself."

Zamir took me in, as if trying to gauge if I was bluffing. "The one downfall of being Ancient is that everything in this life is fleeting, and so things become irrelevant quickly. But you . . . after three hundred years, your scent is still imprinted in my memory. You mean something to me, Alexei, whether or not you want any part in it."

Three hundred years ago, I would have hung on his every word. Even now my stomach twisted with a longing to have a small part of what we used to have. But I couldn't tell what was real and what was an act to gain my affection, to use me as he wished. I didn't know him like I thought I knew him. And so, it was better not to trust anything he said.

I kept my expression neutral and my mouth shut. He would not get to see what his words did to me. I would not give him the satisfaction of an acknowledgment.

Zamir looked away, the slight melancholy of defeat in his grin. "A little advice—you may love her, but you would be wise never to turn that girl. She would be like a vampiric horse, that one . . . except with far too much potential to burn down the world."

Without another word, he shifted into a bat and flew away.

Jerusalem would hate that more than anything, anyway. It's the last thing she would want.

But I would have never said that to him. He didn't deserve to know Jerusalem the way I did. For people like him, knowledge was ammunition to use against you.

I watched him leave before shifting into a crow and finding my group. Julia held her hammer at the ready as I shifted back, startling her.

"Personal vendetta," I said, before anyone could accuse me.

Julia leaned on her hammer like a walking stick with a dissatisfied sigh. "I helped save you from Molly just for you to steal my trophy from me? Those fangs were mine."

"You voted to have me *sent* to Molly *a few hours ago*," I growled. "Or do you have the memory of a goldfish, you little—"

"Hey, now," Augustus said just as Tiny butt in with, "I would've *loved* to see the vamp's head caved in, Jules. But I'd never deprive someone of their personal kill. 'Specially not you, Lex."

By the way she looked at me, she knew what I had done, but she didn't give me away. I wanted to kiss her for it.

Julia scowled. "He's got you under a spell, I swear—"

"You two better get moving," said Augustus, gathering her close as consolation for the interruption, "if you want to reach the plantation in time."

Tiny jumped at them, hugging them both at once—she was so cute, it was almost unbearable. "Thanks for all your help."

And then she grabbed my hand and dragged me toward the woods.

"So, you let him go," she said when she was sure Julia and Augustus had gone.

"He saved my life. I saved his. I don't want to see him again, but it felt wrong to kill him."

"I get it," she said. "I mean, I don't get it, but I get it."

"Thank you, Tiny. I promised to kill him if I saw him again, though. Hopefully, that means we never will." I paused as she stepped in front of me and grabbed my shirt, and when I bent closer, she used my thigh as a step to climb. I loved that she trusted me to do things without her asking—I let her sit on my forearm as she wrapped her legs around my waist, my heart growing far too big as she snuggled against my chest, burying her face in my neck. "Sleepy?"

"Naw, just going to rest my eyes."

I pressed her close. In another life, we would have hours upon hours to do this—Tiny sleeping on me while I wondered how I got so lucky. But this wasn't that life.

And it wouldn't be until Red Mask was dead.

"How you know for sure he won't cause no trouble, though?" she asked, her warm breath gentle against my neck.

Because he's as afraid of her as I am. His words rang through my head: that she was far too ancient for us to face, that this was a fool's errand. But Jerusalem would never listen to that, regardless of what had happened on the battlefield. So I said, "He's very Old World. America is too fast paced for him. He'll go home, I promise." That was true enough without breaking her spirit.

"So he don't care if we kill his girl, huh?" She chuckled. "A thousand years old and no loyalty to be found."

JERUSALEM

I could only doze a good ten minutes before I slid back down to walk, spear in hand. It suddenly hit me hard—we was way too close to finishing this for me to sleep now.

I would catch up when our enemy was dead and buried.

The woods hadn't changed none since a year ago. Not that I knew them that well. I'd only been through once, and that was to leave. But they was thick and wild then in the dark and was just as thick and wild in the day, not that there was much difference with the smoke. Still, I was glad we'd ditched the horses at the inn; they could've never gotten through here. And this was the trees thinned out from decades of gathering lumber for building and firewood. Imagine that. How much more wild and free would it have been if they had left them well enough alone?

"Did you mean it?" Alexei broke our silence. "When you told Julia you love me?"

I hid my face fast. It seemed stupid that the words was more embarrassing than the kissing and touching and holding, but they was.

He chuckled. "You do realize turning away doesn't actually hide your blush from me."

"I ain't blushing," I snapped, even if it was a stupid lie. "And I threatened to kill my best friend for you, didn't I?"

"Excuse me?" He looked really and truly offended. "*I'm* your best friend."

"She's a woman and ain't white. We understand each other different."

He pulled me closer by the waist and kissed my forehead. "I understand you differently."

His tone sent shivers through me, made me blush harder. But now wasn't the time, so I peeled his fingers away from my waist and pressed forward before his touch became a distraction.

"You ever have trouble making your way through society just 'cause you white?" I asked.

He looked confused, and *that* was the point. "No."

"Exactly."

We continued a few paces before he said, "I only asked, Tiny, because I love you more than anything. But you don't have to say it back if you don't mean it. I'd rather you didn't."

I stopped walking. Turned to face him, blush and all. It was hard to look him in the eye . . . why was it so hard? *I meant it when I said it for Dess*, I should've said, but couldn't. I'd never been bashful in my life. That Lex, of all people, could make me out of sorts? *This* dumbass?

I took a breath and forced myself to look at him, my courage growing the longer I did. "I meant it."

The grin he had was so cute, like snail-level cute. "I love you, too."

"Oh, that much is clear." I suddenly wanted his hands all over again, but there wasn't no time. Instead, I continued walking with him beside me. "Feel better?"

"I really thought we were best friends."

I rolled my eyes. "You still on that?"

"After all, I know what you sound like when you—"

"Alexei!"

"Sneeze." He gave me a sly side-eye while I glared at him. "Where was your mind headed?"

"On its way to murder you if you don't shut—"

I tripped to a stop, staring at the ground ahead.

New greenery had grown, new leaves had fallen, covering up the ground that had burned. But the random branches I'd broken was still there.

It'd been dark as the pits of hell the night I'd run away, but a girl could never forget the place where she'd almost been killed. Not to mention what had started it all . . .

We didn't have nothing to clean Lila's body with except water and a pathetic amount of soap. Matthew had offered a small flask of liquor he'd had hidden on him to disinfect, but it wasn't nearly enough to do the job. Lila's flesh had been torn so bad, we'd had to bury her in a rush that same evening. No ceremony, no time to build no coffin, nothing nearly reverent enough for her sweet soul.

The mistress didn't allow them, anyways. Funerals. Mama said the master had never minded them while he was married to his first wife, had treated our time away from the fields as none of his business and allowed everyone to attend real and true funerals with songs and prayers and proper burials. But I guess that had been his wife's influence. 'Cause as soon as she kicked the bucket, and Adelaide showed up, that "nonsense" as she called it was put to an end. She wasn't going to allow us no dignity, not even in death.

I'd done most of the work digging 'cause I could and I'd needed to for my own sanity—plus I was short, so couldn't nobody tell I wasn't where I was supposed to be working. Pa and Matthew managed to get away from their duties, but only 'cause the master had gone out with his sons to celebrate something or other. *Celebrate*, while we was out here mourning my sister. By the time I was done with the grave, it was about time for Mama to be done in the kitchen. And after Pa and Matthew finished putting the devil and his sons to bed, the four of us went about doing a funeral as best we could. The four of us . . . should've been the five.

We buried Lila to the sound of thunder, as if the very sky was mourning her along with us, even if the storm was still a long ways off from bringing rain, if it headed our way at all. The only thing we could do to honor her was placing her favorite belongings on top of the dirt—her sewing kit, her favorite dress . . . all except her doll made of sacks and yarn. That I had folded in my sister's arms before I'd lain her in the grave.

I couldn't stand the thought of her in the darkness alone.

That night, with the sky rumbling with thunder and clattering wind making our small quarters creak, we'd held onto each other like someone might try and tear us apart. Mama had cried herself to sleep in my arms while I'd lain awake . . . thinking and overthinking and crying and seething.

Why did our lives have to be like this? Pain after pain, every day till we died? Or till them monsters killed us, more like. It wasn't fair. And it sure as hell wasn't right.

And, all at once, it clicked for me. Maybe our lives didn't *have* to be like this. I had my abilities for a reason, didn't I? Maybe I was the one who was supposed to set us free. Wish I'd thought of it before . . . but at least it wasn't too late to save the rest of my family.

So, as soon as I knew my family was asleep, I slipped away into the night.

Didn't have no weapon, no plan. All I knew was that godawful, wicked devil of a man needed to pay, and I was strong enough to make him. Adelaide always went elsewhere for the night to hunt and such, but that didn't mean there was time for speeches or humiliation—after all, Donald slept in the same house, and I wasn't about to do nothing stupid that would get me caught. But the thunder booming in the distance and the wind howling like a cat was more than enough cover for me to get in and out without no one being the wiser.

Wasn't real good at climbing, so I went in through the little dog door on the back porch—Lord knew which of their nasty hounds could fit through that, all of them big and none of them allowed inside.

Maybe it'd been placed there just for me.

I tiptoed barefoot across the wood floor and up the stairs— I'd to rush up at the rumble of thunder since the daggone things creaked more than a rusty door. Ain't never been in the big house before, so I didn't rightly know which room I was looking for. I only knew it from the outside, from the window I knew was his, so I had to picture it the opposite way.

Lucky for me, he'd left the door open to keep his room from getting stuffy in the summer heat.

I'd never killed a man before but had experienced plenty of violence. Seen it done, had it done to me. So I knew what would make him squeal and beg and what would kill him quiet-like. As much as I wanted to torture him like he'd tortured me and my family, I wasn't reckless enough to overlook that it would wake the whole house if I did, even if it was only Donald. If that boy knew what was happening, knew it was me, and ran off to get Adelaide or his vamp brother? I'd be good and dead in a few minutes.

I'd have to make sure this man couldn't scream.

Wasn't one candle burning to light my way, but my night vision was enough as I took a shirt that was laid over a chair and carried it with me to the bed. It all happened quickly, without much thought. I crawled onto the bed and sat on the devil's chest, shoving the shirt into his mouth. He startled awake, but by then, my hands gripped his throat, crushing the air out of him.

The thunder growing ever nearer, ever stronger, ever louder, blocked out his feeble efforts to fight. If I'd've thought of it, I would've broken his arms first to keep him from laying any blows on me, but they was weak, anyway. He looked at me, his eyes wild and bloodshot and bulging, as if he was pleading. As if I'd show him mercy. As if I'd let him get away with what he'd done to my sister.

Or maybe he just knew it was over, and a seventeen-year-old enslaved girl was the one to do it. I couldn't rightly tell his expression in the dark. I didn't care.

The wind howled, pounding against the window. It was too long but also not nearly long enough before his body lay limp on the bed. I squeezed harder, breaking his neck to make sure he couldn't be revived. And with not much time to bask in my good work, I left the same way I came.

In hindsight, no amount of precautions would've kept me from being caught. Adelaide would've smelled me on the sheets, tracked me to my house, just like she did. So even though it had felt so satisfying in the moment, squeezing the life out of that demon of a man . . . it was a satisfaction that turned to suffering only a few hours later.

"What is it?" Lex asked, his voice at the edge of a growl.

I twitched, waking from my memories. "We're close" was all I said. That vamp was dead and gone, along with his wicked pa . . . and that was what Adelaide would be when I was done with her. I pulled my eyes away from the scene to look at Lex. "It's going to take us both to bring her down."

I'd learned that the hard way, but there wasn't no point in dwelling on it now. Besides, Lex was a vampire, and that would make all the difference.

He nodded, even if he looked a little unsure.

"In the meantime, kill any white folks you see. No offense, but trust me, they deserve it."

His smile seemed more vampiric, fangs flashing. "Hopefully, at least one of them's worth drinking."

I grabbed his shirt, dragging him down to kiss him, but maybe that was a bad idea. 'Cause all it did was make me feel desperate, make me really realize there was more than just my brother's life on the line. I let myself feel that way for five seconds and then pushed it down. Wasn't no time for doubt and fear, only action.

"You ready?" I asked.

He cringed. "I suppose this will be easy compared to surviving a chimera," he said, but he didn't sound convinced. He handed me the revolver, showing me how to load the silver bullet in before I handed it back. He hid it at his hip.

"We going to make her pay for what she done to us. To my family. To Dess and Gael. To anyone who has suffered at her hand." I didn't bother with holy water this time—it wasn't going to do nothing, anyways, and it would only put Lex in danger. Still, I stepped away from him. I needed to get my head ready for battle. "She ain't taking you back, Lex. I'd never let her."

"I believe you, but . . . I'm still scared."

"Be scared. Fight anyway." I wanted to kiss him again. Chase away his anxiety. But there'd be time for that later after we won. "I need you, Lex."

He nodded, firm and sure, despite his fears. "You have me, my love."

"Till the end of us."

Except there wasn't going to be no end.

"Let's go save my brother," I said.

And we charged forward.

We ran toward the enemy, not too concerned with avoiding

brush and twigs or keeping quiet. It didn't matter that Adelaide would wait till we got there to make an example of Matthew, that he was probably okay for now. This was a year overdue. And besides, that monster knew we was coming—that was why she'd sent Zamir ahead of her.

And quicker than a breeze, we came up on the plantation.

When the war'd begun, they'd switched from growing primarily cotton to also growing crop supplies for the Southern army. It was only July, and the corn was already reaching toward the sky, or at least tall as me.

"The ones on horseback first," I called to Lex. It didn't matter they might hear me—there wasn't nothing they could do about it. 'Cause Lex shifted to a wolf, racing forward like a lightning bolt into the cornfield. I heard some distressed sounds; he must've run past some people. I ran in after him and looked up in time to see him leap out of the corn and pounce on the closest overseer—but all I heard was a short scream when he landed, missing the good part completely as he tackled the man to the ground to finish him off.

I grabbed the closest person I could—a sweet old woman who used to try and love match me up with any and every boy in this daggone field.

Old Miss Kay broke down crying when she got a good look at me. "Bless the Lord, oh my soul." She took my face in her withered hands and kissed it. "Matthew said you'd be back for us."

Another scream—another overseer down.

"Get your things," I said quickly to her and the others around me—there wasn't no time for hugs and relief. The storm wasn't over yet. "Head into the woods till you hit the swamp; there'll be help for you there. Or wait for me, and I'll lead you. Pass the word."

Another scream. Lex wasn't about to save no fun for me, huh? Though part of me was grateful—I needed all my strength for what was coming.

I escaped from her grateful grasp. "Where Matthew at?"

Miss Kay's expression dropped, and I knew.

"Pass the word," I repeated and took off running toward the house.

Please don't let me be too late, I prayed. She wasn't going to kill him, that much I knew. But after learning what she'd done to Alexei . . . who knew what horrifying things she'd put him through while they waited?

My heart tripped as Alexei's wolf form caught up a few feet beside me, racing through the corn—I still hated dogs. That was going to take a while to get used to. But he was still my brutal Lex, and he dashed ahead of me and leapt at the overseer who'd just come from the barn, tearing out his throat before they'd even hit the ground.

I ran on while Alexei kept the way clear, taking out anyone who dared to get in our view—there shouldn't of been so many, with most of the family dead already, but I recognized some as neighbors, and that was good enough for me.

Finally, we reached the front of the house.

A rage built up in me, seeing it again. The fence where that vile boy would tie up his bicycle. The old oak where I'd been whupped within an inch of life. The side window, open and displaying where I'd woke that wicked man up and choked his ass to death the night he'd killed my sister.

The flower garden had gone downhill sometime in the past year, I guess, so the house could be seen for the big, ugly thing it was.

And I couldn't hardly wait to burn it to the ground.

Lex shifted back from his wolf form and wiped the blood from his mouth, his shirt splattered with it. "They're definitely inside."

I nodded.

Even though I knew good and well Adelaide could smell us coming, I still stepped lightly up the porch steps to draw all the attention to myself. The front door and the wire screen across to keep out the bugs was wide open, inviting us in.

I saw Matthew before he saw me. He was at the far end of the living room standing in front of the fireplace, and my throat went tight with anger. She'd put that God-awful metal bridle on him to keep him quiet, his wrists bound together with crude rope. But other than that, he didn't look hurt. Naw, she wasn't fittin' to hurt him yet, not if she had the chance to torture him in front of me.

As soon as he saw me, his eyes went wide. But I'd barely took a few steps into the house when he shook his head, a warning that came too late as Adelaide was already coming down the stairs.

Or would've been too late if that wasn't the exact hag I'd been waiting a year to kill.

Her smile was a vile thing as she locked them dirty blood eyes on me, her voice as cool as snake when she said, "Welcome home, Dido."

ALEXEI

It didn't matter that I'd never seen her face. Her scent was undeniable.

But Zamir was right; mine clearly wasn't—no signs of recognition crossed her expression until she looked at me, her eyes widening in the way one would look at a fancy coat in the window they'd been dying to buy. She'd probably tortured so many—before *and* after me—that my scent was just one more in her queue of victims.

"My, oh my, isn't this a surprise," Adelaide said, laying a hand on her beat-less chest. "I recognized your aroma but couldn't for the life of me place it. My Alexei. It's been far too long."

My stomach roiled at her acknowledgment. I wished I could have turned back when I had the chance. I forced myself not to touch the gun. Better to keep her attention on me, as much as I dreaded it, than to let on I had a silver bullet for her.

"Zamir was always very soft on you," she went on. "I suppose I shouldn't be surprised that he let you through."

"He was an easy kill, honestly," Jerusalem lied casually.

Adelaide laughed in a way that I knew meant pain was coming, and my muscles tightened against it. "I don't know that I believe you, girl, but I do so enjoy your unbridled arrogance. It is my favorite personality type to dominate . . ." Her grin turned almost grossly fond as she locked eyes with me. "Isn't it, Alexei?"

I fought the urge to place my hand against Jerusalem, shift her back to protect her. I couldn't show that I cared for her— anyone or anything I loved could be used against me. Tiny didn't need my protection, anyway, and it showed in the very way she carried herself. I couldn't let her down. I couldn't let *myself* down. Now was not the time to fall apart.

"What are you doing with this little *thing*?" Adelaide asked. The question was clearly for me—she had ceased to find interest in Jerusalem, which was a small relief.

"We have a common enemy, as it turns out," I said, forcing my voice cold.

Detached. Good.

And yet, the monster assessed me as if she didn't quite believe it.

"You know," Adelaide said, so casually that for a moment, I couldn't believe the words coming out of her mouth. "There is a far less bloody solution to this mess you've found yourself in. You, Alexei, could simply return to me."

"Like hell," growled Tiny, undoing all my efforts to distance myself from her.

I felt sick as the monster grinned. "Be mine again, Alexei," she said. "And instead of killing your little subhuman, I shall simply leave her to rot in enslavement with her brother. Where she belongs."

Her words felt like poison in my blood, and the first thought in my head was *This is a trap.*

JERUSALEM

I laughed. Not 'cause what she said was funny—'cause, Lord, it was the worst thing I could think of to have Lex taken to be tortured, to not be able to save my brother. But I'd been free a year. And did she forget what I'd done to her nasty-ass husband and stepson? Naw, this deal was desperation talking. She knew good and well she couldn't beat the two of us at once. Maybe she'd felt cocky when it'd been two Saints against her, but vamps hated facing off against each other.

We had her.

Adelaide looked annoyed as hell at my laughter, and somehow that made it all so much funnier. "Okay," I said, "well, lemme throw another deal out there for you. Me and Alexei kill your sorry ass, and *you* burn in hell."

I glanced at Alexei—it was time to attack, ready or not.

But Adelaide grabbed Matthew's chin, so I paused—too risky with her touching him like that. My poor brother closed his eyes at the contact, like the monster would kill him any second. *She won't,* I wish I could tell him. *She can't torture me if I ain't got nothing left to fight for.*

But who knew what awful things she'd done to him in the year he'd waited for me to come back. Just thinking about it made me tremble with rage.

"Did I pick the right boy, Dido?" she asked. "I never can tell any of you apart, really. He does, however, look so much like your sister." She released him with a small shrug. "Such a shame. The quality of Millie's styling gravely diminished after I killed her."

Every muscle in my body went rigid. This whole time I thought it'd been a doctor, but . . . it must've been my smart mouth that done it. I'd threatened Donald. Adelaide had whupped me. She remembered me and punished Lila for it—

No. It didn't have nothing to do with me. She was a monster, killing without remorse.

Well, she wasn't the only one who killed without remorse.

I could be a monster, too.

"Oh no, is this the first time you've heard?" she asked, a mocking pout mucking up her face, making her red lips look bloodied. "Well, you'll be glad to know that when she was screaming for help, it was your name on her lips—"

I unleashed a war cry, senseless and rageful and murderous, and it was all I could do to keep from crying. The sudden sound did its job—the monster flinched, thrown off for a second. A second long enough to leave her open to attack.

I lunged at her, and she blocked it with one hand, the other unsheathing her sword. I snickered, spinning my spear away from her parry—she was going straight for her weapon, which meant she was already fighting scared. By then, Lex had joined me, and Adelaide blocked his sword with hers. There wasn't nowhere to run in this living room with a couch, chairs, a small table, a big old pillar in the center—exhilarating in a different way than a battlefield ever could be.

And fighting alongside Lex was a game changer, as it always was. He was fast and strong and skilled, and it made me work harder to be better. But the thing about a monster like this was you had to get them quick, or they had too much time to think they way out of it. And Lex wasted no time, parrying only twice, waiting for me to block the next one, before finding just the opening to knock the smug witch straight through the wall.

Literally.

I winced, gaping as she slammed through the outer wall, taking the whole dang thing with her, and skidded along the dirt outside.

"Hell yeah!" I exclaimed, shoving him in the arm in excitement. I wanted to kiss him so bad, but I couldn't lose my head just 'cause my boyfriend was a badass. I rushed over to Matthew and broke the latch at the back of his head, tossing the awful contraption aside. My brother took my face in his hands, even as his wrists were bound, his grip desperate.

"I knew you was alive."

Seeing him, hearing his voice, I wanted to cry. "This ain't over yet, Matthew." I tore the ropes from him. "Find you somewhere to hide till it is."

My brother looked scared, and I wished I had time to soothe his nerves.

Later.

Me and Lex had a monster to slay.

ALEXEI

She's going to punish me.

My muscles tightened to the point of pain as I forced my mind not to give into panic. Because while Jerusalem saw about her brother, I watched Red Mask as she stood up a hundred meters away. Even if her movements were cool as she shook out the skirts of her deep red dress, I could see the irritation in her eyes from here. She wasn't injured, wasn't distressed, and in no rush to attack us—but of course she wasn't. Like little gnats, all we'd done was annoy her.

"We got to keep her in the house so she ain't got no room to run," said Tiny. "I know better than to take her on in an open field."

And I knew better than to face her in close quarters.

But there was no point in debating. Zamir had been right, and it was too late to heed his warning.

All I could do was protect Jerusalem and hope today wouldn't end in her death.

The monster had a far worse plan than death for me. By then, she'd made it back into the house through the busted in wall and leveled a look at me that was half chastisement, half wrath.

"That was rude, Alexei," she said, far too calm.

A shiver ran down my spine, but when Jerusalem rushed forward, I was right beside her.

I would never allow fear to let me abandon the people I love ever again.

Everything was unspoken when Jerusalem and I fought together; we'd been doing it for so long. Red Mask blocked Tiny's attack, but her blood wet my sword before she could manage to push my weapon. My blade wasn't silver, so she would easily heal, but if I attacked quickly enough before she could heal, it would weaken her the slightest bit.

All we had to do was distract her enough to land one gunshot.

And it worked, because the next time I attacked, she parried. But this time I didn't move away for another attack. Instead, I held her blade with mine, hers inching toward her face as I overpowered her.

But the monster suddenly leaned to the side quickly, the risk of being cut by my blade well worth it when I realized far too late that she wasn't reaching for another slash but for my—

The bang of the gun threatened to deafen my sensitive ears, but in the next breath Jerusalem's scream was high and alarmed.

I heard it before I finally felt it, the pain zapping my strength . . . as if my entire body was on fire.

"Did you think I couldn't sense your little silver bullet, Alexei?" asked Red Mask. She shoved me against the wall, tossing the gun carelessly away. "I have to say, I'm disappointed in you."

I slid down the wall to sit, my legs suddenly feeling too weak to hold me up. *Don't touch it* was all I could think, on instinct only, yet my body still fought not to reach inside the wound and yank out the bullet. My hands might never work again if I did.

My vision dipped in and out as I fought not to pass out from the deep, searing pain.

And suddenly the memories threatened to consume me.

Of being bound . . . of the fear and hopelessness . . . of the excruciating pain as the monster's teeth crushed into my neck.

All that newfound courage was gone, and everything in me was sinking into panic.

I couldn't let that happen to the girl I loved.

"Jerusalem," I managed. "Run!"

JERUSALEM

I didn't care what Lex meant. I raced to him instead of away. Adelaide knocked me off course, and I fumbled to keep grip of my spear. Wasn't a fatal blow, so I got to my feet quickly, just in time to realize she'd snatched it right out of my grasp. In the next second, she snapped it in half in her hands like it was nothing but a skinny twig. But there wasn't no time to feel nervous. I snatched up Alexei's sword right as she picked up hers.

"My, you are resilient," she said, looking me up and down. "If you hadn't been born with such an unfortunate complexion, you'd be just the sort of mortal I'd consider keeping as a pet."

"Suck my dick," I growled, charging forward, and her amusement at my vulgarity bought me half a second—long enough to land a cut on her shoulder. Even if the blade wasn't silver, even if she shoved my blade away right after. Lex had taught me to use a sword some before I'd received my first real spear, and I remembered enough to get by. Either way, it didn't matter. I just had to get close enough to lay my hands on her. She wasn't way bigger than me like Lex, so there was no size she could use against me, and I could brawl with the best of them.

That was one side of me I hadn't shown on the battlefield,

and she wouldn't be expecting it. Surprising her seemed to be the only chance I had.

And, lo and behold, I just had to parry twice before her face was nice and open for me—I slammed the heel of my hand up the base of her nose, a satisfying snap vibrating through my hand. Adelaide stumbled back and covered her broken nose, blood gushing from it, her eyes wide with angry shock. I'd made the monster bleed, and if I could do that with one slam of my hand, it wouldn't take much more to kill her. She knew it, too.

"You filthy savage!" she growled, right as I plunged my blade through her stomach.

I laughed as she let out a sound of shock and agony—it was just too good after all her gloating. She looked mad as hell, a dangerous kind of fury that would wither the weak but with an edge of confusion that made me smile.

Yet when I went to pull the blade out, she clamped her hand around my wrist to hold me still, and my stomach soured. Her face was a mix of anger and pain, but the blade wasn't silver . . . and this whole thing reminded me of why I'd chosen a long spear as my weapon in the first place.

I gasped out too much breath as the monster grabbed my throat with her other hand, lifting me into the air. Her grip was crushing, and for a second I panicked—*she going to break my neck before I ever run out of air.* I tried to kick at her, but my efforts were too little. Feeble.

"You still don't know your place," she bit out blood trickling out the corner of her mouth as she pulled the sword out and threw it away.

She slammed the side of my face against the wood floor.

My head swam, my vision blurring to a smudge of color. I blinked and blinked but couldn't see nothing, couldn't hear nothing but my sprinting heart, all of me numb. In the haze, I heard Alexei's voice, even if I couldn't hear no words, yelling while the monster laughed. But a second later, all my senses rushed back at once, and I heard my own body cry out at the pain in my head. I tasted bitter blood, saw blood splattered on the floor before me. Splinters dug into the side of my face. But I couldn't get up from any of it, a heavy palm pressing down on the side of my head, a knee digging into my back, threatening to break me.

"Well, well, well . . ." Adelaide's tone was self-congratulatory. "A year ago, I swore up and down to Garfield that you'd be back for your brother. I thought a Saint would present a fine challenge for me, a little entertainment after all these years." I grimaced as she ground the side of my face harder into the floor, into my own hot blood. "But you're still just a sorry little beast, aren't you?"

I swallowed the urge to cry.

How could I have been so stupid?

I'd lost that fight against Alexei. He wasn't my enemy, but if he had been, I'd be stone dead days ago. And it wasn't just 'cause he was powerful—he was an Ancient. He'd let Zamir go, but it'd taken two Saints and a sasquatch to take the monster down—also an Ancient. Gael and I had been fighting her at the same time, and for some reason, it hadn't hit me then. Adelaide was winning this *because* she was an Ancient, not in addition to it. She was stronger and faster, not to mention smarter from far too many centuries on this earth.

And now she was going to take Alexei back as her pet, keep Matthew in chains, and there wasn't nothing I could do to protect them.

'Cause killing was all I was good at, and I didn't see no way to do it.

Still, if I was going to die, I wasn't going to die no coward.

"I ain't afraid of you," I managed.

Her fingers gripped my neck, her long nails digging into my skin as bad as the splinters, and I barely held in a sob of agony as the monster bent my arm the wrong way. My elbow snapped. Sharp pain made it hard to think, but I kept my senses enough to move with her as she dragged me to my feet, if only to keep my spine where it was supposed to be.

"'Ain't afraid,'" Adelaide mocked. "Your little rabbit heart tells a very different story."

I wanted to vomit but couldn't tell if it was from the dizziness of a concussion or the sharp pain in my arm or just plain old fear. All I knew was it was a familiar kind of scary, the memories of a year ago springing to life all over again. I felt those bony fingers dig against the scalp of my memory as Adelaide's flesh ones grabbed my face with nearly enough force to break my cheekbones. She bared my neck as the monster in my memory did, and I choked on a sob, my vision blurring. Only this time, there wasn't no weapon hidden in my apron pocket. I was broken and useless and going to be eaten alive by the very monster who had killed my family.

"Not like this," I whimpered to God, as the monster's cold lips came near my throat—

ALEXEI

"I agree to your terms!" The words tumbled out of me before I could stop them, as sick as they felt to say. I couldn't watch Adelaide hurt my love anymore—I couldn't sit here being useless to stop her.

Adelaide halted, her fangs hovering near Jerusalem's throat. Waiting.

"Lex, no," Tiny gasped, in pain and fear.

I nearly cried. My memories were as pained as her voice. But I couldn't let this go on. I had to protect her how I could. The first step was ensuring she didn't die. Next was removing this bullet without burning my hands off.

And then . . . I didn't know. We'd think of something. We always did.

"Don't hurt her anymore," I said, "and I'll go with you without a fight. I swear. Leave Jerusalem and her brother alive and unharmed."

"Why, Alexei," the monster said, "I enjoy your begging, but for a *mortal?* Don't tell me it's love!"

"I'll go with you," I said again. I had to leave love out of it, even if Jerusalem was my only reason to continue this existence. I couldn't give that monster further reason to torture her. Not after what she had done to my wife all those years ago . . . what she had made me do. "It's me you really want, anyway, isn't it?"

She considered my words. That, at least, was a good sign. "My pathetic darling. You always were a soft one during conditioning. I see I shall have to break you in all over again."

JERUSALEM

Alexei's expression at her words looked as sick as I felt. I'd been abused enough in my short lifetime to understand exactly what that meant.

My sweet, gentle, brave Alexei. I couldn't let him take this deal. If I let him go, she would treat him no better than an animal, no better than she treated me. Except it would be for eternity, no mercy of old age or death to escape it. I couldn't let him sacrifice himself for me. I couldn't walk away knowing he'd suffer for me forever.

But I didn't have no say, did I?

I tripped to my knees, catching myself on my only good arm as the monster shoved me forward, my head still reeling. I looked at the arm I could barely move, stubborn tears blurring the sight of the useless limb covered in blood with a bit of bone cutting through at the elbow. It hurt bad, but it wasn't the worst I ever had. Still, she'd broken it like dry bread. Like flesh and bone was nothing. I'd been so stupid, so arrogant, to overlook Lex's terror before.

How could I have been so wrong.

Tell him you love him. You ain't never going to see him again.

I couldn't make my mouth work, but I didn't take my eyes from his. My insides felt torn up, messed with. This wasn't the end of us . . . it couldn't be the end of us.

"Remove the bullet from him, girl," Adelaide said. "Then leave. If you look in my direction, make any move to attack, I'll snap your neck like a twig."

"My brother," I managed.

"Will follow you. As agreed."

Like hell. As if a monster who could own human beings and torture her own kind could ever be honorable. 'Specially after keeping Matthew alive a whole-ass year to bait me. She'd let us go now? Just like that?

I needed a plan, and I only had till this bullet was got out of Lex to come up with one. I crawled over to him. He looked paler, if that was possible, and sick with pain. I wiped my vision clear with my arm and looked down at his wound.

"I need some sort of tools, don't I?" I whispered.

He grabbed my hand, trembling, and when I looked in his eyes he shook his head, clearly thinking the same thing as I was—that Adelaide was sure to change her mind about any sort of mercy if I wasted time looking for them tools. "Your hand is the perfect size."

Maybe it was. My hands was small, my fingers narrow, so I wouldn't need to tear much flesh to get in there. Doing it with one hand would be tricky, though.

I reached into his wound, tentatively at first. I'd have to be careful not to shift the bullet—Alexei would heal from whatever my hand did to him, but not wherever the silver touched.

I whimpered and held back a gag at the awful, soft, wet feeling of flesh tearing, as blood pressed out of his wound around my hand. It was one thing to kill with a weapon, but this wasn't natural touching the inside of the body like that—and hearing Lex's small sound of pain made it so much worse.

Behind us, the monster scoffed.

"It's okay, Tiny," he whispered, his voice soothing me. "Do it quickly. It's okay . . ."

I had to think of something else other than this so I wouldn't lose my nerve. Like why the hell did Adelaide want *me* to take out the bullet when her skin could take the silver like it was nothing? What in the hell was she thinking—?

Son of a dick.

I remembered a year ago when she'd had me bound and whupped me, how when I'd torn the rope, she'd said it was 'cause her nasty boys ain't tied it tight enough. I'd seen her look of shocked confusion when Alexei'd knocked her through that wall, when I'd broken her nose. In her mind, ain't nobody was stronger than her—she'd built her whole reality on that. She wasn't used to people beating her, didn't understand it. She was used to people fearing her 'cause of what she was and had gotten comfortable. She was arrogant. So she'd let me remove the one thing slowing Lex down like we wasn't no threat. Her ego was as ancient as she was.

And it didn't matter that she *was* powerful—'cause I wasn't stupid. But she sure as hell was. Her ego had set a goal to torment and humiliate before a kill, and, in a way, that was a weakness in itself. 'Cause it meant she wasn't willing to do *anything* even if she could. If she was, me and Matthew would've been dead already, and she'd've had Lex exactly where she wanted him.

I'd always thought that the more I trained, the better I'd be at killing—and that helped, but it wasn't with sheer strength and skill that we would beat this monster. We had to go for her one weakness: All we had to do was shock her with something humiliating or unexpected that would buy us that one second, and we'd have her.

I saw the moment Alexei caught what I was thinking, that I meant to defy all that monster's plans and attack, and he dropped his gaze to the floor to hide it. But I saw the same fire in his eyes that I felt in my gut.

"You and me, Tiny," he murmured.

"Till the end of us," I whispered back.

Together, we took a breath, and I pulled out the slippery bullet, my entire hand slick with red.

And, as with every fight we'd ever shared, we moved as one.

As I went to turn, I saw Alexei shove to his feet from my

view. But at the same time, I heard a sharp crack, and Adelaide let out a startled yelp without us doing nothing. And when I turned fully, I saw the scene as if it was slowed down but also fast, all at once—the broken chair dropping to the ground and my brother falling right along with it as Adelaide struck him hard.

It was the distraction I'd asked for, even if it was the one I'd never want.

Still, there wasn't no time to scream his name or feel scared for him. I couldn't barely think of nothing as I rushed forward and snatched Alexei's sword up off the ground and plunged it into the monster's heart.

Lord. The bliss as the weapon sank deep though the dense skin, the soft organ, the smell of fresh blood as the blade went completely through her—*that* I relished. She screamed like a caught cougar as I shoved her against one of her grand columns, the house creaking at the impact.

"H-How—?" She gasped as if she barely understood what was happening.

I smiled ear to ear, breaking into an elated laugh.

I did it.

Mama, Pa, Lila, Dess. I did it.

By then, Alexei was behind her, pining her arm behind her back.

I didn't care for the pathetic type of adversary—didn't expect no apology or groveling, and she didn't offer none, neither. But I saw in her face the one thing I'd been dying to witness since the moment I'd set out to kill her.

Disbelieving terror.

"Well, well, well," I mocked, looking her over, unimpressed. "Ain't you just a *sorry* little beast?"

ALEXEI

That monster grabbed the hilt of my shashka as if to remove it, but it was too late for that—her heart had already been pierced. I used the advantage of her being trapped to sink my teeth in the side of her neck, relishing her gurgled cry as blood poured from her wound. No hypnosis for her. No easing her passage to nowhere. She deserved to die horribly, in pain . . . like the pain she'd inflicted on me all those years ago. But I didn't want to linger to savor it—I just wanted her dead before anything could get in the way to stop me.

So I dug two fingers into the bite wound and tore hard, exhaling with relief at the satisfying snap of her spine that told me she would never rise again as I dropped her head to the ground.

14

JERUSALEM

The monster's body slumped against Lex's sword, and I yanked it out to let her body join her severed head on the floor. I looked up at Alexei, both of us panting from too much pain and emotion, the monster's body lying between us. Dead. Never to rise again. Used to be I'd be afraid just seeing him behave like a vamp. But now, even with blood on his face, dripping off his chin and hands . . . I couldn't love the boy more if I tried.

I'd made myself free a whole year ago. But for the very first time . . . I felt it.

And then I heard an agonized moan.

"Matthew!" I raced to my brother, dropped to my knees beside him where he lay on the floor. "Alexei, help!"

My only brother—my only family left—was bleeding from his nose, ears, and mouth, but I couldn't see no injury, no weapon—what the hell did that monster do to him?

"It's an internal injury," Alexei said, kneeling on the other side of him. "From the impact."

"What can you do?" I felt myself crying as I gripped my brother's shirt. "Please, do something, Lex."

"I-I don't know."

"I can't lose my brother! I can't! Not like I lost everyone else—" I choked on a sob. Now that revenge was had, now that Alexei was safe, now that Adelaide was dead . . . Lord, saving my brother was the whole point, and now he was dying . . . and I couldn't do nothing to save him.

I looked into my love's blue eyes brimming with tears, blinking away my own to see him better. "Turn him, Lex. Please?"

He looked sick as he shook his head. "Not if he doesn't consent. I won't."

"He's going to die otherwise."

"He'll be a soulless monster," Alexei choked, taking my face in his hands. "It will destroy you, I know—"

"You ain't no monster, Lex." I gasped, and the emotional weight of my words nearly crashed us, my forehead meeting his.

A few days ago, I had the opposite opinion. Hell, *a* day ago, I was raring to kill the boy. But I couldn't hold onto that narrow thought any longer. I couldn't judge him for the sins of every vamp I ever met. I had to see him for who he was, not what— the way he'd seen me as a Saint, his equal, when everyone else was still laughing at me.

Dess had been right, as usual, and I was so glad I'd come to my senses in time to save my brother.

We lingered there for a second, Alexei's cool skin soothing me, till I could speak again. "I want my brother, soul or no."

I felt Alexei nod against me. "Matthew?" He looked down at my dying brother and gently took his weight from me. "Can you hear me?"

Nothing but a pained sound came out of my brother.

"Blink twice if you understand me."

Matthew did deliberately, even as he gagged up blood, and my lungs tightened in both relief and fear.

"I can save your life, but I'll have to turn you into a vampire. Do you consent to having eternal life on this earth without a soul?"

My brother blinked twice again, but this time he looked at me right after. Who knew if he consented 'cause he was fine with it. *I* didn't know. All I knew was he was doing this for me. My brave big brother, ever selfless.

"Look at me, Matthew," Alexei said gently. The pained expression left Matthew's features as soon as they locked eyes, Lex's hypnosis at work. But I trusted Alexei. If that was what had to be done to save my brother, I'd let him do anything.

"You don't have to watch," Alexei's voice said over me.

"I ain't leaving my brother alone again," I said, and gripped Matthew's hand.

Alexei's stab wound had been cauterized from the silver, but he dug a bit of it open again with a wince and soaked his fingers with his own blood. He put the blood in Matthew's mouth. "Swallow," he instructed gently. He did that a few times to get enough blood into Matthew without moving him.

The old grandfather clock in the hall ticked by painfully slow.

He lifted my brother's arm by the hand, hesitating as he glanced at me . . . and then he sank his fangs into his wrist and began to drink.

I didn't know why I expected it to be . . . well . . . more *frightening* to see Alexei feed. Maybe it was 'cause he didn't go for the neck. Maybe 'cause he graciously didn't make eye contact. But it was odd. It didn't look like nothing was even happening. I let out a heavy breath, relaxing a little. It didn't look like nothing scary. The only scary thing was part of me was worried it wouldn't work. That Matthew was too far gone to come back. That sucking out some of his blood would be too much for his body to handle.

The clock ticked and ticked and ticked.

Finally, Alexei pressed his thumb to Matthew's wrist to stop up the blood.

"It's done?" I asked, holding back one inch from panic. I studied my brother to find a difference, but he looked the same. Human. Dying.

Lex nodded.

"But he don't look okay."

"Trust me, Tiny, he's doing far better than the two of us." He was looking at me in a worrying way. "Your arm is broken."

Him drawing attention to it made me remember the bloody thing hanging beside me. "It's just my elbow. My shoulder and hand still work . . . sort of."

Lex got up quickly—wincing against the silver wound in his belly—and tore a scrap from the throw blanket on the tattered couch. I knew what he was up to, so I lifted my dead arm with my working one, holding it in place as he tied me a sling with the cloth.

"This needs to be splinted," Lex said. "But Matthew is going to turn quickly, and he'll be thirsty when it happens. Is there any livestock you could bring him?"

"I thought you said animals tasted gross?"

"It's better than him trying to make you his first meal."

I nodded, tightening my lips against wanting to cry. My own brother. Seeing me as food.

You asked for this, Jerusalem.

I glanced at my broken spear on the ground, a tool I'd thought defined me for so long, now useless. I got up quick, snatching up Lex's sword instead. "Be right back." I glared at the monster we'd just killed—*making sure* she was dead—but still giving her body a wide berth as I rushed outside.

ALEXEI

I could've sent Tiny upstairs—I could smell two humans in the house. But I didn't want her too close to what was about to happen. And from where I sat, I could see the door, so I would be ready when she came back.

I had to do everything in my power to protect her from what was coming.

Matthew's labored breathing was all too familiar. Even if he hadn't been injured, the burning . . . I remembered the burning through my body as if it'd happened yesterday. I couldn't hypnotize him for this part—he had to be aware so I could tell when the change happened, could know when I needed to be on my guard.

I smelled the change in him first—distinctly inedible. A few moments later, the pained twitching in his muscles calmed. His pulse would be the last thing to go before his thirst hit, but there was still a little time.

And hopefully, by then, the urge to vomit caused by my own burning wound wouldn't be so prominent. Or, at least, I'd get used to it. I didn't know of anything that could heal a silver wound, so it was better to adjust and try to ignore it as much as I could.

"How are you feeling?" I asked.

He groaned and pushed on the ground to sit himself up. I helped him lean against the wall. "Loud in here," he said, his voice quiet and even.

"All your senses will feel a little overwhelming until you get used to them."

He made a sound of acknowledgment, then wiped the blood from his mouth and stared at it. He put his tongue to the back of his hand and cringed. "Nope."

"Almost there," I said. "But, thankfully, yours will never taste good to you."

He seemed unusually calm for a New Blood. Perhaps 'cause I'd spared him a violent turning. Still, I couldn't let my guard down—when his thirst kicked in, it would be a different story.

"Your sister will smell like food to you now," I said. "Let me know if her scent is too much so I can help you regulate your thirst."

"You sound like you got experience at that," he said. "How she smell to *you*?"

I'd encountered many an older brother in my time, and this one was formidable—a stern warning in his voice without coming off as insecure, without aggression, but holding the promise of some in the future if I were to answer incorrectly. I was more accustomed to the ones who charged in like a bull, but he was the calculating type. Honestly, I wouldn't have thought anything of it if I hadn't just made him a physical match.

Circumstances being what they were, I chose my words wisely.

"I would never hurt her," I said.

"But she smell good to you, though."

It wasn't a question. I smiled. He might have been the softer spoken of the two, but he and Jerusalem were definitely related. "She smells . . ." *Perfect. Heavenly. The most beautiful scent in the world.* "Nice. But I know the difference between friends and food. I can control my thirst and will teach you to do the same."

He gave me a narrow side-eye. "What you doing with my sister?"

"It's a long story."

"You know that ain't what I'm asking. You bedding her or ain't you?"

"I love her."

Matthew paused, shaking his head. "All due respect, no you don't. You people don't love us. Can't. You don't respect us enough to truly love us 'cause we ain't even human to you. We exotic playthings to be trampled. Work horses to be misused and discarded."

"Slavery disgusts me. All people are equal in my eyes."

"I don't believe you."

"I adore Jerusalem. She's everything to me, and I would do anything for her. But trust takes time, I know, and I'm willing to earn yours. Just as I did with your sister."

He glared at me, still skeptical.

"All people is equal, huh?" He folded his arms across his chest. "Well, we sure is about to be."

That was a clear threat. I grinned despite it.

JERUSALEM

This place was quieter than a chicken coop after a fox got to it. The bodies of the slavers we killed were scattered across the ground, crows gathering on their corpses. Calamities would find them soon, too. Good riddance.

I rushed over to the stables. Ain't never been near them before, but I knew where it was, and knew there was plenty of horses in them. If I had to give my brother something that would taste awful to him, I could at least make sure it was a noble animal.

Would be annoying wrangling that thing with only one full arm, but I'd been doing far more with far less my entire life.

There was horses in there, all right, but also a very traumatized-looking Donald huddled in the corner, gripping a rifle to his chest. He must've seen or heard what happened in the field earlier—or maybe it was the sight of my bloody sword—'cause when he saw me, he went whiter than fresh cream.

Suddenly, something inside me went giddy.

"You needed at the big house," I said.

Instead of answering, he fumbled to lift his rifle.

I rolled my eyes.

Fighting Adelaide had made me forget how fast I was—or, I guess, how slow regular people was—'cause I walked up and kicked him in the knee, caving it in, before he could fire. The boy screamed like a caught coyote, but I didn't pause, just tripped him to his back, grabbed the collar of his jacket, and dragged him. He hollered and carried on the whole way.

Could've carried him easy. But did I want to touch his slave-keeping ass? Not really.

He was sixteen. Maybe it wasn't too late for him to change his ways, get right. But I remembered how he kicked me, stepped on my hands . . . how he was responsible for the worst whupping I'd ever had in my life, and over a pile of weeds of all things. Naw. If I was old enough to do forced labor under pain of death since the moment I could walk and lift things, he was sure as hell old enough to become vamp food.

I halted, my knees locking painfully, when I got to the sitting room. Alexei had Matthew held in place with one arm around his stomach and arms and the other at his throat. Matthew was . . . growling. Like if Alexei didn't have his head secure he'd bite the very hand trying to help him. Tears burned the backs of my eyes as I looked at my brother, thirst taking over his mind like some kinda—

I closed my eyes, shook my head. No. My brother wasn't no monster.

Alexei would never let him be.

"Leave him there, Tiny," Alexei said, unnaturally calm for the situation. "I'll come get you when we're done."

I swallowed, dropping Donald on his back. He'd been fussing and cussing, but as soon as he turned and saw what was left of Adelaide and Alexei holding Matthew back, he started begging and praying. As if God was going to listen to his evil little ass.

I couldn't see my brother like that no more, so I rushed to the kitchen door, pausing just outside.

"Don't hypnotize my brother's lunch," I said, and Alexei gave me a questioning look. "I want that little monster to suffer."

Alexei grinned. "Anything for you, my love."

As soon as I shut the kitchen door behind me, Alexei must've turned Matthew loose 'cause Donald's carrying on turned from frightened to frantic to agonized real quick. I could barely hear Alexei's encouragement over the screams.

There was a full pitcher of lemonade sitting on the kitchen counter, so I poured myself a glass. Ain't never had lemonade—it was sweet and tart at the same time. Tasted real nice; no wonder white folks kept it to themselves.

I licked the sugar from my teeth, and by then, Matthew's food had stopped screaming.

But I had to wait, even though I was anxious to see my brother. Could be dangerous if I went in there before Matthew was full. I'd seen New Bloods, but never *brand* new. Not behaving that way, completely out of control. The care Alexei took with my brother . . . he really did have a special place in his heart for people like him. It made me feel safe knowing my big brother was not only alive, but in good hands.

After a few minutes, Alexei opened the door. He had fresh blood splatters on him, his hands stained red only in the creases as if he'd tried to wipe them off before he came to see me.

"He do okay?" I asked.

"The first feeding is always a bit . . . chaotic," he said, shrugging. "And he's feeling a bit of shame, which is normal. He has to get used to the fact that he's no longer human. We just have to encourage him."

"I can see him?"

"Give him a minute," said Alexei, entering the kitchen. "Let me take care of your arm first."

"The sling ain't enough?"

He raised his brows and sat me down at the kitchen table, pulling up a chair to sit beside me. He winced as he bent over to get closer to my arm, and I looked down at his bloodied shirt, at the wound in his stomach that was no longer bleeding 'cause it was burned shut. We'd both suffered bad injuries, but despite him being an immortal, I might've been better off than him—at least mine would eventually heal. I leaned over and kissed his face as he worked, feeling grateful more than anything.

"Love you, too," he replied, and I could tell he was forcing himself to stay focused on his task. But he worked quicker than any human could, and by the time he was done, my arm was bent stiff, supported in a better sling. It felt strange, only being able to use one arm. But I had to admit it did hurt a lot less when it wasn't just swinging around freely.

I sighed. "What would I do without you?"

He looked at me like I was the most beautiful thing on this earth. "Die, probably."

"Watch it, dumbass," I said, and he kissed me before I could say anymore. I closed my eyes, basking in his touch. I didn't want to dwell on the thought that I'd almost lost him. None of that mattered, not now that the monster was dead.

I pushed away from him abruptly, remembering my brother. "I can see Matthew now?"

Alexei nodded. "I'll be right behind you."

I rushed out of the kitchen. Lex said a vampire's first feeding was chaotic, but that was putting it kindly. They darn near spilled every ounce of blood all over the floor and furniture, the body it came from torn at more than just the neck. Surprised there'd been any left for Matthew to drink.

Thinking of Matthew, he sat on the floor, blood all over his hands and face, staring at the carnage . . . his eyes wide. Terrified. It was more than shame—he was mortified by what he'd done. I tossed out the flowers from a vase on a corner table and kept the water, then used my foot and good hand to tear off the edge of a blanket that hadn't been spoiled.

"You must be nice and full, Matty," I said, feeling sick to my own stomach for saying it. I didn't know how I was going to encourage him in a practice I found just plain wrong. I cleared my throat, forcing cheer into my voice. "And you killed that little nightmare of a boy, too? Man, I'm jealous."

Matthew twitched, his brown eyes glassy with stubborn tears, but said nothing.

I bit my lip and crouched beside him. "You just getting used to it." I cleaned him off as best I could with the blanket and water from the vase. "It won't be so bad next time."

He grabbed my hand when I tried to clean his, squeezing. My pulse panicked as I yanked away from his grip and covered his hand with mine. He needed my comfort, but he was strong as hell now, and I don't think he knew it.

"Did I do the right thing, Pa?" he murmured into nowhere.

"Pa would be proud of you," I whispered, and hugged him his neck, kissing his cheek. "I'm proud of you."

He swallowed hard, as if on a sob, then cringed.

"Time to get out of this messy room." I stood and pulled him to his feet with me. "A good walk will clear your head right up. And we'll do that as soon as we leave here, okay?"

I'd have loved nothing better than to leave this evil place, no looking back. But my body was starting to fall off from that battle high, and there wasn't no other food for miles around. A few more minutes here, just to eat and get some supplies, wouldn't hurt.

Besides, there wasn't nobody to stop me.

"I'm starved," I said. "Alexei, can you check the rest of the house, make sure no Black people inside before we burn it to the ground?"

"You don't want to stay awhile?" Alexei asked. "Get some rest?"

I grimaced and shook my head. "Won't get no rest till this wicked place is in ashes and Adelaide with it."

He hesitated. "I don't know if it's safe . . ." All he needed to do was glance at Matthew and I knew what he meant. New Bloods was feral. Couldn't control their strength. The remains of Donald proved that.

But he was my brother.

"We okay, Lex." I took my brother's hand, rubbing it with my thumb to get his grip to ease up. "Go on, get."

"Bossy little brat," he murmured as he turned away to go down the hall, and I prayed my big brother heard only the annoyance at being told what to do and totally missed the growl of sexual frustration beneath it.

But when I looked up at Matthew, he still looked distant . . . damaged.

I led him into the kitchen and sat him down at the breakfast table. His arms wrapped around me before I could leave, his grip desperate and trembling. He sobbed into my stomach as I hugged his head with my one arm. And we just rested like that for a while, Matthew crying, me . . . well, I should've been crying, too. But it was like when we'd found Lila. I was thinking it through. Deciding what was best.

Deciding . . . how I felt.

'Cause my big brother was a vampire, and there wasn't no going back. I was going to have to wrestle with that truth. Him and Alexei, the two people I loved most in this world, was both the very thing I hated most. Maybe before all this, I'd've thought it was some sort of punishment for hating so fiercely— for judging them for what they was, not who.

Now I was just relieved we was together.

He moved away to look at me, sniffling and wiping his nose. "Aw, Jer, your face is all cut up and bruised. And your arm . . ."

"I've had worse, Matty," I said, shrugging. "I ain't worried about it."

He sighed, resigned. And then he looked at me as if he'd never get to look at me again if he didn't do it now. "I knew you'd make it out."

"Thought you was dead," I said, my gut twisting. "I never would've left without you if—"

"Don't you go regretting your freedom." He looked like he was going to cry again. "My baby sister . . . knowing you was free was the only thing that kept me going."

"I feel so bad that this was the only way to save you. Like you only said yes 'cause I was panicking."

"Pa always taught me to do everything in my power to protect our family," he said, scratching his scalp. "I wasn't going to die, all selfish, and leave you behind."

"Human, vampire, it don't matter. All I care about is having you back." I kissed his overgrown hair. It was dry and needed a good detangling, but it smelled good. Like him. Like family. "But first, I got to eat something before my stomach starts eating itself."

"Don't suppose I can, anymore?" He watched me walk around the kitchen and collect ingredients.

"Alexei says human food like vegetables or bread can make vampires sick. You can't digest it."

He made a sound to show he'd heard me but didn't like it. "It don't really smell that great to me no more, anyway, to be honest. Nothing smells like it should."

"What about me?"

"Naw." He shook his head with an apologetic look. "Sorry, Jer. You don't smell so great, neither."

I sighed, relieved. At least my brother would never want to eat me. "I guess I just ain't good vamp food. Alexei don't like my scent, neither."

"He told me you smell good."

"He—" I felt a blush building up and turned away—not that it mattered, since Matthew could probably hear my pulse. But hopefully, New Bloods wasn't as aware of their senses 'cause I didn't want him to know how excited I was to hear that. "He did?"

I didn't know why I was happy about that. Smelling good to him meant I was more attractive to eat, but . . . part of me wanted the boy I loved to think I smelled good.

And he'd never bitten me. He wouldn't bite me.

"So he lied to you," he said.

"Probably to spare me the stress. I get it."

He raised his brows. "You don't forgive nobody, Jer, not for nothing. Least of all some white boy."

I shrugged, finding some bread, hard cheese, and pickled peppers in the pantry.

"How'd you fall in with this Alexei, anyway?" he asked as I opened the icebox.

A big old ham. Each thing I grabbed was making me hungrier and hungrier. "He was with the Northern army," I said. "Trained me to fight and everything. He's good people, don't worry."

"Ain't never seen 'good people' that was so . . . blond."

"And a vamp to boot." I dumped everything on the table and took out my knife, slicing everything probably thicker than I's supposed to, but I only had one hand working right and the other only working enough to hold the bread still. Hadn't had a good sandwich since the army had first scooped me up, though, and who knew when I'd get to have one again. "He's perfect. You'll see."

He raised his brows even higher. "Perfect?"

"You okay, right?" I said, if only to change the subject and keep myself from blushing.

My brother wasn't fooled, giving me a disapproving look as he picked up the jar to open for me. As soon as he gripped it, his New Blood strength broke the glass, spreading vinegar and peppers all over the table. He pressed his sleeve to his nose against the stench—it smelled strong even to me; I couldn't imagine what my poor brother was going through.

"Sorry," he murmured from behind his sleeve.

"You don't got to be sorry. Probably wasn't much good, anyway, smelling like that." I took up a dish towel and swiped the mess to the opposite side of the table and onto the ground, away from him. "You feel okay?"

"It scares me to say it, but I feel fine for almost having died. Better than fine. Like I been pumped by a drug that turns all my senses on at once." He sighed and leaned on the table, watching longingly as I bit into my mess of a sandwich. "When you going to turn vamp, too?"

I just about choked on my food, his question and my too-big bite coming together in an attempt to kill me. I grabbed the lemonade and drank it straight from the half-empty pitcher, then cleared my throat. "You talking like you been wanting this."

"I don't know . . ." He shrugged, sheepish as he looked away from me. "Maybe. I mean, most people that turned vamp down South was nasty people in the first place. Wouldn't be so bad to level the playing field with some good."

I could've argued against him—that kind of power could warp a person, the idea of drinking human blood to survive was *sick*, and how could anyone truly be good without a soul? But he was a vamp now, too. There was no sense in making him feel bad, making him regret a decision he made for me.

Besides . . . Alexei existed. Proof that vamps was people who could choose good or evil, just like the rest of us. I was still trying to get used to that, and it might take me a long while yet. But Alexei wasn't no monster, and he'd teach Matthew not to be, neither.

"So you ain't turning?" my brother asked again.

"Never thought about it," I said, which wasn't totally true, but that didn't matter.

"So what, I got to live forever, watching my sister age and die?" he asked while I went back to eating too much.

"It ain't that simple, Matt."

He opened his mouth to say something, but a woman's shrill protest coming from the stairs, along with footsteps, cut him off. He sighed. "Ain't nothing in our life ever been simple, and it clearly ain't about to start now."

"She's the only one in the house," Alexei said, making us look up.

Millie stood in the doorway, pale and gripping a baby to her chest. Though, I guess it wasn't *that* strange to see her. She was the only one left out of her nasty family and had obviously been put in charge of the house while everyone else was gone to war. Now her husband was dead, and she didn't even know it.

Maybe in another life I would've felt sorry for her.

But all I could do was look at the baby in her arms.

"Oh, thank God. Toby," Millie said, her face beet-red from crying or heat or stress or all of them. "Throw this man out. He's trespassing."

"*Matthew* ain't at your beck and call no more," I said. I didn't even look at her. My eyes was still locked on that baby. That baby girl with skin like beech wood—light enough for them to have kept if they was desperate, but sure as hell not light enough to pass. With thick, reddish frizz on her head but with a nose I just knew was going to be beautiful and wide like her mama's when she grew up. Lila could've never denied her if she was still with us, which meant she looked just like Matthew, too. That was my sister's baby, even if she did look a little like the man we used to obey.

"Dido?" The woman gasped. "How did you—?"

"Hand over the baby," I said coldly.

She stared at me, confused and frightened, clinging to a child she had no claim to. "Abigail isn't used to strangers."

"Give me my niece," I said, at the end of my patience. "Or Imma make you give her to me."

That did it. Millie was as soft as her husband. She held Abigail out at arm's length, and the baby started crying as soon as I reached out to her. I sighed and tucked her under my arm like holding a log. I ain't held a baby but a few times in my life, but I reckoned I could get used to it.

The crying, not so much.

Matthew covered his ears with his hands and winced. "Hold her right, Jer," he said—he sounded so much like Pa then I could've cried—and even though the crying bothered his ears, he came to take her from me. But Alexei beat him to it and took the baby.

"You don't know your own strength yet," Alexei said, holding her against his chest. And wouldn't you know it, she stopped crying.

As if that boy wasn't sexy enough already, now he was a baby whisperer, too.

"What are you going to do with her?" Millie asked, her eyes shifting to each of us.

"She's our family," I snapped, and she cowered. "What you think we going to do, eat her?"

Okay, well . . . Matthew might be tempted, but I'd never let him. Yet she stared at me, eyes bulging, as if I was some kind of liar.

"She ain't worth arguing with, Jer," said Matthew, and I took a deep breath. "Let's just go."

Good old Matthew, ever the peacekeeper. Maybe he was right. About the arguing, anyway. But I done killed the rest of her family, why not finish them off? She didn't have nowhere to go no how.

But, for my brother, I said to her, "You might want to get out of here. We fittin' to burn this place to hell."

I turned my back to her. She could do what she wanted at this point—I was done. I reached for the baby. She cowered into Alexei's chest, fussing.

"Come to auntie, little girl," I said, rolling my eyes, but as soon as Alexei held her down to my level, she started crying again.

"What in the hell?" I muttered, glaring at the crying baby.

"You too rough," Matthew said. "She don't want to be held under the arm like that again."

"She ain't even big enough to think all that."

"Well, when *one* of you takes her," said Alexei, grimacing, "she needs a new diaper."

"Oh, that's all you, Matty!" I laughed. "I don't know nothing about that."

"And I do?" Matthew countered.

"Do we really need a baby?" Alexei asked, and his frustration sounded sort of adorable.

Still, I slapped him in the arm, and not playfully, neither. I winced—the quick movement made me remember my other arm was locked up in a splint and sling and hurt like hell. So my tone came out a bit biting when I said, "Shut up, we ain't leaving her."

Matthew rolled his eyes. "Can I hold the baby, please? I don't trust *neither* of you crazy people with her."

But my brother didn't do nothing but step closer, and the baby started crying even harder.

Me and Matthew looked at each other, knowing full well what just happened, while Alexei glanced between us, confused.

"Son of a dick," I growled.

"What's wrong?" my sweet Lex asked, sounding as ready to fight as I was.

"Jerusalem," Matthew warned, "don't do nothing—"

"Oh, Imma do something," I snapped, storming toward the doorway—Millie had long left, but I knew where she lived and could catch her up easy. "She done raised that baby to hate Black skin. Hate her own people. Oh, I'm about to snap that hag in two—"

Matthew grabbed my one good arm, almost yanking it out of joint with his new strength, and pulled me to him. "Don't do it, Jer. Don't give these people no more of us—not our time, not our effort, not even our hate. They don't own us no more."

I shook away from his grasp, panting. My gut raged. I needed her blood like a vampire needed it to live, except spilled, feeding the ground she used to own.

But when I looked at my brother and my love and my baby

niece, all I could think was that I never wanted to leave none of them again, not even to chase that woman down. Not even to kill.

"The baby needs a new diaper," Matthew repeated gently. "And then we can get out of here. Forever."

15

ALEXEI

With all our threats eliminated, I waited alone in the wrecked sitting room while Tiny and her brother went upstairs to tend to the baby.

Well . . . not so much alone.

I crouched beside the bodiless head of my tormentor. Drained of blood, it was dehydrated and skeletal, skin stretched taut against sharp cheekbones and a narrow chin. Without blood, it would decompose quickly with the rest of her body and crumble into dust, a side effect from inhabiting this earth for centuries too long.

I pressed my palm into her face, crushing that monster's skull with a satisfying crunch as easily as crumbling sandstone. I felt myself grin despite the tears clouding my vision, relief tightening my chest.

Before a few days ago, I'd never dwelled on my past. Never thought of those lonely days and nights of neglect and thirst, the way she would torture me just 'cause she could. I never thought of her, never dreaded seeing her.

And I'd never have to ever again.

I got up and set to packing some food for Tiny—she was so anxious to get away from here, I knew she'd never think of it. Most of the food was perishable, so we'd have to find her something else in a day or two. But for now, it was enough.

When they came back downstairs, Tiny had a few oil lamps cradled in her arm, and the weeping baby was tied to Matthew's chest with a torn blanket. His fingers were in his ears, his face a mask of misery as he tried to soothe the baby with soft words.

"This is not a good idea," I said, standing. "He shouldn't have a human baby strapped to him like a portable snack."

"He won't hurt her," Tiny insisted, and threw one of the oil lamps into the center of the room, the glass and metal shattering to seep oil onto the already blood-soaked rug.

"He will if we don't hunt in time. New Bloods become violent and irritable if they are forced to wait."

"It's going to be okay," she said, resting her hand against my stomach. Her words felt true and equally irrational.

Jerusalem lit a match and threw it onto the oil-splattered room, but we didn't stand by to see it catch. The intense heat was proof enough. We rushed outside away from the flames.

"I'll get us some horses," I said, not rin the mood to admit that I really just wanted to get away from the fire, and flew over to the barn.

When I got back with three horses, flames had enveloped the house and the giant oak in front of it. Tiny was running and dancing in its light.

"Die, you evil-ass tree!" she shouted, laughing, while Matthew looked on with half-concern, half-approval. But when she grabbed his hand and pulled him into her dance, he didn't hesitate to join her.

And if that wasn't the personification of freedom, I didn't know what was.

Because we were free, weren't we? Truly free. Not just physically, but . . . I felt myself relax in a way I didn't think I remembered ever feeling. My tormentor was gone forever—not just dead, but eaten away. Never to return. Never to haunt me with her scent or threats or presence ever again.

And so I tied up the horses to the fence so they wouldn't run and joined them. And we laughed and danced as cleansing fire consumed the pains of our past.

JERUSALEM

We led every single Black person away from my former plantation—anyone who hadn't run off sooner on their own, anyway—to the swamp's entrance. Hundreds of people I'd grew up with . . . free. Wasn't no time for hugs and such—it was still daylight, and though anyone who'd bother occupying these woods was dead, it was always better to move quickly. Once inside, a Conductor would find them.

Lila—like hell we was going to keep that slave name, Abigail—had cried her little self out for a good hour then fell into a dead sleep, drooling with a half-opened mouth on Matthew's chest. Part of me was regretting bringing a loud-ass baby along, but I wasn't about to leave my family behind. It was only the three of us, now.

No. Four of us.

Alexei was as much my home as my brother and niece.

We stopped just outside of Underground territory. Me being the only grown human, I was aching something terrible from all the past few days' fighting, and my arm was swelling up even after Lex had properly bandaged it. But it could've been worse—me and my brother could've still been enslaved. That monster could've still been alive. I was counting my blessings, and a broken elbow and some aching muscles was nothing compared to where I'd been.

"What now?" Matthew asked.

"Anything we want," I said, spreading my arm to hug the world. "Free people can do anything."

"Up North maybe," he said, a bit nervously. "Maybe we should go with the Conductors. It ain't exactly safe for us out here."

"Apparently," said Lex, sounding adorably salty, "vampires aren't allowed in the Underground."

I hugged my brother around the waist. "Don't worry, Matty. Me and Lex won't let nothing happen to you."

"I believe you, Jer," said Matthew. "But that don't mean we should stay in the woods of a burning plantation. White folks is bound to start showing up soon."

"Hey, that's a great idea!" I looked between my boys, unable to contain my excitement. "What if we keep this up? Burning plantations. Liberating people."

Matthew never ceased to look like Pa when he was disappointed. "Can we do that? I mean, *how*?"

"With most of the men gone to war, it's going to be pie. Plus, we got friends in the Underground—Julia and Gus will help us, for sure. What you think, Lex?"

Lex raised a brow. "I think *we* is an exaggeration. I'm pretty sure Julia has made it her life's mission to cave my chest in."

"Gus liked you."

"Wait, wait, wait," said Matthew with a slightly frustrated

sigh. "This sounds real dangerous. Y'all can fight—that's great!—but I ain't charging into no plantation to face off with no white folks with guns."

"Guns can't kill you anymore," said Alexei, and my brother looked at him as if he'd lost his mind.

"You don't got to fight, Matty," I butted in. "We can figure all that out. But why should we wait for some war to decide the fate of everyone who suffers like we used to when we can just solve it ourselves?"

Matthew touched the baby's back slowly, as if he thought he might crush her. "We got more than us to protect now."

"That's exactly why we got to do it," I said. "Make a better future for us *and* Baby Lila."

"I do love this idea," Lex said, "but I have to deliver Odessa's and Gael's ashes up North."

Hearing my friends' names, I felt a spot of warmth in my heart. I wasn't upset about them no more—not angry, anyway. There wasn't no need to be. They was together now, where nothing could hurt them. My brother was safe. The boy I loved was here with me. I felt strangely content about it all, leaving no room for sadness.

"We got to do that, for sure. But we might as well free people on the way." I groaned and lowered myself slowly onto my back, cushioned by the brush beneath the trees. "But first, I need sleep."

"Never thought I'd hear those words from your mouth." Alexei chuckled, wincing and pressing his hand to his stomach as he sat beside me.

"For a year, I had one mission . . . and it's done. I don't know what to do with myself."

He caressed my brow with his thumb. "We'll find you

somewhere to sleep." He laughed as I wrapped my arm around his neck and dragged him down to lie beside me.

Matthew did not look pleased. "I feel like y'all ain't really thinking this through. Me and Lila is regular people. You ain't dragging us into all this violent, fighting mess."

"Regular people?" I smirked, but it was hard to turn my head to really look at him since Lex had buried his cool face in the crook of my neck—and, for once, I didn't feel panicked about it. "You a vampire now, Matty."

"Do y'all got to do that?"

I felt myself growing hot and ashamed. God forbid Lex had *kissed* me. My brother didn't need to be seeing none of that. "Why you got to act like Pa *all* the time?"

"'Cause Pa would be boiling like a kettle if he saw a white man touching you like that, and he'd be right."

"I would never hurt her," Alexei said. "I promise you."

And my beautiful, tree-height dumbass did the best and worst thing he could do and kissed my cheek.

"Whoa, whoa, whoa, hey!" Matthew stormed over to us, and me and Lex sprang into action to stop him. There was this strange moment of all three of us holding out our hands, attempting to protect each other from . . . each other.

"It's okay, Matthew." I laid my hand against Alexei's chest to keep him sitting. I guess I could see how it wouldn't look *okay* from my brother's view. Lex had them bright blue eyes and looked powerfully strong and dangerous even sitting. I'd felt the same way not too long ago. I grabbed my brother's hand to keep it busy.

"I ain't letting no white man do to you what was done to Lila," Matthew growled.

His words struck me so hard that for a moment, the painful

memories came flooding back. I had to pry his hands off—he was too strong now and didn't know how to tame it. "Alexei ain't like that," I said, and for the first time, I wasn't just convincing myself it was true. I *knew* it was. "He's sweet and kind, and he don't think of us as lesser or nothing. And I would've never gotten here to save you without him. He's a good man."

Matthew had calmed enough that I could wrap my good arm around his waist, enough to hug me back without squishing the baby between us. "You love him?" he asked to my hair.

"More than love him, Matt. I trust him with my life."

When I turned, Alexei had stood up, and his bright blue eyes were made brighter by the tears brimming them. "You trust me, Tiny?"

I could've kissed him, but it seemed a bad idea in front of my overprotective brother. Instead, I laced my fingers through his and squeezed, looking up into his beautiful face. "Completely."

I positioned us so I was standing between them, forming a triangle. "Hold hands."

"You and your adorable demands," Lex said with a slight smile but held his hand out to Matthew. My brother hesitated, and I held my breath until he took it. He closed the triangle by putting his hand on my shoulder.

"All we have in the world is each other," I said. "Let's stick together, no matter what."

"Like a coven," Lex said.

"I was going to say 'family,' but actually coven might suit us better—sounds dangerous, like us. Agreed?"

"Agreed."

"I ain't letting you out of my sight ever again," said Matthew and side-eyed Lex for a moment. "So, agreed."

Baby Lila made a small coo in her sleep, like she agreed, too, and me and Lex laughed. Matty cringed at our volume—his poor senses—and laid a hand against the baby's back with a small smile.

"Coven, it is," he murmured.

I went to snatch up my spear, then remembered it was useless and burning with the house. Part of me missed handling it out of habit. *Solely* out of habit . . . 'cause for a whole year, it had been a comfort to me, a sense of security in a world of evil. And now I didn't need it. It had served its purpose, a necessary tool for my old life. I'd have to find me a new Saint weapon and soon if I wanted to fulfill my goal of freeing people. But it would be for the new Jerusalem—no longer a vengeful girl full of hate but a Saint on a mission for good. Just like God had always intended.

Still, I was used to my hands being occupied, and so started walking to distract myself. "Okay, boys, but seriously," I said. "I need to get me some sleep."

"First, an inn," said Lex, falling step with me as he wrapped an arm around my shoulders. "Then we take Dess and Gael back home."

"And on the way, destroy some white folks' property. Oh, we about to have some fun."

Matthew shushed me, checking on the baby, and sighed. "Me and Lila going to sit that activity out."

Lex grinned, encouraging me. "And then?"

"And then . . ." I looked at my boys with so much love and contentment in my heart it was almost too much. "Then we find us a place to call home."

AUTHOR'S NOTE

My Dear Reader,

Why didn't you stop me when I decided to write another Black Pain book directly after the trauma-fest that is *Wildblood???* One book was hard enough on my mental and emotional health, but two? This one took me much longer to write because I had to take days at a time away from it to recover. But sometimes, a book idea comes along that is the right combination of important and fun to warrant that degree of sacrifice.

For me, *The Dangerous Ones* is that book.

First of all, I'd been dying to write a vampire novel, and the Civil War felt like the natural choice—after all, my book isn't the first to figure that monsters prone to enslaving people would end up as Confederate soldiers. But I couldn't write a book taking place during one of the biggest historical events to define America without mixing real details into my worldbuilding: Even back in the 1860s, America was a melting pot of ethnicities, and I made sure my cast of characters reflected that. The Russian navy did indeed assist the Union; iron bits were actual historical torture devices used to humiliate and punish enslaved Black people; and the deaths of Black girls and women due to willfully inhuman medical practices was not uncommon (see J. Marion Sims, aka "The Father of Modern gynecology").

But ultimately, *The Dangerous Ones* is the journey of a Black girl seeking vengeance, falling in love, and taking her freedom into her own hands . . . and I also just wanted to write a book about hot, powerful people and include every fantasy romance trope I could think of on my own terms. The result is a fun, emotional ride that is full of just as much Black Joy as pain, and I hope you'll love it as much as I do.

God Bless.

ACKNOWLEDGMENTS

K